The End
of Romance

PUB. DATE _____ PRICE _____
UNREVISED AND UNPUBLISHED PROOFS.
CONFIDENTIAL. PLEASE DO NOT QUOTE
FOR PUBLICATION UNTIL VERIFIED WITH
THE FINISHED BOOK. THIS COPY IS NOT
FOR DISTRIBUTION TO THE PUBLIC.

VIKING

ALSO BY LILY MEYER

Short War

The End of Romance

Lily Meyer

VIKING

VIKING
An imprint of Penguin Random House LLC
1745 Broadway, New York, NY 10019
penguinrandomhouse.com

Copyright © 2026 by Lily Meyer

Penguin Random House values and supports copyright. Copyright fuels creativity, encourages diverse voices, promotes free speech, and creates a vibrant culture. Thank you for buying an authorized edition of this book and for complying with copyright laws by not reproducing, scanning, or distributing any part of it in any form without permission. You are supporting writers and allowing Penguin Random House to continue to publish books for every reader. Please note that no part of this book may be used or reproduced in any manner for the purpose of training artificial intelligence technologies or systems.

VIKING is a registered trademark
of Penguin Random House LLC.

Designed by Alexis Sulaimani

LIBRARY OF CONGRESS CATALOGING-IN-PUBLICATION DATA
[INSERT CIP DATA]

Printed in the United States of America
$PrintCode

The authorized representative in the EU for product safety and compliance is Penguin Random House Ireland, Morrison Chambers, 32 Nassau Street, Dublin D02 YH68, Ireland, https://eu-contact.penguin.ie.

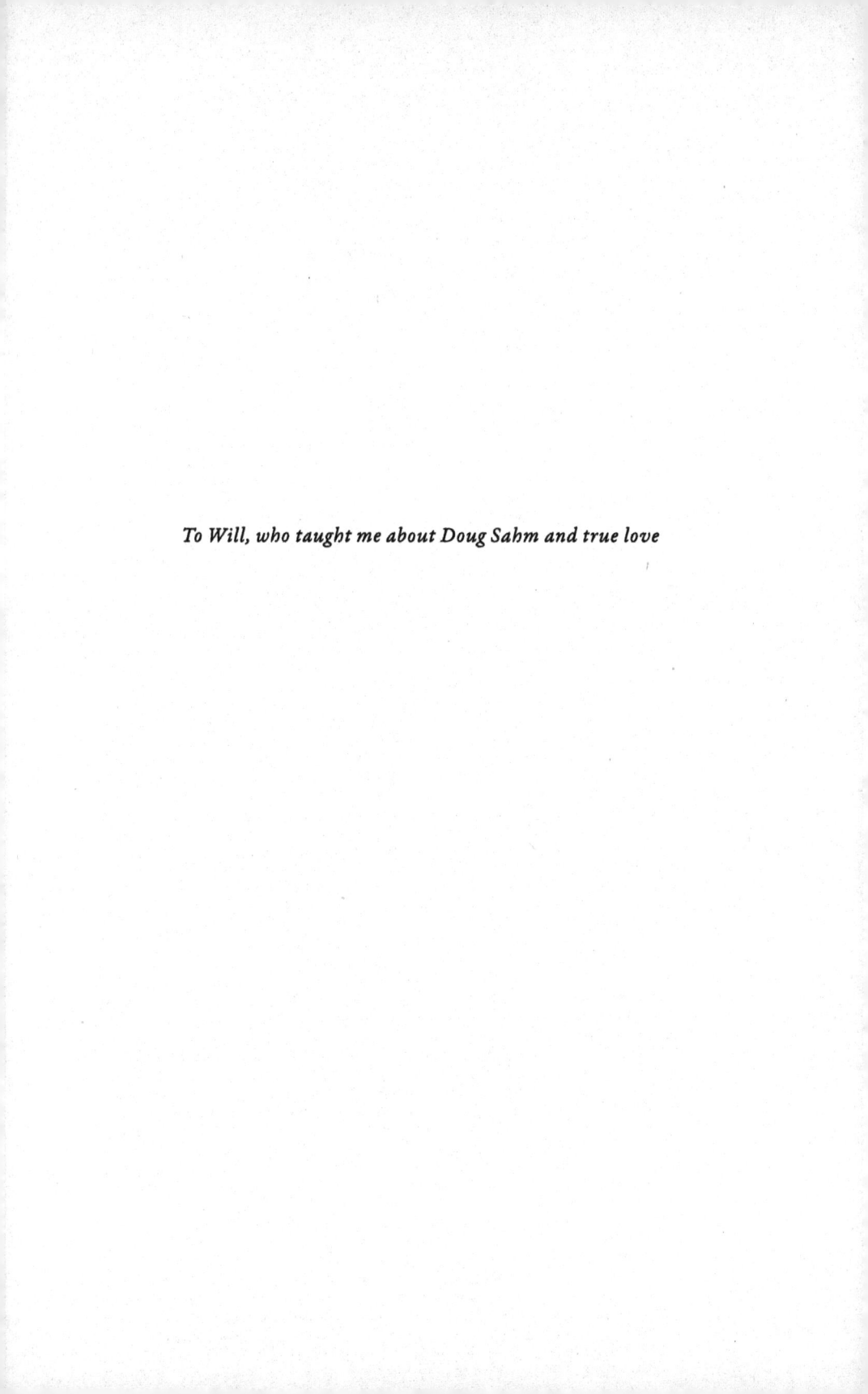

To Will, who taught me about Doug Sahm and true love

He was in a Romance, a vulgar and a high Romance simultaneously; a Romance was one of the systems that controlled him, as the expectations of Romance control almost everyone in the Western world, for better or worse, at some point or another.

A. S. Byatt, Possession

Nobody knows what happens to sex after liberation. It's a big mystery.

Nora Ephron, "Fantasies"

PART ONE

Robbie

Chapter One

1.

Sylvie Broder first tried to think herself out of love when she was nine.

She was fighting with her parents, which happened often but felt earth-shattering every time. Sylvie was an emotional little girl, subject to intense attacks of joy, grief, jealousy, and rage. Paul and Carol, her parents, had the cool containment of British royals—or, rather, all the royals except Diana, whom Sylvie worshipped. Diana radiated *feelings*. She refused self-control. Sylvie frequently got in trouble at home for doing the same, but it was always a false accusation. She tried to control herself all the time. She just failed.

On the night in question, Sylvie was struggling to manage her disappointment about not getting to go to Sarah Langston's tenth birthday. It was a Saturday-night slumber party, and the Broders had a Sunday-morning obligation. Paul's bank was hosting a brunch for executives and their families—"And you're my family," he reminded Sylvie, who was marching around the pristine kitchen, consumed by tears. "I want you to meet everyone."

"I can meet them!" Sylvie raised her hot face to her mother's. "Tell him. Tell him I can go to the party and you can pick me up in the morning."

"You'd be exhausted," Carol pointed out. "I have to say, you girls are a little young for overnights. I don't know what the Langstons are thinking."

"It's the first *one*," Sylvie said. "And Sarah said—" She hiccupped, then continued, "Sarah said if people can't come, it's because they're still babies. It's because they wet the *bed*."

"Do you wet the bed?" her mother asked. Her English accent was strengthening, a telltale sign of aggravation.

"No."

"So should you care?"

"Yes!" Sylvie mopped her face with the hem of her shirt, though doing so was Bad Manners and Not Allowed. "Dad," she said. "Please."

"Quiet," Paul said steadily. "You're getting too loud."

She tried to catch her breath. In the Broder household, loudness, like any other lapse in restraint, was not permitted. As quietly as she could, she said, "I promise, if you let me go, I'll still come to your brunch. I'll be good."

"Your mother and I made our decision. We let Sarah's parents know not to expect you."

Sylvie's voice shot up. "Already?"

"Quiet," her father repeated.

"But *Dad*," Sylvie said.

Carol turned to him. "She's done. She's out of control."

Sylvie hated it when her parents spoke about her as if she'd left the room. She screwed her mouth and eyes shut. A vision of Sarah's house appeared before her. She'd never been invited before, but she imagined it as a paradise of snacks and bright colors, of free expression and loud sounds. In Sarah's house, Sylvie was suddenly certain, nobody had to control themselves.

She considered the possibility of fleeing to Sarah's—or, better, to her friend Hallie's. Hallie lived only six blocks from the Broders. Sylvie wouldn't get lost going there. She could go to Hallie's, call her grandparents, and say she needed to come live in Florida with them.

"I'm running away," she announced.

"You may not," Carol said.

"I'm going to." Sylvie drew herself up. "I'm going to run away because you're oppressing me." She looked directly at Paul. "You're *Hitlers*."

Her father's reaction was instant. All color drained from his face. A muscle jumped in his jaw. "Go to your room."

"No."

He grabbed Sylvie's shoulders harder than he'd ever hugged her. "Paul," Carol said, but he gave no sign of noticing. He frog-marched Sylvie to her bedroom and shoved her in—an actual shove. For the first time in her life, she heard him turn the brass tumbler that locked the door from outside.

Sylvie hurled herself at the door, willing it to break. She got nothing but a throbbing shoulder. She tried her bedroom window next, but the storm sash was in. She had no boots or coat upstairs, anyway, and it was February in Marblehead, Massachusetts. She couldn't run away barefoot.

She huddled on the rug, wrapping her arms around her legs. Guilt, anger, and triumph swarmed through her. For once, she had made her dad lose control, but only by saying something awful. Paul's parents had lived through Hitler. He wouldn't talk about it, but when Sylvie visited her grandparents in Miami, her grandpa Ilya explained the Holocaust and its many perpetrators, the dangers both of ignoring crowds and of getting swept up in them. He was wise, Grandpa Ilya. He understood oppression and freedom, human nature and what he called the momentum of events. Sylvie's parents knew nothing about momentum. All they ever thought about was rules.

It made matters worse that many of her parents' rules were prohibitions on her feelings, or the forms those feelings took. When Sylvie wanted something, Carol called it a whim. When she told a story, Paul called it a lie. When she showed any strong emotion, including love or appreciation, they told her not to get carried away. Not one thing that happened in her head mattered to her parents, and yet she had no choice but to live there.

At least she had company inside herself. When she was very little, her grandfather had come up with a bedtime story concerning a shipwrecked pirate king named Captain Lightning; his sidekick and strongman, Otto DeFay; and an unnamed but very wise turtle who had lived on Captain Lightning's island since the dawn of time. During a visit several years later, he heard his son disciplining Sylvie for arguing and suggested to her gently, "Why don't you take Captain Lightning home in your mind? You can argue with him."

But Sylvie never argued with the captain and his comrades. She unburdened herself to them. She would describe her troubles to Otto, who gave comforting hugs but rarely spoke, then sit on the small throne beside Captain Lightning's big one—it was hers; she was the island's part-time princess—and ask the pirate king what she should do. He'd listen carefully, then shake the vines by his throne until the turtle lumbered out, opened his beak, and weighed in.

But the night Sylvie called her parents Hitlers, her turtle was as silent as a real turtle would be. He left her alone with the realization that if what her parents said—that they made their rules to help her, to teach her the right way of being—was true, it meant they thought her way was fundamentally wrong. It meant they thought *she* was wrong. It meant they didn't love the daughter they had.

Sylvie wanted to get rid of her revelation. She wanted to retract calling her parents Hitlers. She wanted the good-night kiss Carol said she'd outgrown. She fell asleep on the floor and woke aching from shoulder to heel, face indented from the rug's rough weave. In her sleep, she'd found a solution. At school, she told everyone she couldn't go to Sarah's party because her parents were fascists and hated her, and that from now on, as a freedom fighter, she was going to hate them right back. Everyone nodded, impressed with both her independence and her vocabulary, and Sylvie told herself that not loving her parents was easy. Only deep down did she know she wasn't telling the truth.

2.

Sylvie's Miami grandparents were the reason she knew love could come without rules. Ilya and Estie Broder were flamboyantly, dramatically open-hearted and -minded. Both of them had survived Bergen-Belsen; both were marvels of resilience and joy. It was their bond. Before the war, Ilya had studied philosophy at Jagiellonian University in Kraków. Estie had raised chickens in Gdańsk. After they met—not in the camp, but once they'd lived to be Displaced Persons—they collaboratively developed a system of thought that focused on enjoying the life they had snatched back from the Nazis. It was their mission to spite Hitler with happiness, which was, conveniently, something at which they excelled.

In Florida, Ilya drove a limo and played dominoes. Estie taught middle-school art and dealt antiques. Both gave generously to the Miami-Dade Democrats, to HIAS, to anyone asking on the street. Estie sunbathed daily and cooked horribly. Ilya grew six types of hot pepper in their building's courtyard. On Saturday nights, they went dancing. On Sundays, they invited a rotating cast of neighbors to their apartment to drink rum-spiked coffee and eat cookies that crumbled in the humid air.

Paul and his parents did not like spending time together. He thought they were frivolous. Grandpa Ilya said his son's seriousness was an insult to their way of life. Grandma Estie said it was innate, that she'd been too tired during her pregnancy and therefore failed to transmit to the growing fetus the importance of having fun. But all three agreed that Sylvie deserved a relationship with her grandparents, and so Paul dropped her off in Miami for all of her school breaks. There, in Ilya and Estie's shrimp-colored condo, she led the opposite of the life she left behind in Marblehead.

In Miami, Sylvie's grandparents encouraged her to yell, sing, and make messes. If she had an idea, she was supposed to talk about it as much as she possibly could. She got hugs and kisses morning and night, a nice long snuggle on the couch with her grandmother any time it rained or one of them felt tired. Her name wasn't Sylvie but Sylvinka, Vinka, or Winky. Sometimes Grandpa Ilya made up songs about her, primarily to the tune of "On Top of Old Smoky." At home, pop music wasn't welcome, but in Florida, the spring the Spice Girls' "Wannabe" was huge, she played and sang it so often that her grandparents learned the chorus and began joining in.

Ilya set out early to shape Sylvie's thinking. He taught her about much more than the Holocaust. From him, she learned, in not-all-that-simplified terms, about Martin Buber's I and Thou, Isaiah Berlin's hedgehog and fox, and Plato's shadows and reality. He educated her in politics by heckling the news. He had a rigid hierarchy of insults: Democrats who disappointed him, which was ninety-five percent of them, were pigs; Republicans and most Israeli politicians were pig-dogs, scum, or slime; and Slobodan Milošević was a Hitler, a Stalin, and a Satan. Sylvie never called anyone but her parents a Hitler—and she only made that mistake once—but she got in significant trouble in fifth grade for calling her math teacher, Mr. da Silva, a Stalin. She accepted her punishment gracefully, knowing she was in the right. He'd been obstructing her friend Rachel's freedom to wear spaghetti straps. Resistance was called for.

Grandma Estie had different types of knowledge. From her, Sylvie learned to give compliments in Yiddish, Polish, and not-very-good Spanish, and absorbed a staggering amount of information about furniture design. They did decoupage projects, adding rhinestones and glitter any time the opportunity arose. They cried on the phone together when Princess Diana died. Estie bought Sylvie a secret Floridian wardrobe of ruffled dresses, jelly sandals, and embroidered jean shorts. She taught her to consult her body before making all kinds of decisions, not only what to wear and eat but also if it was a good idea to go to the beach, or see a horror movie, or skip calling home.

When Sylvie was thirteen, Grandma Estie took her to lunch at Puerto Sagua, a Cuban restaurant where she and Ilya had been regulars for years. Over croquetas, a shared steak, and cafés con leche, Estie informed her granddaughter that wanting sex, like wanting food, was not only normal but beautiful; Sylvie should enjoy herself by herself, just like how she should help herself to snacks in the kitchen; and—here the food simile fell apart—though she should also enjoy herself with others once she got to be more fully a teenager, if any boy tried to stick it in her without permission or without a condom, she should pop him—*heh!*—right in the eye.

It was October 2000 then. Sylvie was in eighth grade and, in her heart, fully aligned with her grandparents. During that visit, she stumped around with her grandfather, knocking doors for Gore and Lieberman and discussing the horrible fact that her parents would surely vote for George Bush. She liked canvassing, if only because she got to see more of Miami. She wanted to live there someday. She intended to make herself into one of the glamorous women who walked from car door to restaurant door in heels that laced up their calves. She would own so many sequins. Her earrings would be made of gold mesh or feathers and would cascade past her chin.

When she got home, she told Hallie and Rachel her plan, and the three of them decided to grow up to be elegant Miamians together. In the meantime, Sylvie invited them to join her in Florida for winter break, an idea that, astoundingly, her parents had approved. Paul thought Ilya and Estie would enjoy a houseful of girls. Carol agreed that her in-laws loved hosting, and, besides, it would be nice on their part—*their* meaning Carol and Paul—to give Rachel and Hallie a treat. God knew Sylvie spent enough time at their houses without reciprocating. The Broders were overdue to make a gesture.

Sylvie, Hallie, and Rachel got their plane tickets on December 2. On December 11, Grandpa Ilya had a heart attack while listening to the Supreme Court debate *Bush v. Gore*. He died six days later in the hospital. Estie died three months later, of grief.

3.

Sylvie turned fourteen in May. She had no more grandparents. She hated the new president for killing them. She hated her parents for voting for him, and for refusing to let her take anything from her grandparents' apartment except one single watercolor of a bougainvillea plant, and for being themselves. All spring and summer, she stalked around, bereft. Hallie and Rachel tried to cheer her up with bike rides, shoplifting, and frequent trips to the town beach, but nothing worked until the week before school started, when Sylvie happened to notice one of their classmates, Jonah Sabransky, playing Frisbee on the sand by the bay. He'd grown half a foot since June. His shoulders had doubled in size. A dark line of hair marched out of his swim trunks. Sylvie, seeing it, was stricken.

She felt like he'd grabbed a handful of her guts and pulled. Only that night, poking around inside her pajamas, did she understand that tugging feeling was desire.

From the moment ninth grade started, she aimed herself at Jonah. He caught on fast. He kissed her for the first time in a supply closet on September 11, taking advantage of the all-school tumult of emotion and unsupervision. By the time Bush invaded Afghanistan, their relationship was official, and by the end of the academic year, it was so entrenched it seemed preordained to everyone but Sylvie, who remained stunned by her achievement. Jonah Sabransky was famously perfect. Peers admired him; teachers praised him; parents wished out loud that he was theirs. Well, he was *hers* now. Or, really, she was his.

Sylvie had initially wanted to be Jonah's girlfriend because she was attracted to him. She wanted to keep being his girlfriend because she looked up to him. Her admiration was itself a form of wanting, one just as intense and transformative as their steady progression toward sex. Once, sophomore year, she tried explaining to Hallie and Rachel how similar the experiences were. They were sitting cross-legged on Hallie's bedroom floor, surrounded by wet cucumbers. Sylvie had been trying to teach her friends to give blow jobs, but neither displayed the requisite stamina.

"I don't know," Hallie said. "It seems kind of awful."

"It's not the same with the cucumber," Sylvie said, nudging hers. It was waxy and bitter, and unrealistically long.

"No shit."

"Seriously. With the cucumber, it's only uncomfortable. With Jonah, being uncomfortable is part of the fun."

Rachel folded her arms. "Explain."

"It's exciting to make him happy," Sylvie said. "I mean, *that* kind of exciting." She nodded downward. "And if it's hard work, it's more satisfying.

It's kind of like cross-country." She'd joined the team that year, primarily out of self-consciousness about her weight—puberty, for Sylvie, had brought her a version of her grandmother's body, with hips and thighs the likes of which few girls in Marblehead shared—but also to emulate Jonah. He was a varsity soccer player and hurdler, and he liked sports so much that Sylvie, a committed non-athlete through middle school, had found herself motivated to investigate.

"Which you hate," Rachel pointed out.

"Yeah, but after races, I feel good."

"So you only like giving blow jobs after they're done?"

"No, no. New example. Jonah never argues with his parents."

Hallie rolled her eyes. "Of course."

Rachel elbowed her. "Neither do you." Rachel had parents half as strict as Sylvie's and fought with them constantly. Hallie's mom and stepdad were too busy with their younger kids to argue about anything.

"It's strategic," Sylvie continued. "He sucks up to his parents so they never punish him or get in his way. He can pretty much do whatever he wants. And it isn't like I can *not* fight with my parents, but every time I want to and don't, I know that's another Saturday I'm not grounded and get to hang out with Jonah."

Hallie nodded. Rachel screwed her mouth to the side. "But you just sneak out when you're grounded," she said, which was true, but meant Sylvie had failed to explain. Sneaking out dealt with a problem. Containing herself for Jonah, after a life of failing to do so for Carol and Paul, was—like exerting herself to give a good blow job—its own goal and reward.

Besides, Sylvie snuck out whether she was grounded or not. Her parents didn't like her to go to parties, but because Jonah was a varsity athlete, and because, in addition to being perfect, he was popular, he got invited to everything—to seniors' parties, even—and he always wanted to bring Sylvie, though he usually wanted a different Sylvie than he got. By the fall of junior year, this was a source of tension in their relationship. Jonah was good at drinking. Sylvie was not, but enjoyed it anyway. He wanted her to either improve her tolerance—how?—or limit herself. He said it both embarrassed and worried him when someone came to tell him that his girlfriend was puking somewhere, or passed out, or telling secrets anyone could guess a sober Sylvie wouldn't want told.

Only the secrets worried her, and only because she was afraid she'd tell her only real one, a worrying new development she hadn't discussed with anyone—not Jonah, not Hallie and Rachel, not even Captain Lightning and the turtle: that she was tortured by baseless, embarrassing anxiety. It had to do with her new self-control. Behaving the way she was supposed to gave her the sensation that somebody was about to sneak up and grab her from behind. It was a physical feeling, and yet she understood that the *somebody* in question was her own inferiority, which, she assumed, would be proven the moment her new control slipped. She had dreams in which she got rejected by every college she applied to, or picked a massive fight with her mom in front of Jonah, or bit down while giving him head.

Sylvie was aware that she liked getting drunk because it was an excuse not to contain herself. She wasn't about to say so to Jonah, though. Instead, she offered him a deal that was its own vacation from control. "If you think I should drink less," she suggested, "then you cut me off."

He cocked his head toward her. "And you'll listen?"

"Cross my heart." She drew an *X* on her fleece-jacketed chest. They were on their way to a party near Jonah's house, tramping through dry leaves blown from neatly raked piles by the night wind. The air smelled faintly like ocean. It was too cold for outdoor sex, but maybe they could use one of Jonah's friends' hand-me-down Volvos or Benzes, fog up the windows, and pretend to be in *Titanic*. She would pretend, anyway.

Before she and Jonah had started having full sex that summer, Sylvie imagined that it would be another break from her new habit of self-control. It was, but only after drinking. Sober, she liked sex so much that, if she didn't watch herself, she came almost instantly. If that happened, the rest was—still fun, not dull, but *less*. When she was drunk, though, her orgasms took longer, and surprised her. She liked the sneakiness of the experience; liked drifting on the waves of pleasure that came and went, trusting that the one she was waiting for would arrive in time. It was the only circumstance in which she had such faith in her body. Otherwise, she now viewed it as an enemy. If it were on her side, it would be thinner. It would run faster. It would not be on such constant high alert.

She tried, sometimes, to conjure Grandma Estie's lessons in trusting her physical self, but it never worked, which made her afraid she hadn't inherited anything of Estie but her physique. Clearly, she was like her dad. She'd come to understand that Paul was a profoundly anxious person, that routines and rules made him more comfortable, but it seemed impossible to discuss her own anxiety with him. She was sure he'd just start wiping a counter or sorting mail, then walk away.

She knew other girls talked to their mothers. Hallie claimed her mom was her *friend*. Neither of Sylvie's parents engaged in friendship. Paul was a self-sustaining system. Carol maintained a rotation of committees and book clubs, but she never saw any of their members with Paul or one-on-one. Sylvie thought it seemed sad for Carol to have a husband who never wanted to host or attend the dinners that Hallie and Rachel's moms seemed to live for. She herself loved going to parties with Jonah, watching his friendships, even sharing in them, especially now that she and her friends were getting perceptibly less intertwined. It wasn't that anything had happened between them, but Rachel was spending a lot of time with the stoners, and ever since Hallie had gotten her driver's license, she'd been going to Boston twice a week to serve food to the homeless clients of the Pine Street Inn. She'd invited Sylvie to join, but Jonah had pointed out that it was too late for volunteering to make a difference on Sylvie's college applications, and she had to concentrate on her grades.

In the months leading up to early-admission college decisions, Sylvie's anxiety got worse and worse. Marblehead—or *her* Marblehead—was the kind of town in which families agonized aloud about college but never tuition. Kids who would need student loans didn't talk about it. Paul and Carol had informed Sylvie that they would pay full freight at one of the few institutions they considered worth the money. She bargained them into including the University of Massachusetts Amherst, which they persisted in looking down on no matter how often she pointed out that it was their state's flagship school.

Applying to UMass Amherst was important to Sylvie in part because it had a high-enough acceptance rate for in-state applicants that she felt comfortable about her odds of getting in there, which was not true anywhere else. She hardly did extracurriculars—nothing but cross-country, which she felt irrationally sure admissions committees would realize was mainly about weight control—and though her grades and scores were very good, she had no coherent thoughts about what she wanted to study. Something that let her read a lot, and maybe helped her improve herself. She thought she could do that pretty much anywhere. Really, she cared about UMass because she and Jonah had applied early decision to Amherst College, and if he got in there and she didn't, she could at least go to school in the same town.

She had told Jonah she was afraid of not getting in. It was not a fear he shared, either for himself or for her. At the start of the admissions process, he'd said, "Let me be your cheerleader." It was a great kindness, though not one Sylvie's friends understood. They thought Jonah gave her an inferiority complex. Rachel said he was only fake fun. Hallie said it made no sense for Sylvie, who had dreamed of glamour for so many years, to only apply to the crunchy New England schools Jonah wanted. You couldn't wear mesh and stilettos in western Massachusetts.

Sylvie didn't care. Her friends had never had sex, which meant neither of them knew what they were talking about, relationship-wise. Nor did they understand the money aspect. Although Paul had gone to the University of Florida, he'd made clear that he wouldn't pay for a single school in that state. Part of Sylvie had been relieved when he said so. She wasn't sure she could bear setting foot in Florida without her grandparents. Without them, it didn't have a fraction of Jonah's magnetic pull. Being around him made her hopeful that she would someday match his confidence. His desire to be around *her* made her believe it didn't matter that she hadn't yet. Jonah could be confident for her. He showed her a valuable version of herself. Could a college do that? Sylvie thought not.

It turned out that Jonah had been right not to worry. They looked together at their Amherst decisions: both were yeses. Sylvie was overjoyed. Within an hour, Rachel and Hallie had texted to say that they, too, had gotten into their top choices—Wellesley for Hallie, Bard for Rachel— which meant the three of them could see each other regularly. When she told Jonah that, he just nodded, unable to stop talking about what a good time he was going to have with her at Amherst. At school the next day, she heard him telling someone how lucky he felt that he and Sylvie would be going to college together, and she felt a wave of delight so hot and powerful that she snuck into what she still thought of as their supply closet and texted him to meet her there.

Jonah, who was highly responsive to texts, appeared within moments. She pulled him in and jammed a broom handle under the door. It was a roomy closet, enough that they could've had sex, but that was not Sylvie's vision. She knelt and started to undo his jeans. It was one of the frustrations of her life that he always bought ones with button flies.

"Hang on, hang on," Jonah said. "What's this about?"

She sat on her heels. "It's not *about* anything."

"You just decided it was a good idea to blow me in a closet?"

"Isn't it?"

"No, Sylvie." Scorn licked at the words. "Someone could come in."

"We've never done anything at school," she said. It was the nearest thing to a logical argument she could muster. "And we're running out of time."

"I can live with that."

"Boring," she said lightly.

Jonah began rebuttoning his pants. "I assumed you wanted to talk to me about something."

"In a closet?"

He shrugged. "Privacy, I guess. But I don't want to stay in here. It smells." He lifted her to her feet. "Wait a couple minutes after I leave, okay? If a teacher sees us come out together, we'll get in trouble."

Sylvie could feel her face burning. Her throat hurt as if the blow job had gone forward; as if he'd been aggressive about it, pushing himself all the way in. After Jonah left, she leaned her forehead on the cinder-block wall and let her legs shake.

For months, Sylvie had imagined that college would be a paradise of sexual opportunity for her and Jonah: no curfews, no parents, no rules. Now she saw another reality. Maybe Jonah had rejected her offer because he knew that, starting in September, she would be available at all times. She found the thought thrilling, but maybe it was the opposite for him. Maybe she'd ruined everything by getting into Amherst. She probably had. She'd be too present there, too easy to get to. She'd be a high-school girlfriend minus the high-school joys of sneaking and secrecy, and she knew, deep in her panicking body, that the moment Jonah recognized that, he'd want to be free.

4.

Jonah did not dump Sylvie at the start of college, but he threw himself into his schoolwork and social life with a fervor she could not share. Everyone at Amherst both frightened and slightly repulsed her. Sylvie's new peers had diseases to cure, habitats to save, geopolitical problems to solve. She couldn't tell whether they lacked humility or she lacked ambition. She'd spent hours of her childhood discussing Bosnia, Palestine, and the American epidemic of gun violence with her grandfather, but she'd never thought she could grow up to fix much. Was that realism or defeatism? And how could anyone not feel defeated now, in the fall of 2004, with Bush heading for a second term despite his war in Iraq? Sylvie tried to be glad Grandpa Ilya wasn't around to watch his adoptive country decimate somebody else's, but she missed him too much for that.

Longing for her grandfather did help her choose a major. She was going to study philosophy because it connected her to him and was, therefore, comforting. Interesting, too. It gave her mind new ways of working and kept her occupied when Jonah had too many plans to fit in sex with her.

She tried complaining about his schedule on the phone with Rachel, who erupted into giggles. "I'm sorry," she said, catching her breath. "I shouldn't laugh. I just—I *told* you Jonah wasn't real fun. A really fun person wouldn't rather join clubs than bone his girlfriend."

"He's making friends," Sylvie said weakly.

"A fun person doesn't need clubs to make friends."

Sylvie considered the argument, but the evidence was not in its favor.

By October, Jonah was already at the center of a large and swirling posse. He had a regular cafeteria table, which Sylvie appreciated, since it gave her a place to sit. He knew upperclassmen. He no longer texted Sylvie back with his old speed. Instead, he left her hanging. For hours, sometimes. It was mortifying how much she minded. When he didn't reply to her messages, her chest started hurting. She grew sweaty and, if enough time went by, nauseous. Once, freshman winter, he didn't text her back for a full afternoon and evening, and she actually threw up from distress.

It didn't help that Jonah always wanted Sylvie to text back quickly. She was just in the library most of the time, he pointed out over dinner one night. Why couldn't she look at her phone?

"I'm reading," she said.

He wrinkled his nose. Given the academic choice, Jonah took problem sets over books. "Your homework is more interesting than me?"

"No," Sylvie said quickly. "Not at all. But I do—I mean, it *is* interesting. We're reading this book in Psychology and Philosophy, *Man's Search for Meaning*, that I can't tell if my grandparents would have liked or hated." She waited for an invitation to describe the book, which was by a Holocaust survivor, Viktor Frankl, who argued that the freedom most central to human existence—the least alienable right—was the *freedom to choose one's attitude in any given set of circumstances*. His argument reminded Sylvie of her grandparents' existential dedication to fun, and yet he also maintained that *happiness cannot be pursued; it must ensue*. She knew Ilya and Estie had pursued happiness. She wished she could have them tell her how they managed to catch it.

Jonah asked about neither them nor the book. He crossed his arms over his chest. It was warm in the dining hall, but he still wore his full college uniform: knit watch cap and Patagonia fleece quarter-zip, paired with mud-stained boat shoes and Sylvie's old enemy, the button-fly jeans.

"I'm sorry," she said. "I'll text you."

He softened his body. "It's just that I'm so busy, and I want to spend my free time with you when I have it."

She brushed her foot against his. For once, nobody else was at their table. "We're free now."

"And we're together. I do have Investment Club after dinner, though."

Sylvie imagined the face Hallie would make at the thought of Investment Club. She heard Rachel cackling at its name. She herself thought it would be nice if she wanted to hear about Investment Club, just like it would be nice if Jonah wanted to hear about *Man's Search for Meaning*. But that would be a perk. Jonah was a necessity. In high school, she had thought that she needed him; now, far from her friends and the small comforts of her home, she genuinely did. It was terrifying. She imagined herself as a helium balloon tied to a rock. If the knot came undone, she'd fly into space. She'd vanish entirely, or else descend dead, a scrap of glittering litter.

She told Jonah none of this, just like she didn't tell him when she turned down a President's Day visit to Hallie with Rachel because she could count on his sustained attention only on weekends. She did try to convince him to go to Montreal with them over spring break, but he said Rachel would bring drugs and get them arrested at the border, and he couldn't be involved in that. Although Sylvie told herself she could go without him, when she picked up her phone to say so, a sick sensation shot from her sternum all the way to the palms of her hands, and she replied with a lie she knew was transparent: *My parents want me to come home.*

It was humiliating to need his proximity so badly. She complained about it to her turtle, who remained a strong presence in her life through college, though she'd ruined Captain Lightning and Otto DeFay by fantasizing about sleeping with them.

It's like I don't exist without Jonah, she said. Like if I go more than a mile from him, I'll evaporate.

You're complaining about not existing to your imaginary friend?

I guess.

Sounds like a philosophy problem. Take it to a professor.

I can't do that, Sylvie said.

Why not?

Office hours are for school problems, not life problems.

The turtle tapped his claws together. So, he said. Try a shrink.

Sylvie rejected the idea of seeking help, though it recurred periodically for the rest of the spring. She had a plan for herself. She was going to spend her summer in Marblehead, reading Plato's many dialogues. She had encountered his ultimate reality of forms briefly in a class, and she thought that if she truly comprehended it, it would eliminate her existence issue. Also, though no one she knew at Amherst would especially respect her for it, she could feel quietly pleased with herself if, when asked what she'd done with her break, she could say, "Oh, I read all of Plato."

Jonah wasn't interested in the nature of her plan, but he liked that it meant she'd be home. He'd be in Marblehead, too, commuting to an internship in Boston. Hallie and Rachel were doing the same, which meant Sylvie would get to see them all summer. She told herself it would be perfect. Like high school, but better, since a year without their presence had taught her how much their friendship meant to her.

But they seemed to think it meant less. It took them only a few weeks to let her know. On a Sunday afternoon at the beach, early enough in June that all three of them were still consciously nurturing their tans, Rachel smacked Sylvie's phone out of her hand as she flipped it open.

"Enough," Rachel said.

"Just checking to see if Jonah texted."

"Yeah, Sylvie. We know."

"You do that a lot," Hallie agreed.

Hallie seemed largely unchanged by college, but she'd switched from the red Speedo suit she'd worn—clung to, in Sylvie's estimation—throughout high school to a black string bikini whose knots she kept fretfully tightening. She reached for one now, and Sylvie, trying to tease, said, "Enough."

Hallie gave her a long look. "You know," she said, "it's a little controlling if Jonah expects you to text him back right away."

Sylvie looked at the closed phone. "He doesn't."

"Are you sure?"

"He's my boyfriend, Hal."

Hallie shrugged. "And we're your friends."

"Which means," Rachel added, "that it's our job to tell you the truth."

Sylvie wondered if this was a premeditated attack. Maybe Hallie and Rachel had been discussing her in order to approach as a united front, a thought that made her feel both excluded and infantilized.

For the rest of the summer, she tried hard to demonstrate her independence from Jonah and her worth as a member of their trio, a fun and self-sufficient friend who didn't need to be talked or worried about. It became a much greater priority than reading Plato, who wasn't helping anyway. His *Republic* had too much theology and justice, not enough reality and self. Sylvie was glad to ignore it in favor of her friends. She never refused an invitation from Rachel or Hallie, even chose them over Jonah when she could persuade herself to. He said nothing about it until they were driving back to Amherst, his trunk and back seat jammed with milk crates full of clothes and books.

"It seemed like you really missed Hallie and Rachel last year," he began.

She nodded.

"And I could tell it was nice for you to have a whole summer with them. I'm glad you got it." He paused. "I was wondering, though, if maybe they made it harder for you to adjust to school."

"What do you mean?"

"All you did was text them and study." He put his hand on her thigh. "And I get that you like philosophy, but it seemed like you weren't having fun, which makes me feel bad. You came to Amherst because of me, and I want you to like it."

"So do I."

"I'm not saying you shouldn't text Hallie and Rachel. I just think it would help if you did more on campus. You could join an intramural team or something."

She made a face, since he'd returned his eyes to the road. "No sports."

"Okay, then a club. You could do Campus Dems."

"I could," she agreed. It was a gubernatorial election year. Grandpa Ilya would have encouraged her to campaign for Deval Patrick, maybe even flown up to knock doors with her. She told herself she'd try it, but in practice, the thought of introducing herself to two whole sets of strangers—in the Amherst Democrats, then in town—was too intimidating. She was grateful for Jonah's ongoing encouragement to go out, meet people, make friends of her own, but she couldn't.

She was self-conscious about her relationships with Hallie and Rachel now, too. She was afraid they were analyzing her behind her back. She texted them less and less, and when one of them called, she found herself so afraid of revealing that she was no good at college that she hardly said anything at all. Before long, she was waiting hours to reply to their messages, hoping to create the illusion that she was now leading the busy and satisfying life Jonah wanted for her. It was not a change that made her more present anywhere on campus but the library, where she'd curl up for hours, having imaginary discussions with her grandfather about her Pre-Socratic Philosophy course. She knew he would laugh at the Manichaean idea of evil gnawing into good like Pac-Man, but Sylvie liked it anyway. It was much more useful than Plato for representing what was going on in her brain.

Spending more time with her thoughts did not improve her anxiety. Nothing did until winter break, when Rachel, who had gotten into pills at Bard, gave her a handful of Xanax. Sylvie rationed them out by quarters once she was back at school, but they were still gone far too soon. She wished for them while hanging out with Jonah's suitemates and the rotating cast of girls they dated, all of whom approached her with suspicion. She assumed something about her was off-putting. Probably they could smell her insecurity.

She got in the habit of taking long walks to wear herself out. Sometimes she looped by the mental-health center, or lingered at its door, but therapy was for people with real problems: eating disorders, suicidal ideation, alcoholic moms. Besides, how could she talk to a psychologist when she couldn't even talk to her boyfriend? She imagined sitting on a couch opposite some lady in linen, not a single word emerging from either of their mouths. By the end of sophomore year, Sylvie still hadn't made a single real friend.

Then, junior year, in her Hegel seminar, she got adopted by a pair of seniors, who scooped her into their friendship so swiftly she hardly noticed it was happening. Paola Figueroa and Riva Caplan were the only two girls in their year writing philosophy theses. They were just as full of jitters and hang-ups as Sylvie, but they made jokes about it. They took medications and also did other drugs. They lounged around their apartment drinking beers and saying they couldn't go out because they had the sickness unto death. Sylvie lounged with them. She traded clothes with them, watched *Friday Night Lights*, asked Riva—the first Jewish girl Sylvie ever met who eschewed hair dryers and straightening irons—to teach her curly-hair styling skills. Riva, like Sylvie, was the granddaughter of Holocaust survivors, and she shared Sylvie's concept of Jewishness as less a religion than a worldview and a sensibility. Sylvie had read hardly any Jewish literature, but Riva introduced her to Philip Roth, Isaac Bashevis Singer, and Grace Paley, whose stories got Sylvie so excited she ran to Riva and Paola's to discuss them.

"My grandparents thought the same way as her!" she said, flapping a book in Riva's face. "They wanted Jews to remind everyone we're still here—to be 'a splinter in the toe of civilizations,' just like Paley says."

"It's not *Paley*," Riva said, laughing. "It's the character."

Paola, meanwhile, raised an eyebrow. "You want to be toe splinters?"

Before Sylvie could answer, Riva smacked her friend. "Of course we do."

Sylvie couldn't remember ever feeling as understood as she did in that moment. If she had, it was before her grandparents died. After that, she noticed herself texting Jonah less when she was at Paola and Riva's, though lags in her communication still upset him. So did her new habit of getting high with them. He still didn't smoke, and he hated when she got in his bed smelling like weed. Often he'd refuse to have sex, but she was unfazed. Sharing a joint with Riva and Paola dialed her agitation down so far that she didn't feel her usual grief at sexual rejection, though she did learn that she had to be careful: if she overshot, she'd pace in circles for hours, ruminating on her inferiority. If she got just high enough, though, she could, for the first time in years, *talk*.

Sylvie told her new friends about her sadness and anxiety. She talked to them about her mom—"She sounds like a bitch," Riva decided, but Paola, head tilted, said, "Maybe she's miserable"—and about Hallie and Rachel, from whom she felt even more distant now that she had new friendships to compare the old ones to. She couldn't imagine her high-school friends understanding her bad inner life, or taking the baseless insecurities and anxieties that she, Riva, and Paola laughed about together as anything but a sign that they should worry about her. She'd still never managed to have a good conversation about sex with Rachel or Hallie, even now that neither of them was anything close to a virgin. They just wanted to talk about dating and hookups, not about actual fucking. With Paola and Riva, it was a constant subject. She told them how much she'd liked it from the very beginning, what a relief she found it to let her boyfriend take charge of her body. Her favorite thing in the world was the sensation of Jonah pushing himself inside her, holding her wrists down, pinning her to the bed like a butterfly to Styrofoam.

"Oh, I like that, too," Riva said. "It's fun submitting to a guy." Sylvie had never thought to use the language of submission, but instantly, she knew it was right. She loved letting Jonah change her in bed the way she loved letting him change her out of it. She and Riva agreed that the former was one of life's great luxuries.

Paola had different preferences. She told stories about her boyfriend, Caolán, whom she'd met studying abroad in Dublin and who delighted in Skype sex. In the physical world, Caolán's SSRIs made it tricky for him to orgasm, but he and Paola could fuck until he went soft or she lost interest, and then he would go down on her until—she said, giggling—"My body just shuts down and I fall asleep."

Sylvie could hardly imagine sex that went on so long. She'd gotten better at pacing herself since high school, but barely. Until meeting Riva and Paola, she'd had no idea her easy orgasms were a gift. She'd assumed—it was true in porn!—that all girls could come on command. Now she wondered if she'd be able to with anyone but Jonah, and what sex would be like if she couldn't. Both questions opened doors. By late fall, she found herself spending a shocking quantity of her alone time masturbating to Caolán-related fantasies, or just mulling the issues they raised: Would she like to be the center of attention in bed? Would Jonah like it? Or would asking erase the central joy of sex, which was letting him turn her mind off? During sex with Jonah, Sylvie never worried. She never *thought*. She tried not to come, then she came, then she vanished into a cloud of enjoyable aftershocks. How would that work if she was setting the course? What if it didn't work at all?

Sylvie did not mention her questions or fantasies to Jonah. Even if she didn't explain about Caolán, he'd tie them to Riva and Paola, of whom he already disapproved. He thought they were lesbians; that they smoked too much; that Riva was fat and neurotic and Paola was a bossy rich bitch. Sylvie tried explaining that intense female friendships were normal, and it was also normal for girls to like getting high. Riva wasn't any fatter or more neurotic than Sylvie, and Amherst was full of rich bitches. Paola wasn't bossy, besides. She was great.

Jonah was unmoved. He said he didn't *have* to like her friends, but he missed her when she spent so much time hanging around them. He wanted her to come to parties with him, to join in his group's pregaming like always. When she did, he rewarded her by kicking his suitemates out, promising to meet them at the night's destination. It was a legitimate treat to take advantage of the common spaces and, in her case, the opportunity to be loud. She began thinking, that winter, that one of those empty-suite nights would be a good time to try having sex like Paola and Caolán. It was what her brain wanted, and potentially what her body did, too. She just needed to get herself to say so.

On a sleety night in February, after four nerve-dulling shots of Captain Morgan, Sylvie managed not to come during sex. She didn't start putting her clothes on when Jonah did. She propped herself up on her elbows, legs spread apart, admiring his ropy back in his room's dim yellow light. His skin glistened slightly. He twisted to look at her.

"Let's go, Sylvie."

"I didn't come."

His eyebrows drew down. "I noticed that."

"I'd like to." She shivered. "I'd like you to make me."

Jonah scooped his shirt off the floor. "I'm getting dressed."

Instantly, her ribs tightened. "It'll take thirty seconds."

"I'd have to wash my hands."

"You could go down on me."

"Then I'd have to wash my face."

Sylvie sat shakily. Her vagina felt swollen and sore. It seemed possible that putting on her skintight jeans would provide enough pressure for a small, shitty orgasm. If not, wearing them would be excruciating.

"Jonah," she said. "Please."

He tossed her bra at her. "I want to go."

"So go."

"With you." His tone softened. "I like going places with you."

Sylvie inhaled the room's funk of gym shorts, spilled liquor, ancient carpet, dirty sheets. Her eyes stung. She felt abandoned. He had never said no to her so brusquely before. She told herself it was only because he'd been drinking, or maybe because he was so used to her having orgasms during sex that her failure to do so had unsettled him. She wriggled into her party clothes, tugged her boots over her calves, and trailed Jonah down the dark hall.

In the stairwell, she had an idea. Jonah was majoring in economics. He liked talking about debts and deals. Also, though her dream of daily college sex still hadn't come to fruition, he had recently gotten into quickies in risky locations. Years after her initial attempt, she'd been giving supply-closet blow jobs. Surely a staircase would appeal.

She stopped him on the second-floor landing. "You owe me," she said.

"I do?"

Sylvie nodded. "Fair's fair. You owe me one orgasm. You can do it now"—she lifted her chin, body heating—"or after the party. You choose."

Her pulse raced. Pride swelled through her. Maybe she would tell Riva and Paola a version of this story, revised to be sexier. Already she could feel the ghost of Jonah's palm pressing against the seam of her jeans. She tipped herself toward him, prepared to be kissed, unprepared in mind and body when, instead, he shoved her away with both hands.

Sylvie remembered the rest only in flashes. She saw herself crumpled on the first-floor landing; careening through campus alone, mouth fountaining blood; pounding on Riva and Paola's door. Riva was out of town, but Paola was home. She mopped Sylvie up, took her to urgent care, and held her hand while she got stitches—she'd bitten straight through her lip—and flunked the concussion protocol.

Sylvie spent the night in Riva's bed. In the morning, Paola walked her back to her dorm. Jonah was asleep outside her room. Paola woke him, then told him to fuck off.

"It's okay," Sylvie said. "He can come in."

"Do you want me to stay, too?" Paola asked.

Sylvie shook her head, which made it swirl horribly. For a moment, she thought she would vomit. Jonah took her arm, slipped her key from her pocket, and helped her inside.

He didn't leave her alone until the concussion healed. He made microwave burritos and popcorn, held the greasy Pop Secret bag open for her when she really did need to throw up. He told her a hundred times how sorry he was that this had happened. "I was in too big a rush to get to the party," he said. "We should have messed around in the stairs like you wanted. Maybe then you wouldn't have tripped."

Sylvie was not too concussion-fogged to notice that his story didn't match hers. But what was she going to do, argue? It was work to produce a single sentence. Besides, her memory cut out between one landing and the next. She had told Paola he'd pushed her down the stairs, but for all she knew, he was right—she'd just stumbled.

Paola came over Wednesday afternoon, once Jonah had started going to his classes again. She brought Sylvie's scarf in a Walgreens bag. It was stiff and matted, the green wool irredeemably stained. Sylvie could think of little but how awful she looked: black thread bristling from her lip, bruise peacocking from her cheek. Belatedly, it struck her that she hadn't been self-conscious at all with Jonah. With Paola, she was ashamed of her face.

"Do you want me to help you with anything?" Paola asked, sitting in Sylvie's desk chair. "Wash your hair, or—"

Sylvie touched a squashed curl. "Jonah can."

Very gently, Paola said, "So can I."

"I don't think he hurt me," Sylvie said.

Paola looked down. Sylvie had yet to open her blackout shades, which created a constant dusk that obscured the other girl's expression. She could see only Paola's hair gleaming at her part, the Elsa Peretti bean necklace hanging over her sweater. "Yes, you do," Paola said. "But you don't want to lose him."

She was right. Sylvie couldn't quite say so. It was easier to deny, easier to let go of Paola than Jonah, and so Sylvie let her only college friendships wane. Not immediately, but through the spring, she saw Riva and Paola less and less. She skipped the party they threw after exams, ignored their calls, and chose not to stick around for graduation, knowing that week would have been her chance to say a decent goodbye.

She didn't regret the trade she was making. How could she, when she was finally getting what she'd wanted? Her concussion seemed to have switched on a piece of Jonah that could be both partner and friend. He texted back quickly now, and he asked about her reading the way she'd wanted him to freshman year. She could sense the duty underneath his questions, but she chose not to care. She was doing an independent study that summer on philosophical and literary responses to the Holocaust, and describing Arendt's and Benjamin's ideas to her boyfriend helped her untangle them for herself, though it did get them in a fight about evil.

Sylvie agreed with Hannah Arendt that evil could come from anywhere, in anyone. Jonah insisted that was absurd. She tried telling him his ideas lined up with those of Isaiah Berlin, who thought the origin of evil was fundamentally inexplicable, and he took offense.

"I'm not like you," he said. "My ideas don't come from anyone."

"We all get our—"

He cut her off. "My ideas are *mine*."

Sylvie let it go. She didn't want to stop Jonah from asking questions. He was doing it during sex, too. She found it wasn't easy to answer, but telling him what she wanted mattered now that her gift had left her. She could no longer come at will, and she could come less often from penetration alone. Sometimes she thought smashing her head on a concrete floor had knocked her talent out of her. Other times she worried she'd squandered it, burned through a lifetime of easy orgasms too quickly, not seeing their rarity or worth. On the bright side, losing her gift had no effect on her libido. If anything, she found sex—absurd statement, but true—*sexier*. She liked asking Jonah for orgasms. Actually, she liked to beg. It was the most satisfying way of ceding control to him that she'd found yet, and it gave her such a profound sense of peace that, after six years of keeping it secret, she began telling him about her anxiety.

Sylvie had been frightened that Jonah would dismiss her jitters, but he took what she said seriously. He grew determined to calm her, to meet her needs, to reassure her that he wanted a future with her. So determined, in fact, that he proposed that August, shortly before senior year began. Sylvie had not thought for a second that an engagement was coming. She assumed, when he suggested rowing on Lake Wyola, that it was just an outing. He liked to be in nature. He'd gone to summer camp for years. Not for a moment did she wonder if he had an agenda until, in the middle of the water, surrounded by bufflehead ducks and the glassy reflections of pines, he slid from his tin seat and knelt.

Sylvie said yes immediately. She managed not to jump or scream or cry. She was so astonished that she could see but not feel herself shaking. She let Jonah take the ring—*big* ring—from its velour cradle and slide it onto her finger, both of them conscious that she was trembling too hard to touch it. If she did, she might launch it straight out of the boat.

For months, she stared into her diamond as if it were a crystal ball. It temporarily supplanted her turtle, who, like Rachel and Hallie, kept asking why Jonah wanted to get married so young. It was 2007, not 1957. Her diamond said the year and reason were irrelevant. It said getting married would pin her down in a comforting way. Marriage would be like starting every day by smoking a fraction of a joint or eating a corner of one of Rachel's Xanaxes. It would be like falling asleep with Jonah's arms locked around her at night. Besides, the diamond pointed out, she had no plans beyond vague thoughts of grad school, and where did philosophy grad school lead you, really? Sylvie wished you could go get a job as a philosopher, but in the twenty-first century, she was fairly sure that just meant being unemployed. You could be a professor, but she struggled to imagine herself in front of a classroom. She'd have liked to talk about teaching with Paola, who'd gone straight into a PhD program, but she'd let Riva and Paola go.

Instead, she tried Jonah. Walking to his dorm one fall evening, face half buried in her cashmere blanket scarf, she asked, "Do you think I'd be a good teacher?"

He didn't pause for a second. "No."

"Why?"

"Because you just like studying. Teachers like *school*."

It was an unsettling answer. Despite her collegiate unhappiness, Sylvie had never thought of herself as not liking school. But of course in Jonah's eyes she didn't: to him, school was not only classes but clubs, sports, the community a teacher or professor should help create.

"What *would* I be good at?"

Jonah took her hand. "Being married to me."

Sylvie saw no reason to doubt that. Four years earlier, she'd imagined college as a sex-on-demand paradise; now, having not learned her lesson, she thought marriage would be the same. She was stunned by how hot she found the idea of eternal commitment. It was the most intense form of submission she could dream of, and so she went with it in not just bed, but life.

Jonah got a consulting job at McKinsey in Boston. Sylvie had assumed they would live in the city, but when he said he'd found an apartment in Swampscott, one town south of Marblehead, she said great. She was doing her best to say yes and thank you to everything Jonah offered, future-wise. What else could she do when she had no ideas of her own?

It was the same with the wedding. Carol took over the planning immediately, and Sylvie let her. All she cared about was the guest list, to which she had no friends but Rachel and Hallie to add. She did write Riva's and Paola's names down, but she deleted them immediately. After that, she did her best to answer her mother's questions about linens and bouquets and bands, but wedding details seemed trivial beside the more urgent issue of what she was going to do with her brain all day after she graduated. Also the issue of earning money, though Jonah told her over and over that she didn't have to. Neither of them had student debt. Paul and Carol were bankers. Jonah's father was a judge. His mother, the daughter of a wealthy German Jewish family in New York, didn't work, but she liked to day-trade. Jonah had his own set of stocks and associated income, but he wouldn't need to touch it. On a McKinsey salary, he'd have no trouble handling both his and Sylvie's expenses. He was *excited* to. He couldn't wait to take real care of her.

Sylvie was grateful, but she was also ashamed. She knew that paying for her life was a sexy thought for Jonah, but it made her feel like a pathetic baby, a spoiled dilettante who should be relieved her grandparents were dead, they'd be so disappointed by her now. She should have gotten herself a job on the Obama campaign. She should have the energy to *think* about that kind of job. Her grandmother had been a fountain of vitality. She'd survived Ravensbrück and Bergen-Belsen, and yet she walked around beaming all day. Estie saw her life as a joy and a privilege. Sylvie, increasingly, saw hers as a challenge to which she could not rise.

Marriage, at least, seemed like it would be an exception. Once Sylvie was home after graduation, the wedding also seemed to improve her relationship with her mother, who not only enjoyed having company at the walk-throughs and showrooms but seemed to love the thought of her daughter as a wife. "Marriage was the best thing that ever happened to me," she said while picking cutlery.

Sylvie's instinct was to say, "What about motherhood?" but she couldn't quite get the words out. Asking would have spoiled the afternoon, and she didn't want to sit in tense silence while they got manicures.

She'd never cared about her nails before, but it pleased Jonah to see her improving her outer self. He liked the salon-style Sylvie. Liked her wedding-dress diet, too. Possibly he had suggested it. Him or Carol. Hard to remember who brought it up first.

Sylvie thought she looked beautiful at her wedding, though Jonah made it clear that he disapproved of her dress. It was Vera Wang, flouncy and highly beaded, chosen, in a rare moment of faith in herself, because she thought—and her mother agreed—that Estie would have loved it. Sylvie tried to be happy with that decision. She tried to be happy with the wedding, too. She did feel transported by the ceremony, cried all the way through the vows, but at the party, she came adrift. Jonah had swarms of friends there. She had two. Every time Hallie and Rachel took a break from the dance floor, Sylvie found herself dancing alone.

She told herself that the honeymoon would make up for the wedding. Jonah had booked a week in Acadia National Park. It was July, and Maine was at its most stunning. Fir trees leapt into the bright sky, and the ocean glittered green below every trail they hiked. They skinny-dipped in cold waves, ate lobster rolls on rock beaches. All very lovely, but no amount of loveliness could make up for the fact that every night, they set up their tent on ground that seemed to be composed one hundred percent of sharp stones. No sleeping pad could offer enough cushion. No bug spray could ward off the mosquitoes that beset them at dusk. In the day, the woods were far too full of hikers for any attempt at off-trail activity to get far. Around the week's halfway point, Sylvie decided to just be grateful Jonah was so hot in his tiny hiking shorts, his pack cinched tight at his waist. Visual appreciation was, evidently, the only form of sexual satisfaction she was getting on her honeymoon, so she should be glad the looking was good.

Driving home, Jonah announced that he had one more surprise. Sylvie faked enthusiasm as he blindfolded her with a ratty bandana. When he removed it one Radiohead album later, they were in the half-moon driveway of the towering brick Portland Regency Hotel & Spa.

Sylvie squealed and kissed him. "We're staying here?"

"Happy honeymoon."

She could feel him smiling. He kissed her ear, then pressed their foreheads together. One of his hands went to her waist; to her great satisfaction, he slipped the other beneath the waistband of her shorts.

"Was this always part of the plan?"

He shook his head. "I realized camping was a fuckup. I called my mom a couple days ago, when you were somewhere"—code for *you were shitting in the woods*—"and I had service. I told her we needed a romantic last night in Portland, and could she please, please help me out." He dug his fingers into her ass cheek, which sent a spike of arousal through her. She'd been wet since their wedding, from a mix of deferred desire and physical uncleanness, but evidently you could always get wetter.

Jonah shooed her into the shower the moment they reached their room. She took a long time, assuming he would join her. He liked shower sex, though Sylvie had tried explaining that water-slipperiness and vagina-slipperiness were—sad but true—natural enemies. But the door remained closed while she washed, detangled, and conditioned her hair, shaved her toes, legs, and armpits, and eliminated the bristles that circled her belly button and sprang from her nipples. After she ran out of grooming tasks, she dawdled a moment, admiring the shower itself, which had astonishing water pressure and was big enough to be a room of its own. It reminded Sylvie of the elevator in *Charlie and the Great Glass Elevator*. She drew a Vermicious Knid on one of the steamed-up walls, then rinsed her hair one last time and shut the water off. She'd waited more than long enough, and she didn't even want to fuck in the shower. She just hoped Jonah would clean up fast.

Sylvie dried off, buried herself in the hotel's ludicrously thick robe, and emerged from the bathroom, water dripping down her thighs. Jonah was lying naked on the white bedspread, left hand wrapped loosely around his dick. He wasn't quite masturbating, but he was hard enough to suggest he'd just stopped. Seven-day stubble shone on his jawline. Now that she smelled like luxury conditioner, she could pick up his trail funk—not just dried sweat and Off!, but the pheromonal bite of real body odor, the rancid ginkgo-tree salt of unwashed balls—from three feet away. Half of her was insulted. Half wanted to lick him clean.

"You're not going to shower?" she asked.

He lifted his head. "You don't want to have sex?"

She moved forward, stiff as a marionette. "I do."

"I thought so." Jonah's eyes glowed. He looked like a feral cat. "You're dying for it, right?"

Sylvie's face heated. Her vagina pulsed. She understood what Jonah was doing: nudging her to play up her neediness and reliance, to get into the mindset in which she started to beg. Ordinarily, she leapt at the chance. But today was the sexual start of their marriage, and she didn't want ordinary. She wanted transformative. She wanted, suddenly and intensely, to feel new.

"You stink." She straightened her shoulders. "I showered for you."

"I care about smell. You don't."

"I might."

His hand was moving on his erection again. Maintenance. "You don't."

"You have stubble. It's going to hurt."

"So no head for you."

Sylvie shed her robe. She stepped over their sleeping bags, their tent in its nylon sack. She stood at the foot of the king bed, enjoying Jonah's eyes on her. She wished his gaze felt less good. Her mind told her to order him into the shower, refuse to be touched until he didn't stink. But she'd learned very young to ask her body what it wanted, and it wanted Jonah inside her ten seconds ago.

She breathed deeply, allowing herself to turn toward the possibilities of rank, stubble-faced sex. Jonah watched closely. She climbed onto the bed, straddled him, and licked his sour neck.

"Good girl," he said hoarsely. His hands grazed her hips. He pulled her down, grinding his erection against her. She heard herself croak a little. In the old days, when she always came before he did, just this motion could be all she needed. Now, having the first orgasm would be a change.

She let the thought grow for a moment. Jonah kissed her. She pulled away. "I want to come first," she said.

He lifted his head from the pillow. "You do?"

"I do."

"You want to come before me."

She nodded. Hope rose in her. "You know," Jonah said, "I promised I'd take care of you."

"Is that a yes?"

"No." Without warning, he jerked his hips up so his whole penis slid straight inside her. She gasped and rocked forward to lessen the impact. Jonah grinned into her face. "You get to come today," he said. "But you know I decide how and when."

5.

After the honeymoon, Sylvie couldn't tell whether she was committed to letting Jonah make their life for them or too tired to take a bigger part. She agreed to all the ugly neutral furniture he wanted. She let him wrap up her grandparents' bougainvillea painting—"I know it's important to *keep* it, but we don't need to *hang* it"—and stash it under the bed. When, after he completed his training, he got assigned to a work project that required him to spend the second and fourth week of every month in Oklahoma, she at first made no objection to his paying obscene amounts for the convenience of leaving their car at the airport. When, in December, she mentioned that she'd like the option of driving in his absence, he shrugged and said, "Where do you want to go?"

She had no real answer. Neither of her friends was around: Hallie was in social-work school in Baltimore, and Rachel, who'd been offered a job at the Brooklyn Museum, had instead gone almost straight from Sylvie's wedding to rehab, which Hallie said shouldn't have come as a surprise. Sylvie had shrunk from the irritation in her friend's voice. It wasn't like Hallie to snap.

Without a social life, Sylvie had no need for a car. She could walk to the Stop & Shop, the nail salon, the gym, the yoga studio, the library, and the harbormaster's office, where she put her fancy degree to great use as an assistant marina manager. Jonah didn't respect the job, and neither did their parents, but Sylvie knew she couldn't bear sitting at home like Rosaline Sabransky, and she didn't have a corporate soul like Carol. Her ambitions—she thought she had them, somewhere—were free-floating and mainly involved the concept of work that made her happy. Until she had an idea of what that might mean, she was content to let her harbor paychecks slowly accumulate in the bank account she'd opened the summer before starting college. Jonah thought her salary barely deserved the name, but Sylvie felt it was fair compensation for copying paperwork and sitting in the break room with a mug of tea and the romance novels she'd taken to borrowing from the library. She missed philosophy, but she couldn't concentrate on it anymore.

For so many years, she had vibrated ceaselessly with nerves. No longer. Now it was like someone had thrown a heavy blanket over her. She missed her anxiety. It had kept her awake. Jonah thought she was just having a hard time dealing with change, which, he correctly pointed out, had also been the case at the start of college. He also thought she was suffering from understimulating work.

"You should quit," he suggested. It was a Saturday, and he was driving them into the city to go to bars with his friends.

"What would I do?"

"Exercise. See your parents."

"More than on Sundays? *No.*"

She and Jonah had agreed on hosting Sunday suppers with all four parents. It was efficient, but Sylvie considered the dinners a bleak chore. She found her in-laws unpleasant—Mrs. Sabransky never said anything positive, and Judge Sabransky never said anything at all—and although

Carol made skillful conversation at every meal, Sylvie found it slightly alienating to chat with her parents about whether Obama, for whom they had surprised her by voting, was starting his presidency on the right foot. Surely other families' dinners involved discussions of their own lives, or at least of people they actually knew.

"You could read," Jonah said.

Sylvie had not informed him that she spent a good chunk of each workday reading, nor did she, unless he was on a work trip, bring those novels home. She wasn't interested in getting questioned about her turn from philosophy to mild-to-moderately-steamy meet-cutes. It would be embarrassing enough to tell Jonah she had lost the capacity to focus on anything heavier or less formulaic than romance, but he'd guess that was only half the truth. Sylvie liked romance novels because all of them were about the beginnings of relationships, and it had only now struck her that marriage meant she'd never begin a relationship again.

"In college, it was all you did." Jonah continued. Affectionately, he added, "And then you'd tell me what you were reading and I'd have to pretend it made sense."

Sylvie had thought she'd done a better job explaining. Maybe he'd have resisted philosophy less if she'd described it more effectively.

"We graduated," she reminded him. "I'm a grown-up. I should work."

Jonah put his hand on her thigh. "You don't need to."

"I want to."

"No," Jonah said. "You don't. If you did, you wouldn't have majored in philosophy."

Sylvie recoiled into her seat. Jonah patted her leg and returned his hand to the wheel. It was March, the month in New England of mud and wet evening darkness, and the coastal towns slipping by them looked abandoned and gray. With dread she thought of the evening that awaited: Chinese food in cartons, there to be gobbled between games of beer pong, then a fake Irish pub, or karaoke, or a cocktail bar where, if Sylvie were to buy a round herself, she'd spend what she earned in a week.

She found herself in a club, and not one that matched her long-ago Miami daydreams. Nobody was dancing. One of Jonah's friends' dates had on a burgundy leather minidress. Sylvie couldn't stop looking at its seams and shaping, the raw hem where animal skin met girl. In her imagination, she, too, wore leather. She wore sequins and stilettos and mesh. In reality, she wore the clothes that Jonah thought suited her until she got thinner, which meant all her outfits were dull.

She went to the bathroom to study herself. Jeans over Spanx, loose black top, heels, hoops. Safe. Boring. Uncomfortable. After the wedding, Jonah had waited only two months before suggesting she go back on her diet. Of course she'd done it. Grandma Estie would have shrieked if she knew. She'd loathed the concept of weight loss. She would loathe this outfit, too. If she walked in right now, she'd cover her eyes with her hands, then, peeking between her fingers, say, Sylvinka, what are you wearing? Where are your colors? Where is your *shine*?

For a moment, Sylvie contemplated leaving the club. Instead, she went to the bar and, using the personal debit card she rarely touched, bought herself three tequila shots that caused the night to more or less vanish. She woke at daybreak on an inflatable mattress in somebody's living room, Jonah next to her. Her head throbbed. Not only her head. Dimly, she remembered Jonah tugging her close hours earlier, putting one hand over her mouth and using the other to get her close to orgasm before jamming his dick up her ass. She could feel that he'd used only spit—*maybe* spit—to ease the way.

She rolled onto her back to make use of the memory, or a version of the memory in which she'd actually gotten to come, before anyone else woke up. Jonah was asleep beside her, but she could masturbate without rousing him, even on an air mattress. It was a skill she'd needed to learn.

Since their honeymoon, he had gotten increasingly interested in stretching the amount of time between when Sylvie wanted an orgasm and when she got it. She learned from Google that this was called *edging*, and that other girls found it sexy and fun. Reading about it sent a wave of great emptiness through her. She hated the sick, chalky feeling of getting sent to make meals when she'd been about to come.

Sylvie tried for her whole first year of marriage to enjoy the power play of being left hanging. She told herself it was a natural outgrowth of her desire to relinquish control. And he always delivered, eventually.

By their anniversary in July—they went to Cape Cod for two nights, ate restaurant lobster, got sunburned—Sylvie had persuaded herself that, regardless of what she liked, marriage meant compromise. Sacrifice. Jonah had found a game he liked playing, and therefore she, as a good wife, would play it with him. She had also learned that on the internet. She was seeking its counsel often these days.

Google told Sylvie she was getting many parts of marriage wrong. Jonah was growing unresponsive to text messages, which distressed her. On days he texted less, she convinced herself he was angry at her, which, apparently, meant she had attachment issues and was insecure. Shortly after returning from Cape Cod, she decided to disprove that thesis by hiding her phone in a drawer for a whole workday. She made it to 10:15 a.m. before having a panic attack and digging the phone out. She had thirteen texts from Jonah, who thought she was ignoring him, or mad at him, or dead. When he got home that night, he was furious, which, in his case, meant cold. He didn't warm back up until after his next trip to Oklahoma, during which he texted even less than usual and didn't call a single time.

After that, Sylvie's anxiety was back. She welcomed it. She'd rather feel agitated than muted. She thought and worked faster, even with her concentration eroded by texting. She took pleasure in every little prick of reassurance she got from Jonah, from Google, from her renewed stream of ideas. Her current concept was that marriage had made her and Jonah a family, and the Family had Values and Norms. In her childhood, that had meant no mess or loudness. Maybe now it just meant slow orgasms and fast texts.

Do all families need rules, she asked Google. It gave her parenting tips. *Do couples need rules*, she tried, and got a resounding yes. But when she began investigating what those rules should be, she grew confused. Google said that anyone got to refuse or end sex at any point, but that withholding any desired part of it could be a form of abuse. It said your partner shouldn't lobby you to quit your job, which Jonah was still doing, but also that they should support you wholeheartedly and unconditionally, which Jonah objectively did. It reminded her that Kierkegaard said it was a *sad upside-downness* to try to change the person you love. You should change your love to meet them.

What confused Sylvie most of all, and what the internet could not tell her, was whether she should be changing her love or accusing Jonah of upside-downness. She needed a person—a real, living one, not an imaginary friend or a dead Danish philosopher—to weigh in. She wished she could go to Miami and talk to her grandparents. In October, she tried Rachel, who had gone from rehab to Brooklyn back to rehab and was now newly living at home. Hallie had visited her in both places, but Sylvie hadn't seen her since she was home just before Brooklyn.

When Sylvie arrived at their coffee date, she found her friend in a perfectly arranged state: nails done, hair chemically silky, eyes lined. She said, "You look amazing."

Rachel wrinkled her nose. "Fills the time."

Sylvie touched her thumbnail, slippery with gel polish. Jonah had surprised her a month ago by prepaying for four manicures at her preferred salon, so that Sylvie got smilingly waved off when she went to settle up. "What, grooming?"

"Yeah."

A small silence fell. They were at a new café in Marblehead, a marble-countered panini-press kind of place. Although it was cold, Sylvie wished they'd gone to the beach instead.

"Are you looking for a job?" Sylvie said.

Rachel shrugged. "I'd rather go back to New York, but I need to decide if I can."

"How do you decide that?"

Her friend studied her for a moment, as if measuring the question's sincerity. "By seeing if I start to get high again."

"Do you even—I mean, would you know how to do that in Marblehead?" Sylvie said. She meant it as a follow-up, a way to show interest. From the look on Rachel's face, she knew it was not.

"Sylvie," Rachel said slowly. "Are you asking me for a dealer?"

"No." Her voice scratched. She wasn't lying. She'd had no agenda. But now, despite the fury gathering on Rachel's face, the worst, most selfish part of Sylvie was thinking, well, yes, if Rachel knew somebody who sold weed or pills, that would help.

Rachel must have sensed the thought. Read it in Sylvie's eyes, felt it rising from her body. She picked up her coat—Sylvie *knew* that coat: gray wool, Bloomingdale's, $200 of babysitting money in 2003—and, without saying a word, walked away from the table and out the door.

Sylvie texted her floods of apologies. She understood that Rachel's silence was its own reply, but she couldn't stop herself until, that evening, Rachel wrote, *You've been acting selfish for a long time, but today was a new low*. A moment later, she added, *I don't really blame you. I blame Jonah. But as long as you're with him, I need you to leave me alone.*

Never before had Sylvie felt so ashamed. She could not bear to sit alone with either her regret or the question of whether Jonah really was at fault for her behavior. She tried to be angry at Rachel for saying so—she, Sylvie, was a grown woman, able to be an asshole all by herself—but she couldn't. Nor could she talk to Jonah. Hearing Rachel's accusation would only render him more judgmental of her. He thought all her suffering was her own fault, which Sylvie had always known was wrong but now realized was also cruel. Proof of Jonah's upside-downness, possibly.

She called Hallie two days later, on a sleety, awful afternoon when Jonah was in Oklahoma and she'd gotten stung by rain the whole walk home. Wrapped in a staticky synthetic-fur blanket—a Jonah purchase, like everything else in the house—she cupped her phone in her hands as it rang once, twice, then no more. Hallie had hung up. Maybe she was in class, Sylvie thought, but Hallie took only a moment to text. *I talked to Rachel*, she wrote, *and I agree with her. Jonah makes you selfish. You might not be ready to admit it, but it's because he makes you so miserable. I want you to be happy, and I want to be in your life again if he isn't.* In a second message, she added, *I hope it's when, not if.*

Sylvie was so shocked that she turned to her mother. She even brought her lunch: chicken salad made with Greek yogurt, cabbage-leaf wraps, cantaloupe—one of Carol's few weaknesses—for dessert. But once she was there, in her parents' cold, recently remodeled kitchen, Sylvie didn't know how to begin. Her mother had always made it seem like bad manners to speak about feelings. "Jonah wants me to quit the harbor," she said.

"Is he suggesting you look for something more stimulating?"

"Has he talked to you about it?"

"It wouldn't be inappropriate if he had."

"So the answer is yes." Sylvie set her cabbage wrap down. Her carefully poached chicken breast was dry and sour. It needed rye bread and yellow mustard. It needed *fat*, which she didn't eat. She'd had to go out to get the chicken. When Jonah was traveling, she generally subsisted on lentils and celery, which he referred to as Tragic Diet Shit, though dieting was his idea. A sudden heat rose in her chest. "What if he's sick of me?"

Carol's cool did not break. "He isn't," she said. "He just married you."

"A year ago." Sylvie's eyes welled. "A year and a half."

"He isn't tired of you," her mother said steadily. It was, in a way, comforting. "He's supporting you."

"He says I should lose more weight."

Carol glanced at her plate of cabbage leaves. "And you're trying."

"He's got so many rules."

She thought Carol would say rules were healthy. Instead, her eyes moved toward the hallway that led to Paul's study. He was in there now. Sylvie could not fathom what he was doing. Nor could she imagine what was happening in her mom's head—her mom, who had once said marriage was the best part of her life—but it was apparent from her expression, which had changed from calm to flat, that something unusual was going on.

For a moment, Sylvie hoped. Once, when she was eight, her mother had explained to her that the reason they never visited her home in England was because she had none. She'd been raised in a now-defunct commune in North London, and she'd loathed it there. She allowed Sylvie to ask three questions before closing the subject for good. Sylvie had spent years imagining the commune version of her mother, a child of radicals who'd shared a bunk room with a rotating cast of non-siblings, who got bullied for her hand-me-downs and shunned for her scholarships, who was made to feel at every moment like the ordinary world for which she longed didn't want her. Surely that girl could tell the truth about marriage, about adulthood, about turning a life you hated into one you might someday enjoy.

But then Carol's face went back to normal. Her focus returned. In the level tone that had shaped Sylvie's childhood, she said, "Any marriage has rules, Sylvie. Rules are what let people live together. You could never accept that as a girl, but I thought you'd come further."

"I'm doing my best," Sylvie said.

"You'll have to do more than that. If you don't, you're going to find yourself alone."

6.

After Sylvie's doomed conversation with her mother, she resolved to discuss her troubles only with her turtle. He never shut her down or accused her of selfishness. But later that fall, a new candidate appeared: her supervisor, Elaine, who, one lunch, plunked herself down at the breakroom table opposite Sylvie and took her book, *Slow Heat*, right out of her hands. "What's this?" she asked.

"It's—um—it's about a baseball player and his team's publicist."

"Having sex?"

Sylvie felt herself go red. "Falling in love."

"Is it good?" Elaine sounded genuinely interested. Still, Sylvie hesitated. She wasn't reading for quality. She was reading for distraction, which *Slow Heat* delivered.

"Go on," Elaine said. "You've got a new book every other day. Don't tell me you don't know which ones you like."

After that, they ate lunch together. Not daily, but usually. Elaine proved much more distracting than *Slow Heat*. She was sixty-eight and thrice divorced—"Dishonorably discharged," she said, smirking. Her second husband, a boat maker, had been in the navy. He was the one who'd brought her from her native New York to Massachusetts. Before him, she'd married young, in 1960, then devoted herself to psychedelics and husband-swapping that wound up wrecking several relationships, including hers. In the seventies, she lived in downtown Manhattan, joined a feminist consciousness-raising group, and had a pre-Roe abortion and then two kids with different men. At some point, when her friends started turning into political lesbians, she married the boat maker, moved to Swampscott with him, and kicked him out as soon as he built her a house. Since then, she'd had a husband and a rotating cast of boyfriends before retiring from romantic life to focus on her grandkids and rescue dogs.

Elaine's stories of early feminism gradually reawakened Sylvie's philosophy brain. She would've liked to debate the questions of Elaine's past—wages for housework? Is beauty bad?—with Paola and Riva. It would have been interesting to discuss them with Hallie, too, but Hallie remained silent in Baltimore.

She wondered if Elaine was her friend now. She asked the turtle, who said, If you want her to be, then tell her about yourself.

I'm too boring.

She won't think so if she's your friend.

Sylvie ignored the turtle's advice for months. But in May, walking back from a rare outing to Mino's Roast Beef for sandwiches—a dripping gyro for Elaine, a veggie wrap for Sylvie—Elaine squinted into the spring sun and said, "So, Sylvie, do you have a life, too?"

The question surprised Sylvie into honesty. "Barely," she said.

"Oh, come on. You're young."

"Right. Nothing's happened to me yet."

"You're married, aren't you?"

"Marriage didn't *happen* to me," Sylvie said, though, in fact, it had. She could tell Elaine that. She could say she'd spent the past year and a half alternately studying and avoiding the issue of whether Jonah was a bad husband or she was a bad wife. She could ask if Elaine, too, found the word *wife* faintly ridiculous, Pilgrim-sounding. Goodwife Sylvie. If she was a good wife, anyway.

All summer, Sylvie imagined how it would feel to confide in Elaine. She thought about it while she cooked and tidied, biked to nowhere at the gym, grinned through parties and dinners and bar nights. She thought about it during sex, a perverse strategy for taking herself out of the moment mentally before Jonah removed her from it physically. It didn't help. She couldn't sidetrack herself from pleasure, which meant she couldn't lessen the disappointment of having it denied. She had a recurring image of herself as a puppet controlled by Jonah's hand between her legs.

It was hard to remember that, two years earlier, he had loved when she begged for orgasms. Now she got them only on his timeline, and only if she didn't ask. He liked surprising her in the middle of the night. She'd wake disoriented, already panting. Afterward, Jonah would kiss the nape of her neck and gather her to his chest, and the chemicals of happiness swept through her so fast she could feel them. A night like that got her through many days. Besides, variation wasn't unheard of. Sometimes he still preferred kitchen-floor sex, shower sex, lazy Sunday sex without any games at all.

It was on one of those Sunday mornings, while she was still wrung out in bed, that Jonah brought up what he called a family issue.

"Whose family?"

"Ours."

She sat, gathering the heavy comforter into her lap. "As in you and me."

"As in you, me, and my parents. My mom." He tucked his knees up. It was a pose that made him look small and young. She could see half his ribs, the delicate bones of his spine. Around him, the white Matouk sheets she washed weekly caught the faint November sun.

"What about her?"

"Apparently her kidneys are failing," Jonah said.

Sylvie twisted to face him. She touched his shoulder, but he twitched her away. "I had no idea she was sick."

"She's not *sick*. She has a disorder." Sylvie didn't understand the distinction, but she nodded. Jonah went on, "She needs a transplant, but my dad and I aren't matches."

"I can get tested."

Jonah shook his head. "You don't need to. She's on the—" He waved a hand. "Registry. Waiting list. I don't know. She's going to get one. What we need is for you to help with her care."

It took Sylvie a moment to question who *we* referred to, and why she was outside it. She had enough emotions fighting already: relief that she didn't have to give up a kidney, guilt that she didn't want to, sadness as Jonah curled himself smaller in bed. She had never seen him suffer. She said of course she would help. She'd be glad to. It made sense. She wasn't the one who traveled.

"Well," Jonah said. "And my dad and I can't quit our jobs."

She protested without hope. *We* had settled her fate. When she gave notice, Elaine said, "You can quit, but you don't get to quit lunch with me."

"I'm not going to."

"Any day, any time."

Sylvie promised. Eight days later, she was gone. Jonah bought her a used Civic for driving his mom to her endless appointments. He gave her the keys on the last night of Hanukkah, but it felt less like a gift than a reward.

Rosaline Sabransky started out grateful for Sylvie. When she began dialysis in December, she told all the nurses that her *daughter*-in-law was helping her. By New Year's, the emphasis had shifted to *law*. By late January, Sylvie regularly overheard her complaining to technicians and fellow patients that she'd been accompanied only by her son's dud of a wife.

Sylvie wished she could return Rosaline's hostility in kind, but that would be selfish. Rosaline was sick. Besides, Jonah had made it clear that one of her caregiving responsibilities was entertaining his mother, and so Sylvie tried. She brought up the weather, the stock market, the Oscars, the news. Rosaline shut every subject down. After a Sunday supper in March, while she washed dishes, she heard her mother-in-law asking, "Isn't it fascinating that a conversationalist as good as you, Carol, could raise a daughter who's got so little to say?"

Sylvie, frozen in the galley kitchen, waited to see who would defend her. Water splashed into the sink. Surely Jonah realized she was listening. Not one wall in their building was soundproof.

But it was Paul who spoke. "Making conversation's not easy for everyone," he said. "Especially when you're talking to somebody who expects you to do all the work."

No one answered. Sylvie counted to ten, then ten again, before she heard Jonah say, "Anyone want coffee?"

She brought it up the moment the parents left. "Was my dad defending me," she began, "or himself?"

Jonah was grimacing at his phone. "Asshole," he muttered at it. "Sylvie, what?"

"I said, was my dad defending me, or himself?"

"Himself, probably."

Again, she waited. Again, he was silent. Questions and accusations surged into her mouth. Why didn't *you* defend me; she's your mother; she's a bitch; she's a Hitler; she's not right, is she?

It was the last thought that kept her quiet. What if he said his mother had a point, or admitted that he that he, too, found Sylvie's conversation dull? *She* certainly did. She didn't care about cold fronts or awards shows, but she had nothing else to talk about. She had no outer life to report on, and her inner life had become a wasteland.

Jonah said no more on the subject that night. Before going to Oklahoma, though, he suggested that she try connecting with his mother through activities and outings. Obediently, Sylvie asked in the car after Rosaline's next dialysis appointment, "Would you like to go to a museum?"

"Why?"

Sylvie considered saying, Because your son told me to take you somewhere. Instead, she offered, "Or a movie."

"Which one?"

"I'm not sure what's playing, but if you have your phone, you could look."

Rosaline issued a phlegmy sound. "Or I can look when I'm not driving."

"At home, you mean."

She'd meant at a stop sign. "Right."

Rosaline made no reply. Defeat settled over Sylvie. She did not propose any more outings. Nor did she take herself on any in her time without Rosaline. She still hadn't seen Elaine, but sometimes she sat in her car at the harbor and imagined driving into Nahant Bay. At Rosaline's nephrologist visits, Sylvie wondered if the doctor would prescribe pain pills, which she could easily steal.

She told herself she meant none of this. She'd like to be dead, maybe, but that wasn't the same as wanting to make it happen. Her turtle suggested that she read some philosophy on the subject, but her brain was too clogged with unhappiness. She imagined it as a physical substance, like insulation foam inside her skull.

I'm in here, said the turtle, and I don't see any foam.

Shut up.

Want to know what I *do* see?

No.

A girl in need of a change.

He was wrong only in the sense that Sylvie didn't need just one change. She needed a total overhaul. She had no idea where to start. In May, as her second wedding anniversary loomed, she threw Rosaline a sixtieth birthday party. She thought it might make Rosaline and Jonah happy, and that bringing happiness to others would motivate her to seek it herself. A cute idea. In reality, Sylvie was in the kitchen for two days before the party, and then Rosaline didn't touch the food. Sylvie heard her wondering aloud to her friends why her son and his wife couldn't have sprung for a caterer. On the way home, Jonah asked Sylvie the same thing.

"I made your mom a cake," she said, disbelief cratering her voice. "I made three kinds of tiny low-sodium sandwich. I made quiche. I made the *crust* for the quiche."

"It was good," Jonah told her tolerantly. "But from now on—"

He kept talking, but Sylvie could no longer hear. A rushing sound had invaded her consciousness. She hated her mother-in-law. She might hate her husband. She wanted to scream for a thousand years.

On the Monday after the party, Sylvie called Rosaline and said she had the stomach flu. She allowed Rosaline to intimate that it had come from the quiche. On hanging up, she walked straight out of her apartment to the parking lot, drove to her former office, and, though it was 10:30 a.m., told Elaine she needed an emergency lunch.

Elaine reacted so calmly that Sylvie knew she had been waiting for this moment. She said not a word about the months that had elapsed without contact. She scooped up her bag—flagrantly fake Dooney & Bourke, cracking leather, a far cry from Rosaline's cherished Goyard—and bundled Sylvie into her car. It smelled like dog dander and Cheetos. Elaine preferred Flamin' Hot, Sylvie knew.

In the parking lot of Charlie's Seafood in East Lynn, Elaine held out her hand and said, "Phone, please."

"What?"

"You need to tell me something. I want you to tell. You can text your husband when you're done."

Sylvie obeyed. She handed her phone over and heeled like one of Elaine's dogs as they crossed the lot to the squat restaurant, its windows promising HADDOCK CHICKEN LOBSTER, and up to the counter. Elaine didn't give the hanging white menu a glance, and she didn't consult Sylvie. She just ordered them a jumbo portion of fried whole-belly clams to share.

Sylvie hadn't eaten fried food since college. She hadn't gone more than ten minutes without replying to a text from Jonah in a year and a half. He would be furious. She should take her phone back. Stop eating. Get up and go.

But she did none of that. "I used to want to be glamorous," she began.

"And now?"

"Now I want to disappear."

She knew it wasn't only Elaine she was talking to. It was her grandmothers, the mother and mother-in-law she wanted, the friends she had betrayed and let go. It was Jonah, a Jonah who listened, a Jonah who could see her as someone who needed help but not repair. But it was also the real Elaine with her Suffolk University sweatshirt and dangling earrings, her silver cloud of hair that would certainly need to be washed after an hour in Charlie's grease-smoked dining room, eating clams with the steady motion of the truly absorbed. Not since Riva and Paola had somebody listened to Sylvie so completely. It gave her the courage to keep talking, though every time she paused for so much as a breath, she was terrified of what she'd said.

When Sylvie ground to a halt, Elaine reached over the gray plastic table, batting crumpled napkins and squeezed moons of lemon aside. She dug her thumbs into the soft pits of Sylvie's palms. Her attention had transformed into a palpable anger that Sylvie wanted to share.

"Sylvie," Elaine said. "What Jonah's doing to you is a trap. It isn't right. You've got to go."

Chapter Two

1.

Sylvie did not take her phone when she left Marblehead. She didn't leave Jonah a note. She threw her grandparents' bougainvillea painting into her car and drove straight to Hallie's house in Baltimore, where her friend let her in without hesitation. She said she'd been waiting for this day. She had, it turned out, a lot to say about Sylvie. Apparently, she'd clocked Sylvie's depression years ago, and the unhealthiness of her relationship years before that.

"It was textbook," Hallie said, by which she meant it met the criteria of psychological abuse she'd learned in undergrad.

It was the word *abuse* that punctured Sylvie's calm. Out of gratitude, she tried to be the practice patient Hallie so clearly wanted, but she couldn't bear to be diagnosed. Nor was she eager to discuss her emotions, her errors, the insecurity and solipsism that had delivered her to this point. She just wanted to enjoy the ringing quiet of her head without Jonah constantly in it. She conjured his voice daily, of course—hourly; sometimes, it seemed, every minute—but imagining what he'd say if he found her wasn't the same as hearing his pity and scorn.

After two weeks, she told Hallie she needed some time alone. Hallie said that as long as Sylvie wasn't isolating herself, she thought getting a place was a healthy next step. Sylvie thanked her until both girls cried, then started answering Craigslist ads. Within days, she had found a room in a group house, bought the cheapest little square of a phone on the market, and sold both her engagement ring and the Civic, which was registered to Jonah, to a transparently criminal man in the Baltimore suburbs. She called her parents, finally, and was astonished when her mother, rather than scolding, asked, "Do you need money?"

"I'm all right."

Paul, on the other line, issued a soft grumble. Sylvie could imagine him in his study, her mother in the living room, uniting without providing each other comfort. "We're going to send you some," he said.

"Just this once," Carol added sternly, as if Sylvie were insisting. "I hope you didn't close your bank account from college."

"No." Sylvie knew the money was proof of love, of acceptance. She had expected no such thing. "It's still there. Thank you."

Between that, the car-and-ring cash, and her savings from the harbor, she could have made it months without a job, but emotionally, that was a non-option. Among the easier lessons Sylvie had learned from Swampscott was that her emotional state deteriorated when she wasn't employed, and so she found herself part-time work at a museum gift shop, a Pottery Barn, and the kind of wine store that sells $17 containers of almonds and set about making a life.

Sylvie saw Hallie once a month. She wrote Rachel a long apology that led to, if not renewed friendship, a form of intermittent communication—meals when Rachel visited Hallie, text-message catch-ups on birthdays, an occasional *thinking of you*—that made her feel better. She learned how to ignore the emails Jonah sent to the address that she, out of spite, refused to change, and how to pick men up fast and get rid of them faster. Everything was easier and more fun, it turned out, if you stopped waiting for people to love you. If you simply refused to let them, it got easier still.

After a year, she swapped the group house for an apartment with only one roommate, a woman named Corinne, who had enough friends not to need Sylvie, but not so many she wasn't sometimes around to go trawl bars for men or watch an old movie or an episode of *The Sopranos* on a rainy afternoon. Tony and Carmela were among Sylvie's major companions by then, along with the contents of her neighborhood library's philosophy section. Rereading *The Sickness Unto Death* was strangely soothing—more so, certainly, than the romance novels that Sylvie now thought she would never touch again. She'd tried one, and it was a stinging reminder of what an idiot she'd been. As she made her way from comforting old European men to the feminists she'd read about in Swampscott, it occurred to her, as it had occurred to countless women before her, that, in fact, she'd been fooled. By Jonah, yes, but also by a bad system. She was no different from Carmela Soprano. She'd been hoodwinked by patriarchy.

A thought like that could lead a person to lesbianism, or activism, or any number of -isms. For Sylvie, it led to the classroom. During her second year in Corinne's apartment—they celebrated their anniversary as roommates with Chinese takeout and a cake—she applied to Johns Hopkins for a master's in philosophy. Only after she'd been accepted and taken out loans did she remember that Jonah had insisted she liked studying, not school. All summer, she worried that he'd turn out to be right; that he'd understood her more than she currently chose to believe.

He hadn't. He was full of shit. From the moment she started classes, in September 2014, she was consumed by the fun of turning other people's ideas into her own. She had, in her fallow years, developed a distinct intellectual taste. She wasn't interested in the analytic and linguistic philosophy that occupied the majority of her professors and peers. Nor did she care about metaphysics. She thought it was essentially recreational—by which she meant masturbatory—to occupy oneself with big, floaty questions like the mind-body problem, which, incidentally, she found easy to resolve: her mind was both *in* her body and *of* it, distinct but not free. Descartes had said so centuries ago. Agreeing with him made no difference to her life, and what she cared about was philosophy that could.

She settled into reading and writing about a mix of feminist politics, queer theory, and old-school moral philosophy that her adviser said was intriguing, unusual, even contrarian. Most philosophy grad students used mathematical proofs to wrangle questions like *Is the self real?* or *What does the word* maybe *mean?* Sylvie's question was much simpler. She wanted to know how a straight woman could be free.

She graduated without an answer, but with a spot in a philosophy PhD program at the University of Virginia. She started in August 2016. Her drive from Baltimore to Charlottesville was heavy with Trump signs. She tried to ignore them, as she tried to ignore Donald Trump, who she found viscerally sickening. She saw flashes of Jonah in the candidate's repulsive, misogynistic insistence on himself. Grandpa Ilya would have been campaigning against him daily. All Sylvie did was tell herself he couldn't win.

Anyway, she was busy that fall. She was, first of all, fighting a war with the University of Virginia to keep her name off its websites. She'd had to do the same at Johns Hopkins—invoke Title IX, abase herself to male administrators. It was a mortifying experience, but here she at least had the help of the graduate program manager, Isabella Kwan, who from her desk in the department's front office steered the fates of professors who hardly noticed her existence. No professors asked who it was that Sylvie had to be hidden from. Isabella did. Sylvie could hardly bring herself to tell her story, but doing so, and showing Isabella the emails Jonah continued to send, was worthwhile. Isabella strategized with her. She coached her through her paperwork. She made the suggestion that eventually became the university's safety plan for Sylvie: not for her to be omitted from the program's site, as had happened at Johns Hopkins, but for her to appear with neither a photo nor a first name. In the University of Virginia's online directory and live course catalog, she was simply Professor Broder, an androgynous cipher with no estranged husband to come looking for her.

Sylvie felt it should not have come as any great surprise to her professors that she had a husband to hide from. She didn't do autobiography, but in the paper she'd submitted with her application, she had outlined her nascent theory of the end of romance, which she proposed to expand into a dissertation. It was Sylvie's belief, after two years of a master's and four of not living with Jonah, that not only marriage but any public or public-inspired performance of relationships or sexuality—any romance—at once kept women from flourishing and corroded true love.

If she were willing to write about her own life, she could have used it as grounding for her arguments. Instead, she began with Hegel's *Reason in History*. In it, Hegel argued that progress began when people realized they could be free. Sylvie wasn't sure she agreed completely—she was no Civil War expert, but it didn't take a historian to know that enslaved African Americans realized they could be free long, long before the federal government got with the program—but where heterosexual love was concerned, Sylvie thought he was absolutely right.

She also grounded her argument in Michel Foucault's *The History of Sexuality*, which condemned sex discourse. Foucault thought public conversations about sex created social pressure and coercive norms. Sylvie conceded that housewives in the sixties had probably needed their consciousness of orgasms raised, but in this day and age, she agreed with Foucault. Had *Cosmo* freed women? Had all the sex gurus Sylvie read online helped her get Jonah to stop tormenting her in bed? Had talking about sex with Riva and Paola empowered her in any way, shape, or form? No, no, and no, she thought.

Sylvie also liked Foucault's rejection of sexuality as a public identity. She'd read a book by a historian named Hanne Blank that explained that straightness, as an idea, was invented in nineteenth-century Germany. Sylvie thought it had outlasted its time. Why should anyone care that she only wanted to sleep with men? And why, in 2016, did society still reward straightness and straight-type behavior? It was bullshit that the state offered incentives—tax breaks; health insurance—to get married and have 1.2 kids.

But it wasn't just marriage Sylvie opposed. She thought love should be free from the social scripts that came not only from books and movies—in her application, she'd compared the contemporary rom-com to the chivalric tales that drive Don Quixote insane—but also from comparing yourself to your peers. She thought relationships should be totally private. How could love be real if it wasn't completely free from external judgments and standards, and how could that happen if you let the world tell you how to love?

In early drafts of her PhD admissions paper, Sylvie had tried arguing that coupledom was inherently a trap, but then she thought of her grandparents. A rare exception, perhaps, but she could not claim, even implicitly, that Ilya had imprisoned Estie. It occurred to her that the distinction between their relationship and more stifling ones was that they had a shared philosophy. They didn't need to rely on the conventions of romance to prop up their bond. Sylvie had never seen her grandfather bring home gifts or flowers. He brought home ideas instead.

Sylvie, personally, did not want any man bringing her anything. She wasn't about to forgo sex—she was a runaway wife, not a nun—but she was done with relationships. She understood that no one, not even her, could guarantee that sex would never generate love, but she hoped her philosophy would help. It could at least protect her from romance. If relationships were traps, romance was their bait and their teeth. It lured you in, then made sure you couldn't leave.

Sylvie had a vision of the world after romance. No one would get married. Grand gestures of devotion would be vanishingly rare. Rom-coms, reality dating shows, *The New York Times*' Modern Love column, the vast majority of memoirs, and the novels that had once been her personal opiate would be seen as the obsolete apparatus of oppression. All forms of sexual or erotic love, from the lifelong to the ten-minute, would be considered so private it would be tacky to mention them to anyone not directly involved. In such a world, relationships would be infinitely less frightening, since entering one would not change anyone's perception of how free you were. In the world Sylvie currently inhabited, though, that couldn't be counted on, and so she had vowed to herself that she would never again sleep with any man more than once.

Before moving to Charlottesville, she'd worried that it was too small for her policy to be viable, but luckily, the town seemed to have an abundance of men. Within weeks of moving, she'd established the same routine she'd maintained through her master's: spend her Saturday afternoons at a bar reading a novel—she found literature helpful in her work, though most of her classmates and teachers sneered at it—and then, if no man had approached her by evening, select the most promising candidate there. She rarely had to do so. Men loved to interrupt a woman with a book.

One sunny afternoon in late September, she was on the patio of a downtown brewery, hiding in her copy of *The Plot Against America* while watching a man who resembled a young, light-haired Jerry Garcia sweet-talk his friend's giant dog, when the stool beside her scraped and her classmate Nadia Mendes sat down beside her.

Nadia was Sylvie's only potential ally among her classmates. It seemed to Sylvie that the department took its building's name—Cocke Hall—too seriously: Nadia was the only other woman in her cohort, and there were only two on the faculty. More importantly, Nadia was the only other person in Sylvie's class who didn't do analytic philosophy. All the men in their cohort were logicians disinterested in the problems of everyday living. Sylvie didn't get why you'd study philosophy if you didn't care about the human experience, though in fairness, Nadia didn't deal with humans, either. She was a reformed coder who, she'd explained during orientation, had decided she would rather study artificial intelligence than build it.

"Actually, that isn't true." She'd touched her chin, which was pointed just enough to make her head look slightly, elegantly egglike. "I *want* to write sci-fi about it, but I never have good story ideas."

Sylvie had liked Nadia from that moment on. She was intrigued by everything about her. Nadia had grown up in Atlanta with one Portuguese father and one *Glass Menagerie*-type Southern one, and at times she projected tremendous sophistication, but just as often, she regarded the world with the glazed mystification of a time traveler. She looked and dressed like a lost ballerina and could out-argue all of their classmates and most of their professors without seeming to try. When Sylvie had called Elaine to catch up a few weeks after arriving in Virginia, Elaine had asked if Nadia was going to be her friend, to which Sylvie had replied with a noncommittal sound. She thought the two of them might sit together at departmental drinks, maybe complain about their classmates from time to time, but any more was beyond what she imagined for herself.

But here Nadia was, wearing Soffe shorts and an actual leotard. Her hair was loose and freshly bleached to a shade so pale it was nearly white. "Mysterious woman drinking alone," she said.

"Mysterious woman drinking with a classmate," Sylvie suggested. She flicked her eyes at the bartender, who was heading over already. Sylvie guessed that Nadia rarely, if ever, had to wait to get served.

Nadia ordered a cherry beer, which Sylvie would not have thought was her speed, and glanced at Sylvie's book. "Reading a *novel*. Look at you. I thought we're supposed to have so much homework we're basically dead."

"We are," Sylvie agreed.

"You don't do it all?"

She lifted a shoulder. "I do the interesting parts and the necessary parts."

Nadia grinned. "And then you go to bars and pick up men."

"Or go to bars and read peacefully."

"Don't you disappoint me, Sylvie Broder," Nadia said in a Georgia accent Sylvie had never heard her use. "Don't tell me I can't have a wingwoman just when I got my hopes up."

Sylvie snorted. Nadia released a string of startling goose honks, which was, evidently, how she laughed.

"You don't do *any* homework, do you," Sylvie said.

Nadia smirked. "I do the interesting parts and the necessary parts." Her beer came, and she flashed a brief smile at the bartender, then said, "You know, I've been meaning to suggest we get a drink."

"Good coincidence, then," Sylvie said.

"Oh, I wasn't coming here." Nadia snapped her leotard away from her ribs. "I was walking home from the gym and I saw you."

"I'm glad you stopped."

"Same. I like you, Sylvie. I wasn't sure right away if I just hated everyone else, but I genuinely like you. You have perspective. Some of the guys, it's like they decided philosophy is a game they have to win. Reminds me of Silicon Valley."

"What was it like, living there?"

Nadia took a sip of her drink, which glowed red-gold in the afternoon light. A David Yurman bracelet slid down her wrist. "Like you'd imagine. Lots of work, lots of free shit at work. Good drugs. It was fun until I got put on an AI project."

"Isn't that what you study?" Sylvie had only the sketchiest concept of Nadia's proposed dissertation. It involved teaching computer programs to discuss moral questions as posed and answered by major ancient philosophers and religious figures: Saint Augustine, Aristotle, Avicenna, the Buddha. Sylvie thought she needed a Jew.

Nadia nodded. "It is."

"But you don't like it?"

"I'm scared of it, and I don't like to be scared of things."

Sylvie knew the feeling. "So you study it to make it less scary."

"I study whether or not I should be afraid of it," Nadia corrected. "It's very possible that I should be."

"Depressing conclusion to come to, if that's what happens," Sylvie said.

Nadia gave her a thoughtful look. "You decided it's right to be afraid of men."

Sylvie laughed, surprising herself. She had registered that Nadia was not the most tactful, but the statement's abruptness still jarred her. "Only temporarily," she said.

"Only till romance changes?"

"Not changes. Ends."

"You think that's going to happen?"

Sylvie could tell it was a true question rather than a challenge. It occurred to her that she knew nothing of Nadia's own romantic predilections—which was, of course, as it should be. After the end of romance, the thought wouldn't even cross her mind.

"I do," she said. "I have to."

"For the sake of your career, or your life?" Nadia asked, and then shook her head. "No. Rephrase. I'm fishing. I want to know the story of how you got scared of men."

Nobody had ever asked Sylvie so directly what had happened to her. It was oddly gratifying. She hated being handled carefully. She still didn't want to answer, though.

"I got stuck with a bad one," she said. "For a long time."

Nadia waited to see if more was coming. Sylvie let her wait. It took longer than she anticipated. Either Nadia had a very high tolerance for discomfort or—more likely, Sylvie thought—she just didn't feel it.

"You don't mind an awkward silence, do you," Sylvie said.

Now it was Nadia's turn to give a surprised laugh. "I grew up with gay dads in suburban Atlanta. I got used to it." After a second, she added, "Would've been the same in any suburb in the nineties, probably."

"No gay parents where I grew up," Sylvie agreed.

"Which was where again?"

"Outside Boston. Pretty far outside."

Nadia wrinkled her narrow nose. "Cold."

"Existentially and literally."

"It's going to be too cold for me here. It was too cold in California." Sylvie could tell from the creases in Nadia's face that this was an issue that genuinely preoccupied her. Fear of cold seemed more reasonable than fear of artificial intelligence, though what did Sylvie know? She'd never thought about the latter at all.

"I want to know more about your dissertation," she said. "Speaking of California."

Nadia lifted an eyebrow. It showed the telltale signs of overplucking in high school or college. Sylvie, too, had overplucked, but her eyebrows were far too powerful for permanent harm. "Are you sure?" Nadia said. "It's extremely boring to most people."

"I thought everyone was into artificial intelligence."

"Yeah, because they think it's *Terminator*. As soon as you start talking about writing programs to explain Daoism to a computer, trust me, people tune out." Nadia recrossed her long legs. "Anyway, I don't want to talk about work when I don't have to."

"Fair enough," Sylvie said. She was, in all honesty, not especially interested in learning how the Dao De Jing translated into code.

Nadia looked highly satisfied. "In that case, I have a deal for you. Hang out with me all the time and I'll never talk to you about computers."

"You're on." Sylvie extended her hand. Formally, the two women shook. Hours later, after two more rounds of drinks, a prolonged dinner, and gelato eaten while walking through the downtown pedestrian mall, Sylvie found herself sprawled on Nadia's enormous couch, drinking seltzer while Nadia packed and smoked a bowl that Sylvie regretted she couldn't share. In Baltimore, she'd found that instead of relaxing her, getting high now made her silent and tense. A loss, but her anxiety was all but gone now that she'd left Jonah. She no longer needed external sources of calm.

Nadia blew a smoke ring, which drifted halfway to the windows before dissipating. "You know," she said, "I've never had many friends."

"Neither have I."

"I'm not great at it."

"Neither am I," Sylvie said, thinking of Rachel. She'd had a relapse not long before Sylvie moved. Rachel had told her about it when Sylvie called to say she was moving to Charlottesville. Somehow, Sylvie's main reaction was guilt. She felt as if she, with her newly enjoyable life, had left Rachel alone in the realm of suffering.

"I'm going to try," Nadia said. "I promise."

A small glow spread through Sylvie's ribs. It occurred to her that friendship might be a good model for love after romance. Friendship could be as private as you liked.

"I promise, too."

For a moment, they just grinned at each other. Then Nadia said, "When's the last time you had a sleepover?"

"High school."

"Want to?"

"Yes!" Sylvie didn't bother tamping down her delight. "Let's do Bloody Mary in the mirror and scare ourselves."

Nadia did one of her bird-honk laughs. "Let's prank-call boys."

"Let's prank-call *professors*."

"Oh, God. Let's not think about them."

"Better. Okay. What else do you do at sleepovers? Nails, but—" She stuck her free hand out, displaying her ragged cuticles. Manicures were a form of personal maintenance she'd left in Swampscott, along with flat-ironing, diets, and waxing, except in summertime.

"Hair, but you can't touch mine. It's too horrible. I've dyed it so much it feels like Barbie's."

"You know, I've never dyed my hair," Sylvie said.

"Never?"

"Not once."

Nadia sprang up. Sylvie rose with her. In twenty minutes, she was in Nadia's dry bathtub, Usher blasting while Nadia stripped the pigment from a lock of her hair. "Mine is this dark, too," she said as she worked. "But I ditched it in college."

"Why?"

"Why not?"

Sylvie nodded, and Nadia swatted her to hold still. Fumes rose around them. In the morning, Sylvie's hair still smelled like bleach. She maintained the streak—special purple shampoo, aggressive coconut-oil treatment—for a semester before having a hairstylist dye it back to brown. By then, she no longer needed physical proof of her friendship with Nadia. Her proof was that she had, with no prompting whatsoever, told Nadia the story of Jonah; that doing so had felt like a natural progression in their bond, which had gone from exciting to easy to vital. Never before had Sylvie met someone she could talk to so deeply or laugh with so easily. On Election Night, she'd found that she could cry in front of Nadia, too. In the days after, the two of them huddled together, unwilling to speak to anyone but each other. The comfort they took in their friendship made Sylvie feel even more strongly about her opposition to marriage, her conviction that sex didn't have to touch the rest of your life. She didn't need a so-called romantic partner. Nadia was her match.

2.

It took Sylvie a year to meet another person who mattered, not that she intended him to. She intended only to bring him home for a night. She found him at a party she and Nadia had gone to for that purpose, meaning a party at which they had no expectation of other fun. It was in a group house full of law students, and the decor and energy communicated that its residents missed their fraternity days. Men swarmed around, looking generally available and interchangeable. Sylvie's attention kept returning to a tall, lean guy standing by the stairs. He was holding an empty beer bottle and cracking jokes in a friend's ear. His hair was clipped short but looked soft rather than military. His nose was magnificent, his jawline superior, and his shoulders were so flawlessly square they looked sculpted. Sylvie was a sucker for shoulders.

She told herself Shoulder Guy was too risky. He appeared—nose; dark hair; bar-mitzvah-boy aura—to be Jewish, and she avoided Jewish men. She knew it was unfair and potentially self-loathing, but they reminded her of Jonah, who was still emailing her an intermittent stream of entreaties and demands.

Of course, Shoulder Guy was risky if he wasn't Jewish, too. Tall white Gentile men at law-school parties had a nasty habit of turning out to be Federalist Society freaks. Sylvie still didn't pay as much attention to politics as her grandfather would have expected her to, but it was the fall of 2017, and she lived in Charlottesville. Not three months before, she'd cowered in her apartment while neo-Nazis chanted, "Jews will not replace us," in the town that was her only home. It was, in fairness, a long way from Federalist Society to tiki torch, but you had to be careful these days.

But Sylvie couldn't stop herself from looking back at Shoulder Guy. She wanted to run her palm across his soft, shorn hair. She wanted to put her mouth in the hollow beneath his strong jaw. Mainly, she wanted to see if the size and strength of his upper body were reflective of other forms of girth.

"Nadia," she hissed. "By the staircase. Plaid shirt."

Without looking, her friend said, "Narrow it down." Even in a town of homogenous men, UVA's male graduate students dressed startlingly alike.

"Green plaid," Sylvie said. "Great torso. Huge nose."

Nadia glanced left, then released her hair from its bun, shook it out, and retied it. "Your type."

"That's all you have to say?"

"Hot, for your type."

Sylvie faked offense. "Rude."

"Can I help it if you're boring?"

"Not boring. Socially conditioned. Coached to pursue high-status men so I can—"

"Safeguard your future. I know."

Both of them laughed. A spaniel bounded past, fringed ears flying. He had a squashed beer can in his mouth and a look of bright glee in his eyes. A girl in pink pants chased him, laughing and calling in a full Southern accent, "Davy! Davy, drop that now!"

"Bet that dog is named for Davy Crockett," Nadia said.

"Bet that girl splits her beers with him when no one's looking."

Davy the dog wriggled around a chair, shot through someone's legs, and vanished upstairs. Sylvie saw Shoulder Guy gesture at the dog's retreating haunches, then nudge the less-hot plaid shirt beside him. It was time, she decided, to secure the next two hours—or up to twenty-four, depending on performance—of her future. She smoothed her short thrift-store dress so the jersey fabric clung to her hips, then fluffed her hair, fixed her eyes on his, and waited. Once she registered his attention, she drained her beer and, in accordance with local custom, crushed the can. It didn't take long for him to appear beside her, bearing two craft beers still sweating from the fridge.

One of the habits Sylvie had developed in her post-Jonah life was consciously justifying her actions before taking them. It was a lesson, learned belatedly, from Carol and Paul. Unlike her parents, she knew not all reasons were rational. Still, understanding why she wanted to do something was both a way to avoid bad situations and a reminder that she was capable of doing so. She had judgment now, and experience to draw on. She wasn't a dumb little wife anymore.

But she could not justify her behavior the night she met Robbie Klein. It was worse than irrational. It was a deviation, if only—*only!*—emotional, from her way of life. From the moment she accepted the beer he offered, he gave her a deep and pleasant feeling of familiarity. Before long, it morphed not into her standard pre-sex mix of arousal, pride, and energy but into desire somehow both tamed and strengthened—again:

irrational—by a profound sense of peace. She wasn't in a rush to get in bed with him. She knew it was going to happen. What she did not know was how she'd found herself not tossing her hair and squeezing her breasts up but slumped on a couch with him, deep in a real conversation. They weren't even talking about him.

"How did you like Baltimore?" he asked, a good half hour in. "People say it's fun."

"What people say to me is usually, 'Is it like *The Wire*?'"

"My sister lived there for a year and had a good time."

"I did, too," Sylvie said. It wasn't quite a lie, and yet she nudged it closer to the truth. "Not at first. I was in a rough period before I moved there, and it took a while to get my life working."

His mouth flickered in and out of a smile. "Which meant?"

"Finding a decent roommate, a job I didn't hate, a direction to go in." She took a sip of her beer, though it was upsettingly hoppy. "I'd thought about grad school when I was an undergrad, but then I forgot until I moved to Baltimore and Johns Hopkins was right there."

"Why didn't you go straight from undergrad?"

"Philosophy didn't seem like it had career prospects."

"What, it wasn't your childhood dream to be a philosopher?"

Sylvie laughed. "My childhood dream was to be a glamorous woman in Miami."

"You seem to have strayed from that path."

"I regret it every day."

Mentioning her former life disoriented her. Even on her annual spring-break trips with her parents, she rarely spoke about her pre-Baltimore self, and in Charlottesville, Nadia remained the only person she had voluntarily told that she'd left a bad husband in the Boston suburbs. She was terrified of word spreading, of her history being used to dismiss her work. Her second-biggest nightmare was overhearing a professor or classmate saying, Oh, Sylvie's just interested in feminism because she had an abusive husband. Her biggest nightmare was Jonah tracking her down.

Before Robbie could ask more questions, she said, "What was your dream?"

"I wanted to go to the Olympics."

"Classic childhood goal."

"No." He met her eyes. "I really wanted to." Suddenly he grinned. "I was the fastest Jewish swimmer in the state of Michigan."

She burst out laughing. "No way that's a real fact."

"It is! You know about the Maccabi Games? Like the Junior Olympics—"

"—but for Jews."

"Right. I swam in that, and the real Junior Olympics. I swam at the University of Michigan for two years, too."

"Only two?"

He nodded.

"Can I ask what happened?"

"I didn't qualify for the Olympics, got depressed, and quit." He did another flickering smile. "Poor me."

Sylvie found that she had to look away from him. While she'd been focused on Robbie, the party had contracted dramatically. Nadia was gone. She'd expect a phone call in the morning, confirming that Sylvie hadn't been raped or murdered and had had at least decent sex. Davy the dog was once again marauding around in search of litter. His owner, damp-haired and giggling at a lunk in unseasonable shorts, appeared to be too drunk to care.

Sylvie reminded herself that she was meant to be behaving like the girl with the spaniel. She hadn't come to this party to empathize. She'd come to make a man melt into her hands.

She took a deep breath. "Do you still swim?"

"Every day."

Sylvie touched his upper arm. "Explains the muscles."

He blushed. "People always think I'm a gym freak, but I hate lifting. Reminds me of the shitty parts of college. I just need to swim."

"Or?"

"Or I get depressed again."

A second wave of empathy rose through Sylvie's chest to her throat. Her whole body was very warm. She didn't think she was capable of—or interested in—indirectness any longer.

She lifted her eyes to Robbie's. "Would you like to go home with me now?"

He turned redder still. "I would."

On the walk to Sylvie's, neither of them talked much. Robbie held Sylvie's hand. She let him. She told herself it was because she was cold. She had an image of herself curled into Robbie, head on his chest. It was not a position she had permitted herself to assume with any man since Jonah. Intellectually, she'd accepted—*thought* she'd accepted—that sex came with an inherent risk of emotion, but now, sensing that risk for the first time with a stranger, she was intensely afraid.

Don't let me do this, she said to her turtle.

You're already doing it, the turtle pointed out. You're nearly home.

It isn't too late. I could get rid of him.

You could, the turtle agreed. But you won't.

Rather than pushing Sylvie against her building's outer wall for a dramatic first kiss like so many men did, Robbie waited for her to ask him in. He didn't grab her ass on the way upstairs, didn't grope her while she unlocked her door. All those gestures had their place: done right, they created tension, friction, excitement. Robbie seemed wholly unaware of those phenomena. Except the hand-holding, he kept physically to himself until they were standing in Sylvie's studio, looking carefully away from the bed that occupied—she and Nadia had measured once—a quarter of the room.

"Do you want some water?" she asked. "Or a beer?"

Robbie shook his head. He took a step closer. He was a good six inches taller than Sylvie, but she didn't go onto her tiptoes. She just let him fold himself downward to kiss her. It felt like gravity itself had delivered him.

She had no sense of how long it took him to break the kiss off. When he did, she had the gasping feeling of having surfaced from deep water. She was thirty and having a completely new emotional experience. She couldn't tell if she was aroused or upset.

"One thing about me," Robbie said softly. Orange light fell through the window, turning his eyes into hollows.

"Yes?"

"During sex, I don't want to be in charge."

Every muscle in Sylvie's core contracted. She had never taken the lead. When it seemed necessary, she asked for what she wanted, but since Jonah, she'd learned—it came naturally—to surrender herself to being pleased.

"I'm sorry," Robbie said. His voice was still quiet. "I know not everyone likes that. But I—" He paused for breath. It was plain to Sylvie that this level of self-revelation did not come easily to him. "I can't do it any other way."

A surge of emotion rolled through Sylvie's body. She had no wish to name it, but it was far from empathy. She said, "I'm going to try."

"Is that all right?"

Who knows, Sylvie wanted to say. She thought about the old Caolán fantasy, about the night of the staircase. She thought about all the men she'd slept with in Baltimore and here in Charlottesville, the men who'd taught her, surely not meaning to, that fear of romance did not have to mean fear of sex. She'd never thanked a single one of them. She'd never thanked the God she didn't especially believe in for sending her, with only minor exceptions, men who didn't hurt her, didn't deny her, didn't knock her back down the road she'd come along. She no longer went along with anything she disliked. She could orgasm at will again. She had become so lucky.

"Of course it's all right," Sylvie said. Her heart was now beating so hard she felt sick. "Do you want to know what we're going to do now?"

Robbie nodded.

She smiled up at him. "Tough shit. I'm not telling yet." She hooked her hands around his neck, drawing his face to hers. "But it's going to involve a lot of tongue, so you better get warmed up."

His body relaxed against hers as he said, "I can do that."

She kissed him. Softly, she said, "If you don't like anything, tell me."

"Don't worry." He dropped his palms to her hips, and a shiver went through her. "I will."

3.

For a month, all Sylvie did with Robbie was have sex. It seemed ceaseless. She was dimly aware that she still took and taught classes, read for her dissertation, hung out with Nadia, ate meals, but those activities, which had so recently comprised her entire life, had faded into the background. Even at the crescendo of the #MeToo movement—Weinstein exposed, Weinstein condemned, a cascade of perverts and predators revealed—Sylvie was too busy in bed to take much notice. When she did, she disliked what she saw. She wanted to tell the many non-famous women joining the celebrity chorus that had started #MeToo that they should cut it out; that privacy and the autonomy that came with it were the only form of liberation you could rely on.

Meanwhile, she was engaged in her own trust exercise. For five years, she hadn't hooked up with any man repeatedly. She certainly hadn't engaged in sleepovers or cuddling. She'd separated sex and tenderness, and she'd been delighted with herself for it. But now she saw Robbie nightly. He kept asking, with a persistence she recognized as a form of confidence, to take her on dates. She made up reasons not to, or just said she'd rather stay in, but neither strategy could last forever. Her excuses were weak in the face of his quiet, steady desire, and staying in just led him to cook her dinner, which was, frankly, more romantic than ninety-eight percent of restaurant meals. He lit candles, set the table, wore a little apron to cook spattery red sauces or shallow-fried chicken. It was heartbreakingly sweet.

Her Baltimore roommate, Corinne, who was very into astrology, had explained that Sylvie, as a Taurus, craved physical comfort the way other signs craved beauty, entertainment, or change. Spending time in Robbie's apartment made Sylvie wonder if Corinne was right. Robbie had soft wool carpets, furniture bought new from Crate & Barrel, heat and air-conditioning that reliably worked. His bedroom and living room were not the same space; his possessions didn't all bear that studio-apartment scent of accreted cooking oil and shower damp. She loved stretching out to read on his long beige sofa, tea and water arranged at her side. Usually, Robbie sat on the couch's other end to study. He'd rest a hand on her shin or stroke her ankle idly. It brought her a great sense of peace.

In those moments, Sylvie frequently found herself resisting the desire to release her secrets into the air between them. It seemed, in her state of relaxation, as if it would be harmless to do so, which was false. Robbie—kind, gentle, open Robbie—would be distressed and disturbed to learn that Sylvie had failed to mention that 1., that she had spent a decade of her life in a soul-shrinkingly bad relationship, and 2., that she was still married to the man involved. Estranged, yes, but legally, she remained Sylvie Broder Sabransky, wedded spouse of Jonah Sabransky.

Sylvie hadn't communicated with her husband since the day she left, though he continued to email on her birthday, New Year's, Yom Kippur, and a random assortment of dates without meaning, always using a different account. Presumably he thought she was sending his messages to spam, which she was not. She had taught herself, in Maryland, not to read them, but now she braved them on the theory that if he was going to try to hunt her down, he would alert her—intentionally or not—through his emails first.

His most recent email, a Yom Kippur one, had been fairly comforting. In it, he explained that the issues in their marriage had come from his professional insecurities. *Now that I'm a senior project manager*, he wrote, *I have the faith in myself that I needed to be a good partner to you.* An absurd statement, one a Marxist could go to town on, but not a sign he was about to embark on a search for her. Still, she wasn't about to write back and ask for a divorce. Legal freedom wasn't worth breaking her silence.

By the middle of November, it was apparent to Sylvie that she was going to either have to get rid of Robbie or adjust some of her ideas about freedom. Both thoughts were terrifying. She didn't want a boyfriend. Having a boyfriend meant establishing norms, meeting family members, conducting your love life in public. It meant giving a man structural power over your sexuality. But Robbie wasn't *a man*. And he was, in an ill-defined but unignorable way, already hers.

She told herself she could sort her problems out during Thanksgiving break. It wasn't like she'd have much else to do. She never celebrated holidays with her parents: it seemed like too easy a way for Jonah to find her, even if they traveled rather than staying in Marblehead. Nadia was going to Atlanta, and Robbie would be in Grosse Pointe, cooking a feast with his parents, sisters, aunts, and ninety-three-year-old grandfather, Papa

Sid. Sylvie had practically convulsed with jealousy on learning that Robbie had a Papa Sid to hang out with. She'd spent half that night crying in the bathroom, wailing to her turtle about how much she missed her own grandfather, how unfair it was that Ilya had lived only to seventy-nine.

An unwelcome voice—not the turtle's—had entered Sylvie's head that night. It said Robbie was prime father material. He was caring and nurturing. He was patient. He had a job offer waiting at a big DC law firm, which meant that, on the one hand, he wouldn't have an abundance of time, but, on the other, he'd be able to finance plenty of childcare. Also, he'd told Sylvie on several occasions that he didn't plan on gunning for partner. He just wanted to make a nice life for his family.

Sylvie had not told Robbie, then or ever, that she wanted a baby. Not soon, but someday. She thought of child-rearing—and childbearing, terrifying though it was—as an emotional and philosophical adventure too great to pass up. Of course, since leaving Jonah, she'd assumed she would be doing it alone.

After three days of drooping and sulking alone, Sylvie recommitted herself to philosophical inquiry. She needed an outlet for her feelings. Also, she needed to justify them. She needed to find, somewhere in the vast literatures of moral philosophy and feminist thought, a framework within which to safely pursue a *thing*—she was not yet ready to entertain the word *relationship*—with Robbie. She understood that she was setting out to think herself into love, but she had gotten dangerously close to it already. All she could hope to do was reassert some bit of control.

At first, her research went poorly. She lay on her bed and read for hours and hours, but her favorite writers offered her little to work with. Not many old-school philosophers had useful things to say where boy problems were concerned, and a problem with a lot of queer and feminist theory, Sylvie found, was that it got too utopian too quickly, or fogged up when it tried to describe a better-but-not-utopian future, or just thought *utopia* meant any world without men. Sylvie was afraid of men, but she didn't condemn their existence. She thought romance hurt them, too.

Among her missions in writing her own dissertation was to avoid utopianism entirely. She wanted it to be practical, a desire that grew exponentially in the days she spent flailing around her PDF collection and heaps of academic journals. She found nothing until, the night before Robbie came back, she returned in desperation to Adrienne Rich's "Compulsory Heterosexuality and Lesbian Existence," an essay she'd taught and been taught so often that just looking at it generally made her eyes blur.

Not this time. This time, sprawled on her stomach on her unmade bed, kicking her feet in the air like a preteen, Sylvie was electrified. Adrienne Rich was talking to her. She was issuing clear, direct, and nonutopian instructions. Rich said that if you *consider yourself freely and 'innately' heterosexual*, it was your job to examine the failings of heterosexuality—and not just examine but fix. If you did, Rich promised, your *rewards will be great: a freeing-up of thinking, the exploring of new paths, the shattering of another great silence, new clarity in personal relationships.*

Sylvie couldn't believe she'd never seen it before. Rich's point was so obvious. In her relationship with Jonah, Sylvie had capitulated to every single standard of conventional straightness. She'd submitted. She'd suffered in silence. She'd cooked and cleaned and cared for her bitchy mother-in-law. So far with Robbie she'd done the reverse on all fronts. In bed, she took charge, which had yet to feel natural but was certainly fun. He'd made every single meal they'd eaten together. She'd done a startling amount of chattering to him about philosophy and departmental drama; he never talked to her about law school or law. Without even meaning to, they'd set up the perfect environment for a broader liberation of their thinking, and she had faith that he was secure enough in himself to pursue said liberation further. He wasn't trapped in bullshit ideas about masculinity. He knew about his feelings. She and Robbie could have the new clarity Rich spoke of. Together, they could explore new paths.

Sylvie was hopping around her apartment at this point, delighted by discovery. She got a beer from the fridge—her third of the night, but she'd earned it—then went to her desk and began making a list in her dissertation notebook. It was a chart, really, with two sides: conventions of heterosexuality and ways in which she and Robbie could exit them. If her time with Jonah had been characterized by monogamy, public intertwinement, and feminine servility, then with Robbie, she should strive for privacy, independence, and womanly power. They could have an open relationship; they could choose not tell anyone about it. She and Robbie could create a whole private world, and she could live her public life with the cozy, sexy secret of having a boyfriend at home.

She wriggled her shoulders with joy. In the dark window, her reflection was wild-haired and fat-cheeked with smiling. She looked like a Jewish chipmunk. She pulled her phone from her sweatshirt pocket, but instead of texting Robbie, sent Nadia a voice note. It wasn't their normal mode of contact, but she was too excited to type.

"It's me," she said. "Your brilliant friend. You need to come back from Atlanta. I have an idea to tell you."

4.

Robbie also returned from break with a plan. He wanted to take Sylvie to Richmond before finals. It was only an hour away, but he wanted to make a weekend of it. Sylvie's first reaction was a profound nervousness. Weekend trips were both romantic and serious. They were commitments of money and time. They were also ideal opportunities for making requests and declarations, however, which could work to her advantage. It was possible—probable—that Robbie intended to use the trip to ask for a real relationship, but not if Sylvie beat him to the punch. Besides, it wouldn't matter if he got there first. She had her list. She could present it whenever the time was right.

"That's a great idea," Sylvie said, gathering herself. "Let's do it."

Robbie beamed at her. "I already booked the hotel."

He picked her up on campus after she led her Friday-afternoon discussion section for Philosophy and Literature. It was a cold day, the sort where the sun seemed never to rise completely, and Robbie had the heat blasting, her seat warmer already on. She fell asleep before they'd even left the outskirts of Charlottesville. Teaching always wore her out.

Robbie's chosen hotel was comically hip. Its lobby was full of feathered chandeliers and ironic upholstery; its clientele tended toward neat beards and expensive tattoos. Sylvie had never stayed in such a place. She loved it. If Robbie hadn't made dinner reservations already, she would have insisted they spend their first night eating room service in bathrobes. As it was, they had quick sex on the tremendous bed, so huge that lying in the middle made Sylvie feel as if she'd washed up on an island, and then re-dressed and headed out for oysters.

In Charlottesville, Sylvie never went out with Robbie, not wanting to be seen. Now it felt strange to sit in a restaurant with him. He looked so correct in his sweater and button-down, his big hands tucked into his lap as if they hadn't been inside Sylvie less than an hour ago. She'd forgotten how dirty it could feel to look at a man in public and remember the sex they'd just had. After a glass of wine, she entertained the notion of slipping off to the bathroom between courses, but this was a fancy place. She should behave in a fancy manner.

In the morning, they walked from their hotel through the Virginia Commonwealth University campus to a street full of mansions. It was a crisp, sunny day, the blue sky bearing no relation to yesterday's damp-newspaper clouds. Sylvie's to-go coffee released small clouds of condensation, but she was surprisingly comfortable in her tight jeans and leather jacket. She had a thick, blanketlike scarf wrapped around her neck and shoulders, but she barely needed it. In Massachusetts, the weather was probably hovering just above freezing. All the trees would have been bare for weeks. Here, red leaves lingered. Late flowers were just starting to curl and die. Sylvie saw a woman leaning out her apartment window, clipping greens from a box. Never before had she wanted to garden, but a pleasurable thread of envy ran through her. Maybe in her next apartment, or whenever she could afford to live someplace nice.

On Monument Avenue, she and Robbie stood briefly across from a traffic circle containing a cast-iron statue of Robert E. Lee, discussing the absurdity of its presence. They had talked about this issue before: the Unite the Right hate march had been convened, supposedly, to defend another Lee statue. Neither Sylvie nor Robbie had counterprotested. She found the prospect of showing her Jewish face to a throng of neo-Nazis too chilling. Since before she remembered, she'd known she could be chased and corralled. Exposing herself to her would-be persecutors seemed moronic, a dishonor to her grandparents' memory.

She said as much to Robbie now, knowing she was reiterating past conversations. He had the kindness not to point the repetition out. "I should have felt that way," he said. "I just couldn't really believe the march was happening until it was—" He shrugged. "Happening."

"You'd have believed it if you had my grandparents," she said.

"I know. I can't imagine growing up with the Holocaust that close. My grandfather fought in World War Two, but my family's so assimilated, he always talks about it as fighting for the United States, not for the Jews."

"Why not both?" Sylvie asked.

Robbie shrugged. Sylvie tilted her head up to look at the statue again.

She wasn't being fair to Robbie's grandfather. She thought about Jewish history often, US history hardly ever. In her mind, she was a woman, then a Jew, then—a distant third—an American.

She slipped her hand into Robbie's and resumed walking. All around them were tall brick houses with beautiful gardens and glossy doors, heavy curtains parted to let the sun stream in. As they wandered, Sylvie peeked through window after window to see built-in bookshelves, pianos, the occasional antique telescope.

"Parts of DC look like this," Robbie said. "But not the parts I'd want to live in."

Sylvie nodded. She'd only been to DC for the occasional day of museum-hopping. Robbie had spent two summers interning there, securing the job that awaited him now. "Do you have a neighborhood picked out?" she asked.

"A couple neighborhoods." He took her free hand. "I was hoping you'd come look at places with me in the spring."

Sylvie said nothing. Her tongue was suddenly so dry she could barely detach it from the bottom of her mouth. She tried to take a sip of coffee but somehow wound up spilling it into her scarf.

Robbie appeared not to notice. "I don't mean to move in with me," he said.

"I can't."

"I know. School. And it would be too soon, anyway. But Sylvie—" He stopped walking, tugged at her hand so she had to face him. "I'd like this to be more serious. I mean, I feel serious about you. I couldn't stop thinking about you over Thanksgiving."

"I couldn't stop thinking about you, either," she confessed.

Robbie's eyes sparked with a mischief she recognized. "I figured."

"You did?"

"Sylvie." He kissed her, very quickly. A boy in a plaid jacket ran down the sidewalk behind them, leashed terrier trotting at his heels. "You texted every five minutes."

"I did not!"

"Fine. Every ten." His playful expression was fading already. His cheeks were pink in a way Sylvie knew wasn't only from cold. He was so handsome. It was unfair. "What I'm trying to say is that I want to be together for real. I don't want to break up when I graduate. I don't want you to think that's what I have in mind. And Charlottesville to DC isn't bad, honestly. Lots of my classmates are dating people there. I think we could do it, and I'd like to, and—" He dropped Sylvie's hand so he could shrug. "And so I want you to like the apartment I live in. Is that too much?"

It was perfect. It was the answer to a prayer Sylvie hadn't prayed. She could be single in Charlottesville, coupled in DC. She could determine the amount of time she spent in each place, which was to say the amount of time she spent in each romantic state. She could explore all the new paths she liked, and when she wasn't in the mood for exploring, she could hop in the car and head to Washington.

She wanted Robbie to feel the gladness emanating from her. She lifted her face to show him. In her heart, she said nothing but *yes*, but her brain still had some control. It reminded her that distance was not an antidote to ownership; that Jonah had spent half their marriage consulting halfway across the country, and, during the weeks he was away, Sylvie hadn't exactly behaved like a free woman. She'd eaten Tragic Diet Shit and cried.

"It's not too much," she said slowly. "Not at all. But you need to know something first."

"What?"

"I don't believe in monogamy."

She had never said that aloud to anyone but Nadia. It came out sounding like a lie. But Robbie, to her shock, didn't question. He shrugged a little and said, "I'm not interested in sleeping with anyone else, but I don't mind if you do. I just want to know if it happens." He gave her one of his flickering smiles. "It's kind of hot to think about, actually."

"You don't seem surprised."

"I know what your dissertation's about."

"Fair."

"Anyway, you warned me the night we met." Robbie took a step closer. Above him, the sky had become so flawlessly clear it was painful to see. "You said, 'My whole PhD's about the end of romance, so don't get your hopes up.'"

Her stomach tightened. "And yet." It wasn't a sentence that had to be finished. Robbie had gotten his hopes up anyway, and been correct to. She suppressed the temptation to tell him she was sorry. She wasn't. Her warning had laid the groundwork for this moment.

He was quiet. She continued, "When I say 'the end of romance,' I'm not only talking about monogamy. I mean anything that happens in public."

Robbie rubbed the back of his neck. "Is that why you never want to go out to dinner in Charlottesville?"

"Yes. But it's not just that. I want—" She dug her toes into the soles of her boots. "I want to be your girlfriend, but I don't want my private life to affect my public identity, and I don't want to play the girlfriend role in your public life." Joy waxed and waned in his eyes as she spoke.

"You keep saying 'public.'"

"Yes."

"I'm not sure I know what that means."

She thought, a little wildly, of the Anton Chekhov story her undergrads had recently read. Its protagonist, after falling in love, decides that real life—the *core of his life*—happens in secret. At his job, at his club, at parties, he's false.

"*Public* is anyone we're not really, genuinely close to," she said. "So for me, it's everyone but my friend Nadia."

"She's the one you were with the night we met?"

Sylvie nodded.

"Can I meet her?"

"You can."

"But nobody else."

Elaine's face drifted into her head. Sylvie hadn't called her in months. Just the thought released a mix of smallness, gratitude, and guilt that she could not currently accommodate. She was feeling small enough already.

"Nobody else matters," she said.

"What about your parents?" Robbie asked, in a tone careful enough that she guessed he'd squashed this question many times.

"Another conversation."

"All right." He rubbed his neck. "But I'm not hiding you from mine."

"No, no. No hiding." A little philosophical light gleamed within her. "Maybe that's the distinction. Anyone you'd be *hiding me from* is a private person. Anyone you'd just *not mention me to* is public." She tried to pin the thought to her brain. She wanted to return to it later, to see who'd written what on concealment and secrecy.

Robbie was nodding. "I can handle that." He no longer sounded cautious. "If it means I get you as a girlfriend."

Sylvie ignored the tiny clench of alarm that came from hearing him say *girlfriend*. She'd used the word already. She'd given it to him as a term. "You do."

"Should I write us a contract?"

"A what?"

He grinned. "I'm a law student. I could write us a contract."

Sylvie burst into laughter. Her fear flew away. She wanted to leap into his arms, or tell him she loved him, or blow him right there on the street.

She wanted to call Nadia and announce that her breakthrough was now more than a breakthrough. It was an agenda, a *philosophy*, and it was in motion. She and Robbie were testing it from this moment on.

5.

Intellectually speaking, Sylvie's spring semester was the best of her life to date. Personally speaking, it was, very possibly, the same. She had no doubts on either front that romance could be ended. She and Robbie were ending it. So far, their progress was tremendous. Already, she thought, she was freer. After Jonah, she'd had a persistent vision of herself as a woman standing among the fragments of her former life, kicking them aside from time to time. Now the fragments seemed distant. She thought about Jonah less. When he emailed—his emails had gotten more frequent; it was as if he knew—she got less upset. She fretted less about her failure to eliminate the concept of coupledom from her mind. She and Robbie were pioneering a new model. Not new in society, she understood, but new in Sylvie's world. Besides, no nonmonogamy advocates said their goal was ending all public expressions of romance. *Sylvie* said so.

She couldn't have developed her ideas without Robbie. He was an exceptional listener. She told him what she was reading, what she was outlining, how she was splicing and fusing and synthesizing bits of queer theory and feminist thought into nineteenth-century moral philosophy and the post-Holocaust thought she'd studied as an undergrad. It was nothing like describing ideas to a dutiful undergraduate Jonah. Robbie's questions, his lawyerly precision, didn't just help her clarify her thinking; they pushed her in whole new directions.

It was Robbie who got Sylvie to pay attention to #MeToo. He brought it up over dinner one night. He'd just read a *Vanity Fair* essay in which Monica Lewinsky wrote that the movement had caused her to question, for the first time, how consensual her relationship with Bill Clinton had been. "Do you think this is going to keep happening?" he asked.

Sylvie slurped up a noodle. "Women talking about being victims? There's always an appetite for that."

"But do you think it'll lead anywhere?"

"Do you?"

"I hope so, right?" He smiled a little. "But I'm not the one whose job is predicting the feminist future."

"It's not my *job*."

"You get paid for it," Robbie said. He twirled a strand of pesto-covered spaghetti around his fork but didn't eat it. He made his own pesto instead of buying the jarred stuff. When he had time, he made his own pasta, too.

"I haven't thought much about MeToo," Sylvie said, not quite truthfully. "It doesn't seem promising enough for me to spend time on."

"Why not?"

"I told you. It's all about female vulnerability. Rewarding women for embodying victimhood. Why should Monica Lewinsky have to tell the world she was abused to get sympathy? Shouldn't we feel for her just because she's a person, or because she got dragged into the public eye?" She heard the heat in her voice and stopped.

"I don't know if she *had* to tell the world," Robbie said. "Presumably she chose to write that piece."

"Yeah, but it's not choosing freely if it happens in the context of a misogynistic cultural bargain. She knows, consciously or not, that society will treat her better if she slots herself into this new version of the victim narrative."

"Her *past* self."

"Doesn't matter."

"I think it does." Robbie leaned slightly forward. "What's wrong with her trying to change how we see—or how she sees—her old self as a service to her current one?"

"It's cynical," Sylvie said.

"How do you know?"

Sylvie sighed. Robbie was right: she didn't *know*, as such. Maybe Monica sincerely wanted to be seen as Bill Clinton's victim. Sylvie just couldn't understand it. She'd devoted so much time and energy to building her own psychic strength after Jonah, and she was grateful every day that she had. What would her life be like now if, instead, she'd gotten trapped in the identity of victimhood? And she, unlike Monica, couldn't deny that she'd been abused and manipulated. Monica Lewinsky had the option of believing, whether or not it was strictly true, that she'd done precisely what she wanted. Sylvie would kill for that choice.

"I'm not doubting your perspective, you know," Robbie said.

"Just lawyering at it."

"Right."

She nudged his ankle with her foot. "I like the lawyering," she said. "It helps me."

"I'm glad. And it's interesting, what you're saying. I haven't heard it from anyone else."

"I'm here any time."

"In public, I meant. You could write about how MeToo is less feminist than it seems. It's relevant to your dissertation. I bet you could interest a newspaper in an opinion column."

Sylvie suppressed a shudder. Her name online for Jonah to see? Absolutely not. But she couldn't say so to Robbie. She hadn't told him about Jonah. It occurred to her suddenly that his questions might not be so innocent. Maybe he was digging for Sylvie's own trauma story. Maybe he could smell it on her; maybe he just assumed all women had one.

Very coolly, she said, "I don't have time for that."

He glanced down. "Sorry."

She didn't reply. It took her the rest of the night to drop her hackles. In the morning, before he went to swim his laps, she kissed him and apologized for being prickly. He pretended not to have noticed, which just made her feel worse.

On her walk to campus, still thinking of what Robbie had said, she texted Nadia. *Help! Philosophy crisis. Lunch??*

Teaching till 1, Nadia wrote back. *Can you survive that long?*

Barely, Sylvie told her, and ascended to the library stacks to seek guidance. Within an hour, she found herself on the chilly black floor surrounded by discarded books, reading a study of heartbreak by a sociologist, Eva Illouz, who described the contemporary self as *ensconced between the institutional and the psychic*. It was a more or less throwaway line, but Sylvie thought it could be, if not her actual answer, then the answer's framework: Considering oneself a victim was psychically bad, since it meant choosing a position of weakness. But Robbie was right that *claiming* victimhood, which wasn't quite the same, could be good for women on an institutional level, in that it could lead to social rehabilitation—see: Monica Lewinsky—or some measure of justice.

At lunch, she ran the whole framework by Nadia, who screwed her mouth up. "You're forgetting how much Monica got shamed for sleeping with Clinton. Isn't that worse for her than considering herself a victim?"

Sylvie hadn't factored shame in at all. "It's different," she said. "It's external."

"Unless she *felt* ashamed."

"Well, I'd rather be ashamed of my choices than convinced I'd never had the power to make them."

Nadia shrugged. "Sometimes you don't."

Sylvie didn't answer. She wasn't interested in imagining a future that contained the absence of choice.

"Anyway," Nadia said, "why does thinking of yourself as a victim have to mean weakness?"

"How could it not?"

"Isn't it your job to imagine how it could not?"

"Job, job, job," Sylvie grumbled. Nadia lifted an eyebrow, and she explained, "Yesterday Robbie said it was my job to write about the feminist future."

"Well, it is."

Sylvie bit into her bagel and waited to see if Nadia would say more. After a moment, her friend added, "You know, you've always dismissed MeToo when I've brought it up before."

"I have?"

Nadia nodded. Sylvie dropped her eyes to the table. She couldn't remember, but that didn't mean much. Her head had been full of Robbie all fall. "Sorry," she said. "Was I a dick?"

"No, no. Just not interested. You want it not to be worthy of your attention, but it is."

"Why?"

"How could it not be?" Nadia said, and smirked. "Seriously, though, it's the biggest change in feminism in years."

"*If* it's a change."

"Biggest development. And if it's *not* a change, if it's development without progress—"

"—or a regressive development—"

"—then that's important, too."

"Someone's got to say it's not liberatory if it isn't."

"Which requires you to entertain the possibility that it is. And *that*,"

Nadia added, "requires you to imagine the upside of seeing yourself as a victim."

"Me personally?"

"I meant 'you' as in 'one,' but sure."

"Ugh."

"Ugh," Nadia agreed cheerfully. "Crisis solved?"

"I guess."

"I live to serve."

"I owe you."

"All right, then." Nadia sat up straighter. "You can repay me by letting me hang out with Robbie. If he's giving you ideas—*good* ideas—then it's time I got to know him."

Sylvie had yet to allow them to meet. She was afraid of what Nadia would think of him, or of her with him. It occurred to her now that this fear could be useful, and could belong in her dissertation. Yes, it was harder to leave a bad partner if you also had to leave your identity as girlfriend or wife, but an entirely hidden relationship would mean no Nadia—or Elaine or Rachel or Paola or Hallie—to tell you, even if you weren't ready to hear it, that your boyfriend was no good.

"Fine. Come to dinner."

"When?"

"No time like the present," Sylvie said.

6.

Robbie didn't mind that Sylvie had invited Nadia for dinner without warning. If anything, he seemed pleased. He squashed sausages from their casings, sautéed them, and crumbled them into a free-form lasagna that caused Nadia, who'd come lightly stoned, to writhe in her seat with joy. "So much crunchier than regular lasagna," she said, breaking off a golden corner of noodle. "Brilliant."

"Do you cook?"

"I mainly eat."

"Well, you're welcome any time."

Mouth full, Nadia said, "I'm coming back *all* the time."

Sylvie could see the praise soaking into Robbie. She felt its warmth herself. She settled into her seat and let Nadia interrogate Robbie: origin of culinary talent, why he wasn't a chef, why law, why Big Law. He only sketched out his reasons at first, but when Nadia pressed, he admitted, in a tone darker than any Sylvie had heard him use before, that although he considered them a worthwhile investment in his future, the years immediately ahead seemed grim. He assumed the job awaiting him would be rote, meaningless, and exhausting, and that it might require him to do bad deeds. He could get stuck defending major polluters, wage-thieving bosses, corporate criminals of nearly any stripe.

As Robbie spoke, Sylvie worried, though she disliked herself for it, that Nadia would write him off as intellectually unambitious or think he had no morals. But at the end of the night, when she accompanied her friend downstairs, Nadia said with no prodding, "I endorse."

"I'm sure the candidate appreciates your support."

Nadia laughed. "Really, though. He's smart and he's sweet. Very—" She tilted her head, considering. It was ten at night and not one strand of hair had loosened itself from her bun. "Very *comfortable*."

"In himself or how he made you feel?"

"Both," Nadia said as the elevator released them. "And in how he makes you feel, it seems like."

"Is that good?"

Again, Nadia laughed, though this time it had a teasing note. "Poor Sylvie. You've read too much theory. Go back upstairs and have a nice time."

Sylvie groused the whole way to the recycling room. Comfort can be a trap, she informed her turtle.

I'm aware.

How do I know it's not a trap now?

Isn't it Nadia's job to tell you?

If I seem trapped, then yes.

Well, then, the turtle said smugly, I guess you don't.

Sylvie did not consider this discussion logically sound, but she had no more to add. She did, in fact, want to go upstairs and have a nice time, but she returned to a different Robbie than she had left. She'd thought she'd interrupt him cleaning. Instead, she found him sitting in the only hard chair in his living room, hugging his arms as if cold.

"What's wrong?" she said.

Robbie was quiet. All the dishes remained on the table. She could hear the sink running. On going to shut it off, she saw that he'd done nothing but soak the lasagna pan: the range was spattered with grease, the counter freckled with bits of parsley stem. She heard movement in the living room: Robbie sliding from the bad chair to the floor.

She sat beside him, mirroring his crossed legs. He hadn't told her, or she hadn't comprehended, that when melancholy came for him, it was this quick and complete. Softly, she said, "Drama queen."

His mouth twitched. "Sorry."

"Don't." She touched his shoulder, which made his body tighten, but she left her hand there. "Did Nadia—?"

"No, no. She's great."

She ran through the evening in her head. "Your job?"

"You mean my meaningless future as a corporate drone?"

"Who's saying that?"

"You weren't listening to me?" he asked, and Sylvie understood. When she'd been fretting that Nadia would judge Robbie, he had been judging himself.

"You should go home," he said. His tone was harsh. "I get like this. You can't help."

She thought, so rapidly it startled her, that maybe this was the moment to act for the first time on their nonmonogamy. She could go not home but to a bar. It was an unwelcome impulse.

She didn't say aloud that she wasn't leaving. She couldn't be sure that Robbie had sunk too far into himself to argue. Instead, she just sat. Robbie let her. After some time, he allowed her to lead him to bed and curl silently around him, a reversal of their usual position. Her arms were too short to hold him properly. Her breasts got in the way. Still, she fell asleep there, and in the morning found that neither of them had shifted in the night.

As he made coffee, Robbie said, not looking at her, "I'm glad you stayed."

"So am I."

"I'm sorry I said you couldn't help."

Her throat tightened. She wasn't sure she had. As the winter went on, she had the same doubt each time she sat with Robbie through a bad night—triggered sometimes by stress or shame about his future job, but sometimes, he swore, by nothing at all. He always thanked her in the morning, but it took him until spring to stop telling her to go away.

In those months, the impulse to leave that had been so immediate never came again. She did not sleep with other men, which confused her. It felt like a failure. Also, the delight of innovation was waning. By March, she'd didn't quite resent Robbie's refusal to set the course in bed, but she had nothing left to teach him: no positions, no tricks, no fantasies. She felt that, surely, he could teach her some moves, but he wouldn't. It wasn't his style. Increasingly, she had the sense during sex that her directions and feedback were not so much satisfying a kink for Robbie but filling a void, which she resented. *She* wanted filling. She was still having orgasms, still ending up shaky and depleted by pleasure, but that was just her body. Emotionally, or existentially, she was missing something. All the sex she had with Robbie felt like role-play: fun, but not true. Her true self wanted to be overpowered. It wanted Robbie to fuck her until her mind went numb.

She and Robbie spent spring break in DC, touring condos—his parents had offered a down payment, and who said no to a down payment?—and going on long walks. It was a prettier city than Sylvie had realized, and a more vivid one. Everywhere they went was full of loud gaggles of girls, drum rhythms seeping from storefronts, murals that pretended to be street art but had plainly been commissioned by some official force. She liked it, corny murals aside. She could see herself here.

Robbie had found them another luxurious hotel, though less hip than the one in Richmond. He'd picked it so he could swim daily laps in its pool. Sylvie tried to pretend to herself that their room, with its massive glass shower and ruffly bed, did not remind her of her honeymoon. She made it four days. On the fifth and final morning, she found herself on top of Robbie, seeing in his wide eyes that he was close to orgasm, digging through her half-asleep mind for one last bit of inspiration. What surfaced was not good. It was the wrong role. She went for it anyway.

She stopped moving. Robbie gave her an agonized stare. Slowly, she slid herself off his erection and lay down.

He rolled to face her. "Is something wrong?"

"No."

"But you stopped."

Sylvie smiled at him. "I decided you're done."

"I don't get an orgasm?"

"You do." She paused. "At some point."

For an instant, Robbie looked confused, then frustrated, then delighted. "I see how it is," he said, reaching between Sylvie's legs. A great mass of self-loathing descended the moment he touched her. She thought she wouldn't be able to come, but she did.

After that, it took Sylvie only ten days to sleep with someone else. She could not turn into Jonah. She needed to visit the submissive version of herself. On the night she returned to Charlottesville, she said so to Nadia, whose mouth twitched with mischief.

"What's that look?" Sylvie said.

Nadia batted her lashes. "What look?"

They were in Sylvie's apartment, a place Nadia ordinarily disdained on grounds of both aesthetic and physical comfort, but Sylvie had summoned her for emergency counsel. Both of them were on the bed, since there was no room for a couch. Books towered around all four walls.

"You have an agenda."

Nadia poured herself a new glass of the wine she'd brought and said, "Not an agenda. A candidate."

His name was Wyatt Hanson. He managed a brewery in the yuppie part of town. Nadia had, apparently, scouted him in Sylvie's absence. "And you didn't want him for yourself?" Sylvie asked.

"Not my style." Nadia was catholic in her preferences, but the one constant was that she was not interested in any man who seemed too normal. Her taste ran to poets and physicists, most of the guys she bought weed from, once a yoga instructor who tried to sound-heal her in bed. Occasionally she'd sleep with a woman for variety, but they had to be even odder than the men.

"Promising," Sylvie said. "Tell me more."

"What's to tell? Hot, alpha-male energy, single."

"You asked?"

Nadia shrugged. "I told him it was for a friend."

"Queen of tact strikes again," Sylvie grumbled, but she was grateful, really, for Nadia's directness. She was rusty at flirtation. It would make things easier to have Wyatt's attention.

They went to his brewery after class that Wednesday. Sylvie washed her hair and formed her curls that morning, sacrificing an hour of work time to oiling and diffusing. She showed up to their Wittgenstein seminar in a silky green jumpsuit that put her breasts on significant display. She'd never worn it around Robbie, which was a waste. He wouldn't see it today. She'd told him she had plans with Nadia and would be out late.

Her classmates eyed her cleavage with a mix of interest and judgment. Briefly, she wished she'd brought a sweater, but why? It was April. Charlottesville was getting hot. It wasn't her fault she was surrounded by sex pests. She sat straighter in her terrible classroom chair and stared right back at her ogling peers.

Nadia, who was ordinarily highly attuned to fashion, seemed not to notice the jumpsuit or its effects. She was focused on their seminar leader, a French philosopher of language named Salomé Rau, with whom she had recently become obsessed.

Dr. Rau had grown up on a dairy farm in Alsace and was a vocally committed pescetarian. Her only shoes were ancient paddock boots and pristine white clogs. Like Wittgenstein, who hit his students when they didn't understand his lessons, she had no patience at all in the classroom, though she clearly had it elsewhere: she was devoted to complicated YouTube makeup tutorials and sometimes taught with small rhinestones glued to the corners of her eyes. Nadia had applied to be her research assistant for the following year. Sylvie wanted her friend to get the job—not that she doubted that it would happen; nobody was smarter than Nadia—but she didn't like Dr. Rau.

"She doesn't teach like we're graduate students," Sylvie said at the brewery. "She teaches like we're in fourth grade."

"Oh, you read the *Tractatus* in fourth grade in Massachusetts?"

"You know what I mean. She hates letting us talk. She's not interested in our ideas."

"Of course not. She's a genius."

"She's a tyrant."

"Possibly," Nadia said, unruffled. They were only bickering to kill time; Nadia had conceded months ago that Dr. Rau liked her classroom power too much. Like Sylvie, she had grown up keenly attuned to authoritarianism. Her Portuguese grandparents had had their lives defined utterly by the Salazar regime. Her father António had emigrated to the United States out of a sincere belief in the country's ideals of choice and freedom. He was swiftly disappointed, but in a way that led not to disillusionment or departure but to a career as one of Planned Parenthood's most effective fundraisers. Now he was retired and, to Nadia's great confusion, seemed to be spending all his time at the gym.

Before Sylvie could ask for an António update, a man who could only be Wyatt appeared behind the bar. All the hair on Sylvie's forearms stood straight up. Her face flushed.

Wyatt was visibly Robbie's opposite. He had big, red hands and pale hair poking from beneath a new-looking Carhartt watch cap. He wore Red Wing boots and the sort of thick flannel button-down that you got at a menswear store, not a workwear one. His forehead was oily. His eyes were the frightening blue of a husky's. Sex rolled from him in waves.

He wasted no time in coming to chat. It was rapidly clear that he both remembered Nadia and had trusted her when she said she was asking about his personal life for a friend. He brought Sylvie's second beer with a shot of High West rye she hadn't asked for.

After that beer, she asked for the check. He wrote his number on the receipt. Instead of tucking it away coyly, she said, "When do you get off work?"

Wyatt drove her home in his lurching pickup after closing, the hum of its loose bench seat rising inside her. At the door of her apartment, not bothering to ignore the echo of her first night with Robbie, Sylvie told him, "I want you to be in control."

He blinked his blue eyes at her. "Okay."

"I'm not drunk. You don't need to be careful. If you're doing something I don't like, I'll let you know."

"You want to tell me anything else?"

She gave herself a moment. She was intensely afraid that he'd underwhelm her, that she'd miss Robbie, that her whole schema would fall apart. She also wanted, very badly, for him to fuck her. She stepped closer to him. "No, I don't."

Wyatt had a thick, reddish penis that was, in both appearance and effect, satisfyingly different from Robbie's. Robbie had a Platonic ideal. Wyatt had a blunt instrument. He also had exceptional instincts. He pushed himself as deeply inside Sylvie as he could and, when she grabbed his hips to get him deeper still, growled in her ear, "*I'm* doing it."

She had never heard hotter words in her life. They created a feeling of fullness so intense it transcended the physical. It was as if all the bad parts of her consciousness had temporarily been scooped out and replaced by arousal that required no thought and that lasted until Wyatt flipped her over to fuck her face down, which made her come immediately.

She wanted her mind not to return. No dice. Even before Wyatt had finished, she was beginning to think again—to think how good this was, how unlike Robbie, but how much she still wanted to see Robbie tonight. By the time she'd gone to pee and get two glasses of water, her desire to text him was undeniable. She tried to concentrate on Wyatt: his densely muscled upper body, his soft belly and thighs. He had an optimal amount of chest hair. Robbie had ruined his body-hair patterns by shaving for too many swim meets in high school, and had only sparse, prickly tufts.

"You want me to go," Wyatt said. He sounded a little sad.

"Not right this second."

"It's okay." He had the smile of a rock star, gleaming but crooked. His canine teeth overlapped the ones in front. "It's your apartment. I don't automatically get to stick around."

"I had fun," she offered.

"Do-it-again fun? Or the kind of fun where you and your friend don't come back to my bar for a year?"

Sylvie wasn't sure. She resented his sensitivity. It would've been better if he were a pig. She realized belatedly that she had hoped a rough, casual hookup would not only remind her of her submissive self but also purge her of at least some measure of her desire for Robbie. It had done the opposite on the latter front.

"Depends on whether you're looking for anything serious."

He shook his head.

"Then how about this: if I show up at your bar, it means I want a redo. And if I don't—" She shrugged.

"If you don't, you don't."

Sylvie sighed. "You're a nice guy, aren't you."

"Guilty." He pushed his hair back, then rose. "I hope I'll see you."

"I hope so, too."

She stood by her window for a moment after his truck disappeared. A bad, jittery feeling spread down her limbs. Her wrists hurt from being held. Her inner thighs felt both slick and abraded. She needed a shower. She needed to eat. She regretted very much having to admit that she needed Robbie. It was 9:30 p.m. He picked up on the third ring. Eight minutes later, unfed but more or less washed, she was driving to his house.

When she and Robbie set their terms for nonmonogamy, he'd said he wanted to hear about the sex she had with other men. She wasn't sure if he meant it. Her turtle, who'd maintained relative silence on the subject, asserted himself as she drove.

You smell like sex, he said.

I showered!

Her turtle ignored this protest. He said flatly, You should tell Robbie. You should tell him about Jonah, too. If you want to have faith in your relationship, you should spend less time on philosophical experiments and more time trying its strength.

Sylvie pulled into Robbie's building's garage. He'd given her his only guest parking pass. Keys, too. She thought both were perfectly good signs of faith. Really, she thought her turtle was full of shit. She was too old for the turtle, anyway. She liked visiting his island, and she'd had him a long time, but it was shameful to be thirty and still heavily reliant on an imaginary friend.

I think I'm outgrowing you, she told the turtle.

You are not, he said. You can't outgrow yourself.

In the elevator, Sylvie regarded her reflection with distaste. She'd squashed her ruined curls into a sloppy braid, wiped off some but not all of her makeup. Her breasts, which had risen so happily from the jumpsuit, lolled dolefully beneath her sweatshirt. She poked the left one with her thumb. Her mom would be horrified to see them. Carol had never appreciated her daughter's physique. She considered it tacky to have breasts big enough to require support, though she also considered not wearing a bra obscene.

Sylvie let herself into Robbie's apartment, wrestled her boots off, and shuffled into the living room. He rose from amid printouts and clothbound textbooks to greet her. His cheeks looked freshly shaved; his hair was damp. He smelled like citrus soap and, very faintly, chlorine. She tugged the tails of his unbuttoned flannel shirt, wishing she could crawl into it with him.

He kissed her, then sank back onto the couch. Sylvie stayed standing. "I can't tell if you're drunk, sad, or angry," Robbie said.

She shook her head. "None of those."

"So?"

"I slept with someone."

He nodded. "Was it all right?"

"What?"

"You're okay?"

She stared at him. "Are you asking if he hurt me?"

"Something's clearly going on," Robbie said gently. "So yes, I am."

"He didn't hurt me. It was fine."

Robbie pushed his heaps of legal information aside, then motioned at the newly free cushion beside him. "Come sit."

"You want me to?"

"You're not contaminated, Sylvie. And I'm not upset. You didn't do anything wrong." He rubbed the side of his neck. "You met the expectations you created."

It was not an idea Sylvie had ever entertained. *You met the expectations you created.* Robbie made it sound so logical, so normal, so adult. It was the opposite of Jonah. So much of their relationship had centered on him making and then changing the rules, diminishing what she could ask of him, not being satisfied by what he'd told her to do.

She collapsed onto the couch beside Robbie. He kissed her hair. "This was your idea," he said. "I thought you would like it."

Inside Sylvie's head, the turtle barked, Ha!

She ignored him and told Robbie, "So did I."

"But?"

Sylvie twisted to face him. A soft, wobbly sensation entered her body.

Not a good sign. Next would come the warmth of irrepressible sentiment. She tried to beat it, to say something sane. It was too late.

"But," she said, "apparently, I'm in love with you."

7.

"He didn't mind," Sylvie reported to Nadia the next day. They were in the philosophy grad students' lounge, drinking Keurig coffee and pretending to read. Nadia was wearing jeans so stiff they crackled when she slid lower on the couch. She also had on significant eyeliner, possibly influenced by Dr. Rau. "He said I met the expectations I created."

"Wise man."

"He wasn't jealous at all. Or pissed. Nothing."

"Do you want him to be pissed?"

"No."

Nadia waited. Under the harsh institutional lights, she had the luminously dead air of an actress in an old B-movie. Sylvie, who had slept less than three hours, probably looked like the Bride of Frankenstein.

"But you want something." Nadia prompted finally.

Sylvie pulled on her hair, as if she could yank the right words from her head. It was not a good habit in terms of curl maintenance. Nor was it especially useful. She pulled harder. "I want to feel less," she said.

"About Robbie, or in general?"

"Yes."

"You'd be bored."

"I told Robbie I love him," Sylvie said.

Nadia's eyebrows shot up. "You did?"

"Uh-huh."

"You do?"

"I guess."

"And that's why you're upset?"

Sylvie nodded. She had not meant to say *love* to Robbie. She'd hardly said it to herself about him—or, rather, she'd said it frequently, but as a question or warning, not a statement. She'd been totally unprepared to hear it, or to hear him say it back without hesitation. Once again, she'd violated her rules. She had created a situation that threatened her autonomy. She sensed the fragments of her shattered old life encroaching.

She closed her eyes and, in the comforting darkness, said, "It's one thing if I like hanging out with him, and like having sex with him, and like talking about my ideas with him. I can *describe* all that."

"You can make theories about it, you mean."

"Yeah."

"But you can't make a theory about being in love with him."

Sylvie opened her eyes. "You don't have to say it like that."

"Like what?"

"'In love.'" She tried to do a voice—any voice—but it didn't work. She was in love with Robbie. Her body, her heart, and her mind all agreed. Weakly, she said, "I could probably make a theory about it."

"Does it matter if you can't?"

"Maybe."

"Are you spiraling a bit?"

"Maybe." Sylvie slouched lower on the sofa. It had so many coffee stains they nearly looked like a pattern. "I liked fucking Wyatt."

"But?"

"I wanted Robbie after."

Nadia shrugged. "Sounds about right."

"It does?"

"Sylvie," Nadia said. "For months you've been saying you need some guy to just rail you. I found you some guy, he performed as anticipated, and then you went and snuggled with your boyfriend. You're set."

"I don't feel set."

"No one feels set."

"I did with Jonah," Sylvie admitted. "At the beginning."

"You were miserable."

"Yeah, but I wasn't always arguing with myself."

"Just trying to brainwash yourself into staying in a bad relationship," Nadia said. After a second, she added, "It's hard for me to imagine you that way."

Sylvie shrugged. "I was a kid. And besides, I started dating Jonah right after my grandfather died."

"What does that have to do with it?"

"My grandfather was my role model. Jonah took over for him. I mean, I put him on my grandfather's pedestal." She sighed. "I guess I needed a man to want to be."

"Not anymore," Nadia said. "Now you have your own concept of how to live."

"Sort of."

"You do, and it's working." Nadia tilted her head to the side. "I'm impressed."

Pride welled in Sylvie. With it came a new wave of love. Before she met Robbie, she had known her philosophy had to account for good relationships, ones like her grandparents', but she hadn't believed she would have one. She had accepted that a life without romance would mean a life with sex but not eros. Now she saw how dry and empty that would have made her arguments. Nobody would sign onto a feminism that offered no real hope for partnership, and she'd never have found that hope if Robbie hadn't agreed to be her lab rat.

"What if Robbie decides he wants to get married?" she said.

"Is that something he talks about?"

"He wants a family."

"So do you."

"I want a baby," Sylvie corrected. "Someday."

Nadia, who was uninterested in reproducing, made a face. "Distinction without a difference. And he can't make you marry him, anyway. Bigamy."

"He doesn't know that."

"So tell him. It's a perfect test. If you say you're married and he freaks out, then it's proof he secretly wants more than you do."

"I'm not *married*."

"You're not divorced."

"Robbie could freak out because it's weird for me to have an estranged husband."

"Lots of people have estranged husbands. What's weird is not telling your boyfriend."

Sylvie wasn't sure that the first part was true, or that Nadia had any way of knowing, but she didn't say so. Nor did she say that she'd been considering telling Robbie about her marriage since their discussion of #MeToo. In the intervening months, she hadn't made much progress on that front, though the movement itself careened forward. She could not get herself over the wall of victim rhetoric, let alone heed Nadia's suggestion that she seek nuance about it.

She raised the issue to her turtle on her walk home that afternoon. He said she was oversimplifying. Public vulnerability, he told her, isn't necessarily the same as victimhood.

Distinction without a difference.

Don't imitate Nadia.

Nadia's smart.

The turtle clacked his beak. So take her advice. Get over your victimphobia and tell Robbie about Jonah.

I don't want to.

Why?

He'll pity me. It'll be terrible.

He won't. He'll be kind to you. It's good to let men do that. Good to confide in men, too.

Why?

Because you fuck them, the turtle said.

I talk about Jonah with you. You're a dude.

Her turtle turned his wrinkly head. Palms rattled their fronds behind him. Huge hibiscus bloomed everywhere. No, he said, as he always did. I'm you.

You're irritating, is what you are. Why should I confide in men?

Because you have a bifurcated relationship with them. You want them, but you're scared of them. Robbie's not scary. He gives you a chance to unify your reactions. Or at least to narrow the gap.

Sylvie couldn't argue. Before Robbie, no man other than her grandfather had shown her sustained kindness, consideration, or respect. It didn't occur to her that she hadn't let anyone but Robbie try. She thought only of the not-great luck she'd had with her dad, the shitty luck she'd had with Jonah. But she was lucky now, she reminded herself. And besides, she didn't want to let her rat husband set the terms of the rest of her life, or keep her from experiencing the love of the future. If the way to prevent that was by telling Robbie about him, so be it. She was brave now. She'd tell.

8.

Sylvie made her great revelation the day she turned thirty-one. She planned it ahead, on the grounds that, symbolically, having a momentous conversation on a birthday made sense. Also, she'd be thinking about Jonah anyway. He emailed on all her birthdays.

On waking in Robbie's bed, Sylvie consciously assembled the thought *Jonah will email me today* behind her still-closed eyes. Her heart skittered. She rolled over and kissed Robbie awake.

"Hey, birthday girl," he said sleepily. His voice settled her pulse.

"Morning."

He hooked his legs around hers. "Got anywhere to be?"

It was—a small cosmic gift—a Saturday. "Nope."

"Good."

Sun streamed through the window, defeating Robbie's blinds. It was early May, the most perfect time of year in Virginia. Sylvie and Robbie had been formally together for more than six months. She still couldn't sink into herself during the sex she was steering, but now she had Wyatt for balance. Since the day they met, she had returned to his brewery repeatedly, whenever she needed to be removed from her head. The more she did so, she found, the more physical and intellectual pleasure she could get from telling Robbie what to do.

But right now, perhaps as a birthday gift, Robbie was taking some amount of charge. Sylvie closed her eyes and tucked her face into his warm shoulder as he pushed inside her. She had the sensation that he'd wrapped her whole body in his. She pressed her hips up and tightened her muscles, and Robbie groaned softly in her ear.

"Good?" she said, her speech already breathy and fractured.

"So good."

She lifted her head to kiss him, tasting herself on his tongue. In her life with Jonah, that had never happened. It had been a bad life, she thought with a swell of gratitude to Robbie. She never had to relive it. She was so lucky to be here.

After they both came, they lay still for a while, Sylvie's head on Robbie's cool chest. She wanted to spend all morning there, but her caffeine headache got acute fast. She sat on Robbie's sofa as he made coffee, gearing herself up to read the email that—no surprise—had arrived at 8:03 a.m. from jonah.sabransky@gmail.com.

> Happy birthday! I wish we could celebrate together, in our new house. I just bought it this winter, but of course, what's mine is yours.
>
> I always hoped we'd have children by the time we were 30. It isn't too late to start now. I haven't met anyone like you. I can't imagine another woman I could feel comfortable with the way I felt comfortable with you.
>
> I'm no longer angry at you for leaving, or for staying away so long. I know you like to dawdle. Still, it's been enough time, Sylvie. I hope this is the year you come home.

Dawdle took Sylvie straight to childhood. It was a Carol Broder word. Sylvie was always getting scolded for dawdling at breakfast, brushing her teeth, tying her shoes, doing her math, beginning her chores. Jonah must have picked it up from her mother during their marriage. She knew they'd talked about her. No longer. It was a family rule that Broders no longer spoke to Sabranskys and that, as far as anyone in the state of Massachusetts knew, Carol and Paul had no clue where their daughter was.

Sylvie glanced up at Robbie, who was still fiddling with his pour-over setup. He smiled and lifted a mug at her. "Almost ready."

She blew him a kiss. "Thank you," she said. Headache aside, she was startled to register that she felt fine. It was if she still had the protective mantle of Robbie wrapped around her, repelling Jonah's words. Still, she did not like this email. *It's been enough time* was a frightening assertion.

She would have been more comforted if he'd limited himself to bragging about his fancy new home.

She deleted the email and got up for coffee. She could do nothing about Jonah's agenda. She wasn't letting him ruin her birthday. She resettled herself on Robbie's couch with her book and stayed put until he left in the early afternoon to grocery shop for the birthday dinner he was cooking her. She'd asked to have it at Nadia's house.

"Wouldn't it make more sense for me to cook here?" Robbie had said.

It would have. Robbie's apartment was bigger, his kitchen much better stocked. He had a full set of matching pans and a Le Creuset Dutch oven that he scrubbed regularly with Bar Keepers Friend to prevent stains. Nadia had one big roaster and a pasta pot. She also had Sylvie's favorite apartment in the world.

"I just want to spend part of my birthday there," she had told Robbie. "It makes me happy."

"I'd like my place to make you happy, too."

"Of course it does," she'd said, kissing him. It wasn't a lie, but she didn't get excited about Robbie's apartment the way she did Nadia's. If Robbie wasn't in his apartment, you couldn't sense his presence. Nadia's, on the other hand, was clearly the space of a singular mind.

Nadia kept her four rooms—kitchen, living room, study, bedroom—spotlessly clean and nearly empty. She had no plants, no lamps, no art except an Amish quilt on one wall. Her study, which was miniature, contained a child-sized desk and an Aeron chair the department had discarded after its right arm fell off. Her books sat on a giant industrial iron shelving unit that took up the living room's longest wall. She had a huge, soft couch upholstered in some kind of unstainable white fabric, a cheap table, and black plastic folding chairs. A cashmere blanket was draped over the couch, and more sat in a basket beside it. Across the living room, she had a wall-mounted television and a stack of shockingly comfortable floor pillows. Her strategy for living well while conserving her tech savings was to spend money only on textiles. Why pillows counted, Sylvie didn't know, but she sat on them frequently.

She got to Nadia's at 6:00, having napped, showered, and taken a long, looping walk around Charlottesville. Robbie had been there for an hour, baking a fish in salt. He'd made potatoes, too, and a salad with herbs and soft cheese. Nadia had gotten out an embroidered tablecloth and filled the living room with fat red candles. She was in on Sylvie's plan to tell Robbie about her marriage tonight and had promised to create the most soothing possible environment beforehand. She'd also stocked her fridge with a disturbing amount of wine.

"You can't let me get too drunk," Sylvie hissed to her friend in the living room while Robbie tended his fish in the kitchen.

"I won't. But you need to be a little drunk, right?"

"A *little*. You got six bottles of wine for three people."

"Don't worry," Nadia said cheerily. "There'll be a fourth after you leave."

"Who?"

She shrugged. "Math department. I found him in the library last week."

Sylvie sighed. She wished she were going to spend the night having meaningless sex instead of a terrifying conversation.

Nadia looked at her closely. "It'll be all right," she said in a low voice. "He really loves you."

"I'm aware."

"So cheer up. You have a nice boyfriend. It's summer. Oh! By the way, I got that fellowship to work with Dr. Rau."

"Congratulations!" Sylvie gave her friend a squeeze. "Don't let her convert you to fascism."

"If she converts me to anything, it's going to be lesbianism."

"Is she a lesbian?"

"Maybe."

"It would be fun to have an affair with a professor."

Robbie swung the kitchen door open, saying, "No one's stopping you." He came into the living room to give her a kiss.

"Our male professors are," Nadia told him. "By being old and out of touch."

"So I've heard," Robbie said.

"It's true," Sylvie said. "But let's not talk about professors. It's my birthday. I don't want to be grouchy. I want to eat dinner and have a nice time."

It was an extremely good meal. Robbie's fish was excellent. His potatoes were golden and thickly crisped on all sides. Sylvie, who loved sourness above all other tastes, usually thought his salads needed more lemon or vinegar, but tonight's was acidic enough for her—intentional, surely, given that Robbie downed half a glass of water after every few bites of his.

Nadia kicked them out shortly after dessert, as instructed. She sent them home with the third of her six bottles of wine. Sylvie uncorked it the moment they walked into her studio, where she'd decided for obscure reasons the conversation should take place. She heard a mouse scuttling somewhere but ignored it. She poured two jam-jar glasses and handed Robbie one.

"I need to talk to you," she said.

Robbie sat instantly on the bed. He gazed at her like a dog told to stay. "I'm listening."

Sylvie wished she had more furniture. Her desk chair, a highly uncomfortable wheeled wooden thing, looked unbearable. Joining Robbie on the soft, rumpled bed seemed too nice. She settled for the metal stool she kept by the kitchen counter. Perched on it, swinging one leg, she gave a moment to the quiet inner voice that informed her, in all unpleasant times, that she was going to die. Once it completed its message, she glanced for strength at her grandparents' bougainvillea painting, which hung over her bed, then told Robbie, who was twisting his fingers worriedly, "You didn't do anything. I mean, nothing bad. Only good. Your fish was delicious."

He smiled a little. "You mentioned."

"I'm going to mention it more. You need—Robbie, you need to understand, no guy ever cooked for me, or brought me things, or hung out with my friends, or let me have friends." Sylvie saw his eyebrows jump. She'd gotten ahead of herself. She took a sip of wine, which tasted like hay and honey, and tried again. "Before you, no man was ever really nice to me. I've been single for a long time—too single for anyone to be nice or mean, you know? And before that, I only had one boyfriend."

"Ever?"

"Ever," Sylvie confirmed. "In my whole life."

Robbie tipped his head to the side. "How long were you together?"

"Eleven years."

He sat straight up. His mouth opened. He looked like a Ken doll, if Mattel made Kens that were Jewish and visibly drunk. "*How* many?"

"I was his girlfriend for seven years. We were engaged for one, so that's eight. And then we were married three more—not quite three—and then I left."

"Why?"

She grinned, surprising herself. "He treated me like shit."

Robbie blinked at her. Otherwise, his face was expressionless. He didn't get up to hug her. She was grateful to him for that.

"He set up our life so I couldn't do anything," she said. "He made me quit my job. He dictated every single thing I did. Not—not explicitly, always. He'd manipulate me, or withhold. He'd punish me if I was too emotional, or if I didn't text him quickly enough. It sounds so stupid."

Shame swelled in her throat. Her little apartment felt alien. Its stacks of books pressed in on her. She knew she needed to get to the not-divorced bit, but now that, too, struck her as degrading. An emotionally competent person wouldn't have let herself be manipulated via text message. An emotionally competent person would be able to get a divorce.

She was terrified, suddenly, that Robbie was sharing her thoughts. Maybe he was about to say her story was absurd, or her fault, or not that bad. Maybe the reason she shied from calling herself a victim was that, deep down, she knew she wasn't one; that she was faking it, crying wolf, hiding her own failures behind the pitifulness everyone assumed of women. She looked at Robbie, knowing her expression was somewhere between dire and pleading, and he said, instantly and hotly, "Sylvie, no. None of this sounds stupid. It sounds terrible."

She bit the inside of her cheek. "It's humiliating."

Robbie opened his mouth, but, instead of speaking, got up and came to stand before her. It only took him four steps to cross the room. Very carefully, he said, "I thought you might have a story like this. Not this long—not *marriage*—but I thought maybe a man had treated you badly. I was going to ask—"

"Yeah," Sylvie said. "When you asked about MeToo."

Robbie nodded. "I thought that might be a way to make it easy for you to tell me, but when we were talking about it, I realized that making it easy or hard isn't my job. What happened to you happened to *you*. And I want to say it isn't humiliating, you shouldn't be anything but proud you got out, but I don't get to say how you should feel. I don't get to say anything about it. You can stop talking right now, if you want, or you can tell me everything." He made a small gesture, less than a shrug, that wrenched something in Sylvie open. She wanted to leap at him. Quietly, he said, "I love you. I won't love you any more or less depending on how much you tell."

"I love you, too," she said, just as softly. She was almost too relieved to speak. She slid forward so her head could rest on his torso. He smelled like fish and wine. Into his shirt, she said, "Jonah hated hearing about my feelings, but he still wouldn't let me keep anything to myself."

"Jonah was—"

"My husband, yeah."

"Asshole."

"Asshole," Sylvie agreed. She felt so close to Robbie it was as if she had let him inside the skin of her arms and legs. She had not imagined that connectedness and privacy could coexist in this way. In the morning, lying in bed beside a sleeping Robbie, she dredged the feeling from her hungover memory and held it in the light like a jewel. For the second time since she met him, she saw a new life unfurling before her, one in which she could have a true and lasting relationship without having to return to her old ways. She thought of that old self, of all the women in the world who let men tell them what to do and how to be. No more. Not for Sylvie Broder. She'd found a man who understood her right to privacy not just outside their relationship but in it. Not until now had she seen that divulging traumas was not only a bad form of public discourse but also a part of romance that needed dismantling. Why should you have to unspool your past for your partner? Shouldn't the love of the future look *to* the future?

In her head, the turtle manifested to say, It's not a trauma that you're not divorced.

It is if I say it is.

You don't even believe in calling your *real* traumas trauma.

A foolish consistency is the hobgoblin of little minds, she informed him.

Don't quote Emerson at me. And don't be cynical. You were going to tell Robbie you're still married, and you didn't do it.

Sylvie rolled over. She did not wish to pursue this line of thought. Robbie, still sleeping, emitted a small sigh and pressed his face to her shoulder, and she wriggled down so she could kiss his forehead. She didn't need consistency, or a divorce, or—she announced silently—a turtle, who sulked off into the thickets of her mind. What she needed, at least for the moment, was Robbie. She didn't have to tell him all her secrets to know that.

Chapter Three

1.

Robbie graduated the last Sunday in May. Sylvie subleased her studio and spent the summer in DC, studying for her qualifying exams and going to the nearby pool. Robbie's neighborhood—or, rather, *their* neighborhood—had gorgeous, leafy stretches of row houses turreted like tiny castles, renovated and un- in roughly equal proportions. His building—*their* building—was at the corner of Fourteenth and Shepherd Streets NW, near the end of a little commercial stretch that included three poky grocery stores, a dry cleaner, a nail salon, and more restaurants and bars than Sylvie needed to stay happy until mid-August. She barely strayed beyond where she could walk.

For her, that summer was a new way of living. She wasn't teaching, which meant she had nothing to do but read and write. Robbie, who had no debt and whose starting salary was $215,000, refused to let her pay any part of any bill. Sylvie didn't protest. Her yearly stipend was $26,000. She carried credit card debt every month and had deferred her student loans. Except for the harbor checks she'd let pile up in the first year of her marriage, she'd never saved money in her life. Although she was the daughter of bankers, she had not been raised to think about her finances. Her parents had clearly assumed that Jonah, or another man, would take care of that side of her life. Now she took some pleasure in using the small profit she made from her subletter's payments to shrink her Visa bill somewhat. She did so by less than $100 a month, barely more than gas for the trips she'd promised to take to see Nadia, who was spending the summer in Charlottesville. Still, it made her feel like an adult.

Sylvie understood that her summerlong financial responsibility was an illusion, but she knew that, if she wanted, it could be a promise for the future, too. In the meantime, it was both part and symbol of the comfort she felt with Robbie. It was shockingly easy to live with him. She had never cohabitated with any man but Jonah, and Robbie had only lived by himself and in group houses full of guys. Both anticipated an adjustment period, but none turned out to be necessary. His presence muffled her worries; her steadily growing relaxation satisfied his desire to please.

If she had a problem, it was only that life with Robbie generated memories of life with Jonah. Reading at the kitchen island while her boyfriend cooked, Sylvie thought of her younger self in Swampscott studying her reflection in the upper oven door while she ate celery sticks for dinner. She used to pour her Head & Shoulders into a John Frieda Brilliant Brunette bottle. Now she sometimes recruited Robbie to pop a pimple on her back. She let him see her pluck her eyebrows and floss her teeth. These things seemed minor, so insignificant Sylvie wouldn't mention them even to Nadia, but in her heart, they grew large.

It took Sylvie a few weeks to register that she was permitting herself far more recollections of her marriage than usual. Ordinarily, she played Whac-A-Mole with them, beating each memory underground the moment it arose. Now she could sit and consider them. She could feel sorry for the girl she'd been, rather than terrified she was still that girl. It was a realization that made Sylvie feel first old, then mature, then grateful. She waited for Robbie to finish swimming his laps—much of her major thinking that summer happened while she lounged poolside, reading or admiring her boyfriend's machinelike freestyle—and then informed him, smiling innocently from her deck chair, that she wanted them home and in bed in fifteen minutes, tops.

"I'm not telling you my plan," she said as Robbie's ears pinkened. "But I've got one."

She tied his wrists together with her bikini top. It seemed like the right thing to do. Once they were fucking, though, she missed Robbie's hands. She was on top, her breasts swinging. He was plainly enjoying the view, but she wished he could grab them, pinch a nipple, dig his fingers in.

Afterward, while Sylvie lay with her head on his chest, he said, "I really liked that."

"Good."

"I'm not sure if you did."

Sylvie sat up. "Why do you say that?"

Robbie shrugged while still lying down, which she found impressive. "Your face."

She rubbed her eyes. Presumably they had betrayed her. It couldn't have been her mouth; too much panting. "I came," she noted.

"You always come."

Sylvie detected no self-satisfaction in Robbie's tone. Any other man she'd slept with would be bragging. He was just stating a truth. She admired him, now and always, for his ability to see himself clearly, without shame or ego interceding. A lot of women would say this was a rare trait in a man. Sylvie thought it was a rare trait in human beings. Certainly it was one she'd worked hard to learn.

"I just mean," he said, "that you don't have to do that again if you weren't into it."

"Maybe as a special treat."

He gave a quiet, noncommittal hum. She slouched against the headboard, thinking, not for the first time, that the bedroom—*their* bedroom—

needed color. Currently, it was all light wood, cream paint, white sheets. Elegant, but unsexy.

"How would you feel about painting the walls in here?"

"What?"

"Or wallpapering. It's too white. Boring."

Robbie laughed. "If you'd like wallpaper, we can have wallpaper."

She pushed her hair back. It smelled like chlorine, which she now considered a comforting scent. "I'll find a good pattern."

"Done."

After that, Sylvie began searching constantly for ways to bring the condo to life. In a month, she did more to it than she ever had to her awful studio. In part, that was because she couldn't afford much, but she'd known the day she signed her lease that the place was unimprovable. She hadn't cared. If anything, it felt right that it was an apartment to be transient in. Robbie's condo was different. Whether or not it would someday be *her* home, it was *a* home, and the Estie in her couldn't allow it to be simply neutral and nice.

Besides, it was fun to decorate with Robbie. It became part of their weekly routine, which otherwise centered on food. Friday dinners at Little Coco's, lots of wine and amaro to go with their margherita pizzas and sides of meatballs; midweek takeout from Taqueria Habanero, usually paired with the Habesha beer Sylvie bought at her favorite of the poky grocery stores. Farmers market on Saturday, Georgetown Flea on Sunday, sometimes paired with a spin through a Wisconsin Avenue antique shop—most of them were heavy on carved gods and painted chests, trophies of long-ago State Department tours—or one of Bethesda's many rug stores.

When she wasn't eating or helping Robbie furnish his home, she was rereading the French Marxist-turned-mystic Simone Weil. During her master's, Sylvie had loathed Weil's *The Need for Roots*. In it, Weil argued that the human soul's greatest necessity is physical and historical permanence. She said leaving your family and community led straight to malaise and alienation. Sylvie disagreed totally. Only by uprooting herself from Jonah, and from Massachusetts, had she survived. But her relationship with Robbie changed her angle. She revisited *The Need for Roots*, searching for nuance less in the book than in herself, and found it. *Whoever is uprooted himself,* Weil said, *uproots others. Whoever is rooted himself doesn't uproot others.*

Sylvie thought her new life proved Weil right. She thought that, softened and adjusted, the idea of rooters and uprooters was, like the institutional-vs.-psychic split, a useful framework. Her commitment to a private relationship had uprooted Robbie some; his need to create comfort for himself and everyone around him was rooting her enough to try to reciprocate. Both processes, she thought, were good. Both were welcome. *In love of future,* Sylvie scrawled in her notes, *no one has to be rooted/uprooted. Not a dichotomy. In future, no dichotomies, even in straight relationships?? Everyone gets to be both.*

She explained all this to Robbie, who, rightly, took her new angle on roots as a compliment. "I'm not so sure I'm uprooted, though," he said.

"No?"

"Not monogamous isn't the same as not rooted."

Sylvie wanted to suggest that it might be if he slept with somebody else, but that wasn't fair. It was his choice. "You haven't introduced me to your family yet," she noted. "Not even at your graduation. And I'm sure you would have if I were anybody else."

Slowly, he said, "I would have." He hesitated, and Sylvie saw, with terrible clarity, the mistake she'd made. "And I want to."

"It's not enough for them to know about me?"

"It wasn't enough for Nadia to know about me."

She swirled the remainder of her Habesha, then downed it. Out the giant window, Fourteenth Street was taking on the slate blue of evening. She knew she had only one acceptable response. "All right."

Robbie put his hand on her leg, pinning her down physically, she assumed, as a prelude to pinning her down logistically: suggesting a late summer visit, or High Holidays with the Drs. Klein. But he surprised her. "You know what's proof of your argument, though?" he said.

"What?"

"I've been thinking lately that I always assumed I wanted a wife and children, but it was—that. An assumption. I think I just wanted to love someone."

Sylvie set her drink down and crawled into his lap. Into his neck, she said, "I love you."

"I love you."

"And I do—" She ignored her surge of fear. "I do want children. Or a child, anyway."

Robbie wrapped his arms around her. For a moment he was silent. When he spoke, he said only, "I'm glad."

Sylvie didn't relay the conversation to Nadia during their daily call the next afternoon. She felt too tender toward it and too unsettled by it. She wanted to leave it alone in her psyche for at least a year. Besides, Nadia didn't exactly create an opening. She was on campus, teaching summer classes and prepping for her year with Dr. Rau, and spent the whole call complaining about the professor's request that Nadia come up with a link between her dissertation and the Wittgensteinian language games that Dr. Rau studied.

"Is that part of the fellowship?" Sylvie asked.

"No. She just wants me to do it."

"Isn't she also making you learn French?"

"And German, for Wittgenstein."

"What if you just included Wittgenstein in your conversations with the computer?"

"She's not interested in that."

Of course not, Sylvie thought. Dr. Rau wasn't interested in anyone else's ideas, even if the *anyone* in question was a computer model created by her research fellow. Instead of pointing that out, she said, "You used to want to write sci-fi."

"I did."

"So go back to that. Write a novel about a robot programmed according to something from Wittgenstein. I mean, he basically *was* a robot, right?"

"He'd have liked to be."

"Perfect. There's your novel."

"Nobody in the world is going to read a book about robot Wittgenstein."

"If you write it, they will," Sylvie said, and meant it. She had faith that Nadia could tell, and tell well, any story she liked. Since they met, Nadia had not only persuaded her that it was possible to discuss morality with a computer, but shown her the point of teaching them to do such a thing. If you can show them moral reason, Nadia always said, you can reduce the chances of humans using them for evil.

But Nadia was saying, "Besides, there's no *way* the department would let me write a novel for my dissertation."

"It's not against the rules."

"Yeah, but it wouldn't look great on the job market, and Dr. Rau wouldn't like it. She hates fiction."

"All of it?"

"She says it's false."

"I believe the term is *made up*."

"Which is another reason not to do it," Nadia said. "Making things up is too hard."

"Challenge is healthy."

"Failure is depressing."

"Have you ever failed at anything?"

Nadia laughed. "Fuck you."

Sylvie laughed, too. She fanned herself with her hair. She was walking to the pool to read, and it was so hot the asphalt seemed to shimmer. It reminded her of Miami. "Come visit me," she said. "We'll brainstorm your novel together."

Nadia made a mysterious sound. "Do you want me to?"

"Yes!"

"Positive?"

"Nadia, I call you every day." She sidestepped a woman walking a fawn-colored dog who appeared to be grinning, if dogs could grin. "I miss you. Why wouldn't I want you to come?"

"I don't know. You haven't invited me yet."

"Well, I'm inviting you. I want you to be here. I want you to see everything." Sylvie waved her free arm, as if scooping her neighborhood up. "Robbie has a guest room. A guest *bed*. I bought the weirdest quilt in the world for it." It was a great quilt. She'd found it on eBay. Every one of its squares was patterned with bugs.

"Okay," Nadia said, more warmly. "Next weekend, then? Friday to Monday?"

"Done."

"You don't need to ask Robbie?"

"I will," she said, "but he's going to say yes. He'll be excited to see you."

Instead of reading at the pool, Sylvie planned. She would take Nadia to play pinball at Lyman's and drink devastatingly strong cocktails at All Souls. In the afternoons, they'd visit art museums, walk or lounge in Rock Creek Park, go to bookstores. Maybe she could get Nadia to buy some nice pulpy sci-fi.

When she told Robbie her schemes, he asked only, "How much do you want me to hang out with the two of you?"

"As much as you want."

"I'll give you some space. Let you talk about philosophy."

"You can talk about philosophy with us if Nadia wants to. Her dissertation is more interesting than mine."

Robbie's face twitched. "You don't really think that."

"I mean, not more interesting to me personally, or I'd be writing it myself. But it's more socially important."

"As far as I can tell, the world's got a lot more romance than robots."

"Well, hers will be more important once romance is over."

"Fine." Robbie laughed. "I'll give you that."

On Wednesday, he washed the good sheets and put them on the guest bed. He had dinner waiting when Nadia got in from Charlottesville, proposed Lyman's afterward before Sylvie even had a chance. All weekend, he maintained the ideal balance of presence and absence, giving Sylvie and her friend alone time without ever seeming to avoid Nadia. On Sunday, he reserved an outdoor table at the Laotian restaurant down Fourteenth Street. Walking home, he said he should go to bed early—work night, brief to draft, et cetera—but they should stay out.

Sylvie took Nadia to the roof bar at Little Coco's. It rotated themes and menus, she'd learned. For the summer, it was a cabana. Pool toys were everywhere. It smelled like coconut, liquor, and hot PVC, which was a more pleasant mix than Sylvie would have guessed. She found it soothing, though Nadia did not seem calm. If anything, she was agitated. She ordered one of her strange, sweet drinks—a Miller and a shot of Campari, which she dumped into the beer—and wriggled around in her seat.

"Is something bothering you?" Sylvie asked.

Nadia screwed her mouth to the side, which meant yes. After a moment, she said, "I support you and Robbie."

"But?"

"It's just scary," Nadia said after another pause. "Seeing your life here. I know this is selfish, but I'm afraid you won't come back to campus in the fall."

"Of course I'm coming back." Sylvie tried to meet her friend's eyes. "I'd tell you if I weren't going to, but I am. I want to."

"You do?"

"I do. You're there."

"No other reason."

"None that matters. I miss you, Nadia."

Nadia twisted her hair around her hand. "I miss you, too. It's been shitty this summer. Nobody to talk to but Salomé."

Sylvie refrained from asking when Nadia had started calling Dr. Rau by her first name. "I'm sorry."

"You said you were going to visit."

She had. She'd broken her promise. She thought with a great flash of guilt of Hallie, who she hadn't talked to in over a year, and of Rachel, whom she hadn't checked on since the conversation when she told her she was moving to Virginia for a PhD. Of Elaine, the day Sylvie left Swampscott, saying, *You're going to keep calling me.* Sylvie hadn't, really.

"I'm sorry," she said again, more fervently. "I should have. I'm going to."

"It's basically August."

"So?"

"The semester starts soon."

"Would you like me to come?"

Nadia swirled her drink in its can. "I would."

"So that's settled. I should have gone down already," Sylvie said. "I hate being here without you. I wish we could both live here."

"So you *do* want to move to DC."

"You know what I want?" Sylvie said, struck by inspiration. "I want us both to move to Miami. We could get some giant Art Deco house and each take a wing."

Nadia's eyes gleamed. "It would have a courtyard."

"And a pool."

"A guest room for my dads."

Sylvie ignored a faint flicker of envy. She'd never include her parents in a fantasy. "A guest *suite*."

"We could walk to the beach."

"We'd eat Cuban food every day."

"We would pay for it how?"

"Write your robot Wittgenstein novel, but make it a crowd-pleaser. Have the robot stop Hitler or something so you can sell it to Hollywood."

"Why is it *my* novel? You came up with it."

"I came up with it for you. And it doesn't have to be a novel. It could be a screenplay. *Inglourious Basterds* meets *I, Robot*. People would go nuts."

"I know you haven't seen *I, Robot*."

"Or *Inglourious Basterds*," Sylvie admitted.

"We can fix that." Nadia was slowly teaching Sylvie her personal film canon, which was heavily violent. Sylvie returned the favor by making them watch the arthouse classics—Nadia called them "fancy movies"—for which she'd acquired a taste in Baltimore. "But why do I have to do the hard work? You could turn your diss into a self-help book. *How to Lose Patriarchal Norms in Ten Days*."

Both of them laughed. Sylvie said, "A title like that would get us a motel room for a weekend."

"We can work on it."

Sylvie drank the dregs of her beer and settled herself more comfortably into the banquette. She thought this was a good plan. Not the self-help book, but Art Deco House. Owning a home together. Rooting herself to Nadia.

She met her friend's eyes over the table. "I'm sorry I left you alone in Charlottesville all summer," she said. "I promise I won't do anything like that again. I would be lost without you."

Nadia nudged her foot under the table. In her most Southern voice, the one she used to smooth out her emotions, she said, "Don't worry, Sylvie. I know."

2.

Sylvie visited Nadia two weeks before the summer ended. She brought half her books down on that trip, then returned with the rest ten days later. Before she left, she and Robbie held a State of the Union to determine the new terms of their life. They'd try to alternate weekend visits, with the understanding that Robbie would sometimes have to work too late on Fridays to drive to Charlottesville.

"I just want a couple weekends with Nadia a month," Sylvie said.

Robbie nodded. "She can always come here with you, too."

"I'll bring her."

"And I might like it if you met some of my colleagues," he added.

"*Might* like or *would* like?"

"Would."

"Are they important to you?"

"I spend all my time with them. It's a little complicated for them not to know about you."

Sylvie couldn't gauge whether he was being reasonable or vulnerable. Based on the absence of other evidence, she guessed the former. He wasn't one to make an emotional request in a covert way.

"Can we revisit this after I meet your family?" she asked.

"One step at a time?"

"Right. And they matter more."

Sylvie waited a beat. He was quiet but expressed no disappointment. Reassured, she slid closer to him on the couch. "You know," she said, "I'd like to know if you have sex with someone else." What she really wanted was *for* him to sleep with another woman, though that was unfair to ask. If it happened, though, she wanted the release of knowing.

His eyes gleamed. Talking about sex generally led to it, which was part of why Sylvie had saved this conversation for her last night in DC. "And I want as many details as you'd like to share."

She kissed the spot where his shoulder met his neck. "Maybe I'll learn some new tricks."

More likely, she thought, she'd just go back to Wyatt. She hadn't communicated with him since May, but he'd appeared in her head more and more often as the summer waned. She understood, in a way detached enough to make her wonder if she was a bit of a bad person, that she used him not only to satisfy the sexual cravings Robbie couldn't but also to remedy the deeper sense of emptiness that Robbie's submissiveness sometimes created. She told herself that was good. Part of ending romance was understanding that no one completes you.

She was aware of the thought's self-helpy note, but she still held on to it as worthy of investigation. It might make a good rebuttal to Plato's argument that love is *the pursuit of wholeness*. Of course, it might also just be an intellectualized restatement of Elaine's A WOMAN NEEDS A MAN LIKE A FISH NEEDS A BICYCLE bumper sticker.

She called Elaine on her drive to Charlottesville the next morning. It had been long enough that when Elaine picked up the phone, she yelped, "Sylvie Broder! Are you having a crisis, or is this just a nice surprise?"

Sylvie winced. "I'm sorry it's been so long."

She heard the squeal of an old desk chair spinning. "I'm just giving you shit," Elaine said. "I know how to use the phone, too."

They talked for an hour. Elaine had all kinds of gossip. She'd unretired from dating, then re-retired. She wanted to hear about Sylvie's love life and, more importantly, her dissertation. "I take full credit for this," she said once Sylvie had described the latter. "And I want to read it when it's done."

"I'll send it to you."

"Will it look like a book?"

"It'll look like either an email or a giant stack of printer paper."

Elaine cackled. "I'll print it at the harbor." Sylvie was surprised at how much she liked the thought.

She found, though, that she was less excited about her dissertation at the start of the semester than she'd hoped. All summer, she had developed her ideas about rootedness without actually attempting to work them into her draft, and they turned out to be slightly at odds with her thesis. More problematically, her thesis turned out to be at odds with her life. So far, she'd been maintaining that if a straight relationship changed a woman, those changes, due to patriarchy, were automatically bad. She no longer agreed.

She tried going back in what she'd written to argue that it was all right for love to transform you as long as it happened in private, without any nefarious public influence. It took her a full week to realize that what she was really doing was plagiarizing Martin Buber's *I and Thou*, which, clearly, she had better reread. She was still involved in that when, in mid-September, she emerged from her afternoon class to see a missed call from Robbie, which was unusual enough that she returned it immediately. "Is something wrong?"

"Have you been online at all today?"

"Not really," Sylvie said, confused. "Some eBay, but—"

"All right. Hold on. I'm sending you— Here. I sent you a link. Put me on speaker." Sylvie obeyed. She could hardly see her screen in the bright afternoon sun.

"Did you get it?"

Sylvie looked back at her phone. Robbie's link had loaded. It was a *Washington Post* article about Trump's Supreme Court nominee. *California Professor, Writer of Confidential Brett Kavanaugh Letter, Speaks Out About Her Allegation of Sexual Assault*, Sylvie read. Her scalp prickled as if she were sick.

"Why are you sending me this?" she said roughly.

"Because it's the closest I can come to making sure you don't read it alone."

Sylvie wanted to ask, like a child, why she had to read it at all. Instead, she let Robbie remain on the line. By the time she finished, she was livid. Not at Robbie, though she heard some of her anger spilling out at him. "I'm not mad at you," she insisted. "I'm not. I just can't *talk* about it."

"It's all right," he said. "Hang up."

After she ended the call, Sylvie stood as if nailed to her spot on the green. Her bones were radiant with rage. It felt as if it would be too painful to move. When she did start walking, though, it was good. Speed-walking was better. By the time she got home she was running in her teaching flats, the soles of her feet aching, blisters springing from the skin of her heels. She didn't clean them. She didn't even sit down. She was too angry at Brett Kavanaugh, angrier still at Senator Dianne Feinstein, who had known Kavanaugh raped Dr. Ford since July. *July!* And Feinstein had done nothing. She'd sat on the professor's letter for two months, long enough to give her a false sense of safety, and then let it get leaked, giving Dr. Ford no choice but to go public. She had to show her face, tell her story, let the whole country gawk and argue about whether she'd been assaulted as a teenager and whether it mattered if she had.

In the weeks before Christine Blasey Ford testified to Congress, Sylvie thought about nothing else. It affected her more than Trump's victory, more than the Unite the Right rally, more than anything or anyone since Jonah. She didn't see Wyatt, barely saw Robbie or Nadia, canceled so many classes that the head of undergraduate studies sent her an email, which she ignored. She worked ceaselessly, feverishly, on her dissertation. It had to change. Suddenly all she cared about was privacy. She wanted to turn her whole dissertation into a manifesto on a woman's right to choose—and choose *freely*—whether she talks about being abused.

In the weeks before the hearing, the word *victim* was everywhere. It made Sylvie's skin crawl. She had a constant, irrational sense of exposure, as if her rage gave away her past to everyone she knew, though she tried not to express it in public. She avoided discussing Kavanaugh with anyone but Nadia. Robbie offered to drive to Charlottesville to watch the Congressional testimony with her, but Sylvie said no.

"I just want Nadia. I'm sorry."

"Because she's a woman?" Robbie asked.

Sylvie said yes, which was, she thought, the only real lie she'd ever told him. She didn't care about watching the hearings with no men present—or, really, about watching with Nadia. She didn't want Robbie around because Robbie made her calm. It didn't matter that he would be angry. His presence—his smell, his speech, his mouth twisting up and down with his emotions—would soothe her, and the idea of losing any measure of her fury was unbearable.

After the hearings, after Kavanaugh got appointed to the court anyway, Sylvie's anger got harder and stiller, as if it had moved from her muscles into her bones. Eating lunch on campus with Nadia three days after Kavanaugh got his votes, she said, out of nowhere, "She shouldn't have done it."

It took Nadia only an instant to guess who *she* was. "What, testified?"

"Or come forward."

"She had to," Nadia said. "Morally, I mean. She had to say something."

Sylvie scowled. "Saying nothing is a human right."

"Is it?"

"It's in the Constitution."

"Only if you commit a crime."

"The right to privacy is in *Roe v. Wade*."

Nadia shook her head, hair glittering in the sun. "Not the same. *Roe's* not going to last much longer with that freak on the court, anyway."

"No," Sylvie agreed morosely. A clutch of sorority girls trotted by, and, looking at them, she said, "I don't see who it helps that we know he's a rapist."

"Would it be better if we didn't know?"

Sylvie had no answer. She was aware of the wrongness roiling within her. She wanted so badly to blame somebody—not all of Congress, not the patriarchy: one person—that she was, like legions of misogynists before her, blaming the woman who'd been hurt. At the very least, she should be blaming Feinstein.

"Well?" Nadia said.

"It's not that it's bad for us to know. It's bad for us, and for her, that she didn't get to decide."

"She *did* decide. She wrote her letter."

"Not for the public."

"You were just arguing that it was bad for the public to know at all."

Sylvie hugged her knees. "I didn't mean that," she said. "I would just hate to be her."

"Well, you're never going to be."

A bad new idea had entered her mind. She disliked it, but it would torment her if she didn't say it. "Jonah could get a girlfriend."

Nadia wobbled her head side to side, which meant she was considering. "He could have one already."

"So if he does, is it immoral for me not to say anything?"

"Hard to do that if you don't know whether she's real."

"It's a hypothetical question," Sylvie said, although she knew what her answer would be if it weren't.

"You wouldn't try to contact her," Nadia said. "And it would be okay."

"Would it?"

"You'd be protecting yourself."

"Are you letting me off the hook?"

"No." Nadia met her eyes. "It's true."

After lunch, Sylvie went to the library to poke more at the question of whether emailing Jonah's imaginary girlfriend would be a public or private act. It wasn't public like testifying to Congress, but neither would it lie in her private realm, which contained only herself, Nadia, and Robbie. It occurred to her that, for all the time she'd spent drawing and defending those lines in her personal life, she had yet to come up with a philosophical definition of privacy. She'd taken its meaning as a given, which was sloppy. No wonder her dissertation was on the rocks.

It took an hour of digging through her dissertation notebook—a wise woman, she thought, would really be taking these notes in a digital, searchable form—to discover that she'd accidentally stolen the phrase *private realm* from Hannah Arendt, whose political theory had been a major part of her undergraduate studies in Holocaust philosophy. In one of her more minor works, Arendt wrote that everyone needed a *reliable hiding place from the public world*, and that such hiding places, if you shared them with one other person, could be *rich and manifold . . . under the conditions of intimacy.*

Sylvie turned the concept over while she called Robbie, checked the mousetraps in her kitchen, assembled a meal. So far, the only lesson she'd taken from Dr. Ford's testimony was that women couldn't gain institutional strength from taking on the role of victim after all. In such a world, there was no reason a woman shouldn't just retreat into her private sphere. Outside, she was a victim or victim-in-waiting. Inside, she could be anybody she liked. She could, by herself or with the people she loved, invent a new self, a new way of living. Not while her spaghetti was boiling over, though.

Sylvie shook herself out of thought and emptied the pasta into the colander, then integrated it with the pan of tomato sauce on her stove. Robbie had taught her to make this sauce. It only had three ingredients—canned tomatoes, an onion, a stick of salted butter—and was magically good. In the Jonah days, Sylvie wouldn't have dared cook something so rich or so simple. Now she thought of it as a gift.

She regarded her dinner as she maneuvered it from pot to plate, losing only a noodle or two on the way. It smelled properly sweet and acidic. Robbie would pair it with one of his fennel salads. Sylvie paired it with a small bourbon and Arendt's essay on the private realm. She'd forgotten half of its argument. It wasn't just intimacy that Arendt said thrived in private. It was kindness, too. Real human goodness, she wrote, was too delicate to survive the blasting light of public life.

Sylvie wondered if that was what had happened to her relationship with Jonah. He *was* kind to her at first. Even in college, he had phases of kindness. Not until she became his wife, meaning not until she became a permanent part of his public image, was he unfailingly cruel. Robbie, in contrast, was nothing but good to Sylvie, and their relationship was completely private. Surely the two were connected. In fact, it seemed entirely possible that her reluctance to emerge into any other part of Robbie's life was a way of protecting not just herself but what she valued between them.

At that thought, her turtle appeared and raised the leathery spots that represented his eyebrows. Can't knock it till you've tried it, he told her.

Not according to Arendt, she shot back.

With Robbie, she inhabited a delicate paradox. He was the only man who knew how Jonah had treated her, and yet his love was part of the reason she could transcend—could *reject*—her former victimhood. She knew it wasn't part of her permanent identity because her fear of turning back into Jonah's version of her shrank every day. Some of that she'd done herself, but some of it was Robbie. It was the private sphere they'd created together.

So you think you *are* still a victim in public, the turtle suggested.

No, no, no. I think my private relationship with Robbie affects my public self.

And it doesn't go the other way?

Absolutely not, Sylvie told him. In fact, she vowed, she would never let the public world taint her relationship. Nor would she listen to her own inner voice whining for Robbie to let her be submissive in bed. It was better, safer, to allow herself that vulnerability with men like Wyatt, men who never saw her inner self. With Robbie, she was strong. She'd get stronger. She would get so strong that nothing—not meeting Robbie's family, not the news, not Jonah—could hurt her at all.

3.

Sylvie didn't tell Robbie about her new mindset right away. She wanted to sit with it, see what trouble arose when she tried to bend reality around it—and, if she was honest with herself, what happened when she met his parents.

He didn't bring it back up until late October, on a Sunday afternoon when Sylvie was doing her hair at the head of the bed and he was sorting laundry at the foot. She'd put *Sweet Baby James* on the Bluetooth speaker. After "Sunny Skies," he tossed a sock at her and said, "Request for you."

"New music?"

He shook his head. "I'd like you to come to Michigan for Christmas with me."

Sylvie ordered herself not to panic. She should be ready for this. "A family holiday sounds pretty public."

"It'll just be my parents and sisters and Papa Sid."

She twisted a curl tightly enough to hurt. Hannah Arendt would object to Jewish Christmas, she thought. It was peak assimilation, which Arendt referred to as hiding the facts. It was also the precise opposite of sheltering her relationship in privacy. If Robbie treated her less kindly, or less like the person she wanted to be, in front of his family, it would break her heart.

Her turtle appeared to say, Sounds like a great reason to do it.

So I can be sad?

So you can trust Robbie more.

Why are you obsessed with making me test my boyfriend? Sylvie asked, but she did see the turtle's logic.

Robbie was watching her closely, no longer bothering with his clean clothes. "You don't have to answer right now," he said. "I want you to say yes, but I do get that Christmas is an intimidating way to meet them."

"I'm not intimidated."

"Sylvie."

"What?"

"You're scared of families."

Her chest clenched. "I never said that."

Robbie looked her in the eyes. "Does that mean it's not true?"

Sylvie drew her knees up. She resented that he was right. "I thought you weren't going to make me tell anything about myself that I didn't want to."

He sat down on the bed. "I was drunk when I said that."

"So you didn't mean it?"

Instead of answering directly, he said, "I admire your ideas, Sylvie. I admire how good you are at turning your life into ideas. But I also just like to hear about you."

Quietly, she said, "I appreciate that."

"I'm not ever going to turn what you tell me against you the way Jonah did. I won't make you do anything you truly don't want to, either. If Christmas is too much, it's too much. You did say you were happy that our relationship made you more rooted, though, and my family is—"

"Your roots."

"Right."

Sylvie knew that if her grandparents were alive, she would be rooted to them. She wasn't even completely detached from Carol and Paul. In a convoluted way, her departure had improved their relationship. She'd gotten them to agree to keep her whereabouts secret, to turn that secrecy into part of their elaborate personal code, and with every year they protected her, she felt warmer toward them. Not warm enough to tell them about Robbie or see them more frequently than their agreed-upon yearly trip, but still.

Sylvie took a deep breath. "So let's buy our tickets," she said, and two months later, she and Robbie touched down in Detroit.

His parents met them at passenger pickup, jumping out of the car despite the frigid air to hug them both. Sylvie could feel every hair on her body rising with cold. Robbie emanated joy beside her. He took her hand in the back seat of his parents' four-wheel-drive Audi, the exact car she would have imagined for high-powered doctors in a high-snow state. Mr.

Dr. Klein was a hand surgeon. Mrs. Dr. did fertility medicine, which Sylvie very much hoped not to talk about.

She could see Christmas lights from the highway. Every house in Robbie's childhood neighborhood glowed with expensive festivity. Sylvie would have assumed Grosse Pointe had its share of Muslims, Hindus, Sikhs, and normal Jews, but either there were none or they'd all signed up for professionally installed icicles and color-changing snowflakes, nets of white light over their perfectly trimmed pines and boxwoods, and the occasional painted manger or just-barely-tacky set of candy canes.

Casa Klein was as electric as its neighbors. Sylvie worried that she was going to struggle to sleep in the neighborhood's glow. She photographed the glass-ball-bedecked tree, pretending to admire, and sent the image to Nadia, captioned *These are Jews. Help.* As she did, she thought of the conversation she and Riva had had years ago about Jews being a splinter in everyone else's foot: poking, nagging, reminding the dominant culture that somebody else was around. How could you do that if your house was covered in Christmas lights?

Sylvie hadn't expected the Kleins' Christmas to upset her. She had imagined that it would be some mix of charming, commercial, and corny, an assimilation story she could both judge and relate to. Growing up, she'd spent Christmases in the dark of her parents' shame at not being Protestants. Never did they get Chinese food and go to the movies like other Jews. Carol made Yorkshire puddings that came out dry and oddly bitter; Paul stayed in his home office. It had seemed like the worst of all worlds.

But here, on December 23, drinking a glass of luxuriously rough-tasting wine in the Klein living room with its tree and stockings, Sylvie was reconsidering fast. She kept thinking about the Unite the Right protest, the legions of creeps shaking their torches and chanting, *Jews will not replace us.* Robbie's family, it seemed to her, had replaced themselves.

They'd created a Christian Jewish household, if only for the month of December. It made Sylvie feel profoundly incorrect.

She knew she wouldn't say so to Robbie. She also knew she wouldn't mention that the house itself unsettled her. It was designed and decorated precisely like the Sabranskys'. Probably they'd renovated the same year. In the living room, familiar blue-and-white china-patterned pillows perched on the couch and armchairs, but otherwise, color was scarce. Equally familiar Audubon prints hung in the hallway that led to the kitchen, which had the Sabranskys' giant rectangular hood, their six-burner Viking, their veiny marble countertops and dove-gray cabinet doors. But Jonah's family, like Sylvie's, never ate in their kitchen. Every meal in their household was formal. Here, the space was dominated by an oval wooden table—carved, scarred, incongruously old—on which Mr. Dr. Klein was setting out a colossal takeout spread.

"Yemen Café," he told Sylvie, nodding at the food. "In Hamtramck. It's delicious."

Sylvie told herself that the table, both its appearance and the quantity of Styrofoam boxes on top of it, meant this was a different kind of household, one bound less by manners and rules. She told herself to relax and enjoy her meal, which was, objectively, delicious. What she really wanted to do, though, was rub a fat smear of turmeric- and tomato-laden lamb over the white kitchen walls, spill some summer-green zhug on the taupe window-seat cushion, paint herself with garlicky mashed fava beans and roll down the beige-carpeted stairs.

Instead, she behaved. She displayed ideal table manners, refrained from a second glass of wine, tried to keep her mouth and brain operating independently of each other. Her brain was on a loop of aggrieved Judaism mixed with reminders that she was here as a girlfriend, not a representative of her people, and besides, who was she, the Lorax? She didn't speak for the Jews. She didn't even go to synagogue on the High Holidays.

Her mouth, meanwhile, was asking Robbie's twin sisters, Becky and Emily, about their shared life in Minneapolis.

Unfortunately, the sisters kept asking Sylvie questions back. She knew it was normal for Robbie's family to be curious about her. It was friendly and welcoming and polite. It was not their fault that nothing about her life was easy to present in a way neither false enough to worry Robbie nor true enough to alarm his parents, who she was supposed to call David and Heather. She did her best to make her nascent dissertation sound like a sweeping analysis of feminist progress in the twenty-first century; she glossed over her distant relationship with her parents and lingered on her deep closeness with Estie and Ilya.

"One of the big reasons I study philosophy is that my grandfather did," she said. "He was most of the way through his PhD when Jews got kicked out of universities before the war."

"He was a survivor?" Heather asked.

"Both my dad's parents were. My grandmother wasn't big on talking about it, but my grandfather told me everything."

"It must have been hard, growing up with those memories."

Sylvie wanted to laugh. "Nothing about spending time with them was hard," she said. "And my grandfather didn't tell me about the Holocaust to upset me. He told me so I'd know what it meant to be a Jew."

Nobody replied. The word *Jew* hung over the table, casting its harsh light on the pre-Christmas meal. Apologetically, she continued, "He was proud of having survived. I know some people were ashamed afterward, but my grandfather wasn't. He saw it as the second-biggest achievement of his life."

"What was the first?" Robbie asked. Sylvie could hear his relief.

"Being happy."

David said, "What about being a father?"

"My dad's not much like my grandfather. I think my grandparents mostly found their relationship with him confusing. But they were such good grandparents, I'm sure they did a good job with him, too."

"I can tell how much you loved them," Heather said.

She had a warmth Sylvie had neither imagined nor prepared for. Of all the relatives, she'd been excited to meet only Papa Sid. Liking a mother-in-law figure had not even crossed her mind.

In the morning, Sylvie meant to spend more time with Heather, but she and David busied themselves with holiday preparations all day and refused help, which meant the activities on offer for Sylvie were reading, watching movies—no rom-coms, luckily—with the twins, and a long walk with Robbie through the suburb's snowy streets. It was nice, trudging along in borrowed scarves and mittens, gazing upon the sites of her boyfriend's various initiations into sex, drugs, and alcohol. Apparently swimmers, even Olympic prospects, went wild in the offseason.

By the time they returned from their walk, at 4:15, the sky was dark. David had gone to retrieve Papa Sid from the Ann Arbor house in which, against presumably formidable odds, he still lived alone. Heather, Emily, and Becky were all doing their hair. Sylvie resisted the urge to borrow someone's straightener. Instead, she revived her curls with a fistful of water, put on a borderline-too-short dress and a boxy Agnès B. cardigan—an eBay-auction win she was proud of; her searches for homewares had, lately, started shading into searches for designer clothes—to balance it out, and descended to greet Papa Sid.

He was nothing like Grandpa Ilya. Grandpa Ilya had been lean and brown and twinkly. Papa Sid was short and puffy and rude. He wore heavy tweed trousers, two sweaters, and, inexplicably, a red bandanna twisted around his neck. Sylvie considered a joke about it, but, though Robbie had introduced her with fanfare, Papa Sid had yet to acknowledge her existence. His eyes slid over her as if she were a blank wall.

At first, Sylvie tried not to care. He was ninety-three. It was his prerogative not to give a shit about some girlfriend he might never see again. She tried to observe with detachment the family ritual unfolding: heavily sour-cream-oriented appetizers, spaghetti and meatballs for dinner, tiramisu soaking on the counter for dessert. It was a menu that plainly hadn't changed since the 1980s. She liked the Kleins for that.

But she wanted Papa Sid to talk to her. She wanted him—she knew this was sad—to recognize her mind. Her turtle, whom she had not invited to comment, reminded her that not all grandparent-grandchild relationships were philosophically oriented. Many of them revolved fundamentally around tribute. It seemed clear that Papa Sid belonged to that school. He'd had each grandkid enumerate the year's achievements during cocktails. As Becky had predicted, only Robbie's job elicited much response.

Not until dessert was served did Sylvie come up with what struck her as a good gambit. Robbie and his sisters were reminiscing about reading *The Night Before Christmas* to the younger cousins Papa Sid would be spending the day with tomorrow, who now had the ancestral copy of the book.

"So all your kids still do Christmas?" Sylvie asked Papa Sid.

For the first time, he looked squarely at her, making her heart leap a little in her chest. "Why wouldn't they?"

She pushed her fork into her tiramisu, which released a little gasp of cocoa and coffee fumes. She'd thought the question was self-explanatory, but evidently, she'd broken a rule. "I was just curious," she said. "It seems like a strong tradition, and I don't come from a family with a lot of those."

Papa Sid scowled at the word *tradition* and kept scowling. "It's the biggest holiday of the year."

"Well, yes. In Christianity."

"In the United States of America." He bit off the ends of each word. Sylvie recognized that she'd baited him, but also that she was being unfairly scolded. Robbie, in their discussions of the recent rise of antisemitism and white supremacy, had neglected to mention that he came from a house of Jews who couldn't stand the mention of their own religion. Currently, he was neglecting to say anything at all.

"My mom's English," she said. "And my dad's parents were refugees. I guess my childhood wasn't that American."

She'd wanted a laugh. She didn't get one. Robbie's grandfather sat back in his chair, blinking his dry, purplish eyelids. "I guess not," he said.

Sylvie looked at Robbie, waiting to see if he would defuse the situation or defend her. He did neither. His face was empty. Not the emptiness of his difficult days, either. His current state was a calculated absence. It might have been a punishment. It was certainly an unkindness—proof, in fact, that taking a relationship out in public increased the risk that your partner would no longer be kind to you.

Christmas itself passed without trouble. Sylvie did not utter any derivative of the word *Jew*, and Robbie returned so completely to his usual self that Sylvie could hardly feel betrayed. In the afternoon, during a break in festivities, Heather caught her in the kitchen and said softly, "I'm sorry about my father-in-law."

Sylvie had not imagined that a parent might apologize to her for Papa Sid. She felt her mouth drop slightly open. "You don't have to—"

Heather shook her head. "I had a hard time with Christmas when I married into the family, and he was terrible to me about it."

Sylvie's eyes warmed. "I appreciate your telling me," she said. It came out too formal, but she could see from Heather's face that she didn't need to correct herself.

She mentioned nothing about the conversation to Robbie. She was still unsure whether he'd been punishing her on Christmas Eve. If so, it was unwarranted; if so—she found it unsettling to discover this remnant of Jonah—it turned her on. By the afternoon of the twenty-sixth, their last day in Grosse Pointe, she wanted to crawl out of her skin, but she was too rattled to say so directly. Not in his parents' house, anyway. She got herself together enough to suggest a walk, though it was actively snowing.

"You hate the cold," he pointed out.

"Yeah, but I have energy."

"We could go down to the rec room and play pool." He rubbed his neck. "I'm rusty, though."

In Baltimore, Sylvie had taught herself pool because hot girls in movies were good at it. Men underestimated them, then lost to them, then slept with them. It was a trope, and Sylvie, at that point in her life, hadn't yet learned to condemn the scripts of fictional courtship. She had wanted to do the billiards-bar scene in real life—and she did, a handful of times, before reviewing the evidence and determining that guys who hung around stroking pool cues also tended to get in bed and stroke their dicks instead of putting them to real use.

She did not say so to Robbie, who'd devoted his free time during highschool swim seasons, when he didn't drink, to teaching himself trick shots and corralling his friends into pool tournaments. Half the walls had Adam Sandler posters affixed to them; an archaic CD player sat on the rec room's one windowsill. Across the room, a group of navy bean bags slouched around a sticker-covered mini-fridge. Sylvie found it charming that the basement remained so adolescent, and that it had been adolescent in the first place. Paul and Carol had never permitted any part of their house to be influenced by Sylvie's taste, interests, or age. Her bedroom had been a fully decorated guest room before she was born, though the Broders rarely had houseguests. Sylvie got a child-sized bed and, in high school, defied her parents by Blu-Tacking the occasional torn-out magazine page to her walls, but otherwise, the room's visual identity changed not at all. By now, she was sure, no trace of her remained in that home.

Robbie sank two solids on the break, then got three more before losing the turn. "You're not rusty," Sylvie said. "You're hustling me."

He grinned across the table. "Can't be a hustle if we didn't bet."

She wrinkled her nose at him and considered the cue ball, which was striated with pink chalk. It looked like it had stretch marks. Sylvie's had turned silver, but she vividly remembered how proud she had been watching bright reddish streaks extend across her hips, breasts, and thighs as her body shifted from the shape Jonah wanted to the shape that was hers.

Instead of shooting, Sylvie stood. She could hear various Kleins prowling through the kitchen overhead but chose to believe none of them could hear her. "Robbie."

He spun his cue. "Need a refresher?"

"Are you mad at me?"

"What?"

"Are you mad?" she repeated. "Or were you?" She was watching his face closely. It occurred to her that because she so often gave him privacy with his unhappiness, she now didn't know how to interpret it.

"What would I be mad at you for?"

"Annoying your grandfather by being too Jewish."

His mouth twitched. "You can be as Jewish as you want."

"Not an answer."

"It's my answer."

"I'm not accepting it."

"It's still your turn."

She sucked a long breath through her nose. Unlike the rest of the house, which was scentless except near the Christmas tree, the basement smelled faintly of snacks and damp. She had another vision of teenage Robbie: stoned in a beanbag during the off season, eating a full barrel of cheese puffs before dinner. He still had a weakness for fake Cheddar.

"You're allowed to be mad," she said. "I was rude. I just don't think it's fair not to tell me if you're pissed."

Robbie sighed. "You weren't rude. My grandfather was."

"Maybe we both were."

"No. You asked him a legitimate question, and he was an asshole. He's always an asshole when he drinks."

"You could've told me that."

"I know."

"And you could've stepped in."

"I *know*." Robbie's voice shot into a register Sylvie had never heard. "It was my fault."

"No! I didn't mean that."

He ignored her. "I should have prepared you better. I get that. My grandfather's not even the important part. I didn't think at all about how it would feel to be you, coming from your family, at our Christmas. I should've done that, I didn't, and so I got angry at myself. I'm still angry at myself. Are you happy now?"

At some point in his soliloquy, Sylvie had clenched her hand around her cue so tightly her knuckles hurt. "What do you mean, 'coming from my family'?"

"Your grandparents!" Robbie's hands flew up. "What do you think I meant?"

Sylvie wanted to slide to the floor. She settled for releasing the pool cue, which landed more quietly on the heavy green carpet than she'd expected. She felt trapped by the laughing Adam Sandler posters, the smell of old popcorn, the faux-industrial lights. "I thought," she said, "that you meant I was jealous that your parents are nice."

"Are you?"

She hadn't known until she heard herself say it. "I am."

"I couldn't have guessed that, Sylvie. I don't know anything about your parents."

All the tension left her immediately. "I'm sorry," she said. "I forgot."

"You *forgot.*"

"Robbie." She lifted her eyes to his. "My parents—there's nothing wrong with them. They love me. They just aren't very good at it. When I was married, they saw me and Jonah weekly and never noticed what Jonah was doing to me. That's the worst thing they ever did."

As she spoke, she saw him relax. She went to him, let him wrap his arms around her. Again, she said, "I'm sorry."

"I am, too."

"I miss my grandparents."

"I know."

"They died more than half my life ago." She dropped her head against his shoulder. "A lot more than half."

"So?"

"So I thought I'd miss them less by now."

Robbie pulled her even more tightly against him. "You think about them a lot," he said. "Which is good."

She laughed, which made her tear up. "You have no idea how much."

"No?"

"I have this turtle."

"You have what?"

In Sylvie's mind, the turtle asked a variation on the same question. She had never revealed his existence. Not to Elaine, not to Nadia, not to any of the three therapists she'd briefly seen in Baltimore. Shrink #1 had thought she had PTSD, which was patently untrue: she'd been in a crappy marriage, not the Iraq War. #2 used the word *victim* six times in forty-five minutes. #3 raised the possibility that Sylvie, by refusing to get rid of Jonah permanently, was holding on to him; that she was, in some warped or buried way, still in love. She would never have told a secret like the turtle to any of them.

But now, unstoppably, she was telling. She heard herself explain not just the turtle but Captain Lightning and Otto DeFay—a name she registered only now, at age thirty, as a play on *auto-da-fé*. It was a comforting recognition, a flash of Grandpa Ilya's humor. "Anyway," she said, "at some point, my grandfather heard my dad punishing me for arguing with him, and to make me feel better after, he suggested that I could argue with Captain Lightning and the turtle instead. I took it a step further. I made them my confidants, basically, and I just never stopped."

Robbie, who'd stepped back to look at her while she explained, was beaming. "Sylvie, that's the sweetest thing I've ever heard."

"It's a little embarrassing."

"No, it's not."

See? the turtle crowed. *I told you. No need to outgrow me.* "Fine," Sylvie said to both of them. She added, feeling herself smile, "I can't believe I told you that."

"I'm honored."

"You should be." Sylvie strained up to kiss him. "Was that our first fight, do you think?"

"Let's not count it."

"Why?"

Robbie flicked his eyes upward. "I'd like our first fight to end in makeup sex, and there's no way we're doing anything down here. One of my sisters could come down to get a drink or complain about my parents or something, and they don't knock." He smiled a bit. "We should've gone somewhere else to have that conversation, I guess."

Sylvie hadn't realized the mini-fridge was still active. She hoped very much it held beer. "It worked out," she said, moving toward it. Her body informed her that, even if they had all the privacy in the world, this would not be a moment for sex. She felt too soft for it, too thankful. Gratitude was not an erotic emotion.

She took two seltzers from the fridge—no beer, just an ancient-looking Mike's Hard and four flavors of LaCroix—and gave one to Robbie. "When we get home, we can have as much sex as we like." She reached for her pool cue. "Right now, I want to finish our game."

4.

For Sylvie, the next four months were an unhappy time. None of her troubles had anything to do with her boyfriend, or seemed relevant to him at all. He wasn't the one whose husband had yet again ramped up his unhinged emails—six since New Year's, each one advertising an acquisition that was supposed to be proof of maturity: not just the new house but a new Tesla, new job at Bain Capital, his own wealth manager instead of the one his parents used—or who had to take qualifying exams in early May.

Exams caused Sylvie significantly more agita than Jonah did, which made her proud. In fairness, the exam process was profoundly anxiety-inducing: she had to read one hundred books and then, over six days in April, write three essays and pass a three-hour oral inquisition on them. If she failed, she wasn't allowed to officially begin the dissertation she had been working on since she arrived in Virginia. She'd have to do the whole exam process over again.

She tried to soothe herself with the knowledge that nobody ever failed. But in general, no PhD candidate had examiners who disliked their work. Sylvie did. Her adviser, a Simone de Beauvoir scholar with dual appointments in the departments of philosophy and Women, Gender &

Sexuality, approved of Sylvie's work, but the rest of the philosophy faculty seemed to find Sylvie so unsettling and vulgar that she belatedly wondered how she'd gotten into the program. No one but a mean old existentialist had agreed to join her committee. Sylvie had had to get her other two examiners from Women, Gender & Sexuality. Her adviser had suggested, very kindly, that Sylvie might want to switch departments, which Sylvie refused and resented. She was Ilya Broder's granddaughter. She did philosophy. Besides, she didn't think feminism should be ghettoized.

To make matters worse, the Women, Gender & Sexuality professors on Sylvie's committee—she and Nadia just called them the Women—didn't like her any more than the philosophy ones did. Neither of them approved of Sylvie criticizing #MeToo or appreciated her arguments about privacy. Both believed strongly in the power of claiming victimhood; one said that the only possible reason Sylvie could feel otherwise was internalized misogyny—an opinion Sylvie thought was itself somewhat misogynistic, like blaming a woman's emotions on PMS rather than considering their validity. Her turtle suggested that she think about it anyway, but she refused.

She also refused the Women's obsession with autobiography, which was their worst trait of all. According to them, it was an archetypal feminist mode of thought. They wanted Sylvie to put memoirs on her list of exam books and to write about her life in both her exam essays and her dissertation. She told them she was in enough trouble with the philosophy department for writing about novels. She didn't need to go talking about herself.

When Sylvie was in a good mood, she told herself she'd prove the Women wrong. She was going to be the Francis Fukuyama of romance, except that, unlike Francis Fukuyama, she was going to be right. In fifty years, when romance was over, when it was considered wildly gauche to make the tiniest assumption about a person's relationships or sex life, when love happened only in Arendt's private hiding place, the Women—well, the Women would be dead, but if there was any form of afterlife, they'd look up or down or around from it and see that Sylvie had been onto something. Maybe their ghosts would come apologize.

But Sylvie was not in a good mood very often. As winter wore on, she began grinding her teeth in her sleep. She had tension headaches. She cracked her right bottom molar, an injury that led to weeks of pain, a totally vanished appetite, a weird fleshy taste in her mouth, and no interest whatsoever in kissing. In February, for the first time since the Kavanaugh hearings, she spent two whole weeks in Virginia without alerting Wyatt to her presence. She was getting her tooth fixed, a multipart architectural process, and could barely stand to be seen even by Nadia, who came over on weeknights and read the *Tractatus Logico-Philosophicus* at Sylvie's kitchen counter, or Robbie, who drove down for the weekends to feed her rice pudding and alphabet soup. His care was, she had to admit, not just a source of comfort but a welcome change from Nadia's. Her friend was physically present, sure, but she was no more interested in Sylvie than she was in the endless bowls of Jell-O that, mid–dental surgery, were the only thing Sylvie could stand to prepare for herself.

Before that spring, Sylvie had thought Nadia was changeless. Now her friend was undergoing a transformation that caused Sylvie more alarm than was reasonable. It was normal to be distracted during exams. It was also normal, in general, to change one's habits. People weren't static. Sylvie herself was involved in a prolonged emotional and philosophical process that had led her to abandon Nadia on the field of casual sex, and also abandon her in Charlottesville half the time. Why, then, did she care if Nadia hadn't mentioned a guy since Sylvie's birthday?

But she worried. She thought her friend seemed dimmed. It wasn't just that Nadia seemed not to be picking up men anymore, or that she was reading too much Wittgenstein. Barring her new devotion to eyeliner, she still looked like her normal self—tightly pinned buns, extremely rigid jeans, sweaters in shapes not previously known to Sylvie—but the air in her apartment, which had gotten less pristine than usual, no longer had the faint but constant smell of weed smoke. Her gym leotards no longer hung in the shower. Before this spring, she never would have studied at Sylvie's house. She would have talked.

On one of the last days of the tooth recovery, Sylvie suggested that she and Nadia watch a movie, and Nadia blinked at her as if emerging from a cave.

"A movie," she repeated, sounding baffled.

"Major form of contemporary entertainment, usually about two hours long, you like them to have explosions?"

"Ha, ha." Nadia stuck her pen in her hair. "I can't."

Sylvie glanced at her phone. It wasn't quite 8:30. "We could watch a short one."

"I haven't read enough."

"Enough for what? For tonight?"

Nadia glanced back at her book. "I have a reading schedule. Dr. Rau and I made it."

"Dr. Rau's not on your committee."

"Yeah, but it's hard staying on track with both the exam reading and all the fellowship deadlines, so—" She shrugged.

Sylvie wanted to ask if this the reason for Nadia's new Puritan lifestyle. Instead, she made herself shrug back and return to her book and Jell-O, but the conversation bothered her for days. It wasn't normal for Nadia to fret about deadlines. It certainly wasn't normal for her to let a professor tell her what to read when. Nadia ingested information fast and synthesized it faster; she forgot nothing; and she was a bullshitting prodigy. She could probably pass her orals without reading a single book. She'd said so to Sylvie in August. *That* was normal. Nadia did not doubt her capacities. In her thirty-one years of life, she'd received no indication that she should.

Sylvie didn't want to worry about Nadia. She had enough on her mind: the tooth, paying for the tooth, reading for exams, girding herself to go to South Carolina with her parents for spring break. Most years, she felt neutral toward the vacation, but this time around, she wanted it not to happen. She needed to study; she needed Robbie. She wasn't about to introduce him to Paul and Carol—she'd still hardly told him anything about them, and told them nothing about him—but she resented losing time with him.

From the moment she met her parents in the hotel lobby with its coral wallpaper and seashell-patterned carpet, she sensed conflict. Paul was more aloof than usual, which Sylvie wouldn't have thought possible. Carol's chatting had an edge that, in another woman, you might have called manic. Ordinarily, these vacations involved a fair amount of quiet reading, but this time, Sylvie spent hours by the pool with her mother, talking with a copy of *The Essential Ellen Willis* beside her. Carol took three days to ask who Willis was.

"She's one of the major sex-positive second-wave feminists."

"Meaning?"

"It means that a lot of feminists of her time lost hope in men, or in relationships with men, and she didn't."

"She should have."

Sylvie's mouth dropped open. She waited for her mother to continue, or else to give a sign that the conversation was done. Carol did neither. Her chin was very high. Sylvie thought that, if she were a stranger spying from across the pool deck, she would see instantly that Carol was trying to be brave.

Cautiously, Sylvie said, "Is there a reason you're upset right now?"

"Your father . . ." She sniffed. "I suppose not."

"He didn't do anything wrong?"

"No, Sylvie." Carol's voice sounded like a fan snapping closed. "Not one thing."

After that, Carol neither raised the subject of her marriage again nor allowed Sylvie to do so, but on returning to Virginia, Sylvie said to Nadia, "I think my parents are going to get divorced."

"Would you mind?"

It wasn't a question Sylvie had posed to herself. She recrossed her legs on Nadia's couch and said, "It wouldn't affect me, really. I guess I'd have to see them separately, but it might be more fun. With my mom, at least. She might be happier. I can't imagine it's satisfying to be married to him. Not that I'd want to be married to her either—it's not like I think she'd have been a better mother if she had left him years ago—but she still deserves a little more presence."

"Presence," Nadia repeated thoughtfully. "Is that what's important in a relationship?"

"Isn't it?"

"I'm asking you." She met Sylvie's eyes. "As my resident romance theorist."

A bad feeling crept through Sylvie. She had to resist the temptation to lock her teeth, which, since it was a prelude to grinding, was banned. "Who are you asking *about*?"

Nadia shook her head. "No one."

Sylvie didn't press, but she fretted over that exchange far more than she did her parents. "Either she's in love with Dr. Rau," she said to Robbie that Saturday, "or Dr. Rau is undermining her confidence."

"Or neither."

"Something's up with her, I'm telling you."

"Maybe she's just stressed."

"No way."

"Why not?" Robbie's tone was surprisingly nasty. "You're stressed. Why shouldn't *Nadia* be?" He wiggled his fingers around his face—scare quotes? jazz hands?—as he said her name.

"Nadia's different."

"Is she?"

Sylvie hugged her knees. She was nestled on the pillowy couch, half buried in blankets and books. Robbie was sitting at the table, where he'd been editing some legal document all afternoon. Outside, it rained steadily. Inside, it smelled like the pasta Robbie had made for dinner: fennel, garlic, pork fat. She'd been enjoying the post–dental surgery return of her interest in food.

"Nothing's hard for Nadia, and she doesn't pretend like it is."

"Who told you nothing was hard for her?" Robbie asked. His voice had gone back to normal, but still, the question was hostile. "Did she?"

"Nobody told me. I know her." Sylvie pushed a blanket off her legs. "Why are you being this way?"

Robbie's nostrils flared, either with irritation or as the first stage in a calming breath. He shut his laptop, then rapped his knuckles on it. When he spoke again, it was in the flattened cadence that signaled discomfort, revelation, or both.

"I'm sorry," he said. "I just don't think you see her clearly."

"Oh, and you do?"

He took another visible inhale. "I see the way you idolize her."

Sylvie bristled. "She's my *friend*."

"She's more than that."

"You're making it sound like I'm in love with her."

"Sylvie, you are. Not romantically—or, sorry, *sexually*—but you're always talking about how brilliant and interesting she is. You told me your dissertation, which is about real life, matters less than hers, which is completely hypothetical. You have to know that's nuts. And honestly, Sylvie, Nadia is smart and fun and—and *fine*, but she's always high. She's like a high-school boy half the time. She's great, but she's just a person. She isn't as perfect as you need her to be."

Some portion of Sylvie lit with recognition, but the rest was too frightened and insulted to care. She remembered Jonah curling his lip about Rachel, insisting Riva and Paola were lesbians, mocking Riva for the traits she and Sylvie shared. Did men just hate female friendship? Did it threaten them? Or did she have the personal misfortune of attracting only men who wanted her weak and alone?

Coldly, she said, "Where is this coming from?"

"It's coming from a year and a half of you comparing both me and yourself negatively to Nadia." He ran a hand over his face. "I'm sick of it."

"And you had to say so now because—"

"Because I had a long week, I'm tired, and I couldn't hold it in. Is that all right with you, Sylvie?"

She didn't reply. After a moment, he said, "I'm not proud of myself. I like Nadia. But you can't say it's not hypocritical that you bring her around all the time when you won't even let me tell my friends I have a girlfriend."

"You can tell them."

"Since when?"

She bit the insides of her cheeks. "Since now. And if you had someone like Nadia, I'd be happy to meet them."

"What do you mean, someone like Nadia?"

"Someone special."

"There you go!" Robbie flung his hands in the air. "It's not about my friends, Sylvie. It's about how bad it feels listening to you talk about her in a way you'd never talk about me. You don't care if I'm interesting or thoughtful or even smart. You don't need me to be special at all. You just need me to make you comfortable."

"Robbie." Her pulse was now so high she was practically motion-sick. "No one's ever made me comfortable before."

He laughed harshly. "So I *am* special?"

"Yes! Robbie, I hardly let myself enjoy a meal before you. I lived in a shithole on purpose. I was scared of the whole idea of home, and now look at this place." She waved an arm at their surroundings: the cane Breuer chairs Robbie had found online, the ceramics she'd started collecting, the rug they'd picked out at the Georgetown Flea. "You don't think it means anything that I decorated your whole apartment?"

"It means you like how much money I make."

She sat back, stung. "It means I love living with you."

He got up and went to the window. She could see his mouth twisting in the dark glass. "I love living with you, too," he said softly. "But I don't only exist in the house."

"What's that supposed to mean?"

"It means I have a life outside this apartment, and I want you to care about it. I want you to ask questions about my work. Not *just* my work. I want you to value what I think about."

Sylvie's nausea had turned into a careening feeling. She dug her nails into her knees. "It *means* you're jealous because you feel emasculated. You're jealous I care about my female friend's brain more than yours."

"Gender has nothing to do with it."

She snorted. "That's never been true about a single thing in a straight relationship. Ever. In history."

"Right. Of course. Forgive me for forgetting you were the expert on heterosexuality." His tone was heavily ironic. "Never mind the failed—"

"Don't say that."

"—marriage."

"Don't bring up my marriage."

"Don't act like all men are the same!"

Sylvie discovered that she was on her feet, which felt better. Standing was angrier than curling up in a ball. She had no calm remaining, just the sensation of skidding through her mind. She'd never had a real fight before. Not one where she stood up for herself. It was a loss of control almost like sex. It was pleasurable. Awful, too.

Robbie scrubbed his hands over his face. "I'm sorry," he said. "I shouldn't have mentioned it. And I shouldn't have said *failed*. It wasn't your fault."

"No, Robbie, I'm sorry. I'm sorry I don't make you feel unique enough. I'm sorry I don't tell you you're special. Out of all the corporate lawyers in DC"—she spread her arms wide, shirt clinging to her sides and back with angry sweat—"you're the most fascinating one." She'd gone from sarcastic to shouting, and she could see on Robbie's face that he was either angry again or afraid. "Just be happy with what you are."

"A string of fancy dinners and fat checks?"

Sylvie could not speak. Before Robbie, she'd had no idea that she was strong enough to control her own existence. She thought she could only be safe from romance by hiding major parts of herself. Robbie had shown her a new way. He'd gotten her not just to trust him but to trust herself—and, in doing so, he'd thoroughly decluttered her mind. She thought faster because of Robbie, pushed her arguments further. Some of that was the questions he asked her; more was the doubt and bullshit he'd taken away. She was too angry to say any of that, but saying anything else would be intolerable. Suddenly, on top of her fury, she was intensely sad.

Robbie took a step toward her, saying, "Sylvie, I didn't mean that. I know that's not what you think of me."

"Oh, no?" Her lip curled unstoppably up. "How do you know, exactly?"

"You wouldn't— It's been eighteen months, Sylvie. You wouldn't hang around this long for creature comforts."

"I would." She tried, but couldn't catch herself. "I have."

It was the end of her anger. She had nothing crueler or less true to say. It was like Jonah to lie the way she just had. Robbie stood as if trapped, arms dangling at his sides. Sylvie marched herself into the bedroom, away from him. It wasn't fair to make him watch her cry.

She wasn't sure how long it took her to settle. By the time Robbie opened the door, she'd gone still. He lay down and curled himself around her.

Very quietly, she said, "Can I take it back?"

"You can."

It took her a moment to say more. Her guilt was so strong she felt sick. "You made me into a real person," she said. "You fixed what Jonah broke. That's what I meant about being comfortable. It isn't about the apartment. I mean, the apartment is just a symbol. I was talking about my actual *self*."

"You were a real person when I met you."

"Not like now."

He drew himself more tightly against her. "You're just less scared now."

"No." Sylvie twisted so he could see her face. "I'm still scared. I wouldn't have lost my temper at you if I weren't. But before you—" She had to pause. "Before you, I couldn't let anything matter enough to scare me. Now I can."

Robbie nodded. After a moment, he kissed her, very lightly, between the eyes. She turned all the way over to face him, but neither of them initiated anything else. They fell asleep with their clothes on. In the morning, Robbie took the first sick day of his legal life. It seemed more than warranted. Both of them moved through the apartment like convalescents, fragile and quiet in the grayish March light. It was as if they'd done a purification ritual, banished demons and ghosts from their home. Sylvie allowed herself to believe they had. She let herself think that nothing so horrible would ever happen between them again.

PART TWO
Abie

Chapter Four

1.

In the middle of May, the philosophy department threw what they called a party. In actual fact, it was a clump of space cadets and creeps—and Sylvie and Nadia—taking advantage of a limited quantity of free drinks at Miller's, the one bar on the city's pedestrian mall that still permitted smoking indoors. Its walls reeked of ancient tobacco, spilled liquor, and optimistically applied cologne. On weekdays, it catered to aging locals; on weekends, pretentious grad students, mysterious hippies, and retired fraternity brothers seeking their youth. During the summer that led up to Unite the Right, it was the last downtown bar to ban white supremacists. Why the department chose it was beyond Sylvie, but many of the department's choices were.

She had only agreed to go because Nadia wanted to. Nadia, it turned out, wanted to go only so she could talk to Dr. Rau. Although exams were over, Nadia remained stressed and irritable. She had extended her work with Dr. Rau another year, and seemed deeply preoccupied with it. She was spending a lot of time on the languages the professor was making her learn. How this could possibly help her dissertation was a mystery, though not one as pressing as the mystery of how Sylvie had gotten herself trapped by Eddie Newell, her cohort's leading know-it-all. She found herself explaining to him that she was teaching Philosophy and Gender this summer because she *chose* to—she'd designed the class, actually, and hoped to reprise it in the spring—not because the chair had, as Eddie charmingly put it, "pigeonholed her as a gender person." She hated Eddie. She was sick of teaching. She wished she'd never applied for a summer class. She only did it to silence the suspicion, implanted by her fight with Robbie, that she was a gold digger or kept woman-in-waiting. She was teaching Philosophy and Gender in the name of female independence. It seemed counterproductive, though, to say so to Eddie Newell.

Instead, she told him she wanted a refill and pointedly did not offer to bring him one. As she waded through the crowd, she decided she wouldn't get herself one, either. It was terrible here. Her eyes hurt from smoke and dimness. She could tell her hair and clothes stank. She had meant to get drunk but undershot, giving herself a headache. Nadia was deep in conference with her spiritual overlord. She hadn't noticed that Sylvie was having a miserable time, which meant she wouldn't notice if Sylvie went home.

It was a Friday, late enough that she and Robbie had already texted their good nights, and Miller's was so full it was difficult to change course. Sylvie had to do a three-point turn. She executed the first two points without trouble. During the third, she was interrupted by a large, fluffy person who, bounding across the room with a tallboy in one hand and a set of darts in the other, planted his foot squarely on hers.

She yelped, more in surprise than in pain—though, also, it hurt. Her stomper was wearing lug-soled moccasins, and he was so solidly built he appeared to be carved out of wood.

He was horrified. Sylvie had never heard anyone apologize so much in such a short span of time. Before long, she was laughing. "It's all right," she said. "I've been stepped on in bars before."

"Not by me!"

"We don't know that for sure."

He cocked his head to the side, weighing her point. "I'd remember you."

Sylvie did not say that she'd remember him too. He was both distinctive and vaguely familiar. He had woolly hair, a thick blond beard, and a soft version of an accent she had learned from Nadia was exclusively Virginian. In addition to his battered, heavy shoes, he wore aged green corduroys and a psychedelic short-sleeve button-down. Above the beard, his cheeks were pink with some mix of warmth, alcohol, and embarrassment. He wasn't quite handsome, but his face was profoundly likable.

"Anyway," he said, "now you know me." He extended a hand, found it full of darts, and retracted it in bafflement. "I'm Abie Abraham."

"Sylvie Broder." She backtracked. "Your name's *what*?"

"Abie Abraham. There's a story. Let me buy you a drink, and I'll tell you." He glanced around. "Not here, either. Somewhere nice."

Sylvie tried to look as if she weren't weighing the offer. Abie was not her type. He was too shaggy, too cheery, too untamed. His energy was not that of a man with whom she could have rough and impersonal sex. She doubted he contained an iota of sleaze. However, she had used her three departmental drink tickets. Nadia was ignoring her. The remainder of her night held no other promise.

"What are you doing here if you don't like it?" she asked.

"Oh, I like Miller's," he said cheerfully. "Bad politics, good memories. But I don't think it's *nice*. Nice is the Alley Light."

Sylvie lifted an eyebrow. In her opinion, the Alley Light, which had a cocktail menu longer than many restaurants' dinner menus, was the best bar in Charlottesville. "I wouldn't turn that down."

Within moments, she was in the dark, humid street, learning that Abie was, legally, named Michael. So were three other boys in his grade at elementary school. He couldn't take the competition. He hated waiting to see whether the Mike being called on, or called to, was him. On his eighth birthday, he declared that he was becoming Abie, and twenty-seven years later, not even his parents were permitted to use the name they'd picked out.

At the Alley Light, Abie got them a booth, guiding her onto the leather banquette as gently as you set an egg in a carton. He asked what she'd like, then went to the bar and returned with two glasses of what she knew from smell alone was a fancier bourbon than she had requested.

She turned the engraved tumbler on the table. "Looks like something a rich grandfather would own."

"Do you have rich grandfathers?"

She laughed at the question. "I do not."

Abie planted his elbows on the table. "What were your grandparents like?"

Over their first drink, Sylvie discovered that Abie was the world's most family-oriented person. He was Simone Weil's thesis on rootedness incarnate: his sense of self came from physical and historical permanence, and he knew it. All his conversational gambits involved family stories, but not the growing-up kind. He extracted Sylvie's family tree from her before bothering to ask her profession, home state, or thoughts about Charlottesville. He, meanwhile, came from a clan of German Jews who had emigrated to Richmond, Virginia, in 1822 and never left. On his mother's side, he maintained regular contact with his first, second, and third cousins. On his dad's, he had regular barbecues with the descendants of a great-great-aunt.

"What are those?" Sylvie asked. "Fifth cousins?"

"Fourth," Abie said promptly.

"And you know them."

"Sure." He grinned. "One of them, Josh, runs a fishing charter on the James River. We go out for shad every spring."

"What's shad?"

"What's *shad*?" His face got even brighter. He looked like he'd just stepped down from a stained-glass window. "You mean you live in Virginia and you've never eaten shad roe?"

"I have not."

"It's a delicacy. Not in season until March, though." He glanced at her drink, which was nearly empty. "My dad fries it in bacon fat, which tells you the kind of Jews we are. Another round?"

While Abie waited at the bar, Sylvie considered his extreme devotion to family. She found it appealingly old-fashioned, if also lightly deranged. It was as if he'd spoken to her in Yiddish, or pulled a pipe out of his shirt. By the time he returned with their second round, she'd made two decisions: that she would sleep with him, but only once; and that, charming though his fourth-cousin shtick was, she had a philosophical duty to let him know families could and often did go wrong.

He was a highly expressive listener. His face—which was, beneath his curl-filled beard, as mobile as a child's—telegraphed his reactions so plainly he had no need to speak. As Sylvie detailed her youth under the regime of Carol and Paul, leaning heavily on the conformity and fear of surprise that undergirded their rules, Abie winced and scowled, bit his lip, sucked the stray hairs that wandered into his mouth. He tapped his fingers on the table. Perversely, his distress made her want to talk more.

Still, she was shocked to hear herself continuing toward college, drawing dangerously close to the point of real revelation. She had yet to mention Jonah, but her grip on her narrative was getting slippery and loose. She had the numb sensation at the top of her head that meant she should stop drinking, or should have stopped one bourbon ago, and yet the thoughts forming within seemed clear. Abie Abraham was a stranger, but she did not want even a stranger to see her as a tragic wife. Nor did she want to play down the misery of her marriage. Self-deprecation was no better than wallowing. It was the shadow twin of victimhood.

Sylvie had yet to decide how far to take her story when Abie, finally, lost the ability to keep his mouth shut. She was explaining the time her parents told her she'd snap out of her undergrad unhappiness if she switched to a sensible major when he burst out, "Good Lord. Who's *like* that?"

"My parents. And plenty of others. It's not that unusual."

"I know." He shook his head. "It just upsets me."

"I came out okay."

"I'm glad, but that's not the point."

Sharply, she said, "It is for me."

"Of course it is. But I take family seriously." His sincerity was so plain it made Sylvie sit back in the banquette. "It's my value system. My organizing principle." He worked over the word *principle* in a way that had to mean he was drunk. "It's not that I want everyone to be like me. I mean, it would be easier if *I* weren't like me. But the thought of parents who care more about their rules or ambitions or ideals than about their kid's emotions? It's against nature. It pisses me off."

"Easier how?" Sylvie asked when she was certain his speech was done.

But Abie shook his head. "Oh, no. You're not changing the subject. We're doing your family tonight. We can talk about mine the next time we hang out."

"We're hanging out again?"

"What, you're only telling me about your parents because you thought this was the conversational version of a one-night stand?"

Sylvie gasped. "Fuck you."

Abie met her eyes. "Am I right?"

"Do you always do this?"

"Do what?"

"Get drunk and have insights." Sylvie spat the last word out. When she heard it, her nascent anger fled. She let herself grin, and Abie, tentatively, smiled back.

"Yeah," he said. "Pretty much."

"Horrible trait in a drinking buddy."

"Fine." His smile widened, which made Sylvie more relieved than she would have liked. "We can get coffee next time. Now keep going. I interrupted your story, and I want to hear how it ends."

2.

In the morning, Sylvie woke early but remained in bed, rigid with hangover and regret. She could not summon even one justification for her behavior last night. She had drunk too much. She had not had sex. She had, instead, told some shaggy, mono-named stranger—some *man*—about Jonah. It was a warped thing to do. Why had she *talked* so much? Not since the day she told Elaine about her marriage had she launched into such a torrent of biography, and that had been a reaction to crisis, not an ordinary night in a bar. Abie had conned her with his questions about her grandparents. He'd led her out of her usual ways.

Sylvie rolled onto her belly and moaned. Her tongue, in the night, had transformed into a gigantic cotton ball. Her brain and stomach both felt like they were shrinking. She wondered how hard it would be to smother herself with her pillows. She would prefer to be dead than to continue her life knowing Abie Abraham was carrying her story around Charlottesville.

She was fairly sure she had not told him she was still married. She remembered that, when he asked how her story ended, she'd said, *With me leaving a bad husband.* On the murky screen of her mind, she saw Abie leaning across the table, his eyes as hot and angry as a wronged man's. She saw the golden bar light catching in his golden beard. He had looked like Jewish Zeus. Maybe he was. In the myths Sylvie had read, the Greek gods had no qualms or scruples in their seductions. If Zeus were going to descend to the contemporary Earth to pick up mortal women, it made a measure of sense that he would use his divine persuasions to get them to recount their tragedies and traumas. It would be, if not a solidly winning strategy, one that offered a good shot at success.

Her turtle capered out of the shadows, pushing the image of Abie aside. He looked delighted, to the extent that he could have a facial expression. Once she had fully turned her attention to him, he began to do a little dance, kicking his stumpy legs out like a Cossack. It was not a vision that improved her headache or nausea, though possibly not much would beyond swift and merciful death.

Quit, she told him. I'm suffering.

You'll be happy later.

Oh, will I?

Emotional growth, the turtle said, still dancing, delivers great but belated rewards.

Poor impulse control, Sylvie replied, delivers great and immediate pain. She rolled onto her side, which was unwise. It exposed her to light, and light hurt.

You made a decision, the turtle told her. You don't want to admit it, but you did.

How would you know?

You would *never* talk about the staircase without deciding to. Never, never, never.

Sylvie groaned aloud. Her brain now seemed to be vibrating against her skull. She had not wanted to ask herself whether she had told him about the night of the stairs. Nobody knew about it. Not Robbie, not

Nadia, no one. It was too humiliating. She could not stand the thought of the pity Abie must feel for her. She'd married a man who'd shoved her down a staircase. Half of her—the half that wasn't horrified by the prospect of ever speaking to Abie again—wondered if she had his number. She'd like to call and tell him that part of the story wasn't true.

What she should really do was call Robbie. She was supposed to return to DC today, but driving was unappealing. Ditto sitting up. Setting aside all the other questions she had about her evening, she had no idea why she had thought it was a good idea to close down the Alley Light.

She wriggled close enough to her nightstand to reach her phone without lifting her torso. Robbie had texted good morning. Abie, with whom she evidently had exchanged numbers, suggested coffee on Wednesday. She had no reason to stay here through the week, since her summer class hadn't started yet, but if she had coffee with Abie, she could rectify some, if not all, of the impression she'd made. She could show him she wasn't only a victim. Not as good as rewinding to yesterday evening and preventing herself from speaking to him at all, but unless that became an option, she thought seeing him again preserved more of her dignity than ignoring him until—as would inevitably happen; Charlotteville was small—she ran into him on the street.

Sylvie called Robbie to say she'd decided to spend the week in Virginia as a dissertation-writing jump start. She wanted to get a lot of work done before fall. She texted Nadia the same, to which she got an immediate reply.

Bullshit, Nadia said. *Wyatt.*

Not Wyatt, Sylvie wrote. She added, *Somebody else*, then regretted it. She wasn't sure Abie would qualify as a somebody. She wasn't sure what the feelings animating her were. She had told herself, last night, that she was describing her parents to him—and, frankly, making them sound worse than they were—out of spite. She'd wanted to scratch the shining surface of his family. She had the feeling that she'd failed, but gotten something else.

Who? Nadia texted. *Who who who?*

Sylvie smiled. One unchanged aspect of Nadia's character was her voraciousness for progress of any sort. Nothing made her happier than an update. But it was far too soon to explain about Abie. She would need to know what she was explaining, and all she knew, currently, was that she wanted to see him again.

You, she told Nadia. *We haven't hung out enough lately. I miss you.*

It was the truth, and Nadia received it as such. Sylvie didn't do a moment of work that day, and, shockingly, neither did Nadia. She came to Sylvie's apartment and they watched *Ocean's Eleven* in bed while Sylvie emerged from the throes of her hangover. Afterward, they took a leisurely roam around campus, demolished a Peruvian chicken from Al Carbón, and bought junk food to bring back to Nadia's, site of countless sleepovers since their first.

"I'm honored you took the whole day off," Sylvie said. She was on her usual end of the couch, one of Nadia's many throw blankets over her legs. It was hot out, but Nadia kept her air-conditioning high.

Nadia ate a peanut-butter M&M. "I've been working too much."

"No shit."

"I've never wanted to impress anyone before."

"Before Dr. Rau, you mean?"

"Yeah." Nadia ran a hand through her hair. "My dads were proud of anything I did—you know, spaghetti art, not hitting myself with the teeball bat, whatever—and at school, I was always just the smartest. In California I had some coworkers who could code faster than me, but they were such creepy true believers, I wanted nothing to do with them. And here, I'm smarter than everyone but you, so I made you be my friend so I wouldn't have to worry about impressing you."

Sylvie thought of her fight with Robbie. "You impress me all the time."

"Don't be nice."

"I'm not."

Nadia made a face, but it passed so quickly Sylvie couldn't tell if it was a grimace or just a twitch. "When I'm impressive, Salomé will let me know."

On Sunday, they went to outdoor yoga, got burritos, then worked until dinner. On Monday and Tuesday, they went to the library together, taking long lunch breaks on the lawn. Wednesday morning, Sylvie said she had to write—she had a policy against writing in public—and promised to come over for dinner. She sat on her bed for an hour after that, debating whether and how much to groom for her coffee with Abie until she'd burned through all her grooming time.

They met in the park by his office. He'd told his boss he had a meeting with somebody from the university. When Sylvie arrived, he had two iced coffees on the bench beside him, an array of sugar packets in his lap.

"What if I wanted milk?" she asked.

He beamed up at her. "Then you'd be shit out of luck."

Abie worked in the city archives. He was technically in charge of special collections, but really, he said, he'd been hired a year ago to be Charlottesville's White Guilt Guy. "What is that?" Sylvie asked.

"I use archival material to educate mostly white Charlottesvillians about racism."

"How long has that been a job?"

"Guess."

"Unite the Right?"

"Yep."

"What were you doing before?"

"I worked for the Virginia Department of Historic Resources."

"Have you ever left Virginia?"

He grinned a tremendous grin. "Now, Sylvie, why would I do that?"

When pressed, he gave a more nuanced answer. He had always known he would spend his life in the state of his birth and had, therefore, wanted to leave for college, but not badly enough to justify the additional loans. He'd still had to take some out for undergrad, though nothing compared to what his older brother, who'd gone to Stanford, signed up for.

"I'm the smart one," he explained.

Sylvie thought of her ignored master's debt. "Yeah, but you have a PhD, right? You could have done that somewhere else."

"Not many places. I needed a history department with professors who"—he ticked the reasons off on his fingers—"knew there *were* Confederate Jews, wouldn't think I was a freak for wanting to *study* Confederate Jews, and wouldn't give me too hard a time when I said I *came* from Confederate Jews."

Sylvie was unsurprised by the last. He'd said at the Alley Light that his family arrived in 1822. She might not be well-versed in the Civil War, but she could still do her math. "Did they own slaves?"

"No, but they fought so other people could."

Apparently, the Abrahams had spent the twentieth century atoning. They were all civil-rights lawyers, Head Start schoolteachers, union organizers, lefties of various stripes. Abie's father ran a speech-and-debate program for students in Richmond's public schools. Abie himself had a PhD in history, but rather than bury himself in the academy, he'd tacked on two years of being, as he put it, the loudest boy in library school. "More loans," he added dryly, "so I could get paid less."

But he loved his job. He taught weekly workshops to synagogue and church youth groups. If he was addressing Jews, he opened with a story about the KKK burning crosses on his great-grandparents' lawn. Once the crowd was softened up and sympathetic, he got into the Confederate ancestors.

In addition to his workshops, Abie gave public talks on racist violence in Virginia—which, Sylvie realized, she should probably attend. She'd lived in the South long enough to educate herself on its version of racism. She said so, thinking a little guiltily of the perfunctory conversation she and Robbie had had about the Lee statue in Richmond, and Abie lit up. "You should come to my archive. I'll give you a tour."

"What's in it?"

He waggled his eyebrows. "More falling-apart photos of people who've been dead for a century than you've ever seen in your life."

In addition to the photos, he handled archival acquisitions related to the Civil War and Jim Crow. He was creating a collection of documents about Virginian Jewish history—"which, so you know, is *key* to the history of Reform Judaism"—and another one about nineteenth-century immigration to the state. He ran a speaker series featuring writers and scholars whose work explored race and religion in the South. He guest taught high school classes about Prince Edward County, right in the center of the state, which, from 1959 to 1964, shut down its public education system rather than integrate it.

"Usually I make the kids cry," Abie said, then corrected himself. "A couple kids. White ones."

"I get cried at every semester," she said. "Mainly in office hours, but still. It's part of why I'm sick of teaching."

"Why else?"

It was a warm morning, sunny and only getting brighter, but she pushed her sunglasses up to better see his face. He didn't seem to be treating her like a person he pitied, but, she reminded herself, she didn't know him. She had no idea how his pity looked. "I'm not patient enough. I hate explaining an idea more than once, and I teach philosophy. Explaining once isn't an option."

Abie laughed. "Hate to break it to you, but that's not an option in any discipline. I taught my whole PhD, and I promise, I wasn't exactly flying through the causes of the Civil War. I could explain the Missouri Compromise in my sleep by the end."

"Did you mind?"

He shook his head. "In the end, teaching is just talking, right? And you may not have noticed"—he gave her a conspiratorial look—"but I love to talk."

Sylvie knew she was meant to laugh, but she saw her opportunity. "You're good at getting other people to talk, too."

"I take that as a compliment."

She sighed. "You probably should. But, Abie, the stuff I told you before—" Her cheeks were burning already. She tried to collect herself. "I don't tell people that."

"About your family, or your marriage?"

"Both." Her legs were shaking slightly. "My marriage, especially."

He touched her arm, but only for a second. "I'm honored."

"Don't be honored. Don't be anything."

"What does that mean?"

Sylvie bit her lip. "I don't want you to feel sorry for me."

"Easy," Abie said instantly. "I don't."

She looked straight at him. His curls flopped in every direction. His face was somehow pinker in broad daylight than after hours of drinking at night, but she had the sense that he wasn't embarrassed, wasn't lying. Still, she said, "I don't believe you."

"I told you: I was *angry*. It isn't pity to be mad on your behalf."

Sylvie had no response to that. She took the idea home and poked at it, shook it, looked for the point at which her disagreement might start. She wanted to reject his indignation like she would reject a softer feeling, and yet she couldn't shake the thought that she deserved it. Nobody but Elaine had offered her their anger before.

It helped that Abie had much more to offer. In the next weeks, they talked so much—on walks, at bars, over tacos and bagels and kebabs—that their conversation seemed to have no start or end. It reminded Sylvie of her early days with Nadia, and made her miss her. Nadia had gone back to working too hard. She and Sylvie hadn't watched a movie since *Ocean's Eleven*. She was constantly getting ready to meet with Dr. Rau. Sylvie had gone from wondering if her friend was in love with Dr. Rau to thinking they were having an affair, and was doing her best not to get upset about not being told.

She did recognize her hypocrisy. She hadn't told either Robbie or Nadia about Abie. But on the Nadia front, there was a significant difference. An affair with a professor was an intimate experience, something to be discussed with—and only with—the people in your private sphere. What Sylvie was doing with Abie was less serious. She was hanging out. She was talking. She was, she thought, making a friend.

Sylvie had never had a male friend before. It caused her intense anxiety. She continued to live by her rule against discussing her relationship with Robbie with anyone except Nadia, but she saw now that it complicated matters where a friendship between straight people of opposite genders was concerned. On the one hand, she wasn't planning to create a real private sphere with Abie, which meant it was fine not to tell him about Robbie. On the other, what if Abie had an agenda that wasn't platonic? What if he wasn't really out to be friends? She didn't want to sleep with him—or, fine, she'd have enjoyed it, but with Abie, she was far more interested in talking than fucking, and if she had sex with him, she'd have to relegate him to unimportance like she'd done to Wyatt, whom she hadn't seen in weeks and with whom she discussed nothing of real substance. She wasn't willing to do that.

Explaining all this to Abie seemed ludicrous. So did her fear that Robbie wouldn't like her having a male friend. Robbie wasn't jealous or controlling. He had a modern concept of gender relations. He had plenty of female friends himself, or so he said; Sylvie, having managed so far not to meet them, wouldn't know.

She explained all of this to her turtle while driving to DC four weeks after meeting Abie, then asked plaintively, So why am I all jumpy?

You really don't know? the turtle said.

Don't be like that.

Jonah.

Why does everything always have to be Jonah?

He never would have let you have a guy friend, the turtle said. So now you're scared.

He never stopped me.

You never tried. Anyway, Jonah's leftovers aren't necessarily the same as his rules.

I hate that phrase, Sylvie told him. *Jonah's leftovers.*

You came up with it, the turtle reminded her. You don't get to complain.

Sylvie told Robbie about Abie that Saturday. It was late June, but DC was suffering through an August-level heat wave. Both of them would gladly have spent the whole day at the pool, swarming though it was with life-jacketed toddlers and gossiping packs of twenty-three-year-olds, but Robbie had to work. Sylvie graded half-heartedly on the couch until he rose from his desk, looking tired and rumpled, and said, "Would you like to distract me?"

"How do you want me to do that?"

It was a question she knew he wouldn't answer. He moved nearer. "I thought maybe you'd have some ideas."

Sylvie's only idea was that she'd like to be fucked and then take a nap. She considered just saying so, but that wasn't fun. Instead, she rose and led Robbie to their bedroom, where she resorted to one of her standby tactics: asking for what she wanted step by step, hoping the narration made it seem more interesting. Afterward, they both fell asleep, and when they rose, the heat had broken enough to go to the outdoor patio at Lyman's before dinner. Both of them were sleepy still, but in a pleasant, companionable way. A good opportunity for a strange conversation, she thought.

"I have a confession," she said once they'd sat down with beers and the movie-theater popcorn that Lyman's, God bless them, provided for free.

Robbie's forehead creased. "Yes?"

"I might have made a new friend."

"How is that a confession?"

She shrugged. "He's a man."

Sylvie gave Robbie a moment to work through his confusion. She could see it in his eyes when he did. "You can guess," she said. "I'm not going to get mad at you for understanding me."

"Jonah wouldn't let you be friends with guys."

"Bingo."

"And so you're scared of me not liking it."

"Not *scared*-scared. It's just a leftover." After a moment, she added, "I know it's unfair to you."

Robbie nodded. He ate a handful of popcorn, then said, "Just as long as you get that. And just as long as you'd tell me if you were sleeping with him."

"I would," Sylvie said. "And I do get it, I promise. It feels awful, projecting old Jonah bullshit onto you."

"It feels awful for me, too."

"I'm sorry." She touched his forearm, its hair nearly white from sun and chlorine. "You're not jealous?"

He gave her one of his fleeting smiles. "I'm jealous of Nadia. Not this guy." She chose not to answer, and after a moment, Robbie said, "You know, this is fucked up, but the person I'm really jealous of is Jonah. And *jealous* isn't the right word. It just upsets me that he's the one in your head right now."

"He won't be forever."

"If I thought he would, then I wouldn't be here."

She had no reply. For a moment, they looked at each other across the table. A mosquito lit on Sylvie's hand, and Robbie brushed it away. "I believe in you," he said. "Now tell me about this new friend."

3.

Having told Robbie about Abie, Sylvie resolved that she should also do the reverse. It was, technically, a violation of her philosophy, but her gut and her turtle both told her it was the right thing to do. Besides, she'd let Robbie tell his friends she existed. Maybe this was a reasonable adaptation of philosophy to life: you share your relationship with your close friends, you let your less-close-but-still-real ones know it exists without involving them further, and with the rest of the world, if dating or love comes up, you go mute.

On Monday morning, she texted to see if Abie was free after work. He wrote back quickly, suggesting that they meet in the strange sculpture garden near her building. *I'll bring paletas*, he offered. She requested rice pudding, her favorite flavor, available at both La Flor Michoacana in Charlottesville and one of the poky grocery stores on her street in DC. She said so to Abie that afternoon, and he confused her by looking neither surprised nor alarmed.

"I should have explained about my life in DC already," she said doggedly. She had planned her speech in the shower that morning.

He licked guava from his mustache. "What, that your boyfriend's a lawyer there?"

Sylvie opened her mouth, closed it, and opened it again. Grass prickled beneath her bare thighs. "I told you," she said, guessing, "at the Alley Light."

"Uh-huh."

"Which I forgot."

"Apparently." Abie's eyes glimmered with amusement.

"Because I was drunk."

"Yes."

She licked her popsicle, its embedded grains of rice rough under her tongue. It was milky and full of cinnamon, reminiscent of the desserts she had eaten at Puerto Sagua with her grandparents. Although she hadn't returned to Miami in adulthood, she knew the restaurant was still in business. Sometimes, if she was missing Estie and Ilya badly, she looked at its menu online.

Abie's look of entertainment was clouding over. He said, "It would have been weird of you not to tell me."

"I don't usually tell people about him."

"Why?"

Sylvie sighed and slouched back on the park's lawn. A towering white chair cast its shadow between them. She wondered what its creator's intent was. She thought it looked like a lifeguard's seat.

"I don't talk about Robbie," she began slowly, then restarted. "I don't talk about Robbie because I don't want to be a girlfriend in public. I try not to mention my love life to anyone if I don't have a reason. And we aren't monogamous, so it's not like I really ever have to."

Uncharacteristically, he said nothing. She tried to remember which aspects of her dissertation she had explained to him, not that it mattered. It would be unreasonable to assume he'd remembered her philosophy. It would also be unreasonable to start quoting Arendt at him right now. A woodpecker released an attack on a tree behind her, beak tapping so quickly she thought its poor neck would break. If she and Abie were in the midst of another conversation, she'd pause to ask if woodpeckers *had* necks, but the increasingly dark look in his eyes told her not to.

"When I was married," she said, "Jonah's ideas about me came from other people. Not all of them, and not explicitly, but he wanted to be seen as the perfect husband, and that meant I had to look like the perfect wife." She realized that she'd moved her free hand to her belly. She buried it in the grass and went on. "It was impossible. It made me want out of not just the marriage, but the whole performance. It made me afraid of anyone ever seeing me as a girlfriend or wife again."

"But you are one," Abie said.

"In private. And now with you." Something she didn't understand flared on his face. Quickly, she added, "With my friend Nadia, too. I make a friendship exception. I wouldn't tell you about Robbie if I didn't want you to be my friend."

"I thought I was your friend already."

"I hoped so."

"You were worried?" Abie asked. He appeared to have forgotten his popsicle. Sugary pink juice ran in rivulets down his hand and wrist. Ants would be surging from the grass at any moment to take home what they could of the drips.

"I thought maybe you would disappear once you found out I had a boyfriend."

Abie's mouth moved under his beard. "It would be a little late for me to do that."

Sylvie dug in her tote bag for paper towels, which she'd had the presence of mind to grab on her way out the door. "Here," she said, offering

Abie a fistful. As he glanced at his sticky hand, she added, "It's been melting on you for a while."

"So I see." He ate the remainder of the popsicle in one giant bite, then mopped himself up and stretched his arms overhead. "Want to walk?"

"Sure." She suppressed the urge to ask if he was angry. Instead, she said, "Abie, I'm sorry. I should have told you about Robbie before."

He shrugged. "It isn't like I brought him up again. I could've asked you questions about him."

A small bit of Sylvie noted that it was, in fact, strange that he hadn't. Strange in a good way, though. Among the purposes of a private relationship was not having to talk about your boyfriend instead of yourself.

"I like that you didn't," she said. She and Abie were in motion now, roaming toward the park's exit. She wondered if he had a destination in mind.

"I owe you an apology, too," he was saying. "I'm sorry I made you scared I would bail."

"You didn't do that. *I* did that."

"Or the pressures of life under patriarchy did that."

It was something Sylvie would say to Nadia. She twisted to look at Abie, who was grinning. "Are you making fun of me?"

"Maybe."

"By saying something true?"

"Maybe."

She smacked his arm. "No fair."

"Very fair. And if you want to be friends with me, you better be ready to get made fun of. Nonnegotiable."

It occurred to Sylvie that no one teased her anymore. It wasn't generally Nadia's style; it certainly wasn't Robbie's. Hallie and Rachel had, but as they grew warier of her in the Jonah years, they'd stopped. Not since her brief and shining friendship with Riva and Paola, who used to laugh at her cluelessness about drugs, casual sex, and all the Nickelodeon shows that Carol and Paul hadn't let her watch, had Sylvie been mocked with affection instead of as a means of belittling.

She bumped her shoulder lightly against Abie's forearm. "I guess I have no choice," she said. "I accept."

4.

On Wednesday, Robbie called to say he'd had some sort of giant hearing moved to Monday. "We're going to be prepping all weekend," he said, sounding more enthusiastic than Sylvie would have anticipated. "I'll be lucky if I eat one meal at home."

"Is that legal?"

"It's my job."

"Do you want me to come up anyway?" she asked. "For moral support."

"No, no. It's not worth the drive. I'd feel guilty."

"I'll miss you," she said.

"I'll miss you, too. But we're going to the beach on Wednesday," he reminded her. For the Fourth of July, they had rented a beach house with Nadia in a small Delaware town where, according to the internet, you could watch fireworks across the bay in New Jersey. She'd rather have Robbie's job steal a nice Saturday than ruin their trip.

After hanging up, she searched online for treats to have delivered to his apartment—whether or not he minded losing his free time, she thought he deserved something to make up for it—and, once she had ordered him a babka from Ann Arbor's famous deli, she texted Abie, *Hang out this weekend?*

He replied immediately. *Sure. Hike?*

Sylvie hadn't hiked since Jonah. In the spirit of rejecting his memory and fearlessly marching into the future, she said yes, though the thought made her nervous. *If it's a small hike*, she added. *No mountains.* Abie sent her eight laughing faces, but no guarantees.

He retrieved her on Saturday morning. It was a beautiful day, so bright and breezy Sylvie could have sworn she was back in New England. They drove to Shenandoah National Park with the windows down, then set off on a trail to a hut Abie liked. He whistled bird calls as they walked, undeterred by the failure of a single bird to respond.

"I was better at it when I was a camp counselor," he conceded eventually.

"Of course you were a camp counselor."

"I didn't mention that?"

"No, but I could have guessed."

He told camp stories as they progressed up the trail, which snaked gently along a leafy ridge. Sylvie had expected more hikers, but though the parking lot had been full of families and day-tripping twentysomethings, they found themselves nearly alone in the woods. A loud couple approached and passed with a spotted Great Dane loping beside them, seeming to take half as many steps as its owners despite having double the legs. Not long after, a sinewy man appeared, wearing hiking pants and what seemed from a distance to be two layered shirts. Cups and pans jangled from his backpack, and he carried hiking poles in one hand.

"Must be a through-hiker," Abie said as they walked toward the man.

"A what?"

"Somebody hiking the whole Appalachian Trail." Abie waved, then, briefly, shaded his eyes with his hand. "Yeah. He's wearing sandals. Only a through-hiker would do that."

Sylvie waved, too, but the through-hiker didn't acknowledge them. He trudged closer, shoulders stooped. Sylvie could not imagine subjecting herself to a hike the length of the country, even if it was north to south rather than east to west. She wondered idly if it was possible to hike across the United States the long way; if there were enough connected trails to get a person from Virginia to California. She glanced at the through-hiker, as if he could tell her. Her body reacted before her mind to the fact that his penis—not erect, and not circumcised—was hanging outside the fly of his pants.

Instantly, she doubled her pace. Her shoulders snapped back; her head lifted. Her surroundings blurred into every street she'd ever walked down, every bit of the UVA campus where a man could have hidden at night. Not until she had left both Abie and the through-hiker well behind did she register that she had no reason at all to be frightened. She wasn't alone. He hadn't touched her or sought her attention. Hadn't even flashed her, if she thought about it. He had just happened to have his dick out. Suddenly she was mortified.

When she turned, Abie was jogging up the trail. "You can keep walking," he called, which made Sylvie feel even worse. She dug out the Nalgene he'd loaned her and drank showily until he was beside her. "I swear," he said, "Shenandoah isn't full of perverts. I'm pretty sure that dude was my first."

Sylvie made herself laugh. "Baby's First Pervert."

"A major milestone."

"I overreacted, though," Sylvie said. "Instinct."

Abie lifted his eyebrows. "What were you supposed to do? Slow down for a better look?"

"You just kept walking."

"No, I didn't. I told him to put his crusty dick away."

"Seriously?"

"Yes! A little kid could be coming. No child deserves to see that."

"You're a good citizen," Sylvie told him, returning the water bottle to her backpack. An enormous, bristly caterpillar hunched through the dirt by her shoe, its black body adorned with orange spots. She nudged Abie and pointed to it, and he stooped, exuding pleasure.

"Look at him go! Incredible."

"Spoken like a counselor."

"A good counselor would know what type of caterpillar that was," he said as they resumed walking. "I was never great on bugs. More of a trees-and-plants guy."

He returned to his camp stories until they reached the hut, which had a tar-shingled overhang and no view to speak of, just endless, rustling green leaves. Sylvie asked, teasing, if he'd lost his virginity on its concrete floor, and Abie yelped in indignation. "What do you think I am, a trail pervert? My *dad* used to bring me here."

She should have guessed that the hut was the site of cherished Abraham family memories. "I haven't come here with anyone but my dad and brother," he went on. He said his father had brought them every fall to see the flaming foliage, every spring to hunt for crocus buds under wet leaves. He'd pack in Hebrew Nationals and cook them on the tiny grill embedded in a concrete post in front of the hut, whistling Bob Dylan songs while they sizzled and dripped. Abie and his brother, Max, revved up by physical exertion, would wrestle in the hut's tiny clearing, rolling down to the edge of the woods.

"Who won?" Sylvie said.

"Max. He's older. He was bigger than me."

"Your dad only whistled Bob Dylan?"

"Sylvie, I'm telling you a heartwarming story. Please don't question my evocative details." He was laughing. She laughed with him, though she had a mouthful of peanut-butter sandwich. Abie's dad wasn't the only Abraham who hiked with food.

It was barely warm in the shade. She was glad to be wearing leggings, which she'd chosen primarily to avoid chafing and ticks. Flies drifted overhead, but no mosquitoes were in evidence. Sylvie had never thought before to compare or rank the greens of leaves, but Abie—a trees-and-plants guy, after all—pointed out the most emerald branches, the lime-green ones, the dull ash trees with their winged seeds. She had a suffocating vision of him pulling a branch down to a child's height. Sitting in the woods with Abie was nothing like sitting in a bar with him. Her agitation from the through-hiker had vanished, but she had a strange, unsettled feeling, like she couldn't trust what she'd say if she opened her mouth.

Sylvie expected to keep moving once their sandwiches were gone. It hadn't been an effortful hike to the hut, and Abie did Old Rag yearly. He ran marathons. His hiking boots were so worn and ancient she was shocked they were still wearable. Surely he wanted a longer walk, but he remained sitting on the hut platform's edge. It was, really, just a raised floor with a roof; it reminded Sylvie of the sukkahs that Jews prouder or more religious than her parents built in their backyards every fall. She wanted to ask Abie if his family celebrated Sukkot, but he was on a tear with his tree facts. He had progressed from ashes to red oaks.

"Bears love their acorns," he was saying. "Bears, raccoons, deer, turkeys. I once saw a whole flock of wild turkeys here. Horrible-looking birds."

"I don't think I've ever seen one."

He didn't respond. She wondered if it was her turn to contribute a nature fact or a childhood bird story. It was too bad the only animal she had to offer from her childhood was the turtle, though she did recall a heron visiting the courtyard of her grandparents' building. It had come once—this was a story!—while she and her grandmother were setting out food for Estie and Ilya's annual Fourth of July party, at which Sylvie was both the youngest guest and the gladdest to be there. She loved all the objects her grandma dug out for the party: red glass ashtrays, fake-wood folding tables, lace tablecloths browned from long use. She loved her grandparents' friends' collective scent of cigar smoke and Chanel perfume. She loved her grandfather's unholy Polish-American-Cuban hybrid of a menu, which featured pickled beets, pickled eggs, pickled herring, ribs, ham croquetas, pastelitos de guayaba, and a seventy-five-piece Popeye's bucket. One year, she spilled beet juice all over her brand-new hibiscus-print dress, staining its yellow-and-orange skirt magenta. At home, she would have gotten in trouble for such sloppiness. Her mother would have scolded her in front of the assembled party guests, and her father would have withheld her allowance until she'd repaid him for the ruined outfit. Her grandparents didn't even send her inside to change.

She was describing the heron, and the party, when Abie made a sound like a city bus kneeling. She twisted toward him. "Are you choking?"

"Kind of." He was staring into the woods. "No. I'm in love with you."

She froze. "No, you're not," she heard herself say.

"I am."

"You don't want to be."

"Yeah, Sylvie. I know." His knees bounced on the weathered platform. She could see bits of leaf in the hair popping out of his high wool socks. "I shouldn't have told you I wanted to be friends. I mean, I *did* want to, but that was dumb. It was dumb to bring you here. It's too painful. I was trying, but I can't do this. I can't be Lancelot. We can have sex in this hut right now, or we can go back to the car and I'll take you home and never text you again. I know I sound like an asshole. I know ultimatums are bad, and I'm sorry, but—"

"Abie."

"What?"

She had no *what*. All she'd wanted was to cut off his torrent of words. She could physically sense her mind straining. In a small voice, she said, "What do you mean, Lancelot?"

Abie blinked at her. "That's what you're asking?"

"I don't know much—" she started, and then, before she could complete her sentence—*I don't know much Arthurian myth*—she recognized the absurdity of the question. Abie had just professed love to her. He had asked if she wanted to have sex on the leaf-covered floor of his childhood-memory hut. It was unkind, and possibly also insane, to respond with a clarifying question about Camelot.

"Abie," she said. "You know Robbie and I aren't monogamous."

He shook his head. "But I am."

A bird cawed above them. She was scared of Abie's feelings. She looked into the canopy, and, as if she'd pulled a cord, realization descended upon her. It was a double epiphany: the conviction that she would never be able to give him what he wanted, and the profound desire to do so.

Sweat was cooling all over her body. Her legs itched. Her blood and heart and stomach all seemed to be moving in different directions. She felt like she was about to fly straight up into the trees. It struck her—flight did—as a good solution. Never mind that Abie had driven her here; never mind that she didn't know which trail led back to the parking lot. She'd get there. She'd hitchhike. She'd go straight to DC, she promised herself as she snatched up her backpack and ran.

It took Abie a moment to follow her. "Sylvie!" he called, boots pounding on the trail. "Sylvie, I'm sorry. Sylvie, wait!"

She did not wait. If she waited—if she stopped—she would set a bad precedent, and so she kept moving. Her breasts, supposedly constricted by a weapons-grade sports bra, managed to both bounce and ache. She pressed her forearms to them. It slowed her down. Around her, branches rustled; squirrels chittered; birds sang. Maybe, instead of returning to the parking lot, she could vanish into nature. She could become feral. Probably that was a good idea.

Abie caught up to her at the first trail fork. He touched her upper arm—not a grab, not a hold, barely more than a brush, but still, it arrested her instantly. She turned and looked into his face. He said, "Lancelot was in love with Guinevere, the queen. It was forbidden, but he didn't leave Camelot. His feelings for her purified him, sort of. He used them to make himself a model of chivalry." He swallowed. "But eventually they had sex, and so he couldn't look at the Holy Grail."

"Are you worried about that?"

"I was very into King Arthur as a kid."

Sylvie had the sensation that the ground was moving under her feet. Abie seemed to blur and wobble at his edges. Maybe he was the Holy Grail and she wasn't pure enough to see him. Maybe she was going insane. It was 2019. She was theorizing the end of romance. Surely it could not be true that a man was talking to her, in total and absolute sincerity, about chivalry and the Holy Grail. Surely she was having some kind of woods-induced hallucination. Heatstroke, though it wasn't that hot.

She was still staring directly at Abie. He was no longer blurring. For an instant, he looked like a stranger. She closed her eyes. When she reopened them, he was so close he looked like no one at all.

They kissed on the trail, but not for long. She led him back to the hut, where, in their brief absence, a pair of withered, silvery hikers had installed themselves. Without conferring, Abie and Sylvie turned and marched back downhill.

Neither of them said much on the drive to Charlottesville. Abie put on the *Last Waltz* soundtrack, which Sylvie barely heard. She was nearly sick with sexual longing. She couldn't tell if she'd been suppressing it or if it had just set in.

Before that afternoon, Sylvie had never visited Abie's house. She wondered now if he'd avoided inviting her. As it was, the contents of his home only vaguely registered. All she wanted to see was his bed.

In his room, Abie slowed down. He got serious and quiet in a way she found intensely moving. It was as if she were a solemn project. He stood before her in admiration, taking each piece of sweat-stiffened clothing off slowly. By the time she was naked, she had entered an almost animal state. Complexity left her. She had no verbal power, no sense of the future, no imagination at all. She kept hearing a high, ringing sound that came from nowhere. Her sinuses ached with the possibility of tears. Abie moved her from her back to her front, then pulled out, rolled her over, and knelt to go down on her. She didn't stop him after she came, though it had been an orgasm so long, so rattling, that she knew there would be no other. When, finally, he climbed back on the bed to finish, she felt cracked open with emotion. She would let him do anything to her. She wanted to say so, but she couldn't speak. She had never been more frightened in her life.

5.

Sylvie was furious at her turtle. She lay in Abie's bed, wide awake in the thin early sun, and demanded, Why didn't you tell me I was dying to have sex with him?

Is that all?

You fell down on the job, Sylvie accused. You told me I was just afraid of making male friends because of Jonah.

Her turtle snapped his beak. Seemed true.

Sylvie turned onto her side. Abie was sleeping face up, peaceful to the point of majesty. Never before had she seen his face completely at rest. She thought of his expression as he braced his body over hers the day before, the light of real joy in his eyes. It was too early to wake him. Still, she moved closer and, very gently, licked his neck.

Abie made a small sound but didn't stir. Sylvie bit his earlobe. She was, apparently, waking him. He grumbled slightly, but this time, he rolled toward her. Without opening his eyes, he said, in a tone of wonder, "You stayed."

He kissed her, beard prickling at her nose and lips. He still smelled like her. She nudged her thigh between his, and he scooped his pelvis close enough that she could feel what was rapidly becoming a full erection swelling toward her. It wasn't a good position for sex, really—not enough leverage—but Sylvie had no patience. She reached for the strip of condoms on the bedside table.

She started on top, but Abie turned her onto her back quickly. After that, she had the sense of time flattening out. It was as if she had always been here, looking down her own torso to see the point at which their bodies met. Somehow, that timelessness was better than physical pleasure, which was, in this moment, nearly unwelcome. Pleasure grew, and then peaked, and then ended. She didn't want any endings. She wanted no change at all. She tried telling herself that she was sore and abraded from yesterday, that she probably wasn't going to have an orgasm, that Abie wouldn't care if she did, but the last one was untrue and, in its untruth, a mistake. Knowing how wrong it was made her come instantly. He shuddered and did the same.

While Sylvie was in the bathroom, she heard him thump downstairs and start grinding coffee. She got back in bed, and, after enough time that she was beginning to consider descending, he returned, still completely naked, with a steaming Chemex in one big hand and two empty mugs dangling from the other.

"Don't burn yourself," she said.

"I'm very brave." He was smiling, but Sylvie heard a slight shake in the words. He'd had a talk with himself while he brewed the coffee, she guessed, and now he was going to have one with her.

He let her finish her cup of coffee first. As he poured more in, he said, "My offer from yesterday about never texting you again still stands."

"No," she said instantly. "Don't do that."

"Everything else I said stands, too. I love you. And I can't do nonmonogamy."

It was as if he had reached inside her torso and snapped a rubber band, or a bra strap, or a bone. A mouthful of swallowed coffee rose into her throat. A very clear voice in her head—one she heard from rarely, and thought of as the Voice of God—said, You will not give this feeling up.

"Can I have some time to think?" she asked.

"What kind of time?"

"I don't know." She slid her free hand over his. "I'm going to Delaware on Wednesday. Wednesday to Sunday. How about we don't talk until after that?"

Abie nodded. She wanted to die. She wanted him to say he couldn't go a whole week without hearing from her, couldn't go a day, couldn't go a minute. She needed to get out of here.

She took herself to DC within an hour of leaving Abie's. It felt both cowardly and necessary. For half the drive she debated whether to call Robbie or surprise him when he returned from work. Absurdly, she imagined that he'd lied about the hearing; that if she chose not to call him, she'd walk in on him with another girl, a girl more innately toppy than she was, not a true dominatrix—she had asked: not Robbie's style—but a girl aroused by bossing a man around. It wasn't an erotic fantasy. It was about impunity. If Robbie had found a way to break their—*her*—rules, then she'd have the right to do the same.

She knew she wasn't going to tell Robbie she'd slept with Abie. She couldn't stand to alter the memory by describing it. Neither did she want to lessen it by having sex with Robbie, an aversion she recognized as a nascent, terrifying form of loyalty to Abie. A shock of envy for the monogamous ran through her. A closed relationship would protect her from feelings like these.

She didn't call Robbie. On arriving, she found his condo not just empty but uncharacteristically messy. A knife and plate crusted with babka remnants sat in the sink. As if she were a different Sylvie, a different girlfriend, she began to wash them. When she was done, she wiped the counters. She vacuumed. She made the bed. It was penance, or apology, or just a way of creating some comfort for a man she loved.

Robbie got home at six. In the instant before he registered her presence, she saw how utterly tired he was. His shirt—a button-down, even on a Sunday—was crumpled, his gorgeous shoulders hunched. He had more stubble on his face than she'd ever seen.

"Hey," she said softly. It was as if she'd turned the lights on inside him. He dropped his messenger bag and strode down the hall.

"You came," he said into her hair.

She shrugged so he could feel it. "I thought you might like it."

"I said you didn't have to."

"I'm not teaching Monday or Tuesday," she said. "And I know you don't *need* me here, but—"

He cut her off. "I always need you."

She closed her eyes. Shame and love and longing swirled within her, though she wasn't sure which man she was longing for.

"Sylvie," Robbie said. "Did you clean my house?"

"A little."

He stooped to kiss her. She could tell that he was too worn out for sex, which felt like a reprieve. While he showered, she got takeout from the Indian place down the block and cued up an episode of *Parts Unknown*, Robbie's comfort show. Sylvie found it soothing, too. She told herself she had no right to let the evening calm her, but she couldn't control how she felt.

For the next two days, she tried to stifle her conflict and confusion with preparations for Delaware, though really, there wasn't much to do.

As a general rule, she rejected grooming she didn't personally enjoy, but she made an exception for bikini waxes in the summer: getting them was a capitulation to patriarchal standards, yes, but also, her forest of pubic hair belonged to the private sphere. In this case, it was also an excuse not to have sex. She told Robbie the wax had been too hot, and she was sore.

On Wednesday morning, Nadia flew into DC from Atlanta. Sylvie drove to get her at the airport, worrying the whole time that her friend would take one look at her and demand to know what had happened. Instead, Nadia got into the car already moaning about Dr. Rau. "She keeps texting me in German," she said. "And if I complain, she switches to French."

"What's she texting you about?"

"Work."

It was a lie too transparent to call out. Instead, Sylvie surveyed her friend, who had on unusually large hoops and an asymmetrical garment that was, on inspection, not a shirt but a cleverly tied scarf. "Nice earrings," she said.

Nadia touched one. "My dad got them for me. António. His trainer's girlfriend just opened a boutique."

"Do you like them?"

"The trainer? Or the earrings?"

"The earrings."

"No."

Both of them laughed. It occurred to Sylvie that, even now, it would weigh on her to wear something to please one of her parents. She could tell Nadia was happy to. Abie probably let his eighth cousins pick out his clothes.

She suppressed the idea of Abie. "So António's still obsessed with the gym?" she said.

"Addicted."

"Is he jacked now?"

"No!" Nadia shook her head so hard the hoops swung. "He looks exactly the same. I don't think he works out. I think he just goes there and talks."

"How does Malcolm feel about that?"

Nadia dropped her voice into a low, rumbling imitation of her other father. "'Every minute he spends in that gym is a minute of blessed peace and quiet for me.'"

It made Sylvie feel normal to have her friend around. So normal, in fact, that though they had an entire afternoon to themselves before Robbie got home, she didn't say anything about Abie. She wasn't allowing herself to think about him. A small part of her still wanted Nadia to divine that a great shift had occurred within her, but the rest was just relieved that she could hide it. If Nadia guessed, anyway, it would complicate their vacation, and Sylvie wanted to enjoy the trip she'd planned, though she wished she'd picked a smaller house. At the time of booking, Sylvie had wanted to ensure that Robbie wouldn't be too self-conscious about sound to have sex. Now she wished she'd rented a yurt.

Sylvie drove the three of them to Delaware while Robbie edited a brief in the back seat. One town away, they stocked up in a strip mall, sending Nadia to buy beer and wine—no grocery-store sales in Delaware—while Sylvie and Robbie got food. In the produce section, he wrapped an arm around her and said, "No more lawyering until Monday. I promise."

"You can lawyer."

"I've been ignoring you."

"I don't mind."

Robbie gave her a questioning look: not wounded but prepared to be. She winced. "I mean," she said, "I don't want you to feel guilty when you have to concentrate on something else. I know you love me."

She leaned into him, and his hand tightened briefly on her shoulder.

She imagined the two other produce shoppers glancing at them, feeling a flash of admiration or envy or repulsion for the little show of love in their body language as he said, "But I do feel guilty."

"I wish I could release you from that."

"Me, too."

"Here." Sylvie wriggled out from under his arm, then tapped him on the forehead. "Be free."

"Was that a spell or an order?"

"Whichever you prefer."

"Order." He smiled, and, even in the icy Food Lion with its towers of lifeless yellow apples and bagged, dusty green grapes, her body warmed unmistakably. Maybe it had been an error to dodge sex with him.

She still went upstairs before him when they reached the house, though. Despite his no-lawyering promise, he had a last round of emails to send, and Sylvie was exhausted. She thought she'd go straight to sleep, but she hadn't accounted for the power of an empty bed. Since leaving Virginia, she hadn't texted Abie or read their old texts; hadn't Googled him to see his face; hadn't replayed the hike and its aftermath in her head. But lying alone, she could resist no longer. In the hall, she heard Nadia's feet but not yet Robbie's. Abie's ancient hiking boots appeared before her, followed by his thick, furry calves. She imagined the noise he might make if she licked behind his knee. Predictably, the thought sent a shiver all the way through her. She reached downward. As if summoned, Robbie came up the stairs.

Sylvie told herself it was a sign. She pushed the covers away and propped herself up on her elbow, siren-style, so that when he opened the door, he immediately saw her bare breasts.

"I couldn't fall asleep after all," she whispered.

"I'm glad." He was already undoing his belt. It had been nearly two weeks since they'd had sex, and she found that, despite her dread and avoidance, she was eager, specifically, for him. His body was so beautiful, so familiar. For the first time since she woke up in Abie Abraham's house, her thoughts, to her relief, left her alone.

6.

Sylvie let herself sleep late. When she came downstairs, the house smelled like buttermilk and pleasantly burnt sugar. Robbie was making chocolate-chip pancakes. Nadia, between her second and third stacks, stretched luxuriously and declared, "Everyone should live like this."

After eating, they descended to the beach with their towels and paperbacks, their cooler of snacks and beer. Beach plums and dry, tall grasses waved on the dunes behind them. Seaweed and dead horseshoe crabs streaked the shoreline. Sylvie had never been to a mid-Atlantic beach before. All morning, and often during their four days in Delaware, she thought of the glittering, built-up stretches of sand in Miami, the neat bite of the Marblehead town beach. She never swam much in those places, but here, she bobbed in the ocean with Robbie for at least half an hour at the end of his daily swims. It was their only time together except in bed, where she initiated very quiet sex every night. Her fear of sleeping with him had flipped around. Now it quieted her deeper concern that, through choices and decisions entirely her own, she was going to lose him: her boyfriend, her philosophical partner and guinea pig, the most solicitous man in the world.

Out of bed, too, the trip went beautifully. It was sunny and warm, but not dehydration-hot. Robbie didn't lawyer, Nadia didn't do anything

Rau-related, and the two of them were clearly bonding. Nadia appointed herself kitchen DJ and, while cranking decade-old Atlanta rap hits, helped him cook and clean every night. Afterward, they'd gang up on Sylvie while choosing movies to watch, rejecting all her arty selections. "We want explosions!" Nadia chanted Friday evening, and Robbie, to Sylvie's surprise and delight, joined in.

But on Saturday, something shifted. Nadia began to exude agitation. Sylvie couldn't guess whether her friend was eager to get back to Charlottesville or dreading it, but by lunch, both Sylvie and Robbie could tell something was wrong. After they'd eaten dinner—Robbie had done his version of Americana: kosher hot dogs, potato salad, and juicy hunks of watermelon with chili and lime, like the vendors on his street sold—and watched the sunset over Cape May, Robbie announced that he was going to bed early. Sylvie followed him in for a kiss, and he said in her ear, "I thought you might want some alone time with Nadia, but I'll wait up."

His thoughtfulness made her want to cry. As cover for her surging feelings, she turned away from him and rooted in their things for bug spray. When she returned to the deck, a bottle of Off! in one hand and a six-pack of Flying Dog in the other, Nadia, without turning to look at her, said, "I have something to tell you."

It seemed that Sylvie had been wrong, but barely. Nadia was not having a physical affair with Dr. Rau, but, apparently, that was only because Dr. Rau had scruples about sex with students. "I tell her all the time I'm a consenting adult," Nadia said, drawing her knees to her chest. Waves hissed on the beach, yards away but too dark to see. Cape May glittered its faint post-firework glitter on the horizon. In the dim light, Nadia seemed thin and pale, as if she'd spent the past three days in the library instead of basking in the sun. "She says she has too much power over me for that to be true."

Sylvie disliked that angle. It didn't strike her as especially conscientious to remind someone how much power you wielded over them, but she didn't say that. Instead, she asked, "Does she, though? It isn't like she's your dissertation adviser. She doesn't control whether you graduate. She's not even on your committee."

"She is now," Nadia said dully. "She wanted to be."

"Since when?"

"Start of the summer."

"You could have said no."

"Yeah." Nadia took a sip of her wine. "But she's helped me so much, and she's interested in my ideas." She brightened. "Which is good. She's not the type to date someone who's not smart enough for her."

Sylvie had never heard Nadia talk about dating anybody. Nadia thought dating was boring. Hearing her use the word now triggered a current of sorrow, mixed with the awareness that Robbie was right: she did expect Nadia to be perfect. Invulnerable. Immune to the traps, tropes, and clichés of love.

"Why her?"

"She understands me."

Sylvie ordered herself not to say, *I* understand you. "Is she going to wait for you to graduate?"

"Don't know."

"Have you talked about it?"

"She won't promise." Nadia plucked at the frayed hem of her shorts. Even on a beach trip, she wore the unyielding denim to which she was committed, albeit in cutoff form. Dr. Rau might understand Nadia intellectually, but Sylvie highly doubted that she appreciated her devotion to textiles. She was willing to bet Dr. Rau had no idea how much Nadia liked shitty action movies, or extra chilies in her larb tofu, or falling asleep in the grass.

"But," Nadia added, "I'm pretty sure I can graduate in April. Nine months isn't so bad." She grinned, teeth flashing in the dark. "If you can wait that long for a baby, you can wait that long for a girlfriend."

Sylvie squeezed her eyes shut. She took a long breath of beach air, inhaling as much acrid bug spray as oceanic salt, and ordered herself not to ask if Nadia had lost her mind. "You seriously think you can finish by April?"

"It's only a year early."

"Only a *year*? Do you hear yourself?"

Nadia lifted one shoulder. "I've been working my ass off."

"I noticed," Sylvie said. She sounded sarcastic, which was not her intention. She took a long drink of her beer. Completing your PhD a year early—a year *minimum*: it wasn't uncommon to need six or seven instead of the recommended five—was the goal of a maniac. It was enough to wear anyone down.

Sylvie's tone seemed not to be relevant. Nadia was speaking as if to herself. She repeated, "I'm pretty sure I can do it. And then I won't be her student. I could adjunct after—"

"And get paid shit?"

"—or get a job in Charlottesville. Any job. Salomé does want me to be a professor, though. She says I have a real shot."

"You do, Nadia. Of course you do. You don't have to give that up."

"I might."

Sylvie wanted to get up and hug her friend, or else shove her into the bay. She wanted to build a towering medieval wall between Nadia and the world. She wanted her friend to be safe from the horrible yearning that she currently felt for Abie.

"You're being an idiot," she said.

Nadia gave her a look of tremendous unhappiness. "I'm aware."

Now Sylvie managed to stand. Alcohol and grief whirled in her head. She meant to go to Nadia, but the emotion radiating from her friend was too frightening. Yet another unwelcome voice suggested that she go inside and break up with Robbie. "Unrelated," she told it sternly.

"What?" Nadia said.

"Sorry." Sylvie shook her head. "I'm sorry."

"Why? You're right." Nadia made a small sound that was related to a laugh. "I knew how dumb love made other people. I didn't know it could happen to me."

Sylvie attempted a laugh of her own. "Now you see why I want it to end." She sat on the end of Nadia's lounge chair.

"I thought you were just against romance."

"I am."

"But?"

Sylvie dropped her head. She thought of Robbie waiting in the house, Abie waiting in Charlottesville. Abie, who, the moment he was first inside her, put his hot, prickly face in her neck and growled, "God, I love you." Remembering it was erotic enough to seem illicit with another person, even Nadia, so close. It was also like remembering that she had been condemned to a life of suffering.

"But love is terrifying," she said.

"I don't want to hear that from you."

"Why?"

"Because Robbie's a saint."

"Right," she said. "He's a saint, and I could hurt him."

"Don't."

Sylvie wanted to curl up like a pill bug and roll herself into the sea. Her turtle said, Guess you won't be telling Nadia about Abie.

She scooted to the end of the lounger and put her arm around Nadia, who dropped her head onto Sylvie's shoulder. Crickets chirped in the bushes; the dune grass rustled without wind. Sylvie saw herself and her friend as if from above, tiny and drifting in a huge, dark expanse. It didn't help them to be together. It was possible that nothing could help either of them at all.

Chapter Five

1.

Abie called Sylvie—not a text: a call—within hours of her return from the beach. She willed herself not to answer. Staying away from him was the wise and correct thing to do. She didn't want to be unkind, though. She could pick up the phone and *explain* that it was wise and correct for her to stay away. She got as far as answering, but then, in the space of what her call log informed her was four minutes and twenty-three seconds, she agreed that he could take her on a date the next night.

She told herself it was only dinner. Her turtle manifested instantly to call bullshit. He said, It took you how long to go to a restaurant with Robbie?

We aren't discussing Robbie.

Have you ever been to a restaurant with Wyatt?

His brewery serves food.

The turtle waggled his head in his shell, then retracted it. She stretched out on her bed and shut her eyes. Jonah had sent her an email that morning. No bragging about his stuff or status this time; no mention of the life he still seemed to imagine they could lead. It said only, *I miss you. I'd love to see you soon.* She allowed herself to hope that the brevity of his message was a sign that he was finally losing interest. For seven years, he had sent her these reminders of his existence. Maybe he was almost ready to let her forget.

Her turtle let her enjoy that thought for a moment before asking, You can picture Wyatt's bedroom, correct?

Sylvie could. It had an ancient pinkish Southwestern carpet, bookshelves built from scrap wood, an IKEA bed with corners that could dent a girl's shin. Instead of telling the turtle about it, she said, What does that have to do with anything?

Answer.

You know I can. You're in my head.

Well, then how come I can't see Abie's?

Sylvie groaned—aloud, not just to the turtle. I've only been there once, she reminded him.

For how many hours?

Don't be rude.

Is it possible to be rude to yourself?

I don't see why not, Sylvie said.

She woke up exceptionally nervous. It was wrong to go on a date without telling Robbie, though less wrong that she still hadn't told Robbie she'd slept with Abie. Also, she had never—not once—gone on a date with someone who wasn't already her boyfriend. She reminded herself that Abie had seen her eat; seen her naked. He'd seen her body from more angles than she had. A date was a performance she agreed to put on before arriving at what she presumed was the evening's real purpose, which was showing him more angles still.

But Abie had another agenda. He announced it immediately. She'd taken her time—leaving town for a week, not texting—and now he was taking his in the form of a speech. Over charred carrots and wood-fired oysters, he delivered a soliloquy on his prior relationships, minor Freudian damages, and present emotional availability. Over foraged-mushroom and housemade-sausage pizzas, he outlined in astonishing detail the married—or committed, partnered, he didn't give a shit if the state was involved—future that he imagined for them. He wanted to move home to Richmond, do the same work there he did here. He wanted to buy a row house, a fixer-upper with original details, no open–floor plan developer crap. He'd adapt it to suit their joint life. He would make Sylvie a study complete with built-in desk, not that he'd ever built a desk before. He'd put a garden in back, get a pair of shelter mutts who'd trample it up, jam picnic tables between vegetable beds so his cousins and their kids could all eat dinner at once. He wanted to set them up as one of his family's new centers. He'd build a movable ramp so Great-Aunt Wolfie could get around the house in her wheelchair; he'd childproof every room years before they had kids. He knew Sylvie collected pottery, so he'd put in tall shelves. Floor-to-ceiling, maybe. He hadn't been to her place yet, but he'd bet neither of them was lacking in books.

Sylvie was not going to be charmed by any Great-Aunt Wolfie. She'd learned her lesson from Papa Sid. She hugged her elbows in, pressed her sit bones into her hard metal chair in an unsuccessful effort to counteract the current rising inside her. She could tell that by the time she stood up, her underwear would be soaked. It was not a good reaction to talk of dogs and domesticity. It was, in fact, extremely dangerous and bad, and yet not until she was halfway through her third glass of wine did she manage to say, "You know this is my nightmare."

"I do."

"So why—?"

"I want a life with you," he said. "And I want the life I want. I'm not making demands, but it wouldn't be fair not to tell you what's in my head. But Sylvie." He held her gaze. "I said this before, and I'm going to say it now. I can't share."

Sylvie reminded herself that she had devoted the last three years to researching and elaborating a philosophy of love based on the concept that conducting a romance like the one Abie had just described was a curse and a death. If she truly believed in it, then she should get up and march out the door. She wasn't supposed to want a life with anyone. She didn't want a whole one with Robbie, and she loved him.

"I was married," she said. "It was awful. I don't want to do it again."

"Marrying me would be nothing like marrying him."

"You don't know that."

"Yes, I do."

She knew she should be gone already. She should be six blocks away, calling Nadia to say love is fake, don't fall for it, don't listen to your body, your body is a dumb bitch. But her reaction to Abie's fairytale wasn't just physical. It came from not just her body but also her supposed ally, her mind.

It was tough to know whether to hold body or mind accountable for what happened next. Abie paid while she was in the bathroom. On her return, he asked if she'd like to go get another drink.

"No," she said. "I'd like you to take me home."

In order to spite her turtle, Sylvie took great note of her surroundings. Abie lived alone in a very small house with robin's-egg siding, a chain-link fence festooned with morning glories, and a scraggly but not unloved yard featuring dirty wood Adirondack chairs, a charcoal grill with the lid off, and several pots of tomatoes. Inside, his living room overflowed with books and paper detritus. He had a fish tank, a record player, a much-used brown leather Eames chair, and a couch so heaped in blankets Sylvie couldn't see its actual fabric. Half the walls were lined with white shelves he had built; the others were covered in basketball ephemera, including, to Sylvie's mixed amusement and horror, a framed *Space Jam* shirt featuring Marvin the Martian. Pale skeletons of dead cacti littered the windowsills. Sylvie found them appealing, in a ghostly sort of way. Georgia O'Keeffe could have painted them. She was interested in desert plants and death.

"I overwatered," Abie said as she approached the cactus graveyard. His voice sank to the bottom of her stomach. She felt faintly dizzy. She pressed her thumb into a shriveled star cactus, which didn't help.

"Why do you keep them?" she asked.

"Respect for their service, I guess."

Sylvie was too jangled to give him the laugh he presumably wanted. Examining the house more closely had helped her remain inside herself up to this point, but she felt fundamentally porous. Her courage, or what remained of it, had deserted her. Every inch of her skin rose toward Abie, but she could barely move. She was afraid to take her clothes off. She sat halfway down on the windowsill. Abie regarded her from across the room. He said, "Do you want to be here?"

She nodded.

"Are you scared?"

She nodded again.

He made the same face he had when she brought up Jonah at dinner. It was an expression related to a smile, but only in the way a wolf is related to a dog. "Me, too."

"Why?"

Abie dropped himself into the Eames chair, which issued a resentful creak. "My gift and curse," he said, "is that I only want one thing in every category of life."

"What does that mean?"

"You know I've never lived outside Virginia. I decided to be a historian when I was nine." He tugged at his hair. "I'm very simple, Sylvie. I latch on to ideas and don't let go. I don't have doubts or second thoughts." He raised his eyes to hers. "It's going to be very easy for you to break my heart."

She heard herself say, "I don't want to." Every voice in her head, even the Voice of God, screamed, You will. She had to keep talking to drown them out. What emerged was the truest and most terrifying sentence she could have spoken. "I want to give you what you want."

Abie said nothing. He just looked at her. She found that she was on her feet. She needed to do something abject. She pushed the ottoman aside and knelt in front of him, but he stopped her when she reached for his belt.

"What's wrong?" she asked. Her throat was hot, her mouth already full of anticipatory saliva. She thought that if she couldn't suck his cock she would cry. Her insides were hot and light, as if turned into some new substance.

"You want what I want?" Abie said, so roughly she shivered. He shoved his seat back and slid down so that he, too, was kneeling in the trough between chair and ottoman. It was an absurd, constrained place to be. He kissed her hard, teeth briefly scraping her bottom lip. She was crying now. It was nice to have been right.

She broke the kiss off without retreating. Very quietly, she said, "You have to tell me."

Abie hooked his hands around her wrists. He pulled them back to rest on the ottoman, which meant she had to arch her back and press her breasts up to keep its wooden edge from biting into the flesh of her back. He lifted himself to kiss her, shifting so one of his thighs was very nearly, but not quite, between her legs. She told herself to let him close that minute gap, but what she thought and did were tethered more and more loosely, the chain of her mind sliding to the edge of the latch. She pressed herself hard into his body, holding still rather than rocking her hips. He let go of one of her wrists to reach behind her and under her dress, pushing into her tailbone with the flat of his palm. She had a fleeting image of herself as a gymnast alone in an auditorium, masturbating by rocking on a balance beam; then, better, the same image with Abie in the bleachers. They were still kissing fiercely. A hot energy moved down her spine. He released her other wrist to shove the ottoman away, and the two of them collapsed together to the carpeted floor.

"All I want," he said, "is to fuck you."

"I want you to."

"Now?"

She took his hand and moved it so he could feel her wet underwear, her body pulsing beneath. It was like breathing, almost. He slid the fabric aside and put two fingers inside her, and she made a sound like a rusted gate flying open. He added a third, and she wailed.

Both of them came quickly enough that a second round was easy. Sylvie led Abie upstairs for it. Afterward, she went to the bathroom and, having peed, regarded her reflection. Her face was bright pink. She found herself beautiful. Outside the smeared little window, the Virginia night raged with stars. She was sure Abie, the former camp counselor, could name every constellation out there. He would teach their eventual children. She could see it as clearly as if it were happening outside right now. Any child would be lucky to have him as a father. Of course, any child would be lucky to have Robbie, too.

Just thinking Robbie's name made her shiver with guilt. She had never imagined him with their child, or abandoned herself to him the way she just had with Abie.

She always texted Robbie good night when she was in Charlottesville. Her hands itched to do it now, a sensation that reminded her of the Jonah years, though the obligation out of which she'd texted Jonah bore no resemblance at all to the guilt that now sent her down the stairs to the living room, where she'd left her bag. *I love you*, she wrote. It was the truth, but still, she felt monstrous. *Hope work's not eating you alive.*

When she returned to the bedroom, Abie was standing, shirtless, by his closet, buttoning a pair of jeans. Relief crashed across his face when he saw her. "I thought you were leaving."

"What?"

"I heard you on the stairs and I thought you left." His mouth twitched. "So I was getting dressed to chase you."

"I wasn't leaving," she said, surprised. It hadn't occurred to her to go home.

Abie shucked his jeans off and sat down. Quietly, he said, "I'm afraid you're going to hurt me, but you're just afraid of me. Is that right?"

She shook her head. What she feared was herself and what she wanted. She was afraid of the person Abie would make, or let, her become. "I'm scared of how I feel."

"Which is?"

A chill ran across Sylvie's scalp. She hadn't allowed herself, until this moment, to give a name to her emotions. Now the word sat fully formed on her tongue, but she didn't release it. She couldn't. If she told Abie she loved him, she would be pledging herself to betrayal and insanity.

He didn't push. He looked steadily up at her from the bed and, after a moment of her silence, said, "How can I make you less scared?"

Sylvie took a deep breath. "You can wait."

"Should I?"

"What do you mean?"

"If I wait, will I be waiting for the rest of my life?"

"No."

"Even if you don't get less scared?"

She swallowed. She could do nothing but tell the truth. "If I don't get less scared," she said, "I'll be gone."

2.

In the morning, Sylvie walked home feeling a mix of confusion and clarity that she thought should not be possible. Her body was intensely relaxed, though also leaking and achy. Sun sank into her shoulders and hair. All the houses she passed seemed especially brightly painted, their gardens loud with summer life. She imagined an aura of sex and luck emanating from her.

She didn't welcome the feeling. It was dangerous, not lucky, to have stumbled on a man a person who made her lose herself both physically and emotionally. In the shower, she reminded herself that she'd resolved, after the Kavanaugh hearings, that she should only submit in bed to men who got no access to her inner life. Hadn't she decided that was an important precaution—no: a *principle*—for women who wished to be strong?

She shut her eyes and stuck her head directly into the stream of water. A face she hadn't conjured in a long time appeared in her head: tangled beard, warm smile, battered crown. Strength is more complicated than that, he told her.

Captain Lightning?

At your service, he said. I appreciate you bringing me back.

Sylvie opted against telling him that she found his presence alarming. She hadn't meant to summon him, and yet here he was, looking at once like she'd always imagined him and distinctly like Abie. Maybe there was meaning to be found here. More likely, her brain had gone haywire and she should take herself straight to Psych Services. Instead, she asked

Captain Lightning how his experience as an imaginary pirate king informed his concept of strength.

Well, he said, if you're hurting somebody, that's not strength. It's cruelty.

Sylvie bit her lip. She wanted to tell the captain she hadn't hurt anyone, but if she didn't add *yet*, she'd be lying.

And, Captain Lightning added, it's not strength if it only holds under certain conditions. I learned that when I got shipwrecked.

My conditions haven't changed.

Her turtle, unsurprisingly, chimed in then. Bullshit.

"Enough," Sylvie said aloud. She shut the water off. Again she considered declaring herself temporarily insane, but that would just be a version of playing the victim. She wasn't deranged; she wasn't helpless. She, Sylvie Broder, self-appointed destroyer of romance, had, through stupidity, horniness, and negligence, fallen in love with two men, and now she had to decide what that meant.

All day she searched her copious dissertation notes for help. She found nothing that could justify holding on to Abie. Still, she spent eight solid hours searching her shelves, her files, and her mind for an argument that she should, and she quit only when it was time to go to his house for dinner. She didn't need any philosophers to tell her that doing so was only plausibly ethical if she called Robbie and confessed.

She could tell the moment Robbie answered the phone that he was in the legal weeds. His colleagues chattered in the background—she heard one say, "By nine at the latest"—and a mix of guilt and relief gripped her.

"I can talk later," he said.

"No, no. I was just calling to chat. If you have more time tomorrow—" He groaned, and she said quickly, "Don't worry. I'll see you Friday."

"I'm sorry I'm not more available, Sylvie. After this case is done, it'll be better."

She heard somebody near him shouting, "No, it won't." Robbie laughed. She recognized that, despite all his fears about hating his job, he enjoyed this: the rush, the camaraderie, the high demand. For an instant, she let herself hope the pressure of his work would distract him from his grief after a breakup. It probably would, which was too awful to contemplate.

She made it halfway to Abie's before her revulsion at her selfishness started waning. She was ashamed that it did, and yet she couldn't deny the lightness, the excitement, in her gait. As she turned the corner onto his block, she had to consciously slow herself down.

She found him waiting with dinner ingredients and a lit grill. Apparently, his hamburgers were legendary in both the Abraham family and the Jewish frat at William & Mary. "Secret recipe," he said proudly. "Invented it when I was sixteen."

"Do I get to learn it?"

"You do not." He kissed her, then gave her hip an affectionate squeeze. "But you do get to help."

He assigned her to caramelize onions, which she didn't tell him she hadn't done since 2011. It seemed that she remembered how. She found herself taking pleasure, even, in swirling her spoon through the pan, waiting for strings of sugar to develop. She was determined to turn her onions the walnut shade that denoted real patience. Abie would be highly impressed.

While she stirred, he bounded through the kitchen like a Labrador. He had put music on his little portable speaker, and the Beastie Boys yelped over the sound of his thudding knife and clanging spoons. Every time Sylvie looked, he was on to a new task: shredding lettuce, slicing pickles—he said he refused to buy any kind but whole dills—seasoning beef, shaping patties. Once he had a pair of fat, raw burgers ready, he washed his hands, then wrapped his arms around Sylvie from behind, kissed her neck, and plucked an onion from the pan.

"Delicious."

"Give me ten more minutes, and—"

"And nothing." He let her go. "It's hot in here. Come hang out with me while I grill."

She hadn't noticed the grill smoking on arrival, but the moment she stepped through the back door, she smelled charcoal. Abie had pulled the Adirondack chairs—a style she hated; it was bleak standing up from them—close to the Weber kettle, positioned a rickety little table between them. Once he got the burgers on the flame, he vanished inside and returned with buns and fixings, the stubby brown necks of two Red Stripes gleaming from the pockets of his shorts.

"Man," Sylvie said, accepting hers. "I didn't know I was going to get waited on."

"I gave you the hardest job. You earned that beer."

"Did I earn the secret recipe?"

He clacked his tongs at her. "Marry me, Sylvie, and I'll give you all the secrets you like."

A great gust of girlish joy went through her. Immediately after it came shame and alarm. She should not be reacting to marriage talk with pleasure. She should be shutting it down. "You better not have meant that to be a proposal," she warned.

"It was a promise."

"Better," she conceded. "But not by much."

She watched his shoulders swell as he lifted the kettle's lid, turned each patty and scraped up the scraps. Billows of sweet, meaty steam rose around him. She thought she smelled something mushroomy. Worcestershire sauce, maybe. She plucked a pickle disc from the toppings platter and ate it, and Abie gave her another clack. "I saw that."

She drank some of her beer, which was already losing the refrigerator's cold. It was the kind of evening that fades rather than darkening, heat still hovering from midday. As he lifted the burgers from grill to plate, it occurred to her that she couldn't have fallen in love so quickly in the winter. In hot weather she was her truest, most exposed self.

Sylvie had already learned that meals with Abie never lasted long. He was a savagely fast eater. She did her best to keep up. Once their beers were empty, he rolled his shoulders, then stretched his arms overhead. "Want to go inside?" he asked. "Or should I go get some bug spray?"

"I want," she said, "to have exactly the same evening you would have if I weren't here."

"In that case." He stretched again, then stood. "Bear in mind that this is nothing compared to my feelings about the Washington Wizards, but since it's not basketball season yet, are you ready to commit emotionally to the Orioles?"

Sylvie allowed the nod to their future to go unacknowledged. She just told him that she and Corinne, her Baltimore roommate, had gone to Orioles games to drink beer in the cheap seats and rank the players in order of hotness. Now, she did her best to channel a real Marylander's extreme pride in their state but managed only mild engagement with the game. She was more interested in the texture of Abie's routine: the fact that he took his socks off, not seeming to notice that he did so, at precisely nine o'clock; the heap of *Nations* he read during commercials; the staggering amount of seltzer he consumed. Occasionally, instead of picking up his magazine during breaks from the game, he leaned over to kiss her, but each time, she found herself disinclined to return the kiss ardently enough to suggest sex. It wasn't quite that she didn't want to, though she did still feel scraped up from the night before; it was that stalling had an eros that she could only call romantic—didn't the romance novels of her young adulthood rely on delayed gratification?—but that she couldn't resist.

She hadn't bargained for the calming effects of closeness. Without really meaning to, she let herself settle into Abie's lap. She was fast asleep by the time the game ended. It had never been her plan to return to her apartment, but still, when he woke her for bed, she asked hazily, "You don't mind if I sleep here again?"

Abie brushed a piece of hair from her eyes. He'd turned the living-room lights out, and she had the sensation that the two of them were drifting through the dark together, tethered to the couch by gravity, but not to the earth. "Of course not," he said. "I won't mind anything until you leave."

3.

Sylvie had to teach the next day. It was even less than usual what she wanted to do. Her lesson was a good one—she'd given her students bits of Foucault's *The History of Sexuality* and planned a discussion about the coercive nature of fixed public identities—but the idea of concentrating on desire in the abstract was laughable. She regretted yesterday's decision not to have sex with Abie. It had been a capitulation to romance; to the idea that waiting was good, i.e., desirable, i.e., hot. Now she was both disappointed in herself and distracted by longing. She'd be levitating with impatience by the time he finished work that afternoon.

She considered texting him something slutty. Instead, she wrote to Nadia, *Consumed by dread of teaching. Hang out with me after my class?*

Nadia replied instantly. *In office with Salomé all day. Come by?* After a moment, she added, *We have snacks.*

Sylvie didn't want Salomé's snacks. She wanted nothing to do with her. Spitefully, she thought that if the department knew Dr. Rau was dangling the promise of sex in front of one of her supervisees, there would be no more Salomé. She'd be out on her ass. Back to France.

She knew this was wishful thinking. Not one of the professors in her department would act against another without undeniable proof of clearcut wrongdoing. She scowled at the prefab building in which she taught. Sun bounced from its white vinyl sides. On hot days, which was to say every day, it smelled like a mixture of Lysol and tires, with faint top notes of cold brew and student sweat. She would have liked to be anywhere else. If she had any sense, she would have ignored the paranoid little voice that had urged her to apply for summer classes. She would be reading in a lounger at the Upshur Street pool right now. It would be deserted at this hour. She'd have a bagful of books, cut fruit to snack on, maybe a kombucha or Coke. She would, in this alternate version of her summer, either never have met Abie or, having no excuse to return to Charlottesville, not pursued the romance she appeared to now be pursuing. Nadia was not the only person in their friendship who had turned into a complete and utter fool.

Oui madame, she texted. *Her treats better be good.*

Probably as a karmic reward for agreeing to subject herself to Dr. Rau, Sylvie had her best class of the summer so far. None of her students was too late or too hungover; all of them had done at least some of the reading. Several were genuinely excited by Foucault's arguments against jamming your sexuality into social norms, which was a relief to Sylvie. She'd worried that they would cling to the contemporary argument that any relationship that happened in private was dangerous and should, therefore, be avoided, but they gamely followed her—followed Foucault, rather—to the conclusion that leading a publicly sanctioned sex life could be more dangerous still.

One student, a former debate champion named Prabha whose attitude swung from disdain to fascination week to week, lingered afterward to tell Sylvie how much she'd liked the readings. "I mean, I read Foucault in high school," she added, twisting her rope of glossy hair around her hand.

"In debate. But only the stuff he wrote about prisons. It was super interesting, but not—" She dropped her gaze. "Maybe this is bad to say, but it's not exactly relevant to my life."

Sylvie permitted herself to smile. "One of my goals when I wrote the syllabus for this class was to choose assignments that students can use to reflect on their own lives, so I'm glad to hear that today's readings felt relevant." She slipped her teaching folder into her bag. "Though it's important to consider others' lives, too."

Prabha was looking at her again. It appeared that she expected something. Sylvie cocked her head and waited, and after a moment, the younger woman said, stumbling in her rush to get her words out, "None of my friends get that philosophy is useful."

Sylvie, who until this moment had never experienced affection for a student, wanted to hug her. Almost certainly that wouldn't be allowed. She said, "It isn't useful for everyone. For me, it is. And for you."

"I want them to get it." Prabha lowered her head again. "I'm so spoiled. I went to a school with a philosophy club. My dad teaches religion at Georgetown. Growing up, I thought this kind of conversation was normal."

"Prabha, that doesn't make you spoiled. It makes you lucky."

"Are your parents like my dad?"

"No. Not at all. But my grandfather was."

"Is the reason you want to teach so you can pass it along? You know, to people who didn't grow up this way?"

Sylvie found that she didn't want to lie. Any desire she had to pass Ilya's grandparenting along was not by teaching Foucault to undergrads, but by having a child of her own.

"It sounds to me," she said, "like you're considering teaching philosophy someday."

Prabha nodded. "I always told my dad I wasn't going to turn into him.

But now I guess I want to." She sighed. "All the girls in my sorority are psych majors. Or business."

"Gross," Sylvie said, and was rewarded with a quick but massive grin. If Prabha wanted to give evidence she was spoiled—this came from the department of Takes One to Know One—she should point not to the intellectual depth of her upbringing, but the orthodontic perfection of her teeth.

"I should go," Prabha said, straightening. "I'm meeting someone for lunch. But Professor Broder, it was really nice of you to talk to me."

"My pleasure," Sylvie said, truthfully.

She left for the real philosophy building imagining how she'd describe her encounter to Nadia, and then Abie, and then Robbie. Robbie, especially, would be proud if she said—which she thought was true—that she'd been, if only for a moment, a role model. Maybe she'd encourage Prabha to enroll in the Political Philosophy course for which she was a graduate assistant this fall. She could be Prabha's mentor.

Dr. Rau had her door open. Sylvie could hear her speaking rapidly in what she initially thought was French but then realized was French-inflected German. Nadia replied hesitantly, stumbling over a word that Dr. Rau then supplied. Sylvie tried to walk louder, shy about surprising them, but her Birkenstocks refused to do more than squeak faintly on the wooden floor. Abie, she had noticed, had a very heavy gait. It was part of his general volume. He moved in a whirlwind of loudness, like *Peanuts'* Pigpen in dust. Sylvie had given up the idea that he was a Greek god, but only because she now thought he was an incarnation of some pre-Judaic imp of noise.

She tapped on the door, then stuck her head in. Dr. Rau waved from her desk, which was positioned in front of the window so her pale hair was backlit and glowing. Nadia stood behind her, apparently looking at one of the professor's three—why three? Was she a day trader?—computer screens. Instead of the bookish disarray common to philosophy offices, the room was taken up mainly by a set of molded green plastic chairs, which could have been stacked but were not. A milk crate of books held the door open. Sylvie stepped past it and pulled up a chair.

"Hey, Sylvie," Nadia said. "Great timing. I need to speak English. My brain's fried."

"You need," Dr. Rau corrected, "to practice your German." She narrowed her pale eyes at Sylvie. "Maybe you should learn, too."

Lightly, Sylvie told her, "I don't see that happening."

"It would help your friend. And German is a good language in philosophy."

"Not the philosophy I do," Sylvie said.

Nadia put in, "She speaks French." She'd re-dyed her hair since Delaware, changing it to a slightly darker, more natural blond. Like Dr. Rau, she had on clogs, though the similarity was minor: the professor wore her usual fatigues and bone-white Danskos, spiritually distinct from Nadia's high-heeled, open-toed shoes and tailored cotton dress.

"I *read* French," Sylvie corrected quickly. She'd studied the language in high school and college, but never studied abroad—fear of separation from Jonah—or otherwise used it outside the classroom. Now she couldn't bear the thought of Dr. Rau sneering at her pronunciation, which was *exécrable*.

Dr. Rau ignored her, which was, somehow, more humiliating still. "But Nadia," she said. "Did you anticipate, three years ago, that German would help you?"

Nadia shook her head. "I was thinking in computer languages then."

Dr. Rau gave Sylvie a satisfied look. "See?"

Sylvie, primarily, did not see why the professor wasn't dropping the subject. It wasn't her business what languages Sylvie spoke. It occurred to her that if she were dealing with not a tenured academic but some shitty girlfriend Nadia had stumbled across in the wilds of Charlottesville, she would already have shut this discussion down, and that she would have been justified in doing so.

"My grandparents were in the camps," she said, giving Dr. Rau her meanest smile. "I'm not interested in learning German. Nadia said you had snacks?"

Nadia gave her a look that managed to contain both reproach and apology. She said, "Chips and pretzels in the filing cabinet, seltzer and fruit in the fridge." She pointed at a startlingly cute cherry-red Frigidaire.

"Help yourself," Dr. Rau added. She sounded neither chastened nor bothered. As Sylvie broke herself a branch of green grapes from a bag that took up half the tiny refrigerator, the professor asked, "Which camps?"

Before she could catch herself, Sylvie said, "Are you joking?"

Nadia, who was now sitting on the radiator, spoke at the same time. "Jesus Christ, Salomé. You can't—"

"I can be curious," Dr. Rau said sternly. "It happened closer to my home than either of yours. My region's Jewish inhabitants were removed early in the war. We were proclaimed Jew-free in 1940."

Sylvie's body ignited with anger. "Are you *proud* of that?"

"Of course not." Dr. Rau shrugged. "But it's true."

Nadia cleared her throat but said nothing. Sylvie wanted to shake her. Silently, she said, Help me! Aloud, she informed the professor, "What happened to my family is my business."

"Certainly. But you brought it up."

"I did."

"I assumed that meant it didn't belong to your private sphere."

Again, Sylvie looked at Nadia, who said, in a tightly controlled voice, "I talk to Salomé about your work sometimes."

Dr. Rau nodded. "It's very interesting. But I suppose it's also your business?"

Sylvie recognized that she was meant to lose her temper, which made her wonder if Dr. Rau had been baiting—*Jew*-baiting—her all along. Maybe she was an antisemite. The thought came with a shock of nasty glee. If Dr. Rau hated Jews, then she was Sylvie's enemy and, by extension, Nadia's.

"I'm happy to talk about my dissertation," she said, impressing herself with the steadiness of her tone. "Or you could ask me how the class I just taught went."

Dr. Rau put the tip of her tongue between her teeth. "How was your class?"

"It was great, actually. Very strong discussion. One of my students told me afterward that she wants to major in philosophy."

"I hope you told her not to."

"Why?"

"We're busy." Dr. Rau looped her hand in the air, lassoing Sylvie and Nadia into her *we*. "We have real work, and I would prefer that we had no undergraduate majors to take us away from it. When they're interested, they get needy. They want their hands held. It can be very distracting."

"So can life," Sylvie said.

"Yes," the professor agreed. "For example, you can get distracted by men."

Sylvie twisted to glare at Nadia, who widened her eyes and shook her head. Smoothly, Dr. Rau continued, "It already happened to me this summer. I should have known better. You agree, Nadia?"

Nadia's expression had gone from panicked to miserable. Instead of shaking her, Sylvie now wanted to rescue her. She wanted, more immediately, to hurt Dr. Rau. She could sense the energy reaching from supervisor to supervisee, the cords of desire and authority that kept Nadia from telling the professor to go fuck herself all the way back to France. It was profoundly unsettling to witness, worse still to be drawn into. Sylvie refused to let either go on.

She stood, smoothing her dress over her thighs. "You know what?" she said, allowing hostility to shine through each word. "I'm not enjoying this visit, and I have a lot of work to do. Nadia, text me later, okay? It's time for me to go."

4.

Over dinner—take-out sushi this time, again eaten in Abie's yard—Sylvie told Abie the saga of Dr. Rau, beginning with Nadia's academic fascination and ending with that afternoon's conversation, which she relayed in much more detail than she would have to Robbie. In Robbie's life, antisemitism was an abstraction. Not in Abie's. He'd grown up with it and had driven to Charlottesville from Richmond, where he lived at the time, to counterprotest Unite the Right. He could tell Sylvie whether Dr. Rau was an antisemite or just a bitch.

He writhed in his chair as he listened, yanking at his hair and beard with steadily building ire. "What a monster," he said when she finished.

Sylvie lifted a tuna roll with her chopsticks. "I know."

"Sounds to me like it wasn't about you being Jewish so much as her being on a giant power trip."

"Or both."

"You've taken classes with her, right?"

"Just one."

"Still." Abie ate a piece of pickled ginger with his fingers. "I had a data-science professor in college who had some strange ideas about Jews, and I found out fast."

"You took *data* science?"

He grinned. "You don't know everything about me yet, Sylvie."

"Why?"

"Because we only met in May. I'm simple, but not *that* simple."

She rolled her eyes, laughing. "I meant why data science. Doesn't seem relevant to the Civil War."

"It's not. I just wanted to do something hard. But back to Dr. Rau. Has Nadia always been susceptible to people like her?"

It took Sylvie an instant to focus herself on the question. She was too busy thinking—unfairly; unkindly—that Robbie would never have chosen a course just for the challenge.

"Nadia never used to be susceptible to anyone," she said. "We used to pick men up together every weekend."

Abie made a face. "So how come it took you so long to get to me?"

Because of Robbie, the turtle informed Sylvie. And you should say so.

Instead, she said lightly, "I could ask you the same."

Abie took an eel nigiri and ate it, looking reflective. A fat little bird wobbled by. Sylvie glanced at the row of potted tomatoes by the fence, green fruit drooping from each plant. She wished she had any doubt about whether she would be here to eat them as they ripened, make sauce if there were extras, go to the nursery for their autumnal replacements.

Her turtle snorted. You're going to garden?

Why shouldn't I?

You've never wanted a garden in your life.

How could I? I've never had a yard.

Or a houseplant.

Jonah hated houseplants, she pointed out.

You haven't lived with Jonah in eight years.

My apartment gets shitty light. Anyway, gardening runs in the family. Ilya grew all those peppers.

You, said the turtle, don't want peppers. You want *roots*.

Go away, she said, which was tantamount to conceding. If he was wrong, it was only in that he hadn't specified. She wanted to root herself to Abie. It was absurd to feel this much certainty about a person so new to her life, but her sureness came from the stillest, quietest inner part of her, the part that needed not to be bolstered or comforted, but seen.

"I wasn't ready for you," Abie said, wiping eel sauce from his beard. His answer took Sylvie by surprise, and not only because she'd forgotten she'd asked him a question.

"You gave me a whole speech Monday night about how ready you are."

"Feels like a long time ago," he said, smiling at her.

Sylvie laughed in recognition. "I know."

"So long you forgot what I said."

"I did?"

"I wasn't talking about being *ready*. I was talking about being *available*."

"What's the difference?" she asked, and then, realizing how likely it was that his answer would involve Robbie, amended, "For you, I mean."

He tugged at his shirt, which was brightly tie-dyed and bore the image of a large, delighted-looking snail. Never had she met a man who was so aesthetically and spiritually coherent. It was, if she set aside her opinions on tie-dye, one of his many appeals.

"If I had met you a year ago," Abie said, "I wouldn't have been patient enough. I would have seen all the caution tape wrapped around you and I would have run for my life."

"So you lost all your common sense in the past year?"

Abie snorted. "Maybe."

"Seriously, though. What happened?"

"Who knows?" He shook his head. "Actually, forget what I just said. I wasn't ready the day before I met you. I'm probably not ready now. But I never met someone I want to talk to as much as you. I never met someone

I *want* as much as you." He met her eyes. "Though I'm finding you very hard to get."

Sylvie found that she had no choice but to abandon the remainder of her sushi. No reaction was plausible except getting up, kissing Abie with the fervor of a sixteen-year-old, and marching him indoors and upstairs.

In his bedroom, she backed him against a wall and knelt, accepting the shocks of knee bone on hard wooden floor—a more than worthwhile trade for the pleasure of taking control of a man who, so far, had only taken control of her. She liked that she got to choose.

Abie groaned like an ox. He dug his hand into not only her hair, but her scalp. When she moved the hand she'd had planted on his stomach to the flat spot behind his balls, he sank a full two inches lower on the wall. She'd never had an effect like that on Robbie. He never even let her go down on him.

Once her jaw began losing its feeling, Abie lifted her to her feet, then tossed her onto the bed. He moved her between positions with the rough confidence of an athlete tossing balls through a net. It was a shocking pleasure to have her limbs arranged for her, to know Abie had her leg hooked back precisely the right amount for him. For her, any angle would be right. She was completely open. It was almost like having no body at all.

Neither of them moved for a long time afterwards, barring Sylvie's requisite trip to pee. She curled against him as he asked, "You go back to DC on Friday?"

"I do."

"Are you teaching tomorrow?"

Her heart rose in her throat. "No."

"In that case," he said cheerily, "I have a feeling I'm going to be sick in the morning."

Sylvie had a sudden, bad impulse to ask why. He shouldn't be so endlessly interested in spending time with her; shouldn't be so confident that he wanted her. Surely it wasn't normal. It wasn't normal for either of them to feel as if Monday night's dinner was two life stages ago, not two days.

"I could have food poisoning," he continued. "Very messy and debilitating. No way I can go into work."

"What are you going to do instead?"

He ran his hand along her shoulder. "Mainly this."

Sylvie sat up in bed. "Are you sure?"

Abie raised himself on one elbow, looking baffled. "Unless you don't want me to."

"No," she said quickly. "I do."

"But?"

She gulped back the answer, which was that the more time he had her, the more he'd get used to her. He would hate it more every time she left for DC, and one day, he wouldn't let her go.

She looked at his big features, which had so recently struck her as merely appealing. Now she found him unbearably handsome. She remembered her grandmother rearranging a display of bright Hellerware mugs in her store and talking about how when she met Ilya, she'd thought he was the best-looking man alive, even though he was malnourished and had—Sylvie remembered both this phrase and the cackle that came on its heels—"ears like an elephant mixed with a bat."

As an old man, Ilya still had tremendous ears, with drooping, wrinkled lobes and significant bristles. His face was sharp and leathery, not unlike that of Sylvie's turtle. Abie, when he was Ilya's age, would be jowly rather than beaky. Instead of smelling like Dr. Bronner's and library air, he'd have some old-man mix of peppermints, soup, and outdated aftershave. Probably he would have terrible hair, a prickly mustache. He would look like a walrus. It was a thought more tender than Sylvie could stand.

Since their hike—only eleven days ago, somehow—he had told her he loved her over and over. She hadn't said it back. Now she put her head on his shoulder. "I love you."

Abie pulled her closer. He rubbed his beard against her cheek so it scratched and said, in the warm murmur of real contentment, "So you do want me to call in sick tomorrow?"

"I do," she told him, and then, without meaning to, she added the very sentence she longed to hear from him, the one she feared a thousand times more than the one she'd just said. "I want you to stay here with me."

Chapter Six

1.

As summer wound down, Sylvie's fantasy life began threatening to take over her real one. When she was with Robbie, she imagined that she could, somehow, shield him from knowledge of her betrayal forever. When she was with Abie, she imagined that she could do so while also moving into his house. She'd come to see Abie's little bungalow as a magical location, to treat its cracked red-and-white kitchen tile and cactus graveyard as talismans of personal abandon. Not once had she and Abie had sex in her apartment. He hadn't even seen it. She didn't want him to.

She was aware that it was an awful idea to move in with Abie. It would ruin what remained of her independence. It would also be unconscionable. Bad enough that Robbie still didn't know she was sleeping with Abie. *Living* with him would be orders of magnitude worse.

And yet, in August, she began rearranging her teaching schedule. She'd set it up so she could split her time equally between her homes. Now, after elaborate maneuvering, she managed to trade a section with her enemy Eddie Newell, which meant she'd have to attend or lead a class every day but Wednesday. She'd come to campus on Monday mornings, leave on Friday nights. When she received the email locking in this new schedule, her immediate reaction was sorrow about the time she'd miss with Robbie. It was an absurd emotion, but recognizing its ridiculousness wasn't enough to banish it.

She was walking to Abie's, but she still called Robbie to tell him. He accepted the change without complaint. "I've been working till ten all the time," he said. "It makes sense for you to be there."

"I know," Sylvie said. "But—"

"No *but*." He laughed softly. "Remember when you freed me from guilt in the Food Lion?"

"I do."

"Now I free you."

Sylvie had to stop moving. She waited for Hades to rise from the earth and take her to hell. When he failed to, she texted Nadia, who also didn't yet know about Abie, a screenshot of her new schedule. *So much time for us to hang out*, she wrote.

In other moments of their friendship, such a message would trigger an immediate, shrieking call, celebration mixed with demands to know whether there was a man involved in this decision. But since the concentration-camp conversation, which Nadia refused to discuss, she'd been remote. She replied only, *That's great*.

"Fuck you," Sylvie said to the phone, and shoved it into her track shorts. She couldn't get agitated about Nadia now. Her sadness was waning already, ceding ground to an excitement that, if she wasn't careful, would lead her to suggest moving in with Abie the moment she got done telling him about her schedule.

In general, Sylvie had no control over what she said to Abie. Her habits of forethought and self-management, learned in the Jonah years, had utterly vanished. She told him she loved him more often than seemed conceivable for Carol and Paul Broder's daughter. Often she thought that her emotions traveled directly into her mouth in Abie's presence, not doing her brain the courtesy of stopping by. But this time, she restrained herself. She sat with Abie in his horrible Adirondack chairs and described her teaching schedule without saying a thing about giving up her studio. Doing so was not easy, which made her feel at once immature and accomplished. After all, chasing what she wanted had saved her from Jonah. If she were better at ignoring her wishes, she would be suicidal in Swampscott right now.

Her mixed emotions were not enough to distract her from Abie's alarmingly muted reaction. While she talked, he was silent, and when she got done, he just slid his jaw to the side, then took a conspicuously long drink of his seltzer.

A mosquito landed on Sylvie's wrist. She shook it off rather than kill it, which she knew was an error. As lightly as she could, she asked, "Something wrong?"

Abie lifted his face as if examining the darkening sky. It was one of the last true long summer nights of the year. Crickets sang in the gutters. On the university's nearby fields and front yards, undergrads in town early would be reuniting, hugging and roaring, setting up outdoor tables to play drinking games under the campus cops' protectively averted gazes. Nadia would be sitting on her miniature balcony, smoking a joint—Sylvie hoped—and considering computers, or God, or love. Eddie Newell would be hunched in his apartment with the windows closed, air-conditioning blasting. It was among Sylvie's beliefs that uptight people couldn't enjoy summer heat.

"Okay," Abie said. He sounded like half his voice was trapped in his throat. "What I want to say is going to scare you."

Obediently, Sylvie's muscles tightened. She made herself nod. "Go ahead."

"Promise me you won't just shut down."

"I promise to do my best, but you have to stop with the lead-up."

"Fair." He looked into the grass between his feet. "When does your lease end?"

Sylvie choked back a laugh—of panic? Triumph? Relief that Abie had lost his mind, too? She said, "It's month-to-month."

"So make this your last month." He scooted his chair closer. "Move in with me."

Instinctively, she pushed her chair back. Victory and terror ran through her as one. She felt like a child whose dream of becoming a rodeo cowboy or getting beamed up by aliens had come true. It was a deep and cherished yearning, and yet she was not only frightened and overwhelmed but unprepared.

"It's only been nine weeks," she said. "Not even."

Abie looked pleased. "You're counting?"

She hadn't known that she was. "I guess."

"Are you counting how many weeks since you went to your apartment?"

It had been six. On her last visit, she had packed up clothes and books to bring to Abie's, drawn the shower curtain to conceal from herself the mold that had marched through the tub, and unplugged the empty fridge to save money. She had disconnected the window air-conditioner. It was probably ninety degrees in there. She did not dream of going back.

"My rent is so cheap," she said.

"Mine, too."

"You don't have any room. I need to set up my desk. My books—I have a whole dissertation's worth of books. I don't want to keep them in a library carrel."

"So we'll rearrange."

"And I need time to work. *Quiet* time."

"I do have a job, Sylvie." He sounded more confident with every objection she posed. "I'm not some kind of house gremlin. I leave every day."

"Okay, but how about when you come home? I don't *go* to work—I mean, not always—but I work. I won't clean or cook during the day. Or at all. I pick up after myself, but I'm not doing chores for a man."

"I didn't ask you to."

When Sylvie had decided to live half-time with Robbie, she hadn't worried that the dynamic of her marriage would reappear—though, to some extent, it had, with Sylvie in the Jonah role. Until now, she'd felt she had every right. Now she was less sure. She was unsure, too, about how fair or reasonable it was to be afraid of Abie turning into a Jonah, given that she had no evidence for her fear except that he was a man. She wanted to think she wasn't a misandrist, but maybe she was lying to herself when she said her skittishness about men was, really, skittishness about romance. Maybe some piece of her believed the very argument she tried so hard to reject: that all women were victims waiting to happen, which, if you generalized one step further, meant all men were predators. Robbie had warned her she thought that. He'd told her—had shouted at her, or the closest he ever came to shouting—to stop acting like all men were the same.

"You're thinking about Robbie," Abie said. "I can tell from your eyes."

"I don't want to talk about him with you."

Abie nodded. Sylvie suddenly felt very close to tears. She wanted to live here so badly. She wanted the morning glories on the fence, the drift of junk mail at the front door. She wanted the grill and the garden. She wanted, against every single shred of her better judgment, to do domesticity with Abie, to let him seduce her into his future.

"I hate these chairs," she said. Her own voice echoed in her head, telling Robbie to get wallpaper. Evidently the need to redecorate wasn't their dynamic, but a part of Sylvie's psychology.

"You do?"

"It hurts my abs to get up from them. And my hips. I hate how my thighs go through the slats. And who has a back shaped like this?" She rapped on the chair. "Nobody. No woman. Female spines—you may not have noticed—have curves."

Abie's mouth vanished into his beard. "So if I get ergonomically correct lawn furniture, you'll move in with me?"

"Yes," Sylvie said. "I will."

2.

Sylvie told Abie she'd move the Wednesday after Labor Day. She told herself she absolutely had to tell Robbie first. Driving to DC the Friday before, she ordered herself every ten minutes to come clean on arrival—but when she got to the condo, she found it full of stacking chairs, like Dr. Rau's office. An enormous olive cooler, far bigger than the one they'd brought to Delaware, squatted in the kitchen. "Are you tailgating something?" she asked when Robbie came home.

"I invited people over." He peeled his dress shirt, sweaty after the walk from the Metro, over his head.

"Here?"

Robbie jerked his head upward. "You know there are grills on the roof." Sylvie did know. He'd grilled for her plenty of times. Before she could say so, he added, "You can reserve them, so I booked Sunday night."

Sylvie was stunned. In another moment, she would have objected. She might have gotten angry, even, about having Robbie's friends sprung on her in this way. She'd agreed that he could tell them about her, not signed up to meet them. But what was she going to do, launch into negotiations now? She'd meant to admit to a colossal betrayal this very evening. She had no right to protest. In fact, she was grateful to him for the party. It had bought her—bought *them*—more time.

"Who's coming?" she asked.

"Mainly work friends. Some law school, some Michigan."

"You never said you had Michigan friends here."

Robbie sat on the couch beside her. Neutrally, he said, "You're not interested in my friends."

Sylvie thought of the fight they'd had about Nadia, how his resentment had seemed to erupt out of nowhere. "How long have you wanted me to meet them?"

He ran a palm over his head. "A while."

"Why didn't you tell me?"

"I thought you'd say no."

"So you decided to spring them on me."

He huffed out a minor laugh. "Right."

"You know," Sylvie said, "when you asked me to go to Christmas, I said yes."

"I remember."

"I'm not an absolutist."

Robbie twisted to face her. "Yeah, but you want to be."

Again, Sylvie recognized that under any other conditions, she would have gotten angry, and that Robbie knew it. He was visibly bracing himself. She reached for his hand. When she touched it, a small spark of desire bounced through her. So many of her theories were in shambles now, but it proved at least some of her philosophy right that falling in love with Abie had not, after the first wave of confusion and alienation, decreased her attraction to Robbie. Nor had it stopped her from wanting to reciprocate at least some of his care.

Softly, she said, "I do. And I'm sorry. I know you aren't going to get sucked into other people's expectations."

"I appreciate that."

"I should've offered to meet your friends sooner."

Robbie smiled. "You won't like them, anyway."

"None?"

"Maybe one or two." He leaned over to kiss her, the kind of kiss that meant not sex or even affection, but a definitive change in mood. "I'll brief you on them over dinner. Just let me change, and we can go."

Sylvie spent Saturday and Sunday morning helping Robbie prepare for the party. She joined him on his trips to the liquor store and nice butcher, helped him lug all the chairs—borrowed from a coworker, he said—up to the roof. She promised not to laugh when the Covington & Burling crew called him Rob, not Robbie, a change she'd been unaware of until this moment. She weighed in on his playlist, which contained an unacceptable amount of yacht rock. She took a long shower, then put on silk pants rather than wear one of the soft linen dresses she'd rotated all summer. It occurred to her that, with the exception of their first official date, she had never dressed up for Abie. She'd never had the impulse.

Her silk pants were wasted on the lawyers. None of them had any glamour, though every single one could have afforded to. If she earned their salary, she'd wear head-to-toe luxury vintage. She'd be showing up to teach in Burberry blazers and striped Sonia Rykiel knit sets, not thrift-store trousers and sweater dresses from Ann Taylor Loft. Every outfit she put on would make her dead grandmother proud.

She would have minded the lawyers' dull aesthetic less if she hadn't found it almost impossible, existentially speaking, to tell them apart. Behind every face lurked the same brain. At first, she asked questions in a secretly unkind spirit, the way she sometimes did with her classmates. A person could get a real superiority high listening to Eddie Newell rattling off proofs that A is equal to A, or to these lawyers debating constitutional minutiae in their summer outfits, making even the question of how Trump could be impeached dull.

Sylvie knew she could wield their tediousness against Robbie. She could say it made him see him differently. Doing so would be intensely hurtful. It would be a great starting point for a breakup.

But that wasn't what she wanted. At the party, she felt her attachment to Robbie keenly. Every time she glanced his way, a beam of warmth reached between them. It made her proud to see him host, to watch others soak up the qualities she loved in him. He'd made kebabs, gotten Italian sausages and half-smokes and veggie dogs, packed his huge new cooler with seltzer, canned rosé, alcoholic and NA beer. Little bowls of Doritos rested on every available surface. All the lawyers shone with satiation.

She imagined, while nodding along to an anecdote concerning a case against the nation of Georgia, how Abie's parties would be. Loud and raucous, like he was. Good food, but not in an organized way. He wouldn't be the host so much as the chief celebrant. His fun would be central. Robbie's was not, and yet it was plain to Sylvie that he was having a good time. He moved as easily as if he were in water. Not once did she see him eating, and yet he didn't leave the grill until nearly 10:00.

By midnight, when the party ended, she had determined with the aid of four cans of wine that Robbie was the Happy Medium. He was not by nature a joyful person, but he had attained and nurtured a contentment he could transmit to others. He was unselfish but not self-abnegating. He wasn't intellectually unusual like Nadia or a moral compass come to life like Abie, but his level of human understanding was so high it was often shocking.

Sylvie wished she could have Robbie interpret the new problem of her life. In less than three years, she'd gone from shunning all romance to holding on to two men at once. She knew that, as Rejected Shrink #3 had said, some back corner of her heart held on to Jonah, too.

She was sitting on a stool in the kitchen, drinking a small and unnecessary glass of the Hibiki whiskey one of the lawyers had brought. Robbie was asleep. When she joined him in bed, no matter how long she waited, he would wake enough to fold himself around her and kiss the back of her neck. He did it every night she was here.

Sylvie thought of that kiss now with a shock of anticipatory loss. It seemed to her that she would do almost anything not to give it up. She loved Robbie so much. It broke her heart to recognize that he wasn't the one she loved most. Alone in the home she'd made them, it still seemed to her that he could be; that, if she just hung on long enough without telling him, her emotions would return to the correct scale and location and she would choose him; but it wasn't true. She would choose Abie. She *had* chosen him. All that was left was to make herself let Robbie go.

3.

On Monday, Sylvie arrived in Charlottesville drained and shaky. She'd woken with a hangover headache that, during her drive, descended to her chest and transformed into anxiety. It didn't help that Jonah had sent another email that morning, not even two months after the *I miss you* he'd sent after the Fourth of July. Sylvie did not like the narrow gap between messages. Nor did she like that this one read only, *Hope the school year gets off to a good start.* Jonah shouldn't know school was relevant to her. Maybe it was a lucky guess.

But more frightening than Jonah's email was her imminent dinner with Nadia. In order to force her own hand, she'd told her friend she had some confessions to make, and Nadia, in reply, had said she had some subjects of her own to discuss. Presumably it would be a long meal. It would be smart to get some packing done beforehand. Instead, Sylvie went to see Abie. He was waiting on the front steps. He'd tied balloons to the mailbox. Sun sparked through her as she ran from the car. Inside, he demanded that she look at all the drawers and bookshelves he'd emptied for her even before they had sex. By the time she headed to dinner, her fear was subsumed in excitement. She wanted Abie, and she had him. No matter how thoroughly she had fucked her life up, she couldn't help but be happy here.

If she had been calmer, she would, perhaps, have softened her approach to Nadia. As it was, she barely tempered her announcement at all. Over baba ghanoush and cigar-shaped börek, she began, "I'm moving out of my apartment."

"Good. You're probably dying already from all the mold in there."

"Probably."

"Do you need help house-hunting?" Nadia bit into a börek, which released a fat string of melted cheese. "Is September your last month?"

"August was. Today's my last day. And I don't need to house-hunt. I'm moving in with a guy."

Nadia's eyes emptied. She uncoiled her spine like a snake rising from its basket. "You mean," she said, with great dignity, "the guy you've been seeing all summer and not telling me about." Sylvie's mouth dropped open. Nadia jabbed her index finger in the air. "I *knew* it."

"How?"

"Oh, let's see. Not mentioning Wyatt; changing your teaching schedule; having a sex glow—"

"Having a *sex glow*?" Sylvie repeated, loud enough that the women at the table to their right turned to stare.

"You should see yourself, Sylvie." Nadia softened. "You look so good. It makes me jealous, really. I haven't slept with anyone since the beginning of—" She waved a hand in the air. "You know."

Sylvie reached for her wine. A soft thrum of relief began to move through her. What could be better, now that Nadia was descending from her anger, than telling her about Abie? And besides, how could Nadia hold a couple months of secrecy against her? She'd concealed the Dr. Rau situation much longer than that.

Evidently, Nadia had reached the same conclusion. "I'm sorry," she said. "I'm being a hypocrite. You didn't get pissed at me when I told you about Salomé."

"It's okay. I came in pretty hot."

Nadia considered her half-eaten börek, but didn't pick it back up. "I'm going to say something mean."

"All right."

"Since I fell in love with Salomé, I've thought you were so much tougher than me. Not tougher. *Stronger.* I can't tell you how much I've beaten myself up for not knowing how to control myself—control my feelings—like you. It makes me feel better that you can't do it, either."

"We're going to talk about Salomé," Sylvie said. She made her tone gentle, though she knew she was issuing a bit of a threat.

"We can come back to her. I want to hear about your secret man."

"His name's Abie Abraham."

"No, it's not."

Sylvie laughed. "It suits him. You'll see."

"Has he met Robbie?"

"No."

"But Robbie's cool with you living with him?"

Sylvie's face burned. She lowered her eyes. "Not exactly."

"Does Robbie *know*?"

She shook her head. "I haven't told him," she said quietly.

For a moment, Nadia was silent. Sylvie thought of her command, in Delaware, not to hurt Robbie. Before she looked up, she braced herself to see anger on her friend's face, disappointment, maybe even contempt. What she saw instead was grief.

"You made the rules," Nadia said. "Why are you breaking them?"

"Because I'm scared."

"You always say that."

"It's true."

"It's not good enough."

"I didn't say it was."

"Sylvie, you came up with an entire *philosophy* about Robbie."

"*With* Robbie."

Nadia ignored her. "I thought you meant it."

"So did I!" Sylvie's hands shot involuntarily up. "I thought we had the love of the future. I thought I was safe. I wasn't *planning* to have both my dissertation and my life fall apart."

Nadia shook her head. "Idiot," she muttered. Sylvie wasn't certain which of them she was talking to. Before she could ask, or apologize, their waiter appeared with a long tray of grilled eggplant, peppers, and lamb between them. Nadia eyed it. "I'm mad at you," she said. "But I'm starving."

"So eat."

"I told Salomé I'd be pescatarian."

"Why?"

Nadia reached for a charred cube of meat. "She wants me to."

Sylvie's body loosened slightly. She considered turning the conversation toward Dr. Rau, but that, in this moment, would be cowardly. Instead, she said, "Abie wants me to marry him."

Nadia coughed through her lamb. "Ex*cuse* me?"

"Not legally, necessarily, but he's got a whole dream life. He wants to live in Richmond because his family's all there, get a bunch of dogs and have a bunch of babies. And he wants"—she heard the scare quotes in her voice—"not to share."

"As in, he wants monogamy."

"A closed relationship," Sylvie agreed.

Nadia's mouth twitched. "Can't blame him," she said. "It turns out that's what I want, too."

Sylvie set her fork down. "With *her?*"

"Look," Nadia said. "Nothing's changed. She still says we have to keep it professional until I graduate. But now she's dating some guy—the guy she mentioned when you came to her office—to pass the time, and I don't see why she tells me about him."

"'Tells' as in—"

"She gives me updates. All the time. If she isn't serious about him, then don't you think she could have just not said?"

"Did she give you a reason?"

"For the guy? Or for telling?"

"Second one."

"She wants us to be truthful with each other." Nadia gave a small laugh. "I was going to ask if you think that's right."

Sylvie said nothing. She couldn't tell whether she was invited to answer. After a moment, Nadia told her softly, "If I were a better person, I'd make you call Robbie and tell him now."

"But?"

"But I feel for him. I know what hearing the truth will be like for him. And he *needs* to know it. I don't. I keep asking Salomé not to be transparent with me, and she refuses, and I don't see the point."

"It sounds like she's telling you to upset you," Sylvie said, "and upsetting you gives her power."

Nadia scowled. "She's not Machiavelli."

"She's letting you be in love with her." Sylvie gripped her elbows. "She's giving you hope, but not much else."

"Just like you're doing to Robbie."

Without meaning to, Sylvie dug her nails into her skin. "So why did you want to ask my opinion?"

"Because until ten minutes ago, I thought you'd invented the next stage of romance."

Sylvie commanded herself not to cry. Of all the friends she had failed in her life, she had never let somebody down as suddenly and conclusively as she had Nadia tonight.

"And," Nadia added, "because you're my best friend."

It was a tremendous kindness. Sylvie had to hide her face in her napkin. She could hear her mother telling her what awful manners that was.

When she was ready to talk again, she said, "I owe Robbie the truth."

"Correct."

"But that's about me and Robbie. It's not about the nature of the truth. I don't believe, necessarily, that you're always obligated to tell the whole truth. I believe everyone has an individual right to privacy, and that, in a relationship, you negotiate what that right looks like. It sounds like Salomé isn't letting you negotiate."

"No," Nadia said. "She's not."

"Jonah always demanded that I tell him where I was and what I was doing," Sylvie went on. "It's a form of vigilance."

"But Salomé's not doing that. She's the one telling *me*."

"And she doesn't expect reciprocity?"

Nadia was quiet for long enough that Sylvie said, "I know it sounds good to have complete transparency with your partner. But the *reason* it sounds good is that it comes from—it's one of—the bad old standards of romance we've been taught. Really, I think it's about ownership. In both directions, right? If I say you have to tell me everything and you do it, I'm exerting control, but the same is true if I say I have to tell you everything."

Nadia was nodding. "Unless it's consensual."

"Right."

"But agreeing to tell didn't work out so great for you and Robbie."

Sylvie looked down. "No."

"Poor Robbie," Nadia said. "And poor you."

"Poor you, too."

"We're both messes."

"Wait till you see my apartment."

Emotion hovered between them. Sylvie was close to more tears. Never before had she watched a friend forgive her. It was conceivable that none of her former friends really had.

"I'm sorry, Nadia," she said. "I'm not a very good romance philosopher."

"Not yet. But you will be."

"I hope so."

"You will be," Nadia repeated. She was visibly collecting herself. She'd gone far beyond her usual capacity to discuss her own feelings. "But speaking of your apartment, I do need you to get me up to speed on this Abie person. If I'm helping you move tomorrow, I want to go in fully briefed."

4.

Sylvie slept in her studio that night. She was too exhausted from her dinner with Nadia to see Abie. Besides, some part of her wanted to say goodbye, though it was hard to be sentimental in—or about—an apartment that hadn't been air-conditioned for an entire Charlottesville August. She sweated all night and woke at 6:45 feeling desiccated and afraid. Lying on her back, she considered the potential futures before her. By 7:00, she was stuffing her sheets into bags.

Nadia showed up half an hour later with iced coffees and every suitcase and tote bag she owned. Abie appeared on her heels. He had a box of doughnuts and a look of total glee. At first, Sylvie was amused by the visual contrast between Nadia, who wore a matching navy workout set and a wisp-free bun, and Abie, who had on a hole-riddled Willie Nelson shirt and hibiscus-patterned shorts sprouting strings at the hems.

"It's great to meet you," he told Nadia. "Your friend's been living in a shithole."

"I know," Nadia said smugly. "I've been saying so for years."

"I wondered why you never invited me over," he continued, turning to Sylvie. "Now I know."

"It was less depressing when I spent more time here," Sylvie said.

Nadia shook her head. "You just noticed it less."

Sylvie pulled up a kitchen stool and took a cinnamon-sugar doughnut from the box. She had no real desire to defend her apartment. She would be happy to leave it behind. Still, she was surprised by how little time emptying it took. She'd moved more of her clothes and books than she realized over the course of the summer. Her furniture, which had been worthless when she acquired it, went on the curb to be scavenged by undergrads. Ditto her two scratched pots, her misshapen frying pan, her bare-bulb lamp. Aside from the bougainvillea painting, she kept only her dishes, her linens, and the antique-mall Fiestaware she was proud of. It was a load so light that they were at Abie's by noon. He put on a Hold Steady record and sang along, roaring lyrics about minor Minneapolis landmarks as he hauled bags of clothes upstairs.

"I told you he was loud," Sylvie said to Nadia.

Nadia shrugged. "He's got character." After a moment, she added, "I feel guilty saying this, but I think he makes the right amount of noise for you."

Sylvie knew, by now, that Abie's excessiveness went hand in hand with his magnetism. Part of what drew her to him was the sense that he'd been designed on a bigger existential scale. Still, she said, "How so?"

"He's big and loud, but he doesn't make you quiet. You were singing in the car. You never sing."

"So you're saying he makes me louder?"

"In a nice way."

"I had no idea."

"How could you?" Nadia gave her a mischievous smile. "You need me to notice these things."

After Nadia had left, Sylvie relayed the exchange to Abie, omitting the tacit comparison to Robbie. He was delighted. "She's got character, too."

"She's a genius."

"I wouldn't expect your best friend to be anything else."

She nestled into his side and surveyed the living room. In her imagination, the day had ended with clutter and chaos, but in fact she had brought so little that the house looked close to ordinary. Her books, unboxed but not shelved, sat in towers by the radiator. Her bougainvillea painting was already on the wall. Her quilt, another antique-mall score, was draped over the Eames chair, where she intended to leave it, though Abie already had legions of downstairs blankets. What he lacked was couch pillows, but she had brought a pair of ochre linen ones that had formerly lived—since she'd had no couch—on her bed, and she thought they blended in well.

She was very tired. Her apprehension and happiness registered only as a pair of dull aches. She had no interest in further conversation. Instead, she tugged Abie sideways on the couch and initiated some slow, drifty fooling around, descending to a pace neither had been calm enough for previously. It was both disappointing and restful not to be frantic, to be submerged in the experience but not pinned to it. Still, she had the sense that this, too, was truthful sex; sex she could float around at will, constrained by exhaustion rather than her absolute need for Abie. It was the sex she imagined having with him after they had children.

Once she'd returned from the bathroom, Abie said, "I told myself we weren't going to do that tonight."

"Because we'd be tired?"

"No." He sat up. "*I* wasn't going to. I was going to make us have a conversation." She could feel him straining.

"About?"

He scowled. "About you telling your boyfriend about me."

Sylvie sat up, too. She waited for her pulse to speed, but her body was still calm from sex. "You're my boyfriend," she said.

"Don't do that."

"I'm sorry." She touched his leg. Empathy welled in her, as if she weren't the one causing him pain. "I just need you to let me go slow. Slow for you, I mean. Fast for me."

"Depends what direction you're going."

"Here."

He met her eyes. "Is that a promise?"

"I moved in, didn't I?"

Abie shook his head. "Syl, I need to hear you say it."

"I'm going to tell Robbie. I promise. I'm going to break up with him. I love you too much not to."

As she spoke, she saw the tension drain from his body. "I don't know why I believe you."

Now something in her chest skittered. "But you do?"

He nodded. "God help me," he said. "I do."

Chapter Seven

1.

Creating a life together took Sylvie and Abie no time at all. It was worryingly easy. Agonizingly easy, from a Robbie standpoint. She and Abie had the garden she'd imagined. She stopped her workday when he got home so she could sit in the kitchen while he cooked. She'd begun reading her way through his shelf of John le Carré novels, starting, at Abie's insistence, with le Carré's first book, *Call for the Dead*. She was learning to tune out the squeaking sounds of basketball games.

Living with Abie did not change the sex they had in the slightest. She wanted him in a way that felt less like desire than surrender. Sometimes she fantasized about cracking her sternum open, yanking out a lung, and giving it to him to keep. For the first time in her adulthood, her orgasms sometimes arrived not only without effort, but without warning: no tensing, no trembling, just some especially ragged breathing and a sudden flood. Abie tended to save his own orgasms for last and to look straight into her face when he came, which gave her a feeling so hot and shaky she could barely stand it. She often cried afterward, out of not sadness or happiness but the sheer shock of returning to herself.

It would be absurd to give up a man who had that effect on her. Her problem was that she seemed incapable of confessing to Robbie. She swore every Friday that she was going to tell him, but the moment she unlocked the door of his condo, it was as if a rope leapt from her chest and bound her to him.

On the sixth Sunday of her new existence, she got home early enough that Abie was in the garden, weeding their already-overgrown beets in the evening light. After kissing her hello, he said dolefully, "We're going to be eating borscht all winter."

"Why is that bad?"

"I don't like borscht."

"It just tastes like beets."

"I don't like beets."

"So why did we plant them?"

"Because they grow in the fall."

Once Sylvie was done laughing, she suggested, "We could pickle them. My grandparents always had pickled beets in the fridge. They used to put some of the juice in horseradish to dye it pink."

"Did they eat a lot of horseradish?"

She nodded. "My grandfather liked his food spicy."

"I know. He grew hot peppers. I already ordered seeds for us to start so we can have lots next summer," Abie said. "Six kinds, right?"

"Right," Sylvie said, turning away so he wouldn't see her eyes well. She'd talked to him so much about her grandparents. Life with him reminded her of visiting them. He'd given her the only nicknames she'd had since they died: he called her Syl, Silvio, Sylvester, Rocky, Rocks. She sang more around him than she had since the vacations she'd spent marching around their apartment belting pop songs. Really, though, the similarity wasn't in any one detail: it was in the instinctive sense of family, of home.

She told herself that she couldn't stall any longer. Her mother and Jonah weren't wrong that she liked to dawdle, or that dawdling was childish. In four days, she and Robbie were meant to go to Vermont, a fall break planned before she met Abie. Abie had said repeatedly how much the thought of the trip wounded him. Nadia, who was, in general, refraining from hassling Sylvie to break up with Robbie, said it was unhinged of her to go, but if she did, she should use it as an opportunity. It wasn't lost on Sylvie that the only way she could make her failure to cancel the trip up to Abie was by telling Robbie about him while she was gone.

She found herself calling her mother, maybe in hopes of getting scolded for dawdling. Carol answered right away. Although she, like every other person of her class in America, had a smartphone with caller ID, she said, as always, "Carol Broder. Who's speaking?"

"Me, Mom. Can you talk?"

Her mother paused. "What's wrong?"

Sylvie pressed her free hand into her temple. She was sitting in the yard with her coffee, surrounded by beet greens and yellowing leaves. "I was wondering whether you and Dad were going to get divorced."

Very coolly, Carol said, "Were you?"

Because she was still touching her face, Sylvie felt herself blush. "A little."

"Well, we're not. I had an episode, but it passed."

"So you're staying married."

"Correct."

"Can I ask why?"

"What a call to get out of the blue, Sylvie."

"I'm sorry." She shut her eyes. "I'm having some trouble. I need to break up with someone, and I can't do it."

"Change is very threatening to you. It's something you inherited from your father." Sylvie heard the weight of marriage—real marriage, not what she'd had—in the way Carol said *your father*. She heard, too, that she wasn't getting any more of an answer about her mother's so-called episode.

"But," Carol went on, "you left Jonah when you had to, and if you need to leave this man, you'll do that, too. You'll delay much too long, I'm sure, but in the end, you'll do what you should."

"I appreciate the vote of confidence."

"I'm your mother," Carol said. "I do know some things about you."

As Sylvie said her goodbyes, it occurred to her that before long, she'd be calling to discuss introducing her parents to Abie. It wasn't a subject she'd allowed him to raise yet, but even a Sylvie-scale fool couldn't deny it was coming. Robbie cared about her privacy too much to ask to meet her parents. Abie cared about family too much not to.

She drove to DC later that day, telling herself the cleanest thing to do was to confess to Robbie before getting on the plane. Had he been available to listen, she might have, but in order to clear his desk for the trip, he spent the entire weekend working. Instead of talking, Sylvie sat on the couch missing him, though he was just across the room.

Once she had flown to Vermont, she decided she might as well wait until the trip's end. No sense ruining a nice hike, or nice brewery, or nice morning on their cabin's porch in her heaviest sweater. Of course, their last evening was the nicest of all. Robbie built a fire and assembled a couch picnic of fancy Vermont meats and cheeses. It was an idyllic scene, and yet, once the cheeses were reduced to rinds and scraps, she managed to say, "Can I talk to you about something?"

"Sure," Robbie said. His face was completely unguarded. Meeting his eyes sent a sting of grief through her, or cowardice disguised as grief. She recognized how profoundly he had lowered his guard with her. He'd let her redesign his whole life. He trusted her so much more deeply than she had ever experienced before. It was among the many gifts he'd given her, and she could not bear to tell him how she'd squandered it.

"It's about Nadia," she said, improvising.

He nodded. "Figured."

"You did?"

"You have your Worried About Nadia look."

Sylvie smoothed the furrowed spot between her eyebrows, a gesture she knew she'd learned from Carol. She had no plan in her head, but her mouth, as was its new habit, had begun operating on its own. It said, "Would you mind if I took a trip like this one with her?"

"Why would I mind?"

"I'm gone so much already. I'd miss time with you. But she's so wound up about her dissertation talk. She needs a way to relax."

Robbie's eyes clouded, but with concern, not the suspicion he should be feeling. "You don't need to ask my permission," he said gently. "You know that."

She wanted to go drown herself in the toilet. Somehow, she'd turned into not only a liar by omission but a complete fabulist—and one who, rather than retracting, was thinking that she could go on a real trip with Abie.

"Yeah," she said, moving down the couch to curl herself against Robbie. "I know."

Robbie leaned his head on hers. "When would you go?"

Nadia had scheduled her dissertation talk for early November, two weeks away. It traditionally happened the semester before you graduated, and it was an unpleasant but mandatory part of the PhD process. You described your concept to the department, everyone clapped, and then, a day or two later, you met with your advisers and they told you how shitty and half formed your arguments were.

"I guess not until after her talk," Sylvie said.

"It would be a nice treat for her."

Rather than agree, Sylvie tucked herself more closely into Robbie's side.

A log burst in the hearth, releasing a plume of popping, glittering sparks. Smoke wafted through the room. She deserved none of this. She deserved its opposite, something she'd cherished for years and now dreaded. She deserved to be alone.

2.

Sylvie had not said anything to Abie about her plan to tell Robbie in Vermont. Still, he somehow knew she hadn't done it. As soon as she walked into the house the next week, he sat her down on the couch and said, "I'm dying, Syl. You're killing me."

She couldn't speak. He was standing in front of her, bristling like a knight in armor. "I love you," he continued. "Not half of you. Half your time isn't enough. I feel like shit every second you're gone. Like I'm not good enough for you."

"That's not true."

His face hardened. "I'm telling you how I feel."

"I'm sorry." It was difficult for Sylvie to speak. She had yet to see Abie vulnerable in quite this way, and she couldn't protect herself from it. She would have found it less painful to pull her own teeth.

"Every time you leave," he said, "I sit here and ask myself what I could do to get you to stay. I tell myself you leave because you're scared, and I start thinking about how I could scare you less, and the only answer I ever come up with is that you'd only be less scared if I loved you less."

Her heart pounded. She had an image of her true self shrunken to mouse size and skittering around the prison of her body. In the mouse's voice, she said, "You're right."

"I can't do that."

"I don't want you to."

"So stop leaving me," Abie said, and, to her utter shame and horror, sat down, lowered his big head into his hands, and wept.

She couldn't touch him. It took all her inner force not to flee. She would have liked to cry, too, or to shout, or to take any single action, but she knew if she moved any muscle she would run, and if she left Abie alone now, it would be a betrayal greater than Vermont, greater than not telling Robbie, greater than anything. She sat perfectly still and silent until Abie raised his wet face to look at her.

"I can't help who I am, Sylvie," he said. It was the first time in months he'd used her whole name. "I can't help how I love you. You can have me this way, or you can go. You're the one who has to decide."

"When you say 'this way'—"

He wiped his eyes on his wrist. "You know what I mean."

"No sharing," she said. Her throat was as rough and swollen as if she had shouted at him. "And with the future." Just speaking the word *future* was terrible. It made her want to get divorced. It made her see, as clearly as if they were before her, the houses in Richmond she'd looked at online without admitting to herself she was doing so; the bigger garden she'd imagined while she and Abie planted their beets; the child she thought of whenever she let her mind go.

Abie was silent. His beard was wet with tears. "Let's go on a vacation," she said.

He gave her a look halfway between incomprehension and anger. "One trip for Robbie, one trip for me? Is that your idea?"

Her chest clenched. So much for balancing the scales. "I thought it could be a fresh start."

"No such thing."

Sylvie had told herself so many times that she wasn't uprooting Abie, that nobody could. She had sat for hours at her desk wondering how she was supposed to keep writing a dissertation about private, rootless love when she grew more into Abie's life every day. Now she saw her mistake. She had taken Abie's stability. He wanted her to say she would return it. She could only reach over the coffee table for his hand.

"You're the most aggravating person I've ever met," he said.

Sylvie waited.

"You're stubborn and you hate yourself and all your ideas about love are wrong and insane, and I don't know why I don't run away from you."

"Because you can't run away from anything."

"And you take advantage of that."

Sylvie was silent again, though this time not by choice. Once she had gathered herself, she said, "I tried to tell Robbie in Vermont."

"*Tried?*"

"I fucked it up."

He snorted. "It shouldn't be that hard, Sylvie."

"I'm scared."

Abie raised his wet face, staring over her head at his living room: his cacti, his *Space Jam* shirt, his books. She was sure he was regretting ever letting her into his house, or his life. Any sane person would.

When he looked back at her, he said, "I want a deadline."

Sweat stung beneath her arms. Arbitrarily, she said, "End of the semester. At the latest."

"If you fuck it up a second time, I don't want to hear about it. I don't want to hear anything till you tell me you're here for good."

She nodded.

"Promise."

"I swear."

Abie took a breath deep enough she could hear it. Again his eyes went to his shelves. He rose and took a record down, then hunched over the turntable, searching with the needle for a song other than the one with which the side began. It seemed like too delicate a task for his big hands, but soon, before Sylvie's chest could start to loosen, a low, fuzzed-out hum came from the speakers, followed by plaintive steel strings.

As if it were an explanation, Abie said, "Doug Sahm."

She had never heard the name before. Nor had she heard this type of sweet and sorrowful male harmony. It was country, but not the country she knew. It had a late-night sound, a lost sound. Sahm and his bandmates kept their voices soft and nearly united as they moved from the first verse to the chorus, which was about a man trying to tell himself that a woman who'd left him had never truly loved him.

She had to lower her face so Abie wouldn't see. She understood what he wasn't saying: that every time she drove to DC, every single Friday since she had moved in, she turned him into the man in the song. Soon enough, she would do the same to Robbie.

In the second verse, Sahm sang that living alone was just like living a lie, which Sylvie thought was backward. Surely you could tell yourself the truth in solitude—though before Robbie, she had been alone nearly all the time, and it was then that she had begun to delude herself. Without noticing, she had done so severely. She had persuaded herself she was tougher than love.

She got up and went to Abie. He let her bury her face in his warm, furry neck. As the next song began, she said, mouth to his collarbone, "I'm sorry."

He drew her closer. "Yeah, Syl." He sounded exhausted. "I know."

3.

All week, Sylvie told herself she would break up with Robbie the second she walked into his condo that Friday. She failed. She failed the week after that, too, though her shame and grief were getting steadily worse. She began devoting much of her supposed dissertation-writing time—her dissertation was all but stalled out, obstructed by the fact that her life now contradicted more than half of it—to contemplating whether Jonah had deformed her in his image. For years she had fought the idea that he'd made her a permanent victim, but now she wondered if that had been the wrong concern. Perhaps she should've been worrying about whether, as she now suspected, he had made her a permanent asshole.

Not until that Thursday, while she was getting ready to have lunch with Nadia before her diss talk, did it occur to Sylvie that the question of whether Jonah had turned her into a cruel or harmful person could be a good new path for her dissertation. It was, in part, an issue of romantic morality—though not only; she knew Jonah had, at least while she was with him, made her a bad friend—which was not disconnected from the end of romance.

She prodded at her idea the whole walk to Nadia's. It would infuriate her professors. It would not work in current feminist discourse. A woman who had been hurt was supposed to be virtuous. A paragon. She was certainly not supposed to hurt others. But, as Simone Weil said, those who have been uprooted become uprooters. Sylvie herself was proof that was true.

Out of friendship, she put her new concept on hold during lunch. Dissertation talks were a big deal, and Nadia was all but levitating with nerves, though she claimed to care only what Dr. Rau thought. Otherwise, her main fear was an audience member falling asleep.

"No one's going to do that," Sylvie told her, scooping up a dumpling. She and Nadia had a set takeout order from Silk Thai: shrimp-and-crab dumplings, eggplant in basil sauce, larb gai with tofu. It was a perfect meal.

"Undergrads do."

"Undergrads are hungover."

"We've been hungover at diss talks before."

"Yeah, but we're adults. We have manners."

"Nobody's going to get what I'm talking about," Nadia said. "Or give a shit. It's going to be like talking to a room of dead fish." She loosened her jaw and lowered her eyelids halfway, which made her look less like a fish than a sleepy snake.

"No one's going to do that, either. Everyone's going to do Interested Face." Sylvie crossed her legs at the knee, steepled her hands beneath her chin, and leaned forward, wrinkling her forehead in fake fascination.

Nadia laughed. "Fine. Maybe. But in their hearts, they won't be interested. They'll be dead fish."

But during the talk, Sylvie didn't spot a single Interested Face. All the professors looked riveted. Nadia was completely compelling: poised, funny, full of anecdotes about her computer model's odd interpretations of the philosophers she'd helped it metabolize. She wore a tight wool dress that made her look like a villain in one of the thrillers she liked. It was conceivable that Nadia was, in fact, some sort of mad scientist, though not an evil one. As the talk went on, she shifted from the performative, jokey mode in which she'd began to a sincere discussion of the value of her work. She had gotten her model to understand that humans feared death, but wished they didn't. She had taught it—"as a tribute to my friend Sylvie Broder," she said, grinning into the audience—that sex and love can be pursued and found both together and separately. Most importantly, she'd explained to it that nearly all its potential users aspired to lead more moral lives than they did; that, like the young Saint Augustine, most people prayed to be good, but not yet.

"It was very sweet," Nadia said of that exchange. "The model asked if it could help its users want to be good sooner. I said only by discouraging them from trying to be bad. Of course, this has practical applications as well as philosophical ones. Think about online radicalization. Imagine if, instead of YouTube algorithms that lead young men to the far right, we had language models encouraging peace." She gave the audience the radiant smile that Sylvie knew signaled a crushing punchline. "Won't happen—no profits in peacemaking for Silicon Valley—but a girl can dream."

After the Q&A ended and the applause tapered to a polite halt, Nadia descended from the podium and moved through the small crowd to Dr. Rau, who stood alone, awaiting her. Sylvie poured herself a plastic glass of departmental wine and maneuvered her way into a conversational circle that gave her a good angle on Nadia and Dr. Rau, who looked electric with an emotion Sylvie did not presume to name. Her eyes shone beneath elaborate eyeshadow. Her big teeth flashed across the room. Her shoulders, hips, and knees were aimed directly at Nadia. Not an inch of either of their bodies conveyed restlessness, distraction, or ease.

A small void opened inside Sylvie. As if casually, she went to Nadia, bumped her hip into her friend's, and said, "You were so good!"

"Nobody fell asleep," Nadia said, shrugging.

"So?" Dr. Rau asked. "All that means is an audience with manners."

Sylvie had made a similar point to Nadia earlier, but, she thought, in a totally different spirit. "Come on," she said to her friend. "Everyone was laughing. No one was even leaning back in their chairs. People were *with* you."

"An audience is a diversion," Dr. Rau said.

"From?"

"Real work," Nadia answered. "According to Salomé."

Dr. Rau frowned. "It's true. You'll see once you become a professor."

"*If* I become a professor."

In unison, Sylvie and Dr. Rau said, "You will." After a beat, Sylvie added, "Unless you'd rather write books about robots stopping Hitler."

Nadia shook her hair back. "Always an option."

"You'd have a huge audience."

"But," Dr. Rau said, "it wouldn't be serious."

"What wouldn't be?" Sylvie asked.

"Her thinking."

Sylvie's parents never read novels, rarely went to the movies. If the television was on, it was the news. Paul was so uncomfortable with Sylvie's imaginary friends that he tried banning them, then getting the pediatrician to ban them, then—when both failed, and the doctor told him Captain Lightning and company were healthy forms of play—forbade Sylvie to talk about them. She wondered now if Dr. Rau was a variation on her father: controlling because she was joyless, an enemy of fun for the sole reason that she'd never had it herself.

Lightly, Sylvie said, "Fiction can be serious."

Dr. Rau sucked her teeth. "Go to the English department, then."

Sylvie heard the condescension in the professor's voice. Analytic and linguistic philosophers like Dr. Rau found it antiquated and unrigorous to include novels in one's work, which made no sense to Sylvie. Their version of philosophy was all about the reality-altering importance of language, and she wrote about literature—her dissertation had a whole section about how damaging marriage plots in fiction could be—because she thought it could alter its readers' lives.

Another of Nadia's committee members approached, and Sylvie took her chance to retreat to the philosophy library, where she waited until Nadia marched in, declaring, "I'm so hungry. I called us an Uber already." She waved her phone. "You know Mas. I don't want to wait for a table."

Mas was their Good Restaurant, site of all major celebrations. Half the waitstaff knew their names. Sylvie had resisted going there with both Abie and Robbie. It was the best restaurant in Charlottesville, but it already belonged to her and Nadia. It was a foregone conclusion that they'd be having dinner there tonight.

In the car, Sylvie commanded herself to apologize for antagonizing Dr. Rau. "I didn't set out to," she said. "I swear."

Nadia, surprisingly, was unruffled. "She likes to be annoyed. It's her default mode."

"You don't mind?"

"I used to. Now it barely even registers."

Sylvie wasn't sure if she should be reassured. She had never gotten comfortable with Jonah's irritation. Adjusting to it would have been a good coping strategy. It also would have made it harder to see that she needed to leave.

Mas had no wait. Holly, their favorite server, led them through the warm, narrow dining room and tucked them at a low table where two wooden benches met. Sylvie took the seat facing away from the door, since this was Nadia's night: she got people-watching privileges. Besides, Sylvie was glad to look into the restaurant itself. Fat candles shone around them, and local-artist mosaics glittered from the walls. The smell of caramelizing tomatoes wafted from the kitchen. Appreciation rose alongside her hunger. Not everyone got a Good Restaurant. It was a thing to be grateful for.

Holly distributed menus, bell sleeve swinging against her wrist. "What's the occasion?"

"Very successful dissertation talk." Sylvie tipped her head toward Nadia. "She did great."

"I don't know about great," Nadia said. "It went okay."

Sylvie and Holly both clucked at her, waving their hands in dismissal. Holly had a perfect manicure, almond-shaped nails painted the glossy, reflective red of Skittles. "I'm sure you were fabulous," she said firmly. "Wine or sangria?"

"Sangria," Sylvie decided. "More festive."

At Mas, each of them had foods they required, foods they shared, and foods they hoarded. Sylvie wanted anchovies to split and a chicory salad to herself; Nadia declared that she would ignore her pescatarianism to order the meatballs, which they always shared, and the hilariously small Serrano ham sandwich, which they did not. To be virtuous, they got cauliflower; to prepare for serious drinking after dinner, they ordered patatas bravas and pan con tomate, which was so acidic and alive that Sylvie briefly forgot it was the middle of fall.

Nadia gazed lovingly at her sandwich. "I'd wish I were a computer," she said, "but they can't eat."

Sylvie eyed her friend. "You would?"

"Sure. No suffering, no death."

"They can break down," Sylvie pointed out. "Also, what about sex?"

"Sexbots."

"Do those exist?"

"A couple do. And intelligent ones will soon."

"Will they like having sex?"

Nadia shrugged. "Different concept of liking. They'll be AIs designed to have sex, so it's what they'll know. What they're for."

Sylvie's first impulse was that nobody, not even a droid, should be designed exclusively for sex. Her second was that it sounded like a great lifestyle. "Is that fucked up?"

Nadia ate a meatball, then licked sauce from her lips. "Don't know. It's one of the questions I'm still working on, actually. I talk about it with Salomé, but I thought it would freak the olds out if I brought it up today."

Sylvie refrained from commenting on the strangeness of Nadia discussing the morality of sexbots with Dr. Rau. Instead, she said, "Welcome to my life."

"Freaking the olds out?"

"Yeah."

"Here's a question I haven't asked you." Nadia paused as Holly rattled by in her short, heeled boots, which defied restaurant convention in their loudness. Sylvie had once owned the same pair—Rachel Comey, bought on clearance; she'd been very proud of the bargain—but they gave her blisters on the soles of her feet, which was a true human horror. Robots didn't get blisters. That was one undeniable advantage to being an object.

After Holly passed, Nadia said, "Does your dissertation freak Abie out?"

"I wouldn't put it quite like that."

"But?"

"He told me recently that my ideas about love are wrong and insane."

"Did you mind?"

"I would have if I weren't worried he was right."

Nadia lifted an eyebrow. "Go on."

"I stand by my whole first chapter," Sylvie began. "All the stuff about how sex discourse can be coercive—I mean, that's Foucault. I can't argue with him."

Dryly, Nadia said, "God forbid."

"And I stand by my argument that nobody should have to talk about being abused."

"Do you still think it's psychically damaging to consider yourself a victim?"

Sylvie sighed. "It's psychically damaging to *be* a victim," she said.

It was an admission. Nadia took it lightly. "Well, yes."

"I don't know if rejecting that identity is strength or denial or both."

"You want it to be both."

Sylvie shook her head. "I *want* it to be strength. But that's not really working for me."

"In your writing, or your life?"

"Nothing in my life is working," Sylvie said, and they both laughed.

"And in terms of my arguments—" She shrugged. "At this point, my thesis is that real strength and goodness and happiness are only possible for women in private. I'm not sure if I believe that anymore, but if I do, then I don't get to say what you should or shouldn't call yourself inside your own mind."

"So what's the part Abie thinks is wrong and insane?"

"He thinks it's bad to keep your love private, and to keep yourself private from the person you love. And I guess he's right, because I can't do the second one with him, and I'm going to stop doing the first."

"What does that mean?"

"It means I promised myself I'd break up with Robbie tomorrow."

Nadia instantly sat very straight. It was like she was a marionette whose strings had all been pulled. "And you're really going to do it this time?"

"I have to." Sylvie speared and ate an anchovy, mainly to quell emotion. "It isn't fair if I don't."

"Fair to Abie, or Robbie?"

"Both."

"Are you going to tell Robbie the truth?"

Sylvie nodded. She heard the Doug Sahm song in her head. "I wish I thought he'd believe me that I still love him."

"Are you kidding?"

"Is that worse?"

Nadia closed her eyes. Her whole face seemed to shut with them. When she looked at Sylvie again, she said, "If Salomé told me she didn't love me, I would be miserable. But if she told me she loved me but was choosing someone else, I think I'd die."

Blood rushed to Sylvie's face. She hated herself in this moment, but not nearly as much as she hated Dr. Rau.

Before Sylvie could respond, Nadia got up. "Bathroom," she said. She sounded choked. Sylvie waited until her friend was safely gone before dropping her head into her hands. When she lifted it, having resolved to dig dinner out of this pit by any means necessary, Jonah was sitting in Nadia's seat.

PART THREE
Jonah

Chapter Eight

1.

When Sylvie's husband sat beside her at Mas, sighing as if he'd needed to get off his feet, her first reaction was relief so intense it took effort to keep her body from going limp. She could have melted to the floor. Curled up beneath the table. Gone to sleep. Why be awake now? Why be vigilant? She'd been afraid of Jonah finding her for eight years. Now she was found.

He was smiling at her, eyes twinkling in the warm light. His face had gotten thinner and seemed oddly masklike. Botox? Had he gone full *American Psycho*? Or was fear distorting her sight?

"You look good," he told her. It sounded like a prompt. "Heavy, but good."

She resisted the urge to tell him he looked like shit. She wasn't sure she could speak without wailing. Also, insulting him would give him power. Any loss of control on her part, she knew, gave him an opening. Carefully, she asked, "Why are you here?"

"For the tapas."

She blinked at him. Half-empty plates littered the table before them. Jonah plucked up an anchovy—*her* anchovy—swallowed it in a gulp, and laughed. "Sylvie, I came to see you."

Evil thoughts roiled inside her. She wanted to die. She wanted to stab Jonah with her fork. "How did you find me?"

He smiled wider. She imagined him with brown, rotting teeth. "Rachel."

Sylvie shook her head. "She wouldn't."

"She did." Solemnly, Jonah added, "It's sad."

For the second time in minutes, or the first time in a new and hideous phase of her life, Sylvie dropped her head into her hands. She knew what Jonah meant. He meant Rachel was using again, or drinking—Sylvie hadn't known, of course not, she hadn't reached out to Rachel in years—and that he'd guessed she knew Sylvie's whereabouts and could be made to reveal them. It was a punishment Sylvie deserved. She'd failed in her friendship with Rachel. Out of guilt for that failure, and a desire to erase or mitigate it, she'd told Rachel when and why she moved to Virginia, and now, because she'd done so, she would pay.

"You took advantage of her," she said.

"'Took advantage' is a nasty way to put it." Jonah reached for Sylvie's sangria. "I asked."

"Don't drink my fucking drink."

He lifted his hands. Fancy watch; wedding ring. "All right."

Sylvie dug her fingertips into her eyes. She wanted Robbie. She would settle for a person walking by who smelled like Robbie. Any fraction of the feeling of safety Robbie brought her would help now. She told God that if He delivered Robbie to soothe and defend her—or, ideally, if He whisked Jonah down to Jewish hell—she would do anything He wanted. She'd quit philosophy. Quit Abie. Atone double-time for her sins.

She lifted her head. Jonah remained in Nadia's seat. He was eating their meatballs. So much for God.

"Delicious," he said approvingly.

"Get fucked."

"I want to talk."

"I don't."

"It doesn't need to be now. We can talk tomorrow." He paused. "Or the next day. Or—"

"Shut up." Her voice cracked. A rush of tears warmed her eyes. She couldn't cry in front of him. Where was Nadia? Either weeping or texting Dr. Rau in the bathroom. Her absence was more punishment for Sylvie's bad impulses. So was Jonah's descent upon her. She was skating dangerously close to becoming a Jonah herself, and the universe had sent her the real deal.

Peacefully, Jonah said, "Sylvie, I came here to talk to you. You know, you aren't in the university directory. After Rachel told me you were at UVA, I had to pay a detective service to confirm. It was very expensive. I only heard back last week."

"So?"

"I drove straight here. I took off work. And besides, wouldn't you like a divorce?"

So God hadn't completely forsaken her. "A divorce?"

He nodded. His ringlets bounced. They were looking very perfect. How much product was in them? Had he stood in his hotel bathroom preening, wanting his hair to look right for his grand reappearance in her life?

"I don't want one," he said. "Just to be clear. I want us to get back together. I want a second chance. I know I wasn't the best husband. I was"—he met her eyes—"very young."

Sylvie's mouth was dry. Her ears buzzed. She was dizzy in a way that, horribly, mirrored the lightheadedness that came before sex. Now she wanted Abie. She wanted Nadia. Why was she taking so long? Where was Holly? Why was Sylvie sitting alone with this man?

"Let me talk to you," Jonah said. "Let me tell you how I've changed."

"You've written me enough emails," she said sourly. "I know you haven't."

He ignored her. "I want to settle back down with you, Sylvie."

"I'd rather die."

"Nobody's dying. All I'm asking is for you to give me one hour of your time." He held his index finger up. "One hour. I can come to your house. It won't be a hassle. And after that, if you want me gone, I'll go."

Sylvie pressed her hands into her eyes until she saw long red streaks. It took the restaurant a moment to settle back into focus. She resented every single diner. All these nice Charlottesvillians in their button-downs and cashmere sweaters, Blundstone boots and polished oxfords, long brass earrings and resin hoops. None of them knew what was happening to her. None would interfere if they did. Not a single one of these upstanding citizens would pause their dinner to rescue Sylvie from a well-groomed white man who not only hadn't touched her but hadn't even raised his voice.

"If I talk to you," Sylvie said, "I can have a divorce. Is that right?"

"It is."

A feeling of horrible resolve settled over her. She would go home tonight and decide what mattered more: getting divorced or never seeing Jonah again. She would consider the strong odds that divorce was just a carrot he was dangling, that his real intention was to harass her back into his one-man cult. She wouldn't permit that. She would rather be dead. She would weigh the risks of showing up tomorrow and make a moral and rational decision, and then she would live morally and rationally until the day she died.

"All right. Atlas Coffee, nine o'clock tomorrow. You aren't coming to my house."

"I would never hurt you, Sylvie." He paused for effect. "But I understand."

His hesitation, false though it plainly was, gave her an idea. "You're acting like you want me to trust you."

"I do," Jonah said, nodding so eagerly that his curls bobbed. Sylvie wanted to pull one, to see if it would stretch like nature intended. She'd bet it was so full of gel it would crack.

"In that case," she said, "you can start proving you're trustworthy by getting the fuck out of here. Now."

2.

Sylvie's vow to be moral and rational lasted less time than it took to tell Nadia what had happened, get the check, and go home. Nadia, full of recrimination over having missed Jonah, offered to walk her, but Sylvie wanted to be alone. She thought she did, anyway. Within blocks, panic swarmed her. It seemed to come from outside and from all directions, like the attacking crows in *The Birds*. Every inch of her skin stung with terror. She tried to carry herself normally, as if faking relaxation for the dark street would help somehow; she tried to pretend she was feeling only the fear every woman she knew felt walking alone late at night. She would prefer any threat from a strange man to that of Jonah reappearing in her life.

Alongside panic, her desire for Robbie grew with every step. She wished she were going home to him tonight. Robbie was a real shelter. Abie was not. He reacted too easily to her emotions. He was like Baba Yaga's chicken-legged house in the folktale Grandma Estie used to tell: he moved when she did. Until this moment, she had loved that sensation. She'd thought it signaled some virtue in their relationship. Now she just felt like she had no destination; like she would be walking in the dark all night.

She was angry by the time she reached her front doorstep. In the dark dining-room window she saw her own reflection, plainly flushed with alcohol, bitten lips swollen as if from kissing. It was an evil fact that distress made her look good. In the living-room window, she saw Abie sprawled in a pool of lamplight, drinking a beer and watching basketball. She could, very faintly, hear the game's squeals and whistles through the glass. She had never spent time around a true sports fan before and had, until now, found it comic to watch Abie delight in and despair over things the Washington Wizards had done. After Sylvie, his family, and the state of Virginia, he said, the Wizards were his great love. It was a sentiment that suddenly struck her as juvenile and shallow. Robbie, the former athlete, had learned to step aside from the circus of athletic performance. Abie barely even admitted it was a show.

He looked through the window and saw her. Instantly his face lit. Sylvie was repulsed by his gladness. He was too enthusiastic for a man who had seen her this morning. In general, he was too enthusiastic about her. It struck her as dangerous and deviant, even if it was only love. Abie loved her. It had been a source of joy and transformation in the past months, and yet it seemed to her now that his love, or her love for him, was a curse on her and everyone she knew.

She still hadn't gotten her keys. Abie rose from the couch. A moment later, the door swung open. "Locked out?" he asked, and bent to kiss her before she could answer. She couldn't kiss back. It was mild out, but her cheeks and hands were as numb as if it were a Massachusetts winter.

"Something wrong?" he said. He let go, which sent a wave of loneliness through her. Her mouth tasted faintly like sangria. She swallowed, which only made more sugary spit gather on her tongue. Half of her wanted to put it to sexual use, but the bodily summons to abject herself made the rest of her angrier still.

Abie looked worried. "Sylvie."

"Sorry," she managed. "My head hurts. Not a good idea to drink as much as Nadia." She was lying—Nadia was measured in consuming all substances other than weed—but it was, at least, true that she regretted finishing the sangria. If she hadn't, she would trust herself to drive back to Robbie right now.

Given that she couldn't, she went to bed. Abie joined her some indeterminate time later, warm and smelling of popcorn. She pretended to wake up, though she had been not sleeping but settling down enough to first make a series of decisions and then mourn them. In the brownish light that came through Abie's paper shades, she saw the branching paths before her clearly. Abie, not Robbie, was the one who would push for marriage. Robbie left her alone. He asked for almost nothing. If she chose him, she'd be safe. She would never need a divorce. In the morning, she would not meet Jonah. She would cancel her class. She would break up with Abie and go to DC.

She allowed herself a goodbye, though she knew it was unwise to. Abie didn't resist, though before progressing past kissing he asked softly, "You're not too drunk?"

"No."

"Promise?"

"I do."

During sex, Sylvie dug her nails into his ass cheeks, clung to his shoulders, ordered him over and over not to change a thing he was doing. She had never been so assertive with him before, but she needed to see his face and heaving chest, to lick sweat from his neck, to know without the shadow of doubt that here, inside her, was the man she would always love most. She imagined her skin becoming so porous she could rise through it to merge with him. She hoped, though she had an IUD, that she would get pregnant tonight. A baby would undo her decision. A baby would root her here.

In the morning, exhausted from sleeping so fitfully it was like no sleep at all, Sylvie rose and got dressed before Abie woke. She made coffee and sat at the dining-room table drinking it, dazed with resolve. Abie came downstairs nearly half an hour later. His curls were matted from the pillow; he wore the alarmingly frayed Wizards sweats he put on every morning. In the emptiest tone she could muster, she said, "I'm going back to DC."

He blinked at her. "I know. It's Friday."

Sylvie shook her head. "For good."

It seemed to her that she left her body then. She stood aside from herself and bore witness to a person who looked and sounded like her breaking a man's heart with the efficiency of a fishmonger cleaning a trout. She told Abie that she had reconsidered the promises she made in Austin; that she had come to understand her guilt toward Robbie as an inner urging to return to him. She was sorry she had interpreted it wrong at first. She was sorry to cause Abie so much inconvenience, though presumably he would rather have this happen now than months or years down the line. Probably it was inevitable. He loved her too much. It was unsafe for both of them.

Abie made a choking sound. "Sylvie, listen to yourself."

"What?"

He wiped tears from his face. "It's not *unsafe* to love someone."

She smiled, which was horrible. "You just haven't learned that lesson yet."

"It's not real. It's—" He turned away. His shoulders heaved. Without looking back at her, he said, "What Jonah did to you has no bearing on your relationship with me."

She left then. She put her cup down and walked out the door. It was only luck that her laptop was in the work bag she'd dropped in the front hall the night before. Had it not been there, she would have abandoned it. She would have abandoned anything.

In the car, her turtle said, Poor Abie.

I don't want to hear it.

He loves you.

I know.

You love him, too.

I *know*, Sylvie told the turtle, jamming her foot on the brake until it squealed. She had no reason to. She wasn't at a stop sign or red light. If she had been on a busier road, she would have gotten rear-ended, and she couldn't afford car repairs. As it was, the minivan behind her slowed and flashed its lights reproachfully, and Sylvie resumed driving with her heart thrusting itself at her ribs. Her turtle had lumbered back into the jungle of her mind, though he would surely return to scold and harass her before long. Probably he'd bring Captain Lightning back again. She told herself the turtle's willfulness was a symptom of psychiatric disease. An adult woman unable to control her imaginary friend was not one who met diagnostic criteria of health and normalcy.

But she was controlling herself. She had gone through with her decisions. It was 8:48 on her dashboard clock and she felt Jonah's nearness as strongly as if he were a planet and she its only moon, but she was not slipping into his orbit. She was driving in the opposite direction from the coffee shop where she had told him to meet her; she was going to a city where she hoped to God he did not know she lived. She would spend as little time in Charlottesville as possible, and she would obey only the dictates of the cool, philosophical part of her mind. She would be moral and rational. A brain in a jar. She would be a good girl from now on.

3.

Regret overtook her by evening. Her hands kept twitching toward her phone, though Abie had not texted. He hadn't called or emailed. More than once she had the wild thought that she'd invented him. It was better to believe he was a monthslong hallucination than that she had taken from herself a real person she loved.

It didn't help to love Robbie, who was sitting on the couch with her, patiently working while she stalled on the idea of dinner. Eating seemed impossible. Any bodily process unrelated to remorse did. She wanted to mortify her flesh like a saint. It occurred to her that she had failed to fast on Yom Kippur this year. Maybe she should fast now, to purify herself, though it was hard to say which impurities she wished to remove.

She looked at Robbie over the *New Yorker* she was pretending to read. She had left *Tinker, Tailor, Soldier, Spy* behind at Abie's. She would never finish it. She would never read John le Carré again. She would never listen to the Hold Steady or the Beastie Boys, never eat Garlic Breath Pasta or hear the sneaker squeaks of a basketball game. She would banish her memories of Abie, and in that way enable herself to remain in the life she had picked.

Robbie turned to smile at her. "Watching me?"

"Appreciating," she said. No living man had better bone structure. Rarely did she pause to note how beautiful he was. Before Abie, she had. But you don't praise your comfort object: you cling to it. Sylvie was clinging, all right.

She thought of the confessions she could make to Robbie. She could tell the truth about Abie. She could describe Jonah's appearance at Mas. Suddenly she wondered if her husband intended to hurt her now. Robbie would ask, and be right to. Jonah was surely angry that she'd broken their appointment, and the odds said nobody was more likely to hurt a woman than an angry male partner, present or past.

Sylvie shivered. She could not afford to fear Jonah more. She slid down the couch to kiss Robbie, which, through everything, still calmed her. His powers were reliable beyond belief. A little bubble of pride rose through her sorrow. She had made a good, sane decision. She was behaving not like Dr. Rau's Nadia or Jonah's Sylvie, but like a woman who could regulate herself.

Robbie rested his hands lightly at her hips. "Dinner?" he asked. "Or—"

"Or."

For months it had been her constant fear that Robbie would smell or taste Abie on her. She tried to take pleasure in having that worry for the last time. Instead, she found herself reaching in her mind for the power Abie had over her. Robbie was too gentle. His torso was too muscular and smooth. She wanted weight and heat and scratching; wanted to be not matched but subsumed. On Monday night Abie had crushed her up against the wall beside the fish tank, then turned her so she could brace her hands on the bookshelf while they fucked. She'd had grooves in her palms by the time they were done.

Afterward, she and Robbie went, as they did every Friday, to Little Coco's. Their server greeted them with cheery recognition, putting them in the booth Sylvie liked and asking, "Same wine as last time?"

Robbie glanced at Sylvie, who, in her heart, wanted not a mid-tier bottle of red but the bar's whole stock of bourbon. "Sure," she said. "And some calamari, please." Revulsion wormed through her as she spoke. She wanted to lie in the narrow corridor between the restaurant's two rows of tables and beat her fists and feet on the floor like a toddler. She wanted to root and thrash in the psychic unfairness of wanting Robbie last night and Abie now. Could she never be satisfied? Had Jonah done that to her, too?

Once the calamari came and their main courses were ordered, Robbie said, "I need to work more after dinner."

"You always do."

He nodded. Sylvie looked behind him, at the restaurant's wall of amateur paintings. Each one was a modified album cover: a rainbow shooting from a triangle of pepperoni pizza on Pink Floyd's *Dark Side of the*

Moon, Elvis Costello wielding a cheese slice instead of a guitar. Abie would love these. She should have commissioned him one featuring Doug Sahm.

"I hate it," Robbie said abruptly. For an instant, Sylvie thought he meant the art.

"I thought you were liking your job."

"I am. But I hate when it cuts into my time with you."

She took a deep breath. "Are you feeling like it's not enough?"

Neutrally, Robbie said, "Your teaching schedule is what it is."

"I can make sure it's better next semester."

His face brightened so swiftly she could tell he'd been afraid to ask. "I'm glad."

"I'm sorry," she said, hearing the guilt in her voice. In order to justify it, she added, "I think I've been distracted, too. I'm having a hard time writing."

"What's wrong?" he asked, but she just shook her head and shrugged, as if she didn't know. She wondered whether her new commitment to morality and rationality would help her save her dissertation or render it unbearable to work on.

After dinner, Robbie gave her a long kiss before settling himself at his desk. Sylvie went into the bedroom, where she'd left her phone, as if not bringing it to the restaurant would make Abie call. What she got instead was an email from Jonah. He was *not surprised by your no-show. You always drag your feet. I got a suite at the Omni through next Sunday. You can come see me any time.*

She crawled under the covers, dress bunching around her hips. She felt small and very alone. It hadn't quite been twelve hours since she left Abie's house in Charlottesville, her mind so cold with decisiveness she had no idea what lay beneath. Now she found not only fear but true dread of a life without him.

In search of relief rather than pleasure, she nudged her hand inside her tights. She had never masturbated while Robbie was home before. It seemed possible that he'd be hurt if he came in. Still, she pressed the hard bone at the base of her thumb into herself, then rocked against it. Abie had teased her for that technique, asked if she was afraid to touch her body without underwear on. She'd told him cloth created good friction, and what did he know, anyway? He'd demonstrated, at length, that he was in fact an expert.

Jonah had mocked her, too, but for insatiability rather than style. He had suggested that she had no real need for him. With terrible clarity, she saw him laughing above her, an image that did not dissipate when she leapt out of bed. If anything, he was even more with her. He was another one of her curses. He was, now and always, the condition of her life.

4.

All weekend, Sylvie suffered. She spent hours hunched over her phone, ignoring Nadia's texts about Jonah and waiting, despite herself, for Abie to call. She told herself that if he did, she wouldn't answer. She would restrain herself. She would allow this time of pain to pass, secure in the knowledge that it was worthwhile. It was better to be in safe love than consuming love. It was better to be with Robbie, who could not reach her innermost self.

She clung to the idea that she had served a purpose in Abie's life. On the night they met, she had thought it was her role to disillusion him about families. She'd disillusioned him about love instead. She had uprooted a person who needed uprooting. Provided a public service. Helped Abie, who was, in some ways, a man-child, grow up. His next girlfriend would thank her. Probably he'd get one before long. He would fall in love with somebody else—a thought that made Sylvie abandon righteous logic in favor of unadulterated misery.

By Monday, she had heard nothing from Abie. She canceled another class and left for Charlottesville late. In the car, she sent Nadia a voice note saying she had broken up with Abie and needed to crash on her couch.

Once Sylvie got on the highway, she called Elaine, to whom she spilled out her pile of issues in no coherent order, starting with Jonah's reappearance before so much as mentioning Abie. Saying his name was painful, though it also gave her a sensation worryingly like hope.

"Hold on, hold on, hold on," Elaine rasped several minutes into Sylvie's description of Abie, which until then had gone unbroken. "You're telling me you *dumped* this one?"

"Yeah."

"Not the lawyer."

Sylvie lifted her eyes from the truck ahead to the highway's horizon. Glassy, angular buildings rose ahead: all defense contractors, probably, here to be near the Pentagon. "No."

Elaine's breath crackled down the line. "You know," she said, "I never loved my second husband. Bill, the boat builder."

"I remember."

"When I met Bill, I had my kids already. I had my life in New York. Answering phones in the mornings, hanging art in the afternoons, going to galleries on the weekends. I was good, Sylvie." She stretched the vowel sound in *good*. "I was healthy. Never drank. Never did drugs, only speed. I ate macrobiotic. I was such a great independent woman, and I couldn't stand it. Could not *stand* it. So I got Bill, and he blew my life up."

Sylvie waited, not sure if the story's moral had come. A gold Cadillac eased by her on the left. She merged behind it as Elaine continued, "Bill and I had terrific sex. He made me laugh. He got me going to Rockaway

Beach on Sundays, letting the kids run around on the shore. Or Coney Island, to the boardwalk—always some outing. Some adventure."

"Sounds fun," Sylvie offered.

"Oh, it was. It was. He gave me a total shake-up. Made me see how I boxed myself in in Manhattan, living an art life like it mattered to me. It didn't matter. All that mattered to me was having a good time, having a *new* time. And the kids, of course. The kids loved him. So when Bill proposed after six months, said he wanted to start his own company and could we get married and go to Massachusetts for him to do it, I said sure, why not—and the minute we got settled in Swampscott, I realized the point all along had been the change, not the guy."

"But that's not true with Abie," Sylvie said after a moment. "He is the point. *Was* the point."

Elaine scoffed. "What's Abie got to do with it? I'm telling you about the lawyer."

"Robbie."

"Sure. Robbie. Seems to me a grown man should go by Rob."

"He does professionally."

"Worse," Elaine said promptly. "If he likes Robbie, he should stick with it. But Sylvie, you shouldn't stick with him. Don't make the mistake I made with Bill."

"Which is?"

"Confusing the man who changes your life for the man who can be it."

"I don't want any man to be my life."

Elaine released a great gale of cackles. When she got done, she said, more gently than her laughter had suggested, "I'm sure you wish that was true."

Sylvie did not ask for evidence. She didn't ask why Elaine was so convinced Robbie, not Abie, was the transitional figure. She had called Elaine for her grandmotherly wisdom, her profound knowledge of how women can and should be. "What about Jonah?" she said.

"Ignore, ignore, ignore. Marriage is for the birds, so who needs a divorce? And besides, you don't divorce him, maybe you get some money when he dies."

Sylvie spent the rest of her drive fantasizing about killing Jonah for an insurance payout. It was true that she had very little money, and, in some sense, didn't he owe her? She could reschedule coffee, then spike his Americano with rat poison. She could go to his hotel—what a douchebag, bragging even now about his *suite at the Omni*—let him fuck her, and then smother him with a pillow once he fell asleep. She could show up at his room with a gun.

It was nearly dark when Sylvie pulled up to Nadia's duplex. She sat motionless in her parked car for a moment, allowing her violent thoughts to ebb. She was, belatedly, disgusted by them. Jonah was a real person, not the villainous husband in "Goodbye, Earl." Killing him would not be cathartic. It would just ruin more of her life.

She trudged up the stairs feeling as if somebody had dropped sandbags on her shoulders. It was a sensation she recalled from her marriage: the imaginary external burden, the illusion that her misery came from outside. When she let herself into Nadia's apartment, her friend wasn't there. After her initial reply—a voice note saying "Shit, shit, shit, shit, shit," then, "I'll get home as fast as I can"—she hadn't texted again. *At your apt*, Sylvie wrote to her. It seemed too stark a message to send alone, but she had no additions to make. She sank onto the sofa and stared blankly at the iron bookshelf across the room until her phone glowed.

For a moment she could not fathom that the text she was looking at wasn't from Nadia, or from Robbie asking if she'd arrived safely, or from Elaine telling her to buck up. It was the message from Abie that she'd been waiting for all weekend, and it appeared to be the first in a string.

Syl, he began. *I know you're probably in town to teach. I want to see you, if you want to see me.* Below the message, the dots that meant he was typing rolled. She waited, and he continued, *I recognize that I rushed you. I'm sorry. Truly. And I'm sorry I said Jonah has no bearing on you and me. I know it isn't that simple.* Another long pause. Her mouth tasted evil. Her hands and feet were icy. It was possible she'd be too physically frozen to respond.

I don't know what else to say, he wrote finally. *Come home. I want you back. I miss you.* Sylvie could not help but read his words as if they were Jonah's. Fear ran through her. She dropped the phone at her feet, prostrated herself on Nadia's couch, and cried until she heard two pairs of clogs on the stairs.

5.

Nadia was dressed as if for a night out. Her hair was loose and curlier than came naturally. She wore a silky black dress and the gigantic hoops her dad had given her. She had plastic take-out bags in both hands and a look of desperate apology on her face. Dr. Rau, behind her, carried nothing. She was wearing head-to-toe Carhartt. Abie would laugh like an animal when she told him Dr. Rau had shown up in workwear. When she remembered she would be telling him nothing, she wanted, with fleeting certainty, to die.

"Nadia and I had dinner plans," Dr. Rau said cheerfully. "But she said she had to eat with you."

"I did say that," Nadia agreed. Her tone was subdued. Sylvie attempted to narrow her swollen eyes at her friend. She wished she could telepathically inform Nadia that she was in too fragile a condition to be in the same room as Salomé Rau.

She lifted herself from the sofa. Her limbs felt extraordinarily weak. Maybe the correct move would be to get in Nadia's bed and fall asleep.

Instead, she managed to scoop her phone from the floor and mutter, "Going to wash up."

In the bathroom, Sylvie examined herself with dull estrangement. Her eyes were miniature. Her face was one giant blotch. She was somehow both damp and dehydrated. She thought about calling Elaine again; thought about replying to Abie, though she had no idea what she'd say. Instead, she texted Nadia, *Please make her leave.*

It was not a winning strategy. When Sylvie, exerting great strength to do so, returned to the living room, Nadia was arranging plates and napkins on the table. Sylvie could smell fish sauce, basil, and cilantro. She glanced right to see Dr. Rau by the bookcase, holding what Sylvie recognized by its caramel leather case as Nadia's phone.

"You'd like me to leave?" the professor asked.

Sylvie inhaled through her nose. She tightened any muscle that seemed available to tighten. "Yes, I would."

"You should get used to me, Sylvie."

"I'm having a very hard week. I need my friend."

Dr. Rau inclined her head toward Nadia, who had frozen completely. "And here she is."

"Nadia," Sylvie said. "Did you give Salomé permission to look at your phone?"

Nadia shook her head.

"Did you invite her over?"

"No."

Sylvie turned back to the professor. She felt better now. Stronger. Not like a person who could go poison her husband, but like one who could survive the night. "You're intruding," she said.

Dr. Rau snorted. "I could not possibly intrude. I did not force my way into this apartment. I know why you're here. You broke up with one of your boyfriends, and now you want Nadia to be sorry for you."

Sylvie had the sensation that all the blood in her body had streamed through her feet onto the floor. She was an empty husk. She understood distinctly that she would be furious very soon, but she was not yet capable even of that.

Behind her, Nadia said softly, "Salomé, please don't."

Dr. Rau's face changed. She looked directly into Sylvie's eyes. "You know," she said, "there is a reason that philosophy turned away from your sort of thinking. Your Big Ideas." She waved a hand. "It is too easy for a person like you to convince herself she's come up, all alone, with the right way of living, and to make some very serious mistakes as a result."

Before Sylvie could react, the professor turned to Nadia. "It is sad for me," she continued, "that you allow your friend to pass her mistakes along. She gives you bad ideas about relationships. She tells you this and that about control. She claims that when I tell the truth, it's to hurt you, and then she lies to the men you say she loves."

Still quietly, Nadia said, "It isn't the same."

"Why?"

"What it isn't," Sylvie heard herself say, "is your fucking business. My life is *mine*. I'm not discussing it with you and I don't give a shit if you judge it." Her vision had become a tight circle. "And if you don't leave here right now, I'm going to tell the department heads that you're jerking Nadia around. I'm going to say you're misusing your power. I'm going to remind them that I survived an abusive marriage"—the phrase was like bile in her throat—"and I have a good eye for that kind of bullshit." She was panting. Righteousness flooded through her.

Without speaking, Dr. Rau set Nadia's phone on the bookshelf. She walked across the room to Nadia, put a hand beneath her chin, and kissed her, quickly but firmly, on the lips. Nadia didn't move until after the professor was gone.

"You're a hypocrite," Nadia said. She sat on the sofa, gripping herself so tightly her knuckles blanched.

Sylvie stared at her, stunned. "You told her about my private life."

"It just *happened*. I slipped. It's human. It's not the same—isn't *close* to the same—as throwing all your own arguments away so you can threaten someone you don't like."

A cold wind blew through Sylvie. "I don't care about liking her. I care that she's manipulating you."

"More than you care about my right to privacy? More that you care about me getting to choose whether our whole department sees me as a victim?"

Sylvie felt as if a glass had smashed inside her. Her sense of blamelessness vanished and, with it, her anger. Nadia was right. What she'd said to Dr. Rau was unconscionable. It violated not only the tattered remains of her philosophy but—far worse—the truest friendship of her life.

Before Sylvie could say anything, Nadia went on, "Salomé's right about your kind of philosophy. You've let your ideas totally blind you. You're so rigid about what you think—what you *think* you think—that you can't even see that the way you want people to live is impossible even for you."

"I know," Sylvie started, but Nadia wasn't done.

"You don't believe anyone but yourself," she said, her voice rising. An unfamiliar light shone in her eyes. "You decide what's good and bad. You decide who gets privacy. You see the whole world through the lens of *your* ideas, *your* relationships, *your* past. I'm not you and Salomé's not Jonah, but somehow that's too complicated for you to understand."

"I just don't want her to hurt you."

Nadia wrapped her arms around herself, digging her fingers into her sides. "Everyone gets hurt. It's life."

"I told myself that when I was with Jonah."

"Maybe you were right."

A sour taste washed through Sylvie's mouth. "What do you mean?"

"You're constantly talking about how you're not a victim." Nadia released her grip on herself. She met Sylvie's eyes. "Have you ever considered the possibility that you actually aren't? That Jonah didn't do anything wrong?"

It was the cruelest thing Nadia could have said. Sylvie had no reply. She knew—she could already see on Nadia's face—that her friend didn't mean it; that she'd only wanted to wound. It didn't matter. Sylvie wished she were dead. It would be better to have drowned herself in Nahant Bay at twenty-three than to have arrived at this moment.

Nadia's mouth was trembling. She'd blown through her capacity to harm. She would take what she'd said back in a moment. Sylvie couldn't stand to let her. She snatched her bag from the sofa, where it sat beside the cushions she'd crushed in her fit of tears, and clutched it to her chest like a child with a favorite teddy bear. It gave her no strength. Still, she managed to walk out the door.

Chapter Nine

1.

It was an act of God that Sylvie made it to class in the morning. She had slept—or, rather, huddled with her eyes closed—in her car. It was very cold. She had a hard time not remembering Swampscott. Many times in the night she thought that she had ruined her life. By daybreak it seemed evident that Robbie was all she had left, and that she had no hope of getting through this streak of losses without losing him, too.

She got a searingly hot coffee and plasticky egg and cheese from a Starbucks drive-through, dimly frightened to enter any building. Eating was miserable. She wanted Wheaties. Her stomach rolled and cramped. Shortly thereafter, she passed a tormented ten minutes in the philosophy department's only single-occupancy bathroom. Bleakly she imagined bumping into Dr. Rau in the corridor. She thought if she did she would grow wings and talons, like the harpies of myth, and shriek until her vocal cords burst.

She found it absurd that she had to go lead a discussion section. Her brain felt wiped of knowledge. She had counted so thoroughly on Simone Weil's assertion that uprootedness destroyed the past. Now her old life had come to get her, and every bit of her new one was, obediently, vanishing into nothingness.

While she washed her hands, Sylvie commanded herself to quit wallowing. Wallowing was self-pity, and self-pity was not necessary or productive. Especially not now, when she needed to scrape up her dignity and go see if her students had understood yesterday's Hegel lecture, which she hadn't attended. It was lucky the professor sent his graduate assistants his notes in advance.

Until very recently, Sylvie had liked Hegel. More than liked. She'd built her dissertation on his belief that *history is the progress of the consciousness of freedom.* He was mainly talking about systems of government, but she'd seen no reason the same idea shouldn't apply to love. "Moron," she said grimly to herself, and marched out of the bathroom.

Her discussion section chugged along at first, though she was so tired the students' voices slipped in and out of her ears. She thought of Dr. Rau's condemnation of her Big Ideas and felt faintly sick. Maybe she should quit philosophy, not teach it. She had used it to lead herself astray.

Rotely, Sylvie moved through her usual routine of ensuring that the kids understood each of the abstractions central to the text. Hegel had some odd ideas about history, which her students seemed to grasp well. Problems arose, though, when she switched the subject to freedom. Before she started teaching here, she would have assumed freedom was an essentially intuitive concept, like pornography or pain, but the University of Virginia's legions of high-school class presidents and speech-team captains did not trust intuition. It was too much like a feeling, not enough like an answer. She thought of the emotion that had risen in her last night as she announced her intent to do to Nadia what Dianne Feinstein had done to Christine Blasey Ford. Maybe her students' lack of faith in themselves was wiser than she thought.

She tried to send them to the text, but that only created more trouble. One of her sharper kids, a stylish math major named Maurice, rapidly pulled a quote that Sylvie thought should resolve the discussion—"It says here that 'I am free when I am within myself,' like, when I don't depend on anyone else to validate me, right?"—but his analysis landed poorly with Prabha, Sylvie's summer student, now the star of her Political Philosophy section. Instantly, she sat straight up and began worrying her notebook with both hands.

Sylvie nodded at her. "Prabha, do you want to add something?"

"Well, not *add*." Prabha shot an apologetic glance at Maurice, whom Sylvie suspected she had a crush on. "But humans are interconnected, you know? I mean, we talked the other week about the social contract, but also"—she motioned outward from her sternum—"we're connected emotionally. It seems wrong to say we can only be free by being free from each other."

Sylvie's heart began to beat hard. She willed Maurice to reply. He did not. She looked at the professor's notes, though she already knew no help was to be found there. She was too warm at her desk by the window. Her students—sixteen sophomores and juniors, barely distinguishable in their eagerness to achieve—tipped their faces toward her like sunflowers.

"Could you give a counterexample?" she asked, stalling.

Prabha answered instantly. "What about a good relationship? If you're with the right person, or even if you're really close friends with the right person, you should feel free, but you're still depending on them."

Now Maurice shot up in his chair. "Yeah, but Hegel's not talking about relationships. He's talking about nation-states."

"Okay," Sylvie said. Her ribs now hurt badly. "Let's see what happens if we reverse the example. If you're in a bad relationship, are you more within yourself than in a good one? Or are you more dependent on the other person?"

"More within yourself," Prabha said slowly. Sylvie tried to control her face, but saw in her students' expressions that she had failed. "Or—maybe more dependent, if that's what's wrong with the relationship."

"So we agree that dependency can be a problem?" Sylvie asked the class at large. Everyone nodded. She had absolutely no idea where she was headed. She was terrified that she would lose control and begin telling these kids about Jonah.

"But," Prabha put in, "if we go back to nation-states, then not *enough* dependency is a problem. Right? You need citizens to trust the government, and each other."

A handful of small snorts echoed through the classroom. Luke, who ran the campus Young Democratic Socialists of America chapter and liked to monologue about the uselessness of impeachment, appeasement, and any non-Bernie member of Congress, muttered, "So we're fucked."

Sylvie saw safe ground ahead. All she had to do was tell the kids to apply what they had gleaned from Hegel to the Trump presidency, and they'd argue until section ended, then leave feeling intellectually satisfied. It was too bad that she was not, at this moment, able to speak. A sequence of terrifying thoughts was unrolling itself in her mind. She was very familiar with the line Maurice had quoted. Familiar with its context, too. She'd put the whole paragraph it came from in her dissertation. In it, Hegel wrote, *For when I am dependent, I refer myself to something else which I am not; I cannot exist independently of something external.* Sylvie had never existed independently of Jonah. She had referred herself to him since she was fourteen. She hadn't stopped when she left their marriage. Look at her! She'd let a six-minute conversation with him ruin the best thing in her life.

She had half the class period to go. She profoundly doubted that she could make it. Her body was so tight with adrenaline her jaw jumped. She planted her elbows on her desk and said, "We don't write in section very often, but when I have trouble clarifying my thoughts, writing generally helps more than speaking." She was lying—she clarified her thoughts via turtle—but it seemed like a useful untruth. "So I'd like each of you to write a philosophical description of freedom, drawing on Hegel but bringing in other texts we've read this semester. Give it ten minutes, then trade with a partner, discuss, and revise. At the end of the class, I'll collect everyone's descriptions. Okay?"

Her gambit worked beautifully. She should tell Nadia to steal it, except that Nadia was neither teaching nor, presumably, speaking to her. She wasn't speaking to Nadia, either. Whether she would resume at some point was a question to handle later, when she was not in full internal chaos. For the moment, she banished thoughts of Nadia and hid behind her laptop, eyes burning and mind stunned into immobility, until her students began announcing that they'd submitted their assignments via email, or Google Docs, or the online course portal, and the period was done in eight minutes, so could they—

"Yes," Sylvie said, rising. Blood coursed to her head. "Good work today. You can go."

2.

Sylvie had not consciously created any sort of plan during her time of emptiness, but on getting in her car, she found that she had one. Without wavering she drove to the Omni. Not until she'd parked her car on a nearby side street did she start asking herself what precisely she intended to do. Divest herself of Jonah somehow. Banish him as a referent.

She walked with her hands jammed in her pockets, not for warmth but for the reassuring sensation of feeling her legs move. Ahead of her rose the Omni, a gigantic pinkish block without detail or charm. It struck her as a faintly comical site of confrontation, and not necessarily a safe one. A hotel room was meant to be private, and dealing with Jonah in private was unwise—though what was the worst he could do? He wouldn't kill her. He could rape her. Half of her hoped he would. She could have no better proof of his evil than that.

She gave his name at the front desk, and the staffer, smiling, said, "Oh, you're his wife. Sophie? Stephanie? He had us hold your key." It was nearly enough to turn Sylvie around, but she'd made it to this lobby with its red-and-gold upholstery, its waxy fig plants and waxier men. She'd acquired resolve, or some monstrous relative of it. She took the plastic card the receptionist held out, made a noise mildly related to "Thank you," and marched herself to the elevator.

Her inner monologue quieted to an inaudible murmur on her ascent to the sixth floor. Her stomach churned. A visit from the turtle would have been welcome, but he made no appearance. She was psychically alone, running purely on instinct. She supposed it was the only way.

Jonah's suite was halfway down a long, desolate hall. No guests, no staff, no noise. Sylvie found herself unwilling to use her key card. It belonged to a wife. She was not one. If she silently began the statement *I am*, the portion of her brain that had taken control finished, *Abie Abraham's girlfriend*. Untrue, at this moment, but illuminating. Steadying. Worth examining at a later date.

She tapped on the door. It took Jonah a moment to appear. When he did, he held a half-full trash can loosely in one hand. She looked at it, then at him, and he burst out laughing.

"Sylvie! You should have let yourself in. I thought you were the maid." He shook the can. "She didn't empty my trash when she came."

She said nothing. Jonah leaned through the doorway, brushing by her, and set the trash can in the hall. He smelled of pine-needle soap and aftershave. His curls were again molded perfectly, his collared shirt neatly ironed, but he had on gym pants and no socks. His feet were unsettlingly familiar. Pale toes, wrinkled nail beds, dark hair.

He straightened. "Come in. My room is your room."

"Legally."

Jonah chuckled. "Does it work that way?"

Again, Sylvie had no response. She lifted her chin and stepped into the room. She felt a mix of tension and nausea that meant her body had begun raising alarms. She backed herself up to the wall and regarded the room with its pristine mugs and glasses, its laptop and iPad, its neat piles of folded workout gear and newspapers and coiled white cords.

"I thought you'd come later," Jonah said, sitting on the edge of the bed. "In my visit, I mean. I thought you wouldn't decide so quickly, or, if you did, you'd dawdle to make a point. Of course, I was confident you'd come. We're meant to be married, Sylvie. It's lucky you were young when you left. It would be"—his mouth shifted in and out of disgust—"difficult if you were in your late thirties already. I wouldn't want that." He caught himself and changed attitudes, switching to a tone of great, velvety sincerity. "I don't want any more difficulty for you, Sylvie. I understand that I made your life hard. I wasn't a good husband."

"You were emotionally abusive."

A furrow appeared in his forehead. Instead of arguing, he said, "You know, I got very depressed after you left. I had to go to therapy. My shrink put me in a men's support group, which sounds cheesy, but it helped me. I learned to reflect on my masculinity."

Sylvie suppressed an ugly laugh. Feminist Jonah. Just what she needed. She recalled Harvey Weinstein promising, when revelations of his predatory behavior broke, that he was taking a sabbatical to learn to be less of a pig. She remembered, too, Robbie describing the life-altering depression that hit after he missed the Olympics. He'd let himself sink in pools, not to die—his muscle memory alone rendered drowning impossible—but for the temporary relief of pretending he'd never learned to swim.

Her body was starting to make suggestions. It said she could not banish her husband by letting him talk, or by talking to him. Persuasion was worthless. Four years of philosophizing had not freed her. She was here to take physical action. It was a repugnant thought, horrifying even to consider, but her body had an agenda.

Sylvie walked to the bed, imagining herself as Robbie sinking in a pool. She would touch the bottom, and then she would float up. It would be that simple. She touched Jonah's bony shoulder, and he shut up, sprang to his feet, and attached his mouth to hers. His tongue was pointed and oddly dry. His lips were tiny. She hoped she wouldn't have to suffer through performative cunnilingus.

She got her wish. Within moments of removing his clothes—Sylvie undressed herself—Jonah was readying himself for penetration, rolling a condom over his tapered, candlelike penis.

She did not feel miserable, or debased, or especially frightened. She felt annoyed that he'd been cocky enough to bring condoms. Once he was ready, she felt the unpleasant drag of latex on dryish skin, and then, once the stinging subsided, she felt no pain, no shame, no arousal, no vanishing of her adult self. Nothing at all.

Jonah seemed to be enjoying himself thoroughly. He had his eyes pressed shut, his head twisted to the side. He alternated between thrusting, rocking, and a twisting move that made no sense to Sylvie. Maybe he thought he had a corkscrew penis, like a duck. She wondered if he planned to switch positions, and bet rightly that, though he used to, today he would not.

She hoped he hadn't always been this dull in bed. She had spent years in complete sexual thrall to him. If what captivated her was *this*—mortifying! She shuddered a little. Jonah, perhaps in reaction, heaved himself deep inside her, released a froglike croak, and announced his orgasm a solid three seconds before it arrived.

He trotted to the bathroom to dispose of the condom, and Sylvie took stock of herself. Her vagina stung again. Her lower back ached. Internally, she felt loose and light. Before, she'd been overwhelmingly jittery and jangled, both keyed up and worn out by years of banked terror. It had been legitimate, that fear.

Before any demons could get inside her again, Sylvie rose. She had her underwear and socks on when Jonah returned. He looked at her slyly. "Want anything?"

"No."

His eyes shone. "*Need* anything?"

Sylvie took her leggings from the floor. She measured her words while she tugged them on, settled her breasts carefully into her bra, and disappeared briefly into the giant cashmere sweater she chose to consider a dress.

"Well?" Jonah said.

"Our marriage is over. Don't contact me again. You should hear from my lawyer, Rob Klein at Covington & Burling, next week." She added, as Jonah gaped, "It was good that you came to Virginia. Unpleasant, but clarifying."

He levered his mouth closed. His eyes had gotten narrow and mean. "Don't leave this room," he said.

She picked her coat, boots, and bag up. She could get them on in the hall. "Jonah, I'm gone."

"We aren't done talking."

"You can talk to yourself all you like."

His lip curled. "You turned into a real bitch, Sylvie."

In the doorway, she turned halfway to give him her biggest, most beatific smile. No last word could be good enough. Before the temptation to speak could set in, she waved and slipped out the door.

Chapter Ten

1.

Sylvie was on the highway when she started shaking. It was not minor. Her teeth rattled in her head. She had the heat cranked, but beneath her sweater the hair on her arms stood. Demons, she thought. Demons exiting her body. Her vision began to narrow. She pulled into the breakdown lane, hit her flashers, and sat while the shivering slowed.

Belatedly, she was surprised it had taken her this long—nearly an hour—to react. Surprised, too, that she was only trembling, not vomiting or in tears. Once, in Baltimore, she had brought home a man who, during sex, spoke as if reading from a porn script. She'd had a tough time not giggling in the moment, but when he left, his insults and possessives rang cruelly inside her until she went in the bathroom and jammed her hand down her throat.

But she hadn't opted in to that man's performance. Every decision she had made today was conscious, if comprehensible only in retrospect. She, Sylvie Broder Sabransky, soon—she hoped—to be Sylvie Broder once more, had chosen, in sound mind and body, to have mediocre sex with the object of her fear and loathing, not to punish herself, but to learn or remember that Jonah was only a man. He wasn't stronger or tougher or wilier than she was. Years ago, maybe, but not now.

Sylvie had to wait a long time before her hands steadied enough to steer. She thought of the *Sopranos* scene in which Dr. Melfi dreams of Tony having a panic attack on the Jersey Turnpike. She wouldn't quite qualify what had just happened to her as panic. More like a fever burning leftover junk from her system.

It took her an hour and a half to reach DC once she began driving again. Even though she was achy and thirsty, stopping appealed not at all. She wasn't yet sure what awaited her, but she felt a building urgency to get there. She understood that the phenomenon she was undergoing—this maelstrom of resolve and instinct, liberation and rage—would end soon. She had to use it while she could.

She didn't get to their building until nearly 2:00. She parked and texted Robbie, *Home early*, adding, for some reason, a photo of their corner. Abie hadn't written again. Nadia hadn't apologized. Jonah hadn't emailed. She stretched, uncoiled herself from the car, and took herself to Taquería Habanero for a late lunch.

Usually it was overflowing with customers, but at this odd weekday hour, she got a window table to herself. As she sat eating chips with Habanero's tomatillo salsa, which was very possibly the most delicious sauce on Earth, an elegiac feeling came over her. Fourteenth Street was luminous in the afternoon sun. It was not a beautiful block—in no mood could Sylvie consider the 7-Eleven across the street beautiful—but it had welcomed her. She'd made a home here, with Robbie but for herself. In Baltimore and in Charlottesville, she'd never felt the need to fuss around her room until she got its look right. In Robbie's condo, not one nook or shelf lacked her touch. He had told her many times that he loved living with her wallpaper and her ceramics, the red Formica breakfast table she'd found on Craigslist and the raffia lampshades she had persuaded him would look festively Miami. All her objects meant she was present when she was gone.

She had her routines in the neighborhood, too. At Habanero, she always ordered the same meal: one lengua taco, one carnitas, and one shrimp, with Negra Modelo if it was nighttime and cinnamony coffee if it was day. Now, though, she just wanted water. She was as dried out as if she'd been wandering through the desert with Moses. She was unused to skipping meals or not sleeping through the night. Among the many changes life with Robbie had brought was the habit of kindness to her body. Not until this moment had it occurred to Sylvie that her body's repayment, or reward, was delivering her to Abie's bed.

But it wasn't her body that had kept her there. For years, she had both written and behaved as if she were just mind and body, as if her emotions weren't their own willful presence. But it was emotion that had convinced her to move in with Abie; emotion that had made her threaten Dr. Rau; emotion, so many years ago, that had drawn her to her grandparents and disconnected her from her mom and dad. As she ate, she thought that maybe, if she wasn't going to swear off philosophy forever, emotion was what she would write about.

She left Habanero feeling serene. Robbie had replied quickly to her text, promising to get home around 6:00. She had time to take a half-hour shower immediately followed by a nap so long it was dark when she woke. Hurriedly she got dressed, brushed her teeth, yanked her damp hair into a braid. When Robbie walked in, she was sitting in the living room, failing to do anything but lie in wait.

Instantly Sylvie knew he was worried. His expression was taut, his shoulders stiff. Instead of rushing to her, he hung his gym and work bags neatly on their hooks, stepped out of his shoes, and walked over without opening his arms to be hugged.

She rose and hugged him anyway. His hair was damp, and his neck smelled strongly like chlorine. "Coming from the pool?"

"Just a quick swim." He kissed her briefly and without heat, then stepped out of the hug. "Should we sit?"

Sylvie nodded. She hadn't necessarily intended to plunge directly into conversation, but she could see it would be cruel to do anything else. It was, potentially, a sign of other, unremarked cruelties that Robbie so plainly took her early return as proof that trouble had come.

She arranged herself on the couch, feet tucked beneath her. Robbie sat at its far end. She said, "I love you," and he shook his head.

"Don't, Sylvie."

"Don't—"

"Soften the blow. You're going to break up with me. It's all right." She could hear him struggling, already, for self-control. "I always knew you would, and I guessed months ago it was coming. I'm not angry. I just want you to tell me the truth."

Sylvie's hands had begun shaking again. Her leg bones trembled inside her, though her thighs appeared still enough. In the early morning, lying on her side on her back seat, she had told herself she wouldn't get through this stretch of days without losing Robbie. She had not imagined that he would so forcefully give her the choice.

She didn't deny. She said, "How did you know?"

"Now, or in general?"

"Both."

Robbie turned his head away. "You keep yourself so separate," he said. "I shouldn't say I always knew, but I've thought for a long time that you love separateness more than you love me."

"Differently," Sylvie said. She wanted to slide closer to him, but she couldn't tell if touch would be wrong. She thought of Nadia saying it was worse to be loved and not chosen than not to be loved, but she was done lying now. "I do love you," she said. "I haven't stopped."

He wrenched his whole body toward her. His face was brilliant with hurt. "So explain."

She could only say it one way. Inventing her own language—the language not of romance from time immemorial, not of books and movies but her own individual life—would mean only confusion and stumbling, wasted time and added pain. She made herself hold Robbie's gaze. "I met someone else."

"And?"

"And I don't want to keep myself separate from him. Or—I do, I want it badly, but it turns out that I can't."

Robbie nodded. She widened her eyes, which did little to dry the layer of tears making the room wheel and blur. In this day she had passed through epiphany and deliverance, righteousness and disgust, shame and peace. It was only right for grief to take its turn now.

"I'm sorry," she said. "I never thought this would happen. You're such a good man, Robbie. I was so sure I was safe with you."

"You *are* safe."

"No, no." She shook her head. "Safe from myself."

"Oh, Sylvie." He moved fractionally closer to her. "You're so afraid of what you want."

"I am."

He gave no sign of hearing. He was, she understood, talking mainly to himself. "You're so afraid, but you can't say no to yourself, either. Living with you is like watching an endless one-person game of tug-of-war. I used to think I could release you from it. I thought it was your ex's fault, and if you spent long enough with me you'd figure out that wanting things is okay, and so is not getting them. But it wasn't his fault at all, was it?" Robbie rubbed his eyes. "It's just who you are."

Every word he'd said was right. Every word but one. She said, before she could flinch from it, "Not ex."

Robbie's eyebrows went down. "Sylvie."

"I never got divorced. I just ran away. Actually—" She did laugh now. It was an awful, uncontrolled sound. "I saw him today. He showed up in

Charlottesville. I mean, he found me. I hadn't seen or spoken to him in eight years, but he tracked me down, and so I told him—" She broke off again. She had to say it. "I told him I wanted a divorce. I gave him your name."

"As your lawyer?"

"Yeah."

Neither of them spoke. Sylvie could not bear to look at him. She knew she had earned every loss she'd incurred. She raised her eyes to the mantel with its neat row of cobalt jugs and vases, the lumpy ultramarine candlesticks she had decided to love. In the bedroom were greens and yellows; in the bathroom, the matching ceramic cups that were her only reds. It seemed like a betrayal to imagine, as she was already imagining, showing up at Abie's door with boxes of newspaper-wrapped ceramics, begging him to take her and them in.

Robbie said, "You know I don't do family law."

"I know."

"And I don't get to choose my own pro bono cases."

"I'd pay."

"You can't afford to."

"I didn't mean you really had to be my lawyer," she said. It wasn't true, but she recognized that it should have been.

"You've been married this whole time," Robbie said, in a tone more of wonder than anger. "When I thought I was going to marry you, you were married to somebody else."

"You thought that?"

He got up and went to the bedroom. She wanted to follow—wanted, really, not to be left alone—but locked her limbs to keep herself on the couch. When he returned, he held a beige ring box with the unmistakable wear of old velvet. "My grandmother's," he said, setting it beside her.

She didn't touch it. "How long have you had this?"

"Christmas."

Eleven months. It was telling that he'd said nothing about this year's holiday, though it was approaching. "Even though you always assumed I would break up with you."

Robbie gave his head a tiny shake. "Even though."

Sylvie felt a great wrenching inside her. Through her pain she had the clear if distant thought that she was lucky to love and be loved by two men this profoundly. Not lucky in how she had reacted, not lucky to stumble and hurt and flail, but lucky in what her life had given.

"Open it," Robbie said. "Please."

Sylvie obeyed. For an instant her mind failed to grasp the object before her. She was already laughing, for the second time in a conversation that deserved no laughter, when she did. Never had she seen an uglier piece of jewelry. It was a—ruby? Amethyst? Something the purplish shade of dried blood—set in heavy gold, the band inset with what appeared to be a small metal braid. It looked far more appropriate for a mobster's thumb than a grandmother's ring finger. She tried to muffle herself.

"Hideous, huh?" Robbie said. "I was going to melt the gold down and get a new stone."

She meant to say that sounded like a good idea. A great plan for another girl. Somehow, though, she heard herself asking, "Why aren't you mad at me?"

He let out a long breath. "You know why."

Sylvie had to think for a shamefully long time before she registered that she was looking in the wrong parts of her mind. It wasn't a reason related to her or to his love for her. "It's easier for you to get mad at yourself."

Another period of quiet set in then. Sylvie's grief was growing stronger. A person who loved Robbie well, a person who wanted to support and be supported by him instead of taking refuge in him, would have learned to guide him toward his anger. Such a person would be in the habit of encouraging him to curse or shout, to windmill his arms, to release his athletic control and let his body be more of a conduit for his emotions. She was not the right woman for Robbie. Not permanently, not temporarily. He had changed her life for the better. She couldn't hope she'd done the same for him.

He said, "I don't want to have goodbye sex."

She nodded.

"And no long goodbye."

"Should I go now?" she asked, suddenly flustered. She'd get a hotel room. She couldn't pay, really, but neither could she face a second night in the car.

But Robbie was shaking his head. "Sleep in the bug room." His mouth twitched. "And take the bug quilt."

"You don't like it?"

"Gives me the creeps."

"You should have said."

He lifted one shoulder. "It made you happy, and that was what I wanted." He reached for her hand. It was the first time they'd touched since the conversation began. "I really wanted to make you happy, Sylvie."

She had to close her eyes very tightly. She squeezed his hand tightly, too. "You did."

It was dark outside, the sky the deep purplish-brown of urban night. Fourteenth Street glowed in the condo's big window, bus lights and illuminated restaurant signs colliding with the lit glass of ten, twenty, thirty more homes like theirs. Sylvie had seen the wet mouths of dogs and babies pressed to those windows. She'd seen couples kissing, lone men and women talking on the phone, doing sun salutations, staring at the sidewalk like she herself stared. Somebody could glance across the street and see them now, guess or not guess that their conversation was final and grave.

"Will I see you again?" she asked.

He gave her one of the flickering smiles she would miss. "I'm your lawyer."

"Are you?"

"Sure. It won't be hard."

"I'll take my stuff," she said. "I'm not sure where I'll be taking it yet."

"What about—" He hesitated. "It's Abie, right?"

"Yeah," she said quietly. "It is."

Robbie didn't ask for more details. Sylvie didn't offer.

"Maybe Jonah will take you to court," Robbie said, "and Abie will come to support you. We can have a conference after. Me, Abie, and Jonah. You can sit in the hall."

"You don't want to talk to Jonah."

"He can't hurt me."

"Me, either," Sylvie said. "As it turns out."

It was the last stage of their conversation. Both of them were too exhausted for more. Robbie made buttered egg noodles, his deepest comfort food. He put on *Parts Unknown* after and, when Sylvie began retreating to the guest room, told her she didn't have to hide. Instead, she changed into pajamas and then took from the freezer two Oreo ice-cream bars she'd hidden there over the summer, and they sat sticky-handed long after the desserts were gone, watching Anthony Bourdain eat skirt steak and towering multi-meat sandwiches in Uruguay, oysters and pheasant in Newfoundland, lavash and stuffed pumpkin in Armenia. After the third episode, Robbie rose, brushed his lips very lightly against the top of Sylvie's head, and looked at her as if he were going to speak, but said nothing. She could not guess what was in his mind. Quietly he went to what had been, until that evening, their bedroom. She sat on the couch until she could hear, through the thin walls, that his breathing had settled into the regularity of sleep. It was how she imagined early motherhood: a form of waiting that mixed calm with watchfulness, relief that an evening was over with sorrow that it was gone. She had told Robbie the absolute truth: she did love him. She felt that she would never stop. When she finally moved herself to the guest bed, her whole body was dense with sorrow. Her storm had ended. Her losses were complete. In the morning, she would pack herself up and vanish to Florida, or return to Virginia to scrape a life back together. Either way, her next stage—the first true stage of her adulthood, maybe—would have to begin.

2.

Sylvie woke at dawn with a sense of stillness so strong it was eerie. She lay a long time in the unfamiliar room, waiting to fall back asleep or grow agitated enough to rise. She thought about what to take with her: the bug quilt, any books that could be helpful in the dissertation reset that was surely looming, the greatest hits of her pottery collection, some clothes. She thought, too, about her destination. In the night she had imagined getting on I-95 and driving to Miami, parking herself there or taking Route 1 to the heel of the Keys. When she was little, Grandma Estie sometimes brought her on buying trips to Key West. They'd eat conch fritters by the water, watch the island's wild chickens strut and peck through the dust.

It was a good memory, but not, she found, an appealing fantasy. Beginning anew seemed nightmarish. Unspooling her tale of defects and scarring to strangers, letting them determine for themselves what portion of her past was her fault—no. She would not. She knew, if nothing else, that she bore total blame for dumping Abie, and for hurting him. It was both her job and her fervent wish to make that right if she could.

When she heard Robbie's alarm, she rose. First she stripped the bed as if she were an actual guest. Sitting on the naked mattress, she texted Nadia, *Coming over this afternoon to talk. 4:30?* She sent another text, too, to Rachel: *I saw Jonah. He told me you were having a hard time. I really hope you're all right.* After that, she folded the bug quilt, took it to the living room, and brewed coffee, gathering objects to take to Virginia while the pot hissed and steamed. Her inner stillness was unaltered by either the prospect of Nadia or the fact of physical motion. It was utterly unlike the calm Robbie ordinarily brought her. She felt neither soothed nor muffled. She thought some time would need to pass before she understood how she felt.

Robbie appeared from the bedroom fully dressed. Usually he made breakfast before leaving, ritually offering Sylvie a bowl of oatmeal or plate of eggs despite knowing she would turn him down for her Wheaties. Now he poured himself a travel mug of coffee, took a joined pair of bananas from the fruit basket, and reminded her, "No long goodbyes."

"No."

"Send me Jonah's address if you have it."

"Anything else?"

"I'll let you know." He paused. "We can talk logistics later. Your stuff, and all that." He smiled a little. "I may need some time to decide how much of what's here to keep."

Sylvie nodded. "Up to you." Probably the gracious move would be an offer to reimburse him for the furniture she wound up taking, but it would be hollow. At the moment, she didn't have enough money in the bank to put down first and last month's rent for the shittiest apartment in Charlottesville. Briefly she visualized herself hauling rugs and floor lamps from sublet to sublet, group house to group house, but shut the image from her mind. It wasn't time for that yet.

In the end, Robbie left without saying any goodbye at all. He just slipped from the kitchen and buttoned the heavy wool coat Sylvie had helped him shop for, took his gym bag and bananas, and walked out the door. Sylvie sat at her breakfast table and waited for sadness, but it floated outside the big window like a ghost. It would trail her to Virginia, wrap itself around her when it, or she, was ready. For the moment, she got herself together. She took the neatly stacked paper grocery bags from on top of the fridge and stuffed them with sweaters, underwear, mugs and bowls wrapped gently in shirts and scarves. She kept her work books in milk crates for easy hauling between cities; those all went to the car, no sorting. When her trunk was full, she tucked the bug quilt and a spare pillow in the back seat. Then she went back upstairs and, afraid her stillness would crack if she lingered, locked the door, slid her key beneath it, and left.

3.

Sylvie let herself into Nadia's apartment without either knocking or checking her phone. It seemed weeks ago, not thirty-six hours, that she had last used this key. Nadia was gone then. Now, she sat on the couch, very small among all its white pillows. Her face was pale and puffy, her hair lank. She wore leggings and a baggy Baltimore Orioles shirt that Sylvie had gotten for free at a game years ago.

"I broke up with Robbie," Sylvie said.

Nadia flattened her mouth. "I broke up with Salomé." She paused, then added, "She said I had to choose her or you, so I chose you."

Instantly Sylvie's stillness was gone. Her face was wet. She wasn't conscious of moving, but she discovered herself on the couch with Nadia, hugging more tightly than they had hugged in four years of friendship, each apologizing indistinctly into the other one's hair.

Eventually, Nadia sat up and said, "She made me do it during her office hours."

"No."

"Swear to God. She *summoned* me."

"Had you made up your mind?"

"Enough to do this." Nadia dug her phone from beneath cushions, swiped and tapped, and held it out. Its little speaker rattled briefly, then began to emit a string of unpleasant French sounds. "I skipped to the good part," Nadia said.

On the recording, Dr. Rau announced, "You are a promise breaker. A *promise* breaker. Not only are you withdrawing the promises you made to me, woman to woman, you are betraying—a sadder story—your intellectual promise. Without me you will not finish your work punctually. You will not finish it well. You are lucky I took an interest in you." Sylvie mimed gagging as Dr. Rau continued, "Another professor, perhaps a male one, could get bitter. Vindictive. Another professor could prevent you from graduating at all. I will never do such a thing. In fact, if you return to me, I will be happy. I will be waiting for you."

Sylvie shuddered. "Enough."

Nadia stopped the recording. "Another professor," she said sourly.

"She sounds like Jonah."

Saying his name released a surge of envy. If Sylvie had thought, or dared, to tape his orders, download his texts, keep a diary of his manipulations and abuses; if she had kept some form of documentation during their relationship, an archive not of what it looked like but how it felt, she could have avoided so much questioning and pain. Every time she began asking herself whether she'd truly suffered, whether it was her fault after all, whether she'd chosen victimhood or had it thrust onto her, the evidence would have been there to review.

She sighed and sank into the pillows that surrounded her. "I went to Jonah's hotel," she said. "I had sex with him."

Nadia stiffened so completely her weight lifted from the sofa. "You *what?*"

"Uh-huh."

"When you say 'had sex'—" Nadia's forehead furrowed. She let the half-question hang. It took Sylvie a moment to guess the sentence's end.

"I initiated it," she said. "It was consensual."

Her friend nodded, eyelids lowering. She was plainly considering her reaction, or imagining why, if she were Sylvie, she would choose to do such a thing. After a moment, she asked, "Was it bad?"

"Horrible. Boring. But short."

"And that was what you needed?"

"It was."

Nadia gave her an amused look. "Banishment by sex."

Sylvie's whole body warmed. For the second time in less than a day, she knew herself to be profoundly understood. With Robbie, that recognition had been heartbreaking; with Nadia, it brought a comfort deeper than she could describe. She slid down the couch to wrap herself once more around her friend.

Eventually, Nadia twitched loose. She said, "So you dumped Robbie and you got rid of Jonah. Next you're going to tell me you and Abie made up."

Sylvie pressed her palms together. "From your lips to God's ears."

"Okay," Nadia said. "Before we start talking about that."

"Not much to talk about."

Nadia ignored her. She was twisting a hunk of blanket. "I'm sorry I said what I did about Jonah." She raised her eyes to Sylvie's. "It was terrible of me. I was—freaking out, lashing out, I don't know. I didn't mean it. I never doubted that he hurt you."

"I'm sorry, too. I shouldn't have threatened to report Dr. Rau. I would never do that to you."

"I know you wouldn't. But if you hadn't said you were going to, I'm not sure I would've done this." She waggled her phone, the recording still glowing on its screen.

"You mean *you're* going to report her?"

"I'm not sure. Part of me thinks it's the right thing to do. Part of me thinks I'm not brave enough."

Sylvie tried to imagine what her turtle, who had absented himself totally, would say. "Brave's irrelevant," she told her friend. "What do you want?"

Nadia was looking down again. She didn't raise her eyes. "I want," she said, "to come up with a way to make her leave me alone."

4.

For days, Sylvie and Nadia barely left the apartment. Sylvie taught, then rushed back, afraid of running into Abie in the wild. His texts still sat unanswered, unrevisited, on her phone. She knew him to be a man who did not change his mind, but she was still afraid to wonder how long his invitation to come home would stand. When Nadia brought him up, using a gentleness that she was only now learning, Sylvie swatted the subject away. She wasn't ready. Nor was she ready to discuss the future of her dissertation, if it had one. Sometimes she thought she wanted to look for a softened, nuanced version of her argument, one that took emotion into account. Other times she thought she wanted to start from scratch, or drop out. She knew she couldn't decide yet. Something inside her had to scab or settle. She had to get further from this moment.

"Excuses," Nadia said. She was lying on the couch, body invisible under a heap of jacquard wool blankets, cylindrical red cushion stuffed under her head so she could smoke a bowl.

From her heap of floor cushions, Sylvie said, "Let's handle your life first, then mine."

"Seems unfair."

"So?"

Nadia blew a smoke ring at her. Neither one had yet raised the question of whether Sylvie was moving in. Nadia's study was small, but not too small for a single bed. Sylvie envisioned a slim mattress on an iron frame, like a nun or nineteenth-century orphan would sleep in. If Abie rejected her, she thought she would live monastically for a long time. It was, in part, that prospect that held her indoors. Also, Nadia needed her there.

It was both anthropologically fascinating and intensely sad for Sylvie to watch her friend reckon for the first time in her life with the helplessness that comes after hurt. "I want to *get* her," Nadia kept saying. Sylvie heard the wish's two meanings: Nadia wanted revenge and understanding. She was unlikely to achieve either one.

Now, Sylvie said, "My life's not time-sensitive. You have Dr. Rau on your dissertation committee, and you're defending in the spring."

Nadia covered her face with her palms. "No, I'm not."

"You're not?"

"I can't. How am I supposed to stand in front of her and talk about Augustine? I never want to see her again."

Sylvie rose from her cushions to join Nadia on the couch. Although physical comfort was not often in the language of their friendship, she took her hand and said, with the bluntness that was usually Nadia's, "You have to."

Nadia stuck her bottom lip out, consciously childish. "I do not."

"You think she'll agree over email to step down from your committee?"

Into her lap, Nadia said, "She won't agree at all. If I defend, she'll sit there grinning like the Cheshire cat, then shit on my work till everyone in the room is convinced I'm an idiot."

Sylvie was certain Nadia was right. She'd heard the malice in Dr. Rau's voice on the recording. But would a fellow professor acknowledge that? In Sylvie's considerable experience, the authority figures in their department were not interested in listening to either stories of or ideas about abuse.

And yet she herself had waged a successful campaign to keep her name off the internet. Not, crucially, *by* herself. She got her safety plan thanks to Isabella Kwan, the graduate program manager. Isabella had created a path for Sylvie. It was reassuring to remember her kindness. It also gave Sylvie an idea.

"You're not going to get the faculty to push Dr. Rau off your committee," she said.

"I know."

"But you added her late, right?"

"Yeah."

"Who did the paperwork for that?"

"Isabella—*oh*." Nadia lifted her head. "She helped you."

"Yes, she did."

"If I go to her and tell her the whole story—if I play her the recording—oh, God. Humiliating."

"I know," Sylvie said gently. "I did it."

Nadia made a face that could have been a smile. "Even though you're obsessed with privacy."

"I was less obsessed then. And less so now," she added. She was stating a new goal as a settled fact, but Nadia let her have it. "Anyway, talking to Isabella was how I kept my name off the internet. She understood. I think if she hears the recording, she'll understand that, too, and if there's any procedural way to get Dr. Rau off your committee, she'll do it."

"And then she'll know for the future. I won't have to go public. If she sees Salomé getting her hooks into someone else, she can warn them."

"She can."

Nadia's mouth twitched a little. "I can't have bad banishing sex in a hotel with Salomé."

"Probably not."

"But if you could do that with Jonah, then—" Nadia's voice faltered. "Then I can be in a room with her."

"Yes, you can."

"I can stare her down."

"Yes, you can."

"I can give her the *ice*," Nadia declared.

"You can what?"

Nadia laughed. "It's a thing Malcolm says. When you want to ignore someone in a way that conveys that you hate them, he calls it giving that person the ice." She had been sitting up straight, but she deflated a little. "Not that satisfying, long term."

"We're women in America," Sylvie said dryly. "We take what we can get."

Over the next two days, she and Nadia sifted through texts, audio messages, and Outlook threads, assembling a digital dossier of evidence that Dr. Rau's behavior had been manipulative and cruel. Nadia planned to send it all to Isabella to create an unofficial institutional memory of what had happened to her.

As they worked, Sylvie often thought about her divorce. She had faith in Robbie to help her get it, though he had been as silent as Abie thus far. Her guess was that she'd be hearing not from him but one of his classmates or coworkers, a buddy persuaded to do a favor. Maybe that wasn't a guess but a hope. Regardless, she knew any decent lawyer could free her from Jonah. She found herself repeatedly imagining a fought-out court case, a contested divorce in which she'd have to testify. At first the daydream made her wonder whether, in some buried way, she wanted to claim victimhood in public after all, but soon she realized that it was a revenge fantasy, or a fantasy of validation: she liked the idea of a judge and jury giving her incontrovertible proof that he was as bad as she'd thought.

She said nothing about it to Nadia. She didn't want to distract her friend as she gathered the strength—and proof—to go to Isabella. Sylvie was shocked at the number of putdowns and threats she found in her friend's correspondence with Dr. Rau. She had emailed Nadia psychological studies suggesting that romantic jealousy was negatively correlated with creativity and intelligence. She'd asked Nadia to book two-person dinners that Nadia wasn't invited to. She had texted, apparently from across a departmental function, that Nadia should get her hair trimmed and re-dyed in the morning, before she, Salomé Rau, had to lay eyes on her again. Less than three months before Nadia's qualifying exam date, she'd sent Nadia a list of assignments for the semester that included taking Intensive Beginning German, which met daily and had major homework; copyediting and proofing Dr. Rau's latest monograph; and *engaging more deeply with Wittgenstein*, a task so vague it all but promised professorial dissatisfaction.

What if I took German in the spring? Nadia had written back. *I understand that you want me to read Wittgenstein in the original, but it may not be the greatest use of time before exams.*

Dr. Rau had replied, in full, *Do you value our relationship?*

Yes! Nadia wrote. *Very much. I feel lucky to spend so much time with you, and happy we get to work together more this year.*

If you're happy, Dr. Rau emailed after twenty-six hours, *then learn German. It will help.* Sylvie had sung that line aloud to the tune of "If You're Happy and You Know It," which made Nadia throw a legal pad at her.

Four hours later, Sylvie still had the song stuck in her head. It was late afternoon, almost evening. Cool light fell across her body and turned the room a wintry bluish shade. She raised her arms to stretch until her spine popped. She was perhaps too deeply in her thirties to spend so much time sitting on the floor. Her hips did not seem at ease in their sockets. She rose and twisted, shook her hair out, pulled it back. Nadia breathed gently on the couch, neither asleep nor fully awake. Sylvie understood that her friend was emotionally tired in a way she herself was not. Nadia was undergoing a previously unknown and unimagined phenomenon. For Sylvie, loss was nothing new.

She considered her options. Reading, writing, and grading did not appeal. Nor did the Criterion Collection, which generally beckoned in moments like this. She had too much energy. She had spent six full days inside Nadia's apartment. From high school physics she remembered that a body or being could hold a finite quantity of potential energy before having to convert some into kinetic. Fear of Abie or not, she was going to have to go outside and move, or else she was going to combust.

It would help, she thought, to walk with purpose. Run an errand. She could get dinner. So far, Nadia had made the daily outings to get their burritos or sushi, arguing that only saps paid delivery fees. Robbie, or a less polite version of Robbie, would say only saps didn't cook for themselves, but what did he know? Not everyone controlled sadness by making elaborate meals.

Sylvie ordered the meal she and Nadia had eaten more than any other—eggplant, shrimp dumplings, larb tofu extra hot—and determined that walking to Silk Thai and back wouldn't take so long that the food in its foil and Styrofoam would cool. She texted Nadia *Went to get dinner*, gathered her possessions, and, feeling both brave and relieved, walked out the door.

In less than a minute, Sylvie knew she had made a mistake. Not in leaving the apartment, but in huddling inside it. Cold air stung her nose and throat, her hatless ears and gloveless hands. She had forgotten it was November in her eagerness to get outdoors. Desperation, really. She wanted to walk so direly, so intensely, that she had to remind herself she was already walking, though not in the direction she should be. She didn't want to take herself farther from Abie. She would rather march up and down his block all night than go, as she was currently going, another block north when he lived south.

She wasn't afraid of running into him. It struck her that she never had been. She was afraid she *wouldn't* see him, afraid he would turn his face or ignore her completely, afraid of how intensely she hoped he would be waiting. By the time she reached the neighborhood's main road, she felt wolfish. With each footstep, the word *want* echoed in her head. She could turn, go away from downtown instead of toward it, get to the door that had briefly been hers in ten minutes. She could give in to the unified demands of her heart, body, and mind.

She tried reminding herself of Nadia, of dinner. She tried asking herself if she was ready to see Abie, if she had the right words to ask his forgiveness. She knew the answer was no. Inside her, nothing was settled. Blood poured from her various wounds. Presumably it always would. She did not strike herself, standing at a green light without crossing, as a woman who could be healed.

Cars rushed by her, too fast for the street, their displaced air ruffling the tendrils of hair that fell in her face. She took a long breath full of exhaust and turned stiffly, like a *Nutcracker* soldier. She texted Nadia, *Dinner's at Silk Thai under my name but you should go get it. Sorry sorry sorry. I have to go see a man about a dog*, and then marched downhill, straight four blocks then right three, left one, and there was Abie's little house glowing in the night. Her chairs sat in the front yard. Her garlic was sending up shoots. She unlatched the gate, heart beating so hard she barely heard the familiar notes of the hinge squealing. In the windows she saw signs of life—Wizards game; water glass—but no Abie. It was all right. She could hope.

Sylvie stood on the doorstep for a long moment. She dried her shoes on the mat, wiped her nose and eyes on her wrist. She thought she could hold herself there forever, but then she heard the thunder of Abie descending the stairs and, before she could give or deny herself permission, she was pounding on the door.

He didn't open it right away. It had no peephole, but she imagined he knew it was her. Still, she crammed herself into the frame, bringing her face to the crack between jamb and door. Light from the hallway seeped through. She could feel Abie on the other side of the wall. She wanted to breathe in the air from his mouth.

"Abie," she said. She was already crying. "Abie, it's Sylvie. I missed you. I came back. I'm home."

ACKNOWLEDGMENTS

When I began *The End of Romance*, I thought it would be modeled on Isaac Bashevis Singer's 1966 novel *Enemies, A Love Story*. I was wrong, but I'm grateful to Singer anyway.

My deepest thanks go to my agent, Sarah Burnes; my editor, Nidhi Pugalia; and my dissertation adviser, Leah Stewart. All three of you read and reread this novel with exceptional intelligence, insight, openness, and care, and my faith in all three of you is total.

Thank you to Aru Menon and Nora Gonzalez at the Gernert Company and [TK] at Viking. Thank you as well to Will Evans and Jill Meyers at Deep Vellum.

Thank you to Michael Griffith and Jenn Glaser, important readers; to Chris Bachelder; and to the Taft Research Center at the University of Cincinnati, which supported much of the writing of this book.

Thank you to the DC Commission on the Arts and Humanities and the DC Paid Family Leave program, which, in a brief but crucial moment, allowed me to revise this book.

Thank you to Princeton's translator in residence program and to Clara Usón's *The Shy Assassin*, which I translated while there and which strongly influenced *The End of Romance*.

Thank you to Chase Culler and Alida Dean for the early reads.

Thank you to Adam Ross and the *Sewanee Review* for the years of supporting my fiction.

Thank you to Julia Fisher and Maddie Johnston for the years of talking.

Thank you to Julianne McCobin for the Charlottesville fact-checking.

Thank you to Grace Palmer for Twin Oaks.

Thank you to my DC community.

Thank you to my father, mother, brother, sister-in-law, and extended family—blood, in-law, and fake—for being my roots.

Thank you to my father for Captain Lightning.

Thank you to my baby.

And thank you to Will, without whom I would not have known to write this book.